8-2021

DATE DUE

PRINTED IN U.S.A.

Hayner PLD/Large Print
Overdues .10/day. Max fine cost of
item. Lost or damaged item: additional
$5 service charge.

DAUGHTER OF CANA

DAUGHTER OF CANA

ANGELA HUNT

THORNDIKE PRESS
A part of Gale, a Cengage Company

Thorndike Press, a part of Gale, a Cengage Company.

Thorndike Press® Large Print Christian Historical Fiction.
The text of this Large Print edition is unabridged.
Other aspects of the book may vary from the original edition.
Set in 16 pt. Plantin.

LIBRARY OF CONGRESS CIP DATA ON FILE.
CATALOGUING IN PUBLICATION FOR THIS BOOK
IS AVAILABLE FROM THE LIBRARY OF CONGRESS

ISBN-13: 978-1-4328-7977-8 (hardcover alk. paper)

Published in 2020 by arrangement with Bethany House Publishers, a division of Baker Publishing Group

Printed in Mexico
Print Number: 01   Print Year: 2020

The Old and New Testaments are filled with stories of daring men and noticeably few courageous women. This is not surprising, for the inspired writers could not recount every story of each man, woman, and child who encountered God. But even though few women's stories are recorded, they are still worthy of consideration. The JERUSALEM ROAD novels are fictional accounts of real women who met Jesus, were part of His family, or whose lives were entwined with the men who followed Him.

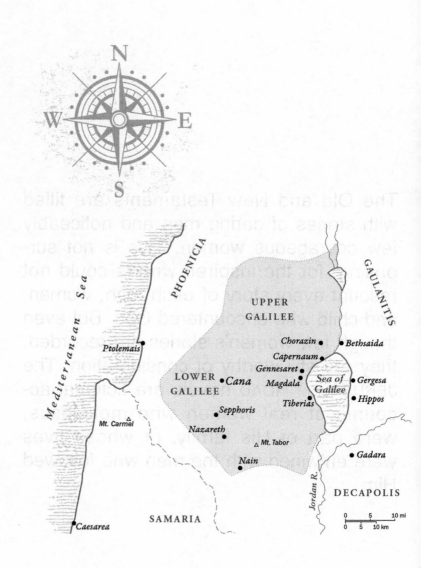

Mediterranean Sea

Sidon

Tyre

PHOENICIA

Ptolemais

GALILEE

Cana

Capernaum

Sepphoris

Mt. Carmel △

Tiberias

Nazareth

Sea of Galilee

SYRIA

Damascus •

△ Mt. Hermon

Caesarea Philippi •

GAULANITIS

Trachonitis

Batanae

Bethsaida •

Hippos •

Auranitis

Caesarea

DECAPOLIS

Pella •

SAMARIA

Sebaste •

Antipatris •

Sychar

Mt. Gerizim △

Joppa

Gerasa (Jerash) •

Jordan R.

PEREA

Philadelphia •

Emmaus •

Jericho •

Jerusalem •

Qumran •

Bethlehem •

Medeba •

Ashkelon

Azotus •

JUDEA

Hebron •

Machaerus •

Dead Sea

IDUMEA

Masada •

Beersheba •

NABATEA

Herod Antipas
Philip
Archelaus and
successors

We, Hermia, like two artificial gods,
Have with our needles created both one
   flower,
Both on one sampler, sitting on one
   cushion,
Both warbling of one song, both in one
   key,
As if our hands, our sides, voices, and
   minds,
Had been incorporate. So we grew
   together,
Like to a double cherry — seeming parted
But yet an union in partition —
Two lovely berries molded on one stem.

William Shakespeare,
A Midsummer Night's Dream

CHAPTER ONE:
TASMIN

The First Day of Nisan — 27 A.D.

"That," my father said, nudging me as the smiling groom led his veiled bride through the courtyard gate, "should have been you."

I ignored Abba's comment and struggled to keep a smile on my face. My father had promised to help me manage this feast, but chiding me about my lack of prospects was not helpful.

"The groom managed to collect quite a crowd," I said, counting the guests as they streamed into the large courtyard of the house belonging to Etan's father. "Forty, forty-one — where did Etan find so many?"

Aunt Dinah, who stood at my other side, waved to a woman among the new arrivals. "Cana is a small town, but I wouldn't be surprised if our groom knows everyone in it."

I stepped back, pressing my spine against the wall, as a pair of young boys barreled

11

past me, hurrying toward the table where Dinah and I had spread a selection of my best honeyed breads. My brother was supposed to have set out a plate of figs, but I hadn't seen him since we heard the marriage party approaching.

"Not only Cana," Abba said, lifting his torch to peer at another group outside the courtyard gate. "But apparently Etan knows people in other villages, as well. I do believe I see Mary, widow of Joseph the carpenter. She and her family have come from Nazareth."

"Mary." Dinah's voice softened with affection. "I have not seen her since Joseph died. What has it been now, six years? Seven?"

"Seven," Abba replied.

Sighing, I followed my father's pointing finger and spotted a woman standing at the center of a dusty company — they must have set out from Nazareth as soon as Shabbat ended. She appeared to be surrounded by everyone in her family — several adult children, in-laws, and grandchildren . . . at least four little ones, by my count. And all of them would be tired, dusty, and thirsty.

As they stopped by the tall water jars inside the courtyard, I turned to look for Thomas. "Where is my brother?" I asked, not bothering to cloak the irritation in my voice. "He was supposed to put fruit on the table."

"There." Dinah pointed toward the torchlit gate, where Thomas was joking with a group of men among the newcomers. One of the hired servants held the guests' sandals while they splashed water over their dusty feet.

"Must Thomas greet every guest?" I asked. "Is he going to help me or play the host?"

"He will help you." Abba patted my shoulder. "But he likes to mingle. Do not scold him for being hospitable."

I pressed my lips together, hearing my father's unspoken rebuke: *Unlike you, he enjoys meeting people, so let him be.*

"When he has finished being convivial" — I gave Abba a pained smile — "please remind him that we were *both* hired to work at this banquet. I will be baking every night, and now with extra mouths to feed —"

"Do not worry about your brother," Dinah said. "I have never met a more responsible young man."

I glanced at the table, where my sweetbreads were rapidly disappearing. If the children didn't stop taking them, the adults would never have a chance to sample their light texture and delicious filling.

At least the children would not raid the wine barrels.

"I hope," I muttered, "Etan's father purchased enough wine or we will be forced to water it down."

"Who plans a wedding feast without wine?" Dinah's smile widened. "Now, I must go greet my friend."

She strode toward Mary of Nazareth, who had just accepted a cloth to dry her feet. I turned to check on the bride and groom — Etan and Galya had taken their places at the head table, and Etan's broad smile, dazzling against his tanned skin, confirmed his happiness. Galya's slender fingers crept out from beneath her long veil to clasp Etan's hand. She had to be pleased with her groom, because rarely did I see such obvious signs of affection at a wedding feast.

I blew out a breath and looked away. They must be in love, whatever that meant. Though Etan had taken nearly two years to build a home for his bride, he told my brother the weeks had passed like days, so strong was his love for Galya. I couldn't help but wonder if he would have felt the same if he'd had to work the seven years Jacob invested in Rachel . . .

I crossed my arms as Thomas broke away

from his friends and strolled toward me. After catching my eye, he waggled his brow, sending a silent message I had no trouble deciphering.

"Yes," I whispered when he reached me. "Abba has already hinted that I should be having a wedding of my own. But he doesn't understand."

Thomas leaned against my shoulder. "He only wants you to be happy."

"So he says. But I *am* happy, so why can't he leave things alone? I have a home, I have work I enjoy, and I have you, my other half. What more could I want?"

Thomas snorted. "Perhaps he wants grandchildren."

"He can enjoy Dinah's. I cannot get a proper Shabbat rest when her wild ones come to visit. Children should be quiet on Shabbat — no, they should be quiet *all* the time. And —" I caught my breath as the two little boys raced by again, their hands filled with the fruits of my labor — "children do not belong at weddings."

Thomas cast me a teasing smile and did not argue. We stood in companionable silence until Thomas turned toward the guests from Nazareth.

"Is that Mary? Aunt Dinah's friend?"

I nodded.

"And she brought — how many?"

"I counted nine additional adults. Nine more mouths to feed, plus a handful of children. After coming from Nazareth, you can be certain they'll be famished."

"The daughters are married, so of course there are children —"

"Are you hinting, too?"

Thomas leaned toward me, his face twisting in mock surprise. "Me, tease you? I know better. I've been with you since the womb."

"Exactly." I crossed my arms again. "Marriage must be wonderful for people who have no one else, but I fail to understand its appeal. I suppose some people love children, but I wouldn't know what to do with a baby."

Thomas smiled but with a distracted look, as if his attention had shifted to something more interesting.

"Brother? Are you still listening?"

He inclined his head toward the contingent from Nazareth. "I was thinking about Mary's family — I have heard interesting rumors about the eldest son. That one." He pointed to a man who had bent to talk to a little boy. "He is called Yeshua."

I studied the man as he straightened, patted the boy's head, and turned back to his brothers. He did not appear particularly interesting to me. A dusty cloak covered his shoulders, he wore his shoulder-length hair tied back with a leather strip, and he was not tall. Taller than his mother and sisters, certainly, but one of his brothers was at least a handsbreadth taller than Yeshua. Being a tall woman, I preferred men who could look me in the eye when we spoke.

The boy who had been talking to Yeshua scurried away, probably to raid another of my carefully arranged tables, and Yeshua turned to speak to his mother, a middle-aged woman whose hair had begun to gray at her temples.

In a sudden silence, Yeshua shifted and his gaze caught mine. I stiffened, momentarily embarrassed to be caught staring, and lowered my eyes. I thought he would do the same, but when I lifted my head, he was still staring, with the suggestion of a smile on his lips. He nodded, almost imperceptibly, as if we shared a secret, and then he pointedly shifted his attention to Thomas, as if he were trying to tell me something about my brother. Though Thomas was looking down, I felt a shudder ripple through his frame as Yeshua's gaze brushed him.

The moment ended when someone from

Yeshua's family called his name. When he turned and addressed the one who had spoken to him, a roar of sound rushed in to fill the dense quiet.

"What rumors, Thomas?" I asked, barely recognizing my voice as my own. "What have you heard about Mary's son?"

Thomas swallowed hard, the knot in his throat bobbing as he turned toward the group from Nazareth. "Various stories," he said. "I heard he left home several months ago and went to the wilderness to see John the Immerser. He asked John to baptize him, and at first John refused. But then he agreed, and some say that when he came up out of the water, a dove flew down and settled on Yeshua's shoulder while the heavens thundered in approval."

I wanted to know more, but just then Dinah tapped my shoulder and declared that more guests were coming toward the house, men she had never seen before.

"Did Etan invite everyone he's ever met?" I looked past the gate, where more than half a dozen torches bobbed in the darkness. "Who *are* these people?"

For the first time that day, an edge underscored my aunt's voice. "I hear they are followers of Mary's son," she said. "But I cannot imagine anyone being so thoughtless.

Etan's father did not expect to feed half the people in Galilee."

"But we cannot turn them away." A host was duty-bound to welcome any guest who responded to his invitation, so anyone who entered the flower-bedecked courtyard would be welcomed, fed, and housed for the duration of the seven-day feast or as long as they wished to stay.

Perhaps, if HaShem had mercy, some of these people would grow tired of the dancing, interesting conversation, and free food and wine. Perhaps some would go home early.

But I was more likely to wake up as empress of the Roman Empire.

Darkness had draped her ebony wings over Etan's house by the time the bride and groom slipped into the bridal chamber. The smell of woodsmoke filled the air as the groom's male guests sat quietly on wooden benches near the fire, relaxing and occasionally belching. Inside the house, the women gathered in small groups to whisper stories of their own bridal chambers.

Since I had no such stories, I remained in the courtyard and focused on the work I had been hired to complete. The sweetbreads had disappeared, along with the

19

raisin cakes and boiled eggs. I would have to bake before going to bed and boil every egg Etan's hens had laid. Tomorrow morning, Thomas could fetch more salted fish from the market, and he had promised to seek out a deer or a gazelle for roasting over the open fire.

Finally, just as the fire was dying down, the bridegroom emerged, a sheet in his hand. He held it aloft, displaying a small sprinkling of blood, and the guests erupted in joyous shouts and renewed calls for wine.

I stood back and bit my thumbnail as the servants carried fresh pitchers among the crowd, pouring drink into every uplifted cup. I knew how much wine Etan's father had purchased, and at this rate of consumption it would not last a full week. I could order the hired servants to pour water into the wine barrels after everyone had gone to bed, but wouldn't the difference in quality be noticed?

I lifted my head as a masculine figure approached, then relaxed when the moonlight revealed my father's worn face. "You look tense, daughter." He leaned against the wall of the house and rested his folded hands on his protruding belly. "Your hard work has been noticed and appreciated. The rabbi himself complimented your fig cakes."

"I will have to bake tonight, probably every night, but that is not what concerns me most." I managed a wavering smile. "I'm worried about the wine. I can always bake more cakes and add vegetables to the stew, but I do not think there's enough wine in Cana to satisfy this crowd's thirst."

"Etan's father must have underestimated the number of guests." Abba barked a cough, then caught his breath and looked out at the courtyard, still crowded with men. "He did not expect so many from outside Cana. Joseph's family, yes, for his widow is related to Etan's mother, but all those men who followed her son . . ."

A crease appeared between his brows as he studied Mary's eldest. Yeshua had pulled away from his family and sat in a circle of men I'd never seen before. Four of them wore rough garments, not proper wedding attire, yet one of them looked —

I blinked, stunned by what my father must have already noticed. "Thomas is with them?"

Abba sighed, then drew a wheezing breath. "Your brother is a man full grown; I do not command him."

"But surely you do not want him associating with these ill-bred fellows. Look how they are dressed! And they came without an invitation."

"Etan's father invited Mary and her children; Yeshua invited the others. Etan was happy to welcome them."

"He didn't have a choice." I shook my head. "Thomas should not be associating with these — these worthless rascals. I am going over there to pull him away. He ought to be helping me."

Abba's hand closed around my upper arm. "You will not interfere. You must think of your reputation. If you ever want to marry —"

"I am not thinking about marriage. I am thinking about my twin!"

Abba looked at me with something like pity in his eyes, and his voice softened as he released my arm. "I know how much you love your brother, Tasmin. But you are a grown woman, well past the age when a girl should be wed. It is time both you and Thomas married and established homes of your own. You have been together a long time, yet it is time you pulled apart. People are beginning to think your attachment is odd."

I turned away, my eyes burning with angry tears. Odd? I *did* love my brother, but how dare anyone accuse us of being anything but twins. We belonged to each other because we had been like two halves of the same person since the womb. He was male, I was female; he liked being around people, I liked being alone; he acted on impulse, I liked to plan; he was active, I was calm. Yet despite our differences, we could communicate without words and feel what the other felt even from a distance.

Our father did not understand our connection, though I did not expect him to. He had been one son among many. He had not shared his mother's womb; his soul had not been entwined with another since the moment HaShem breathed life into him.

But Thomas understood me, and I him. We had endured the same life experiences, so we had been molded together. And neither of us would ever need anyone else.

The crickets had gone to bed by the time I finished cleaning the cooking area at the rear of the courtyard. The local guests had gone home, while those who had come from a distance were sleeping anywhere they could find a place to stretch out. People loved a wedding, and though local guests split their time between the celebration and tending to their animals, children, and work, others traveled from miles away and enjoyed staying overnight, even if it meant sleeping on the floor.

Thomas, Dinah, Abba, and I were staying at our host's home because we would be working late and rising early to tend to the guests' needs. Before heading to the house, I checked the basement where the groom's father had stored the wine. He had purchased seven barrels for the seven-day feast; we emptied three of them on the first day. Only four remained, yet the feast was far from over . . .

Thomas should have spoken to Etan's father, but I had not seen him for hours.

Inside the house, I found one of the hired servants and shook her awake. "I am placing you in charge of the wine," I whispered. "At sunrise, when you fill your pitchers, make sure the pitcher is one-quarter — no, halfway filled with water. Do not let the guests know what you are doing. If we are fortunate, and if the guests are content, perhaps they will not notice that the quality of the wine has suffered."

The girl chewed her lower lip for a moment, then nodded.

"Rest well," I told her, lifting my lamp. "Tomorrow will be another busy day."

I walked to the back of the house, where Dinah had bedded down on a thick pile of blankets. She was on her back and snoring when I stretched out beside her, but she woke when I released an exhausted sigh. "Tasmin?"

"I'm here."

"Good." She rolled onto her side to face me. "You worked late. You must be tired."

"I am."

"You should take some time to enjoy the guests. A wedding should be a celebration, even for those who have to work. After all, Galya is a friend of yours, no?"

"She is. So I will try, Aunt." I folded my hands over my stomach and stared at the ceiling beams. My aunt probably wanted to share all the gossip she'd gathered from the other women —

"It was good to see Mary," she said, pillowing her cheek on her hands. "I haven't seen her in years. How strange to see her children now. The youngest was all arms and legs when I last saw him; now he is a man."

"Hmm. Her husband was a carpenter, no?"

"A good one. Mary hopes her younger sons will continue in the trade. They have taken over Joseph's business, but she does not think carpentry suits them. Their hearts, she says, are not in the work."

I stifled a yawn. "Why doesn't the older

one take his father's place?"

"Yeshua?"

"Isn't he the eldest?"

"He has done much of the work since Joseph's death — in fact, she says, he is the most skilled of them all, especially with carving. But Mary thinks he is destined for something else. She says HaShem has a special plan for him."

I snorted a laugh. "He seems to have a gift for attracting strangers. We used three times as much wine as expected, thanks to the crowd who came with him. Why are so many men following in his wake? Even Thomas seemed captivated by him."

Dinah chuckled. "His brothers aren't captivated, I assure you. I was talking with James and Jude, and they think their brother is odd. His sisters think he's spoiled."

"Spoiled?"

"Anyone can see his mother favors him. Whatever he says, she does. Pheodora, the youngest girl, says Mary thinks Yeshua can do no wrong."

My heavy eyelids scraped like sandpaper over my tired eyes. "Really."

"He is not married," Dinah went on. "And he's thirty years old."

"Hmmm." I could not summon the energy to reply with words.

26

"You should be thinking about marriage," Dinah continued. "And Thomas, too, though it always seems to take sons longer to come around to it. He will have to build a home for his bride, take over the family business . . . But if you should happen to wed one of Mary's sons, Nazareth is not far away."

"Aunt Dinah?"

"Yes?"

"I need to sleep. Tomorrow will be another long day."

I heard a sigh, then felt her hand cup my cheek. "Sleep well, dear girl. We will speak again in the morning."

I did not want to talk about marriage now or ever, so when daylight broke, I would rise before Dinah and go straight to work.

CHAPTER TWO:
TASMIN

I wiped my hands on my apron and blew out a breath, blowing away the frizzy hank of hair that kept escaping my braid. The butcher was supposed to deliver a skinned goat after sunrise, and though I had started the fire and assembled the spit, I still had no goat for the second-day dinner.

I turned, narrowing my eyes, and spotted Thomas laughing with the men from Nazareth.

"Thomas!"

He turned at the sound of my voice and came over. "Sorry," he said, flushing. "What do you need me to do?"

"Everything." I blew hair out of my eyes again, then gestured to the fire. "I need you to make sure the coals stay hot while I search for our goat. I also seem to be out of leaven, which I'll need for the bread. And don't mention it to anyone, but we are watering down the wine today."

Thomas made a face. "What if Etan notices?"

"If he says something to you, remind him it was his guest who brought so many people that we had to use three barrels on the first day." I propped my hands on my hips and looked around. Outside the small area that served as my kitchen, the out-of-town guests were munching on the fruit I had set on trays and dispersed around the garden. The local guests, thank heaven, had slept in their own beds and would eat food from their own kitchens.

"So" — I turned back to my brother — "would you rather mind the fire or go check on the meat and leaven?"

He looked from the fire to the guests, then back at me. "I'll tend the fire. And I'll keep an eye on the wine."

"Good. All right." I pulled off my apron, tossed it onto the table, and hastily smoothed my hair. "People will be ready to eat by the sixth hour and I'm afraid nothing will be ready —"

Thomas lifted his hand, silently shushing me. "Don't worry," he said, understanding flickering in his eyes. "Everything will be fine, and I'll handle things here. Has Etan's father ordered more wine?"

I shook my head. "I'm not sure he can afford to buy more."

"Then the situation can't be helped. And don't worry about the leaven — people eat flatbread, too. Serve that, and they won't know you had something else in mind."

Bless him; my brother had a gift for helping me think more clearly. As my anxiety drained away, I blinked back unshed tears and managed a small smile. "Right." My voice cracked on the word. "I'll go check on the butcher."

"I'll be here."

Fortunately, I knew the butcher well, and the man's home was not far from Etan's. I lengthened my stride, carefully avoiding uneven areas in the street and nodding to familiar faces who were returning to the wedding feast. By midday the crowd might be larger than it had been on the first day.

I walked through the butcher's gate and looked around. Nothing moved in the small courtyard save a pair of nesting hens, who cocked their heads and warily eyed me as I walked to the door. "Butcher!" I called, rapping with my knuckles. "Etan the bridegroom needs meat for his feast!"

The door opened, but the butcher did not answer my call. Instead, I found myself face-to-face with the man's wife, who regarded me with bleary eyes.

"We . . . are not well," she said, one pale hand clutching a shawl around her shoulders. "We were up all night . . . Something we ate."

I took a half step back. "But you are supposed to deliver a goat to the wedding feast this morning. The fire is ready."

The woman's eyes widened. "You cannot expect my husband to work today. You will have to find another butcher."

"Here?" In a fit of exasperation I turned toward the street, looked left and right, and held up empty hands. "There *is* no other butcher in Cana!"

"Try Nazareth," the woman said, slowly closing the door. "Or Tiberias. But you will get no meat from us today."

I heard her latch the door, then turned and walked out to the street. The hour was yet early; the sun had only begun to climb the eastern sky. I could go back to the wedding and tell Thomas to douse the fire and find some salted fish . . . or I could send him to the butcher in Nazareth.

In either case, I would have to hurry.

The dancing had begun by the time I returned. As musicians played the lyre, cornet, flute, and cymbals, the men linked their arms around each other's shoulders and made a colorful, dizzying circle around the bridegroom. Thomas lifted his chin when I waved for his attention, then continued to dance.

Forced to wait, I crossed my arms and leaned against the wall. I glanced toward the fire, where the once-hot logs had gone dark. No matter — better to let them cool, because they would never remain hot until Thomas returned from Nazareth with meat for our dinner.

I sighed and studied the dancing men. Too many guests and not enough food. Perhaps some of our out-of-town visitors would go home early? I searched for signs of boredom, but Mary's sons and sons-in-law were among the most eager dancers. The eldest, Yeshua, seemed particularly enthusiastic. His eyes snapped as he danced, his head tilting back as laughter bubbled up from his throat. Did his passion spring from his happiness for the groom, or did he always overflow with the joy of life?

Finally the music ended, the musicians stood, and the circle of dancers broke up, some moving to congratulate the groom again, others heading toward the tables that offered fruit and pitchers of wine.

I walked directly to Thomas, who stood apart from the others like an overgrown boy afraid to join a group of strangers.

"The butcher is sick," I told him, getting straight to the point, "so we'll need to get meat from Nazareth. Will you go? If you leave now, you can be back before midday, which gives me time to boil the meat and serve a stew."

Thomas tilted his head and gave me an uncertain look. "Must we have meat? We could serve cheese and bread —"

"Not for a wedding dinner. I need meat, and Nazareth is the closest place to find it."

"Can't we find a family in Cana who would sell us a goat? We could do the butchering behind the house . . ."

I moved closer to him. "My livelihood," I reminded him, lowering my voice, "comes from arranging the details of wedding feasts. What family in Cana would hire me if it were known that I had to beg for meat on the second day of a celebration?"

"But it is not your fault —"

I shook my head. "No matter. I will not have anyone think I neglected my planning. I will get meat from Nazareth and no one will know the difference."

Thomas looked toward the other men, who were gathering around Mary's oldest son. "Fine, but I don't want to leave. Could you find someone else to go?"

I laughed to cover my annoyance. "Would you have me send our aged father? Or perhaps Aunt Dinah?"

"Well —"

"Why don't you want to go? Etan's father hired us — both of us — to work at this feast, and now you don't want to do the work."

"I am the headwaiter, not the errand boy."

"And I am?"

"You could go. It's not so long a journey."

His words dropped into the space between us like stones, leaving me shocked and irritated. "Yes, I could go, but you would have to see to everything else. And I still don't understand why you won't do this for me. Have you hurt your foot? Are you in some kind of pain?"

A tide of red crept up his throat. "I know you won't understand, but I want to stay and listen to Yeshua. He has fascinating ideas."

I stared at my brother, surprise siphoning the blood from my head. Thomas had always been a thinker and sometime-philosopher, but never had I heard him express interest in hearing from a Galilean. The sages? Yes. The Greeks? Yes. A Nazarene? Never.

"What," I asked, my voice trembling with

repressed anger, "has he said that fascinates you so?"

Thomas glanced around, then pulled me away from the others. When he was certain no one could overhear, he crossed his arms. "He said we should pray for Caesar."

I winced. "As when David prayed, 'O God, break their teeth in their mouths'?"

Thomas shook his head. "He said we should pray for Caesar so we could live in peace. He said we should pray for all in authority."

I drew in a sharp breath. "I think you should go to Nazareth instead of listening to such nonsense."

"I'm not going, Tasmin, not when I could be listening to Yeshua. I'll do whatever you need me to do here, but I don't want to leave."

I stared at him, perplexed and more than a little frustrated by his answer. Thomas and I were not always in perfect agreement, but never had he flatly refused one of my requests.

"All right," I finally said. "I'll go. But I'll need an escort, so I will leave that to you. And I need to go soon, so please take care of this."

"Never fear," Thomas said, already looking at Yeshua. "I will take care of everything."

I drew a long, quivering breath, struggling to master the anger that had nearly spoiled my day. Thomas did not want to leave the wedding — fine. Perhaps I should be relieved, because now he would be overseeing the many details while I enjoyed a nice walk to Nazareth. He would sit with a group of sweating, belching men while I inhaled fresh air and stretched my legs.

Perhaps I would get the best part of the bargain.

I checked on the servants, set out more fruit and cheese, and pulled a scarf over my head to block the sun on the hour-long walk. By the time I returned to Thomas, a man and woman stood with him. I had seen them with Mary, but both were strangers to me.

Thomas greeted me with a broad smile, then gestured to the couple. "Damaris and her brother Jude are willing to walk to Nazareth with you. They are children of Aunt Dinah's friend Mary."

Damaris clasped my hands in a warm grip. "I am glad you need to go to Nazareth." She stepped closer and lowered her voice. "I am with child again, and my husband has given me leave to return home. All this merriment is too much for me."

I squeezed her hands. "Are you all right? Should you be walking?"

She smiled. "I walked every day with the first five, so I will be fine. And when we get home, I'll be able to rest. That's what I need most."

Five children? She couldn't be more than twenty-six or twenty-seven.

I glanced at her brother, who did not appear thrilled to be leaving the wedding. "I am sorry to ask this of you," I said, "but my father will not let me leave Cana without an escort. He has heard too many stories of bandits."

"I understand," Jude said, his voice gruff. "And if there is nothing else to discuss, let us be on our way. I want to get Damaris home."

We set off at a brisk pace, quickly leaving Cana behind. I had not often traveled the narrow path that lay between our two cities, but the scenery held no surprises. The land outside Cana was hilly, dotted with low brush, and looked as though an archangel had opened his mighty hand and spilled rocks over the terrain. Few trees grew in the area, and those that did manage to take root were sturdy — tamarisk and palms and terebinth.

"So," Damaris said, adjusting her head-scarf to block the morning sun, "I suppose you and your brother are friends of the groom? You seem to be about the same age."

"We are." I surveyed the horizon, where scrubby trees rose above the flat line of the earth. "Etan and my brother attended Torah school together."

Jude grunted. "I studied Torah with my brothers, and we were always competing. I'd memorize one passage and someone else another, and then we'd see who could recite without making a mistake. I did well, but Yeshua never missed a word."

I cast the man a sidelong look. "My brother seems fascinated by him."

Jude sighed. "Many are, and I wish I understood why. He is a man like any other, but when he speaks —" he paused and gave a shrug — "you've seen how they listen. I don't understand it."

"My brother says Yeshua wants us to pray for Caesar."

"And your brother agrees?"

"I don't know. Thomas is not the sort to make quick judgments. But those other men seem to have accepted what Yeshua says."

For the first time, Jude looked directly at me. "Did you meet Andrew? He was a disciple of John the Immerser. John said his work — baptizing people as a sign of repentance — was only a taste of what would soon come."

"We all know HaShem is going to send a king to release us from Roman tyranny. We have been waiting ever since the return from exile."

Jude nodded. "Exactly. But Andrew and the others believe my brother is the promised One."

I took a wincing breath. "The one — those men believe your brother is the *messiah*?"

"They are convinced of it." Jude shook his head. "Andrew was with the Immerser the day Yeshua went to the Jordan and asked John to perform his *mikvah*. John didn't want to."

"Why not?"

"I don't know, but Yeshua said he wanted to be baptized as a sign — to give Adonai an opportunity to show His glory. As if Adonai needed any help."

I laughed and waited for more, but Jude did not seem inclined to elaborate. "Well, what happened?"

He drew an exasperated breath. "Depends on who you ask. Andrew says Yeshua went down into the waters and came up, then the clouds blew apart and the *Ruach Elohim* descended like a dove and sat on Yeshua's shoulder. Then he heard a voice from heaven saying, 'This is my Son, whom I love; with Him I am well pleased!' "

I shook my head. "A more likely story is that the sky thundered and Andrew only *thought* he heard those words."

Jude smiled, satisfaction shining in his eyes. "That is what I told him. Yet he insists others heard *words,* not thunder."

We walked in silence for a moment, and I wondered if Damaris was listening or too sick to care about our conversation. She walked behind us, her head down, but she had not fallen behind.

I had to know more. "And after that?" I asked Jude. "Why are Andrew and all those other men with your brother now?"

He shrugged. "Andrew says John's disciples were sitting around the fire that night and John said, 'I have seen the *Ruach* coming down like a dove out of heaven, and it remained on Him. I did not know Him; but the One who sent me to immerse in water said to me, "The One on whom you see the Ruach coming down and remaining, this is the One who immerses in the *Ruach ha-Kodesh.*" And I have seen and testified that this is *Ben-Elohim,* the son of God.' "

I stared, tongue-tied, but then a retching noise cut into my thoughts. I turned in time to see Damaris lean over and vomit on the side of the road.

In an instant, Jude was by his sister's side, holding her shoulders as she retched again, then spat the remnants of bitter taste from her lips. "Sorry," she said, taking the linen square Jude produced from his tunic. She wiped her mouth and patted perspiration from her brow. "I should not have eaten this morning." She managed to laugh. "At least I got sick here and not before all those guests."

As Jude cared for his sister, I tried to make sense of what I'd just learned. Andrew's belief that Yeshua was our messiah and future king seemed farfetched but not outside the realm of possibility. And yet to believe he was the *son of God*? Impossible. Inconceivable.

Every morning and evening, as part of our prayers, we recited the *Shema:* "Hear O Israel, the Lord our God, the Lord is one."

Israel had only one God, and HaShem had no sons.

My heart twisted in pity for Jude and Damaris — for all of Mary's children. I couldn't imagine being caught up in such blasphemy.

"I am sorry," I said, catching Jude's eye.

"I cannot imagine what you must be feeling."

"It's nothing," Damaris said, wiping her mouth on her sleeve. "The sickness will pass in a few weeks."

I wasn't talking about nausea, and Jude caught my meaning. He nodded slightly and shifted his gaze to the road ahead. "When John the Immerser returned to the river the next day, Andrew kept watching the road. When he saw Yeshua walk by, he called out, 'There he is, God's Passover lamb.' That's when Andrew left John. He's been with Yeshua ever since — he and his brother, Simon Peter."

I shook my head. "How could they leave their families, their work . . . ?"

"They are fishermen, so they can work anywhere they find water. But yes, they left everything. Peter has a house and family in Capernaum, though he does visit them as often as he can."

I waited until Damaris was ready to walk again, then resumed my place by Jude's side. "A few fisherman from Capernaum — not exactly the companions you would expect to be keeping company with Israel's future king."

Jude chuffed as we walked. "My brother's followers are from all over Galilee. There's

Philip from Bethsaida, and Nathanael, who wholeheartedly believed the moment Yeshua said he had seen him standing under a fig tree."

"But anyone could see a man standing —"

"Nathanael had been standing under a fig tree in his walled garden, trying to determine what was wrong with the leaves, two days before Yeshua came to Bethsaida. When Nathanael realized Yeshua saw what no one could have seen, he declared him to be the Son of God and King of Israel."

While I had no explanation for that, I did not need to supply one. When I looked up again, we were passing the watchtower that stood outside Nazareth.

Fortunately, the butcher in Nazareth was healthy and more than delighted to provide meat for a wedding feast in Cana. He had no goat available, but he had a lamb.

I reluctantly accepted his offer. The lamb would work well in a stew, and it was meat — a luxury rarely enjoyed by the average family but expected at a feast.

"I have heard about that wedding," the butcher said, tying a bleating lamb to a post. "A few families from Nazareth have gone for the feast."

"Yes," I said, turning to avoid the sight of

bloodshed. Though people slaughtered animals every day, I had never been able to stomach the sight of blood. When I prepared chicken for our Shabbat dinner, I made Thomas kill the bird because I simply could not bring myself to cut its throat.

"The carpenter's family is in Cana," I said in an effort to avoid talking about the lamb. "Mary, her children and grandchildren —"

"Nice family." I saw the butcher's knife wink at the corner of my eye and turned again, but could not escape a swishing sound and the wet splat of blood spilling on the ground.

My knees nearly buckled. Desperate to talk about something else, I said, "The eldest son, Yeshua —"

"I know him well," the butcher said. "Talented craftsman. Everyone thought he would take over his father's work, but he left a few months ago and the work fell to his brothers." He looked up at Jude. "I would imagine you fellows are not very happy about that."

Jude showed his teeth in an expression that fell far short of a smile. "We are not. But we hope he will return when he grows tired of . . . whatever he's doing."

"For a son, what is more important than the work his father left for him to do?" the

44

butcher asked. "Four months ago, my wife ordered this worktable from your family. It finally arrived, though I know you younger brothers had to finish it. And if you'll forgive me for saying so, the craftsmanship is not what I expected from the sons of Joseph the carpenter."

I shuddered at the heavy sound of the lamb being dropped onto the table. "Do you want me to clean and skin it?" the butcher asked. "Or would you prefer to do those things after you arrive in Cana?"

I frowned, not understanding why he would ask.

"Leave it as it is," Jude answered. "I do not want to carry a dripping carcass all the way back to the wedding."

I closed my eyes, amazed at my stupidity. Of course. I had given no thought as to how we would transport the animal, but since Jude would be carrying it . . .

Once we returned to the wedding, I would ask Thomas to do the messy work.

"Thank you," I told Jude. "I wasn't thinking."

I glanced at Damaris, who stood at the gate, facing the street. "Are you all right?" I asked.

She nodded. "I can make it home," she whispered. "And then I want to nap. My husband and children will be home tonight, and after that I will not be able to rest."

I paid the butcher and smiled my thanks as Jude draped the carcass over his shoulders. Then we walked Damaris to the house where she lived with her husband, their children, and his parents. The building was large and grand, with an addition that had obviously been built to house the son's family.

"You should come in," she said, opening the gate that led to the smaller house. "I will give you lemon water and let you rest before you walk back."

I bit my lip, mentally calculating how long it would take to return and prepare the stew. Fortunately, a stew would cook more quickly than a roast, and we had plenty of vegetables to fill the stewpot.

Damaris went first and threw open the shutters that opened to the central courtyard, allowing a wave of sunlight to flood the front room. Jude strolled inside with the comfortable air of a frequent guest, then pulled a piece of burlap from a basket and spread it on a table. He lowered the lamb onto the rough cloth and wrapped it to keep the flies away.

Then he dropped into a chair and propped his elbows on pillows, gesturing for me to do the same. "I like visiting Damaris," he said, grinning at his sister. "I enjoy seeing how wealthy people live."

Damaris felt well enough to toss a pillow at his head, and then she went over to the cooking area and brought out a pitcher of water flavored with lemon. "My father-in-law is wealthy," she said, filling a cup for me. "He owns a vineyard and exports a great deal of wine. He is always traveling to exotic ports and buying things we are not likely to see in Nazareth."

I gestured to a colorful pillow that shimmered in the sunlight. "Like that?"

She looked up and smiled. "Oh, yes. That fabric is really too fragile for daily use, so I don't know why he bought it. I forget where he found it — probably Rome, since everything seems to come from that city. But my children have already stained that pillow and rendered it — well, if not useless, at least unfit for my father-in-law's house. That's why it now lives with us."

She poured water for her brother and placed a cup in his hand, then sank onto a sofa and fanned her face with a palm frond. "My father-in-law is always telling us about the things he has seen in Rome. Exotic animals, amazing aqueducts, and beautiful statues."

"Not likely to see those here," Jude added. "Only the Herods would be brazen enough to erect a graven image in Judea."

Damaris turned to her brother. "Have you nothing to fetch from home? Wait — didn't Mother ask for her blue cloak? You could go get it, and by the time you return I am sure Tasmin will be ready to return to Cana."

"A good suggestion." Jude stood, kissed the top of his sister's head, and strode cheerfully away.

"He was never one for listening to women," Damaris said, her eyes softening as she watched him walk toward the door. "But if I had to choose, I'd say he was my favorite brother. Pheodora would say the same."

"Your other sister — she lives here in Nazareth, too?"

Damaris shook her head. "She is married to Chiram, from Bethlehem, and she has four girls. Chiram desperately wants a son, but Pheodora told me —" she lowered her voice to a confidential whisper — "she would be happy if Adonai stopped sending babies. Her little girls are a handful."

I looked around at the fine furnishings — Damaris had certainly married well. "Did Pheodora also marry a merchant's son?"

Damaris made a face. "No. She married

into livestock."

"What?" I laughed. "I don't understand."

"She married a *shepherd*." Damaris spoke the word as if it had a bad taste. "He watches flocks outside the city, and he is away from home most of the time. I hate to say it, but every time I've seen him, he —" she lowered her voice — "he smells like animals." Her dark eyes darted to me. "So . . . you are not married?"

I sighed and braced myself for the usual questions. "I am not."

"Don't you *want* to be married?"

I lifted one shoulder in a polite shrug. "I have not thought much about it. For as long as I can remember, our family has been Abba, Thomas, and me. Thomas and I have always done everything together."

"But he is your brother." She shuddered in mock horror. "As a grown woman, I could never live with one of my brothers."

"He is my twin. Abba says we are like two sides of a coin — completely opposite but bonded together."

"But, Tasmin, you are missing so much." She eyed me with something very fragile in her expression, then looked away toward the open windows. "What was it Agur wrote? 'Three things are too amazing for me, four I do not understand: the way of an eagle in the sky, the way of a serpent upon a rock, the way of a ship in the heart of the sea, and the way of a man with a maiden.' " A blush ran over her cheeks. "You will not know what married love is until you experience it."

I took a deep breath and flexed my fingers until the urge to cover my ears had passed. "I am content with my brother," I said easily. "We are happy with our family as it is."

Damaris lowered her hand to her belly. "Still, surely you want children. HaShem created women to have children and commanded us to fill the earth —"

"Your brothers are not married."

She lifted a finger, acknowledging my point. "I believe they will be, eventually. At least I hope so. Because I adore children and want to have lots of nieces and nephews."

"Well . . ." I searched for words, not wanting to sound as if I disapproved of her choice. "I have never really thought much about children. Thomas and I have no other siblings, and we were never around them growing up."

"But you had a mother, and every child loves her mother."

"Thomas and I lost our mother when we were young. Abba asked Aunt Dinah to help care for us, but she had a family of her own. We learned to be content with having only a father."

A tremor of compassion knit Damaris's brows. "I am sorry. Forgive me for rattling on about things I know nothing about."

"Do not worry." I hoped she would not ask anything else, because I did not want to horrify her with the truth.

I took advantage of her momentary silence to drink the water in my cup, then stood. "Thank you for your company and your hospitality," I said. "I know you need rest, so I'll be going."

"But Jude is coming here to get you —"

"I'll wait for him outside."

"But —" She pointed to the wrapped lamb on the table. "Your meat."

I grimaced. "Thank you. I nearly forgot about it."

She might have protested further, but I walked over, slipped my arms beneath the lamb, now neatly wrapped, and carried it to the door. Thankfully, the animal was not heavy and I would not have to go far.

Struggling with the dead animal in my arms, I got through the doorway and went outside to wait . . . where my secret would be safer.

■ ■ ■ ■

I waited several minutes outside the house, then decided to see if I could find Jude's home myself. Nazareth was not a large town, and the first woman I saw on the street knew immediately which family I sought. She waved me toward a narrow, curving lane that lay like a pointing finger around the rocky knoll that supported the city. I started walking, ignoring the newer homes and barely glancing at the ornate ones, knowing Mary and her family could never afford a showplace.

Finally I slowed my steps in front of a row of houses situated cheek by jowl together, each nearly indistinguishable from its neighbor. I squinted as I scanned the row of sand-colored structures. Surely Joseph the carpenter had lived in one of these.

The two-story homes along this road were made of mud brick and not at all ostentatious. Each had a small walled staircase that opened onto the street and led up to the second floor. Unfortunately, none of the staircases had been marked with the name of the family.

I stepped back and squinted to block the glare of the sun.

"Have you tired of my sister's company so soon?"

I blinked, searching for the source of the sound, and spotted Jude at the top of the fourth staircase. I was about to stammer an explanation when I saw his warm and friendly smile — he was teasing.

"I wanted to let her rest." I moved slowly toward him, not wanting to place him in the awkward position of inviting me in. If no one else was at home, he might not want to entertain a strange woman before the neighbors' prying eyes.

"And why are you carrying the lamb? I was on my way to fetch it."

"I . . . I didn't want to trouble your sister, since she was not feeling well. And" — I crinkled my nose as a pair of flies buzzed around my face — "it is not heavy."

"Not at first. Set it down and rest a moment. I will get water for you to wash up."

I did as he said, setting the lamb on a stone bench, then looked askance at my arms, covered in sweat and bits of fiber. At least I saw no blood.

While I waited, I studied the carpenter's home. The house Joseph had built for Mary was not particularly large, despite the number of children who had been born under its roof. Though I could not see inside the windows, I imagined it was like others I had visited: the first floor featuring an open courtyard with a fire pit at the center, single rooms for animals and their feed along two sides, storage jars for washing and cooking along the back. The family lived upstairs — one room for the women, one for the men, and a communal space for guests to mingle with the family. Another mud-brick staircase would lead up to the flat roof, where the night breezes could cool a thirsty forehead and ease an overheated body to sleep.

A cozy house, but not exactly the sort of dwelling I would expect for a man who would be king of the Jews.

A moment later, Jude returned with a pitcher, which he poured over my arms, washing the filth away. After giving me a linen cloth to dry myself, he set the pitcher on a step and picked up a folded square. "My mother's cloak," he said, handing it to me. "And I will carry the lamb."

"If there is nothing else," I said, managing a smile, "let us be on our way."

CHAPTER THREE:
JUDE

Tasmin did not talk much on the way back to Cana. I set a faster pace than before because we did not have to be mindful of Damaris's condition, and I knew Tasmin had to prepare dinner for the feast. The woman might be opinionated and overly squeamish about slaughtering animals, but she did work hard.

A woman who worked hard, Abba always said, was worth her weight in gold. A woman who worked hard *and* knew when to keep quiet was worth a king's fortune.

The date farmer's daughter was a pleasure to behold, as well. Taller than most women, with a slender waist and sturdy hips, she had been blessed with a pleasing appearance and seemed oddly unaware of it. She did not wear her hair elaborately curled like most of the women at the wedding, but had woven it into two braids that beat softly against her back with every step. Soft, damp curls hid behind her ears and at her hairline, especially when her forehead gleamed with pearls of perspiration as it did now. And her ear, decorated only with a small gold circle, looked like one of the elaborately swirled honey cakes that had melted in my mouth when I bit into it . . .

"Jude."

I lifted my brows, startled to hear her voice. "Yes?"

"Do you like being a carpenter?"

The question caught me off guard, and I laughed. "No one has ever asked me that before."

She gave me a bright-eyed glance, full of shrewdness. "Why not? You have five brothers. Surely Nazareth does not need five carpenters. Have you never wanted to do something else?"

I adjusted my grip on the lamb across my shoulders and squinted into the distance. "I have never thought about it. Our father taught all of us how to use tools and work the wood . . . though some of us are better at it than others."

"Really?"

When she did not look up, I suspected she did not care what I said; she was only making conversation to pass the time. Still, as long as the conversation did not get too silly, I was willing to answer.

"Yes," I said. "Yeshua is the most skilled at carving. When he was younger, he used to carve gopher wood into animals that appeared so real you almost expected them to run away. He has carved cups and trays and pieces of furniture. He's very good."

Her eyes sank into a delicate net of wrinkles as she smiled. "Can you carve?"

"Not as well as Yeshua."

Weary of talking about myself, I turned the conversation around. "What about you? Have you always wanted to bake for weddings?"

"No."

"But you do it?"

She shrugged. "My father owns date palms. We harvest dates. What am I supposed to do with so many dates? I hate them, so I dry them and sell them at the market. Dried dates are good for baking, and the cakes are so festive that people want them for weddings. So now I bake for weddings."

"And your brother? Does he bake, too?"

Another sharp-eyed glance, then she shook her head. "Thomas helps Abba in the grove because our father can no longer climb the trees. One day the grove will be his, and we will continue to work together.

Like you, we have never considered doing anything else."

We walked in silence a moment more, then her brow wrinkled. "Why does your brother think he is the messiah? Did someone tell him he is? Did he dream it? Or did he just decide to call himself Israel's promised king?"

I pursed my lips and slowly blew out a long breath. Should I ignore the question or confess my ignorance of Yeshua's motives? I did not want to get into a long discussion about Yeshua. I did not want to talk about him at all.

"Have you," I said, matching the rhythm of my words to the steady tramp of our feet, "ever heard a question so many times you could happily die as long as you knew you would never hear it again?"

She examined my face with considerable absorption, then nodded. "Yes."

"Then let's enjoy our walk and not speak of things that weary us. Agreed?"

Her eyes warmed slightly, and the hint of a smile acknowledged the success of my hunch. "Agreed, Jude ben Joseph."

CHAPTER FOUR:
TASMIN

By the fifth day of the wedding feast, my emotions about Thomas had shifted from concern to anxiety. For the first four days, after he helped me with the work — with an unusually distracted air and minimal effort — he hurried to join his new friends: Andrew, Simon Peter, Nathanael, James, and John. Whether Yeshua joined them or not, they sat in a small circle and talked, their heads bent together, their voices low. Aunt Dinah joked that they must be planning to overthrow the Romans. Though I managed a polite laugh, her jest made me wonder.

What topic held them so spellbound, and why did they lower their voices to discuss it? Whenever I approached, usually on the pretext of serving them lemon water or barley cakes, they snapped their mouths shut and avoided my gaze — even Thomas, who usually told me everything.

My brother and I shared everything growing up: our opinions, which were often opposite, our thoughts, secrets, and fears. We spent every hour of every day together until Thomas was old enough to go to the synagogue for Torah study. That was when Abba sent me to Aunt Dinah's house so I could learn how to cook, sew, grind wheat, make bread, and keep the fire pit coals glowing. While I was with Dinah, I also received lessons on how to be an obedient wife, how to persuade a husband by subtle means, and how to pique the interest of a man. Dinah's daughters were apt pupils, yet I barely listened. Why should I? HaShem had put me and Thomas together in the womb, and we had already experienced things that had bonded us more closely than most of the married couples of my acquaintance. I could tell what my brother was thinking from across the house, and he understood my moods better than I did. Why would we ever need anyone else?

So when Thomas took up with a group of strangers — especially when he was supposed to be helping me — of course I was bothered. Irritated. And distressed.

Not even Yeshua proved as distant as Thomas. Though he spent a good deal of time with the men he brought to the wedding, he also spent time with his mother, with the bride and groom, and with others who sought him out. Once I walked over and pretended to adjust an awning while I eavesdropped on his conversation with Etan and Galya. Yeshua congratulated them on their marriage, wished them every happiness, and offered the blessing of Rachel and Leah — the typical sort of thing anyone would say at a wedding.

So why did my twin find him so fascinating?

One afternoon, when the women had gone inside to rest and most of the men dozed in the sun, I walked over to the shady area where the friends of Thomas and Yeshua had gathered. Yeshua was not with them, for he was out walking with his mother. While the remaining men talked, I picked up a broom and slowly swept the cobblestones, though my halfhearted efforts did little but stir the dust.

A new face had entered the circle — James, Mary's second-born son. Tall and rangy, in his late twenties, James was past the age of marriage, but perhaps he was following his older brother's example.

"Tell us, James," Peter said, "about growing up with Yeshua. Surely you have interesting stories to share."

James gave Peter a skeptical look. "I don't know what you want to hear. We are like any other family."

Andrew shook his head. "But your brother is the promised king of Israel."

James guffawed. "My brother has always been a dreamer. When there is work to be done, you will find him wandering in the hills. When we are cutting lumber, he is likely to be sitting on the slopes of Mount Tabor."

Andrew's face fell. "But surely there is something you could tell us. Something unusual that happened."

A corner of James's mouth twisted. "There was one situation . . . I'll never forget it. I thought our father would punish him severely, but instead our parents withheld their rebuke, almost as if they were afraid to offend him."

"What?" Andrew said, grinning. "Give us details."

James's chest rose and fell as he drew a deep breath. "The incident happened on a Passover trip to Jerusalem. After the feast, we gathered our things and started the journey home with a group from Nazareth. I was ten, so Yeshua would have been twelve. Anyway, we traveled all day, and as we were bedding down that night, our mother searched among our friends and family for Yeshua. She asked me and Damaris if we'd seen him, and we told her no — we hadn't seen him since Jerusalem. Ima became hysterical. Abba calmed her down, but he couldn't stop her tears. I couldn't sleep after that, because all I could hear was the sound of Ima's weeping. She kept saying, 'It is our duty to protect him. How could this have happened?' "

James shot Andrew a pointed look, but the fisherman's face remained impassive.

"She was extremely upset," James went on. "And the rest of us couldn't understand why Yeshua would be so foolish, so inconsiderate as to upset our mother and father."

Andrew nodded. "So what happened?"

James shrugged. "The next morning, Abba sent the rest of us home with a neighboring family, because he and Ima had to go back to Jerusalem. I had been hoping they would leave Yeshua in the Holy City, but no, they insisted on returning. So we said good-bye, and the rest of us had to go home with people we barely knew. I was so upset I didn't speak to Yeshua for weeks afterward."

A heavy silence fell over the group, then Peter spoke. "So . . . ?"

"So what?"

Peter blew out an exasperated breath. "So what had Yeshua been doing in Jerusalem?"

"Does it matter? He deliberately stayed behind when it was time to leave."

"But perhaps he had a reason."

"What twelve-year-old boy has a reason to ignore his parents?" James's jaw clenched and his eyes narrowed as he continued. "Abba said they searched everywhere — the house where we stayed, the marketplace, and finally they went to the Temple. That's where they spotted him — sitting on a stool, surrounded by learned Torah teachers. They were questioning Yeshua, and he was answering as if he were more highly educated than the elders. The Temple teachers were amazed at him."

James glanced around the circle and saw what I saw — his listeners, flabbergasted by the story. "Abba said he and Ima rushed over and asked Yeshua why he hadn't stayed with the family, and he said, 'Why were you searching for me? Didn't you know I must be about the things of my Father?' "

Peter blinked rapidly. "About the things . . . of Joseph the carpenter?"

"His *heavenly* father." James's voice dripped with derision. "He spoke as if HaShem were his father, not Abba. After they returned home and I heard the story, fury rose up within me, for not only did Yeshua act irresponsibly but his answer disrespected our father. And how could Yeshua speak as if he knew more than the Torah teachers? Now that I am a man, I know Torah teachers don't always agree, so how could a twelve-year-old give them definitive answers?"

"But you said the priests were amazed," Andrew interrupted. "So surely —"

"Wouldn't you be amazed if a child tried to explain some of the prophets' most perplexing prophecies?" James asked. "They were amazed by *who* spoke to them, not by the answers. If Yeshua had been sixteen or twenty, they would have turned away or told him to remain silent lest he be thought a fool."

At this, I turned my head and smiled, happy to know that another of Yeshua's siblings had not been swept away by the man's strange ideas. If Thomas would listen to James or Jude, who knew Yeshua better than any of the men seated in that circle, he would remain safe. My brother would not be carried away by whatever brand of treason the carpenter's son wanted to foment.

I moved my broom to a new area so I could study Thomas, but the look on my brother's face was anything but reassuring. He was frowning, which meant he disagreed with something James had said. He would need the benefit of my perspective to fully understand how radical this Yeshua might be.

A perspective I would share at the earliest possible opportunity.

When I finished cleaning, I went into the house to rest. The only available spot was on the floor next to Galya, so I stretched out on a blanket beside her. When she stirred and opened her eyes, I told her I was surprised to find her in the women's room.

"Oh." She gave me a drowsy smile. "Etan is outside with the men, so I thought I'd slip away. A woman cannot spend *all* her time with her husband."

Grateful to find her alone, I asked a question that had been much on my mind. "Is marriage all you hoped it would be?"

"How can I know?" She dimpled. "When the celebration is over and I learn how to be his wife, then I will know. After I have lived a year next to his mother and brothers and sisters, then I will know. But now, of course, marriage is wonderful. Ask me again when I am older."

She dropped her head to her arm and

peered at me through half-lowered lashes. "You should be thinking about a wedding, Tasmin. Do none of the men here interest you?"

"I do not look at other men as potential husbands." I resisted the urge to yawn as a warm tide of exhaustion swept over me. "I will leave that decision to my father."

Galya laughed. "Everyone knows the matter of marriage is up to you! I have heard your father say he has suggested many fine young men, but you refuse them all." Her voice softened. "If you had not lost your mother so early, I am sure you would be eager for a future with a husband and children."

A cold panic chilled my shoulder blades and prickled down my spine. Her comment about my mother, coming so soon after her talk of marriage . . . but she could not know. No one knew, no one but me and Thomas.

I drew a deep breath to calm my pounding heart. "I have my father and Thomas. I need no one else."

"Oh, Tasmin." Galya's dimple winked at me. "You do not know what you are missing."

I closed my eyes, hoping she would take the hint and let me rest. "I know about men and women. But I don't need that. Not every woman needs to be married."

"You may be right. But didn't Adonai make Eve for Adam? And didn't He create a female for every beast on earth?"

"I am not a beast." A profound weakness settled over me like a blanket. "But I am tired. If you have any compassion for me at all, please let me sleep."

"Of course," Galya whispered. "But you are still mistaken."

CHAPTER FIVE:
TASMIN

By the sixth morning of the feast, the celebration had quieted, although I knew the calm would not last. When the final feast day began at sunset, the musicians would play, the dancers would begin to whirl, and appetites would return. Tonight's dinner would be the most extravagant, because it would fortify the guests who would return to their homes on the morrow. The food would be plentiful and the wine would flow . . . but my wine barrels were empty.

I had meat, fruits, and vegetables. I had been baking breads, savory and sweet, for the last two days. The feast would be everything the bride and groom expected, but the groom's money had run out along with his wine.

I was pacing in the courtyard, debating whether or not I should throw myself into the fire pit, when I heard a soft voice behind me. "Are you all right, dear girl? You seem anxious."

I turned to see Mary of Nazareth regarding me with a concerned expression. I had barely spoken to her during the week, but Dinah must have mentioned that I was a kinswoman because Mary's eyes shone with sincere compassion.

"I am exhausted," I admitted, spreading my hands over the glowing embers of the cook fire. "I have done the best I could for this feast, yet somehow . . . I must have miscalculated. We have run out of money, and we have no wine for tonight's dinner."

Mary smiled and turned, calling for her eldest son. Yeshua was sitting with his followers beneath a tamarisk tree, and I expected him to ignore his mother's summons. But he broke away from what appeared to be an intense conversation and came over, nodding at me before he gave his mother a questioning look.

"They don't have any wine," she whispered.

Yeshua glanced at me and looked again at his mother. "Woman" — he lowered his voice to match hers — "what does this have to do with you and me? My hour has not come yet."

Mary turned to me, the warmth of her smile echoing in her voice. "Do whatever he tells you to do."

I stared at her. What did she mean? Was her son going to give us money? Did he have connections with a local wine merchant?

Yeshua did not explain, but looked at the tall water jars standing near the gate like sentries. They had been filled when the guests first began to arrive, but after days of frequent use, most of them were now empty.

Yeshua pointed at the stone jars and looked at me. "Fill them."

Whatever for? I was about to protest, but in a few hours we *did* expect a large crowd. The guests would have dusty feet, so we might as well refill the jars. Still, I would not send servants all the way to the village well for foot-washing water. We would use the rainwater from the family's cistern, an underground container that tended to collect insects and algae.

And how would filling the foot-washing jars solve our wine problem? I stared at Yeshua, considering the question. Perhaps this was a test — maybe he wanted to see if I would obey this simple instruction before entrusting me with the name of his wine-merchant connection.

In any case, I had no choice and nothing better to do.

Sighing, I summoned three of the hired

71

servants and pointed to a row of buckets by the stairs. "Go down to the cistern and bring up water," I told them. "Then fill the foot-washing jars by the gate." I sighed, knowing the servants would not be thrilled by the thought of climbing stairs while carrying heavy buckets. "If you see my brother, ask him to help. You might have to remind him that he was hired to be the headwaiter."

I left Yeshua and his mother and moved toward the stairs, watching as the servants jogged down the stone steps and returned, slowly hauling buckets of water from the cistern. They crossed the courtyard, their young shoulders sagging beneath their loads, then lifted the buckets and poured them into the elegant jars. Etan's family had six of the enormous vessels, and each required five buckets to fill it.

Finally, the last jar overflowed. The exhausted servants stood nearby to wait for my next order, so I turned to Mary's son. "We have done as you said. Now will you explain how we're supposed to —"

"Tasmin!" Thomas hurried toward me, his face flushed. "Sorry to be late, but I've just heard you needed me. What do you want?"

In answer, I looked at Yeshua, who gave me a casual, relaxed smile with a great deal of confidence behind it. "Take some of the water out," he said, "and give it to the headwaiter in a cup."

I still did not understand, but I was too frustrated to argue. I walked to the closest jar, slipped a copper cup beneath the spout, and let the liquid flow. When the cup was halfway full, I closed the spigot and offered the cup to Thomas.

Completely unaware of what had transpired before his arrival, Thomas took the cup, sniffed it, and brought the cup to his lips.

I grimaced. "Thomas, no!"

My brother's eyes went wide as he swallowed and then lowered the cup. "Where did you get this?" he asked. "And why are we serving it now?"

I drew a breath, about to denounce Yeshua's poor attempt at a joke, but Thomas did not give me the opportunity. Instead he shouted for Etan's attention, lifted the cup, and declared, "Everyone usually brings out the good wine first, and whenever they are drunk, then the worse. But you've reserved the good wine until now!"

Had he lost his mind? I whirled to face Yeshua, but he was already walking back to his circle of friends.

But Mary and the servants had realized what happened. Without lifting a finger,

Yeshua of Nazareth, son of Joseph the carpenter, had turned dirty, stagnant rainwater into wine . . . of an extremely fine vintage.

I couldn't stop myself. After taking a quick sip to be sure Thomas hadn't gone mad — yes, it *was* good wine — I flew down the circular staircase until I reached the cistern. The air in the underground chamber cooled my cheeks as I descended, and a wet trail marked the path of those who had filled their buckets to obey Yeshua's command.

Water — especially stagnant water — did not become fine wine because it had been poured into a stone jar. How had Mary's son managed such a trick?

A wire screen normally covered the cistern to keep rats and other vermin from falling inside. The servants had slid the screen aside, making room for their buckets. The top edge of the cistern came up to my waist, so I gripped the side and peered into its depths. Sunlight from the opening overhead glimmered on the surface, and a line on the stone marked the height of the water an hour before. A faint green smear marked part of the wall — scum. To my knowledge, pond scum had never been a vital ingredient of fine wine.

I bit my lip, considering the problem. Even if it were possible to create wine from water, Yeshua could never have done it in the time that passed between drawing it out and serving it to Thomas. So how had he done it?

I lifted my gaze to the sky and waited for inspiration to strike. Thomas would probably describe it a miracle, for he had already begun to believe this Nazarene was something more than a man, perhaps even our future king. But kings were mortal; they could not turn water into wine. They might, however, have hidden wineskins in this cellar . . .

I searched for telltale signs. Yeshua or one of his brothers could have hidden wineskins down here at any point during the feast. They might have heard Thomas voicing his concern about the wine supply, and under cover of darkness Yeshua could have gone to buy more. He could have hidden the wineskins or even a barrel, then bribed one of the servant girls to pour wine into the other servants' buckets when I asked them to fill the water jars.

I smiled in satisfaction. Such a simple plan, and easily accomplished. But Yeshua had not had time to come downstairs and hide the evidence, nor had any of the servants done it for him — I had been with them ever since they came up that last time, and none of them ventured near the cellar stairs afterward. So if evidence remained, I would find it . . .

Moving methodically around the subterranean chamber, I overturned storage baskets, moved wooden boxes, and fumbled through folded bags used for grain and seed. I ran my fingers along the wall, looking for a loose brick that might hide a secret compartment, then considered the pipe that angled away from the cistern and led up to the roof. The pipe was too small to hide an empty wineskin, and a metal grate covered the opening. The grate had not been disturbed.

I crossed my arms and chewed my thumbnail. No barrel or wineskins here. So how had he done it?

I was about to screech in frustration when I heard steps on the stairs. I flattened myself against the wall, half hoping the Nazarene would appear to remove the evidence of his supposed miracle. But the man on the stairs was not Yeshua, but Jude, his brother.

At first he did not see me, but studied the cistern as intently as I had, scratching his scalp as if to urge his mind to greater effort. He leaned over and peered into the cistern, then pressed his hand to a damp spot on the stone and tasted the liquid on his palm.

I stepped out of the shadows. "It is not wine, if that's what you suspect."

He startled, then turned a vivid scarlet. "I did not know anyone was down here."

I crossed my arms and pointedly looked away. "I thought you had come down to hide the evidence of your brother's trickery. I was convinced he had hidden wineskins here, but I have not yet found them."

Jude's dark eyes widened for a moment, then he laughed. "Wineskins? I can assure you of this — my brother could not afford to purchase the wineskins necessary to fill so many cups. I have been with him nearly every minute since you and I returned from Nazareth, and I have seen no wineskins."

"If you are not looking for wineskins, then why are you here?"

His gaze sharpened. "Because I wondered if you and your brother were up to some kind of mischief. Your brother is the steward of the feast, no? And he supports Yeshua. I thought he might have brought in a barrel of wine and hidden it. Or perhaps he had you procure more wine while you were in Nazareth. After all, we were not together the entire time."

I gritted my teeth. "Why would I be

interested in helping your brother trick these people?"

We stared at each other a moment, and then I turned and walked around the cistern again, bending to search every cranny in the bricks. Across from me, Jude did the same thing.

"Your suspicions surprise me," I said, still searching. "Because Thomas has been listening intently to Yeshua. Your brother seems to gather more followers with every passing day, and most of them are young, impressionable men like my brother." I stopped and straightened. "I would not want Thomas to join Yeshua's company."

"I do not blame you." Jude faced me, his eyes flashing. "The things Yeshua says — he did not learn those things in our family. The rest of us hold no illusions about who we are."

"And what, exactly, is he saying?" I crossed my arms. "We have seen too many false prophets and messiahs in Judea. They begin with a few followers, stir up trouble in the villages, preach revolution, and before long Herod sends soldiers to stop their sedition. They die, mothers mourn, and we turn our thoughts back to our work. You would think our people would learn to keep our eyes down and our ears closed —"

"Goodness, but you are full of words!"

I blinked. "How else am I going to make you understand? But if you can't tell me where the wine came from —"

"I was hoping to get that information from you."

I gritted my teeth again. "Clearly, we have both wasted our time. You should leave now. If we go upstairs together, people will think we were conspiring."

He took a step toward the stairs, then halted. "Why would I leave and give you time to hide whatever evidence you have?"

"What will it take" — I spoke slowly, as if to a dull child — "for you to believe me? I had no part in your brother's trickery. I would like nothing better than to expose the hoax."

He waited, his eyes searching mine, and finally nodded. "I will go first," he said, moving toward the stairs. "You may stay down here as long as you like."

CHAPTER SIX:
TASMIN

After a night of fine wine, dancing, and renewed congratulations for the newlyweds, the wedding feast ended. The guests rose early the next morning, broke their fast with bread and fruit, and stopped by the bridal chamber to bless the bride and groom. After myriad prayers that Etan and Galya would prove to be as fruitful as Isaac and Rebekah, the guests departed on foot, donkeys, and in mule-drawn wagons, eager to arrive home before sunset and the onset of Shabbat.

The guests from Nazareth were among the last to leave. As I tapped my foot, eager to begin the hard work of cleaning up, Thomas lingered with Yeshua and his followers. Jude, who had refused to meet my gaze ever since our encounter in the cellar, stood with his siblings near the courtyard gate, apparently impatient to be on his way.

Yeshua said something to Thomas, Simon Peter clapped my brother's back, and I hoped they had completed their farewells.

Then Thomas lowered his head and walked toward me. "Tasmin," he called.

Something in his tone lifted the hair at the back of my neck. A note in his voice reminded me of the time he had to tell me one of my friends had died. I had learned to dread that sound, but there it was, discreetly announcing that my twin was about to deliver news I would not like.

I wouldn't give him the chance.

"I'm glad you're finally ready to work," I said, speaking so quickly my words ran together. "We have to return the tables to the neighbors. We have a wagon loaded with trash to be burned outside the city, and I have several pitchers and lampstands that must be washed, dried, and polished. You can return them at the end of the day, then I'd like you to —"

"I've been invited to go with Yeshua."

The words struck like stones against my chest. I had been dreading them, fearing them, and had almost managed to convince myself I would never hear them, yet here they were, pummeling my weary heart.

"Of course you told him no." I mustered a smile and pressed a cleaning cloth into his hand. "There is too much work to be done, and I can't do it without you."

Thomas draped the cloth over my shoulder. "I'm going with them, Tasmin, because I must. I don't expect you to understand, but I hope you will . . . eventually. Yeshua is important. I have been chosen, and this is something I must do."

"Thomas." I put a hand on my hip and forced a smile. "I don't know how he turned the water into wine, but you can't trust a trickster who does things to amaze a crowd. You can't trust a man who works wonders without explanation."

"I don't think he did it to amaze." Thomas spoke in a calm voice. "I didn't know he had anything to do with the good wine until I heard the servants talking."

"But that's my point — he *knew* the servants would talk. Before the night was over, everyone had heard the story."

"True." Thomas glanced over his shoulder, then met my gaze head-on. "Listen — I'm not completely convinced he is the one we've been waiting for. But how will I know unless I go with him? So I'm going. I'll stay with him until I see something that convinces me he is not the man he says he is."

I opened my mouth and looked at our father, who stood with Etan and Galya. I was hoping Abba would see my stricken expression and help me, but he did not turn in my direction.

So I appealed to Thomas's sense of responsibility. "You would leave me in the middle of a job? We were both hired to manage this wedding feast."

A smile twisted the corner of my twin's mouth. "And you have done most of the work alone. So accept all of the wages, sister. You have earned them."

He began to walk away, but I was not finished. "Thomas, what will I do without you? Your place is here."

He was no longer listening, but waving to Abba and Aunt Dinah. He picked up the small leather bag he had packed for the wedding, then followed Yeshua and his followers through the courtyard gate.

I felt as though half of my limbs had been ripped away.

Mary and the others in her family lingered to say farewell to the bride and groom. I turned, embarrassed to be seen with tears in my eyes, but a moment later I felt a gentle hand on my arm. Mary stood behind me, a compassionate smile on her face.

"We are going to Capernaum, where Yeshua is living now," she said. "You are welcome to join us."

I shook my head. "Thank you, but I can't. I have to stay and clean up."

"After your work is done, then. After Shabbat." She glanced toward the road, where Yeshua and his men were disappearing in a cloud of dust. "I don't know how long we'll be in Capernaum, but we shouldn't be hard to find. Bring your father, if you like. We would love to see you again — and I know Thomas would be delighted to see his sister."

The mere mention of my twin's name made me flinch. Did she know what I was feeling? How could she understand how it felt to have your other half, your wombmate, walk away without a proper warning?

"I know how it feels to lose someone," she whispered, leaning toward me. "When I lost my Joseph I thought I might never smile again. But HaShem is faithful, and while Joseph is no longer at my side, Adonai has never left me. He will not leave you, either."

I sniffed. "I know HaShem is everywhere," I answered, struggling to restrain an unexpected rush of tears, "but He does not have a face."

"Perhaps He will show himself to you." Mary squeezed my arm and smiled, then stepped away. "Come to Capernaum, if you will. We would love to see you again."

I turned from the gate through which my

brother had disappeared and stared at the pile of bowls and pots I would have to clean and return to their owners. A sense of emptiness washed over me, robbing me of the joy I should have felt for successfully completing a job despite a host of difficulties. My butcher had been sick, Thomas had been only half present, and the groom's father had not purchased enough wine . . .

A tear trickled down my cheek, and I swiped it away, irritated by the sign of weakness. I never felt weak when Thomas was with me. He would always laugh if he caught me crying, and I could not abide his mocking laughter. He had made me strong, yet how could I be strong without him?

My father must have realized what I was feeling, because he was the first to approach after Thomas departed.

"Would you like some help, daughter?"

"Thank you, Abba, but no. You need to rest."

"I am fine. Let me help."

"Well . . ." I forbade my chin to tremble as I gestured to a stack of planks we had used as a table. "Those will need to go into the wagon. We borrowed them from a carpenter on the north side of town. But get someone to help you because those planks are heavy."

"I can return them for you."

Without a word about Thomas, Abba hitched up the hem of his tunic and called for Etan. Together they gathered the heavy planks and shoved them into the back of the wagon.

Galya joined me a moment later. "Let me lend a hand," she said, rolling up the sleeves of her tunic. "You shouldn't have dismissed the hired servants so soon."

"I thought I'd have Thomas to help," I said, dismayed to hear a sharp edge in my voice. "I never dreamed he would leave before the job was finished."

Galya shook her head. "I don't understand the attraction. Yeshua seems a nice enough fellow, but I spent some time talking to his sisters, Damaris and Pheodora, and even they think he is strange."

"Has he always been unusual?"

"You mean mad?" Galya laughed. "His sisters said he is a good son, dutiful and devout, and devoted to his mother. A few months ago, they said, he went down to Jerusalem, where he spent time with some of their relatives. John the Immerser is a kinsman, and some say *he* is mad, too. He lives in the desert and wears camel skins. Maybe this John influenced Yeshua. They say the Immerser is a prophet."

I snorted. "Thomas thinks Yeshua is the promised king of Israel. The messiah."

"I've heard that, too. If he is" — Galya dumped a pile of bones from a plate into a bucket — "I'm not sure I'd want to be associated with him. Anyone who hints about unseating Herod usually ends up dead."

I pressed my lips together, realizing the truth in her words. Herod the Great had murdered anyone he even suspected of aspiring to his throne, including several of his own sons and dozens of baby boys in the village of Bethlehem. Herod Antipas, another son, now ruled over Galilee, and he was only slightly less paranoid than his father.

"My father," I said, "says we did not pray with enough faith when we begged HaShem to take the first Herod away. We rejoiced at his death, but he was like a worm — with one part cut off, three others grew to take his place!"

Galya sighed and handed me a silver platter. "Still, I do not suppose there is anything we can do. Men will do what they want, while we women stay behind and worry about them."

I took the platter and stared past it at the spot where Thomas stood only an hour before. Stay behind and worry about him? I had kept up with Thomas since we first began to walk. I was not his wife, expected to remain at home to tend his house. I was as unencumbered as he was, and equally as stubborn.

"I will go after him." I spoke the words aloud, not really intending them for Galya's ear, but she heard them nonetheless.

"Go after him?" She released a delicate laugh. "That's why I like you, Tasmin — you are utterly spontaneous."

I shrugged. "What else have I to do? Your wedding is done. I have no other feasts to manage."

"Not now perhaps. But *how* will you go after your brother? Decent women do not travel alone. You will need a man's protection — no, you will need the protection of a caravan because these are restless times. And before you do anything, you will have to secure your father's permission to undertake such a journey."

"Mary invited me to join them in Capernaum," I said, as if that solved all my problems. "Capernaum is not such a great distance. I could travel there in a few hours —"

"Many things can happen in a few hours, and I'm certain Mary did not intend for you to set out alone. And if you're not going to wash that tray, let me have it." Galya took the silver platter from my hand and lowered it into a basin of water. "I'm sure she thought you'd travel with your father and a few friends."

I picked up some soiled dishes and held them until Galya had finished washing the platter. "I could find someone to go with me," I said, thinking aloud. "And Abba wouldn't care if I went. Indeed, once he realizes that Thomas could be following a false messiah, he might urge me to go."

"He wouldn't go with you?"

I shook my head. "His health is not what it once was. He tires after walking even short distances."

Galya took a bowl from me and scrubbed the inside. "What will you do," she asked, her brows knitting, "if Thomas won't return?"

I bit my lip. "I will wait. I will watch this Yeshua, listen carefully, and be quick to point out anything he says that goes against the Torah. I will put my mind to solving the mystery of the wine and I will figure out how he tricked us." I gasped as a sudden thought occurred. "Did Etan help him? Did he realize how little wine we had left?"

She gave me a reproachful look. "Etan and I had just completed our first week as husband and wife. Do you think he spent much time thinking about wine?"

"I don't know, but he wouldn't have wanted his family to be embarrassed. So did he help Yeshua? Or perhaps Etan's father brought in more wine?"

Galya shook her head. "The family spent all they had on the wedding. Even if they had wanted to buy more, they could not."

I inhaled a deep breath, then dipped my head in an abrupt nod. "I am going to do it," I told her, setting more dirty dishes next to her washing bucket. "I am going after Thomas and I will convince him to leave. The moment I find a flaw in this Yeshua ben Joseph, I will peel my brother away and bring him home. To my father. To me."

Galya handed me a dripping bowl and draped a piece of linen over my arm. "Then you'd better get busy drying these dishes," she said, humoring me with a smile. "Because you have a lot to do before you go."

CHAPTER SEVEN:
JUDE

I walked slowly into Nazareth, well aware that several of my neighbors were peering out their windows and casting curious looks in my direction. One neighbor — a compact man who walked with a spring in his step — finally stepped outside and flashed a smile. "Jude, shalom! Good to see you, my friend. How was the wedding? And where is the rest of your family?"

I tried not to reveal my irritation as I stopped. "The wedding was blessed. My mother and brothers have gone on to Capernaum. Damaris is home, as you probably know. She and her husband spent a short time at the feast."

"Ah, yes, the children." The man nodded. "A mother bears a heavy responsibility."

"As does a father. But they were happy to bless the bride and groom."

I started again toward home, but my nosy neighbor bounced along at my side. "Did anything unusual happen at the wedding?"

Still walking, I cast him a sidelong look. "Etan and Galya of Cana were married."

"And?"

"And they had a feast."

"And?"

Exasperated, I stopped. "What is it you wish to know? It was a wedding like any other."

"Not from what I hear."

I crossed my arms. "Suppose you tell me how it was different."

The man lifted his gaze to heaven, then clasped his hands. "I heard the story from the butcher, who heard it from a woman at the wedding — a cousin of the bride, I believe. She said the wine became more and more watered down as the feast continued, until it was barely more satisfying than water. But on the last day, when she feared they would have nothing to drink, the servants filled their cups with the most exquisite wine imaginable! She couldn't believe the headwaiter would withhold the best wine until the end of the feast."

I sighed. "Indeed. You have heard the truth; the steward waited until the end to serve the best wine."

"But why?"

I shrugged. "Perhaps he forgot he had it."

"Or . . ." The man leaned close enough to blow his sour breath in my face. "Perhaps it was a miracle! One of the servants told a woman at the wedding that your brother had the servants fill the water jars with runoff from the cistern. Rainwater! But as the servants served the water, it turned into fine wine!"

I stared at the man, whose enthusiasm was all but squirting out his ears. "I know nothing about the servants or a miracle," I said, careful not to inflame the man's fervor. "I was there for the groom, not the wine."

"Did you drink it?"

"I did."

"Was it unusual?"

"It was . . . good."

"Oh, to have a sip of it myself!" The man clapped his hands. "I don't care where it came from, a poor man can only dream of such delights! Perhaps it was from a heavenly vineyard!"

Blowing out a breath, I snapped my chin in farewell and walked up the curving lane that led to our home.

As we left Cana, my mother could tell I was not enthusiastic about going to Capernaum, so she suggested I go home to tend to the house. I had been only too happy to accept her suggestion and leave the others behind.

At the top of the staircase, I opened the front door and breathed in air that smelled of dust and disuse. I walked through the house and opened the shutters, then went downstairs to be sure the chickens had not eaten all their feed. I gathered several eggs from the shadowy corner behind the door, placed them in a bowl, and took them upstairs. The donkey had been loaned to a neighbor, so I would not have to worry about cleaning the dirt floors.

I had just unfastened my sandals when someone knocked. When I opened the door, I saw a man I recognized from the synagogue — Chanon Phineas, a wealthy merchant who specialized in trade between Magdala and the city of Tiberias. Why he chose to live in Nazareth, I would never understand.

"Chanon Phineas," I said, bowing slightly. "Shalom."

"Shalom to you," he answered, returning my bow. "May I come in?"

I could not imagine what business he had with me, but I stepped aside and invited him in. He strolled into the house, spotted a chicken who had followed me up the stairs, and adjusted his outer tunic as if afraid of getting dirt on the fabric.

"Next year," he began, his lips parting in a dazzling display of white teeth, "I will celebrate an anniversary with my wife — we will have been married thirty years."

I folded my arms. *"Mazel tov."*

"Thank you. I want to make her a bed — an ornate bed, in the Greek style, with pillars at the four corners and elaborate carvings on the headboard. I have seen the work that comes out of this house, and I am certain you are the family to make my anniversary bed."

I tugged on my beard, thinking. Our father had taught his sons how to use an axe and hammer, a grindstone and measure, for he wanted us to be skilled in his chosen trade. But as our ages differed, so did our abilities, and Yeshua was the only one qualified to do the sort of intricate carving this man wanted. James *might* be able to do the work, yet it would take him at least twice as long as Yeshua . . . "When do you want the bed delivered?"

"Next year. My beloved wife and I just celebrated our anniversary, and this year, to mark the occasion, I gave her a beautiful horse."

I lifted a brow, wondering at the petulant expression on his face. "Was your wife not pleased with her gift?"

"My wife does not ride," Chanon Phineas answered, "so no, she did not appreciate the magnificent stallion in our barn. She was full of temper and would have railed against me all night except for my promise that I would do better next year. I would give her something truly spectacular, something no one else would have. And that" — he shrugged — "is the anniversary bed. Can you and your brothers have it finished in twelve months?"

I stared at the wall, mentally picturing my brothers' faces and their capabilities. Joses, Simeon, and I could easily build a frame and cut and carve the pillared supports in twelve months' time. The headboard, however . . . Yeshua could surely do the work in that amount of time, but James? I turned back to my customer. "How intricate would you like the headboard to be? Have you seen something we could use as a model?"

"Good question, young man, and yes. When we were last in Rome, I had an artist draw an illustration of what I expect to receive."

"Do you travel to Rome often?"

"As frequently as necessary for business. I am always telling the Roman craftsmen that our people do equally fine work."

I took the parchment he offered and unfolded it. The bed looked just as I had imagined it, although the headboard was more detailed than the image in my head. On a solid slab of wood positioned between two wooden Doric columns, someone had drawn a multi-petaled flower rising from the base of the headboard like the morning sun. Rows of symmetrical petals outlined the flower's center, and where the petals stopped, twisting leaves and vines filled the remaining space with intricate patterns, whirls, and curling stems.

I returned the sketch to its owner. "I am not certain, Chanon Phineas, that we can do this work for you in the time allotted. My elder brother, the most skilled at this sort of carving, has been traveling throughout the region —"

"I will pay ten talents for the bed. You and your brothers can divide the sum as you please."

The figure snatched my breath away. Ten talents was more than we would earn in our lifetimes. Ten talents was enough to buy sixty thousand sheep. If we completed this job, we would never need to work again. Our mother would not have to fear old age. We could build a bigger house, one where we could all live comfortably under one roof. My brothers would be able to afford dowries and take wives, and so could I, if I wanted to . . .

I found myself nodding in agreement. "We can make this bed."

"I must have your word on this," Chanon Phineas said. "I cannot risk failure in this venture. I have promised my wife an extraordinary surprise, and if you cannot deliver . . ." He opened his hands and shrugged, indicating that our fate would be dire indeed.

"We will do it," I promised, gripping his outstretched hand. "We will deliver your anniversary bed one year from now. But I will need a deposit, for I must purchase tools and materials."

"Of course."

Chanon Phineas pulled a purse from his robe and took from it two silver talents. I accepted them, grateful to have coin in my hands. I would need money to find my brothers and convince them — *all* of them — to come home and begin this work at once.

I walked my guest to the door, bade him farewell, then stood in the silent house and considered the agreement I had just made on my brothers' behalf. James, Joses, and Simeon would be delighted by the news.

Our mother would worry that we would not be able to complete the work, yet I would set her mind at ease.

Yeshua, however, might be a problem. He had not picked up a lathe or a blade in over a year, and he no longer lived in Nazareth. When I did see him, he seemed pre-occupied, as though his thoughts had wandered far from the family business. But surely a project like this — along with its tantalizing reward — would bring him back to us.

I moved to the rear of the house, where we stored our tools. I would prepare everything and clear out a space to do the work, then order wood for the bed. Once Shabbat was over, I would set out for Capernaum. Since I would be walking north, I would have to pass through Cana. I could stop at Etan's home, certain that he and Galya would be happy to loan me a beast for my journey. My own donkey would have to remain in Nazareth because my neighbor needed him.

If by some chance I happened to see Tasmin again, I would ask if she wanted me to give her brother a message. Surely she would. So I could not leave meeting her to chance, but would have to stop by her house and speak to her.

I found myself looking forward to the journey.

CHAPTER EIGHT:
TASMIN

How odd that preparing for Etan and Galya's wedding could be invigorating and clearing away so depressing. I had worked other weddings and had energy to spare when the festivities ended, but by the time I had returned the last platter and serving bowl, I was so exhausted that Etan and Galya insisted I remain with them over Shabbat. Abba and I accepted their hospitality, though I suspected Abba did so because he wanted another opportunity to debate Etan's father over the Shabbat meal.

After the candles had been lit and the Shabbat blessing given, we ate a simple dinner. Abba and Etan's father argued over whether the kingdom of God would be established in this world or the next. I did not join in the conversation, for I cared little for discussions about the finer points of the Torah, as no one ever seemed to have a definitive answer. The Pharisees took one position, the Sadducees another, with a host of Torah teachers and Essenes holding varying opinions that ranged from idiotic to impractical.

As for me, I was content to know that God reigned in heaven and gave us four regular seasons. Except for granting me the blessings of Thomas and Abba, He had never done anything unusual for me . . . or for anyone else of my acquaintance. He had healed us from no serious diseases, He had not made us rich, and He had not saved my mother from death. While the people of Cana lived and died and Israel suffered under Roman and Jewish tyrants, Abba insisted that I love HaShem with all my heart. For what reason, I wondered, was I supposed to love Him so?

In all my years, I had never received a satisfactory answer.

When dinner was over and the men too sated to debate further, I walked out to the courtyard. The garden, which had overflowed with life only a few hours before, now seemed desolate. The dancers had worn circles in the sparse ground cover, and the flowering shrubs had been picked clean.

But I found solace in the silence because I needed to think. I wanted to set out for Capernaum as soon as Shabbat ended, and I knew Abba would not approve of my travel-ing alone. He *would* approve of my task, for he did not trust Yeshua any more than I did, but a woman should not travel alone on the roads, especially after dark.

So I would have to convince him I could manage alone.

The next morning I awoke, dressed, and braided my hair because the sun would be hot on the road. I strapped on my sandals and gathered the few things I had brought with me to the wedding. I went to the synagogue as usual with Abba. Then we said farewell to Etan and Galya and returned to our home, where I gathered what I would need for my journey. As soon as the sun set, I planned to light a torch and walk as far north as Jotopata, no more than an hour's walk. I would find a place at the inn or sleep under a tree, then rise with the sun to continue walking north. If all went well, I would reach Capernaum by the end of the day.

After dinner, I stood in my chamber, my hands pressed to the door as my father's booming voice seeped from the crack be-neath it. From his tone I knew he had company, and when his guest departed he would prepare for bed. He would want to bless me before he went to his room, so if I was going to make my case, this was the time. If he became adamant about refusing to let me go, perhaps he would suggest a friend or neighbor who could be persuaded to keep me company on the walk north.

I opened my door and startled Aunt Dinah, who was about to sit on the couch. "There she is!" She smiled as she lowered her considerable weight to the seat. "The one who baked so many delicious foods for the wedding. They will be talking about your cakes for years to come."

"You will get many requests now." Abba waggled his brows at me. "Your services will be in high demand. Every bridegroom's father will want to hire you."

"Hire me and Thomas," I added, keeping my voice light. "We are a team."

"Thomas does supply the strength," Dinah said, nodding, "but I have never seen him bake anything worth eating. And the food, dear girl, is why people come to a feast. They want to eat and drink." She frowned at Abba. "About that wine — have we solved the mystery of its origin?"

"That reminds me." I sank to the floor by Abba's chair and propped my hands on his knee. "I am concerned about Thomas."

"As am I." A melancholy frown flitted

across my father's features. "I do not understand why he wanted to leave with that man from Nazareth."

"I believe that man is a rebel," I continued. "I spent some time talking with Jude, Yeshua's brother, and he does not think much of Yeshua's work, either. So I have decided to do something about it."

Abba's brows shot up to his hairline. "What would you do?"

"Before they left, Mary invited me to join her family in Capernaum. I want to go there and speak to Thomas alone. I'm sure I can make him see how risky this venture is. If he doesn't believe me, I'll remind him that we three are a team, and we need him to help with the grove. And I cannot manage a wedding feast alone."

Abba's forehead knit in puzzlement. "You want to go to Capernaum?"

"Is Thomas in trouble?" Dinah interrupted. "Do you know something we don't? I know you can sense when he is in trouble—"

"I'm not sensing anything, Aunt, but I am not at peace with his decision to follow this man Yeshua. Has a prophet ever come out of Nazareth? What do we know about him?"

Abba tugged on his beard. "Apparently he turned rainwater into wine."

"Did he?" I sat back and crossed my arms. "I spent an hour looking for the barrel or wineskins he must have hidden away. No one has the power to turn water into wine."

"A prophet from Adonai could." Dinah lifted a warning finger. "You cannot prove he is not a prophet."

"With respect, Aunt, can you prove he *is*?" I shifted my attention and looked into my father's eyes. "Please, Abba, I am worried about Thomas. I will not be able to rest until he is home where he belongs."

Abba narrowed his gaze for a moment, then sighed. "I would be happy to go with you, daughter, but I am no longer a young man. The journey would be too much for me."

"I'll go alone, then. I will sleep at inns and —"

"You will not travel alone." Dinah stamped her foot. "Only indecent women prowl the roads alone. The road is not safe for a woman, especially a righteous woman. There are Romans and bandits and murderers, and above all, the *lestes.*"

Her caution provoked a shudder, despite my urgent desire to make the trip. The lestes were not ordinary roadway bandits. Their attacks were particularly violent, often resulting in murder, and were usually aimed at Romans or Jews suspected of collaborating with Romans.

"The lestes will not be interested in an ordinary woman. And if it will persuade you to let me go, I promise to find a passing family and travel with them. Please, Abba. If I leave now, I should be able to reach Jotopata in an hour or —"

"Leave *now,* in the dark?" Abba shook his head. "If Adonai meant for you to go to Capernaum alone, He would have made you a man. I cannot allow this thing. Sometimes your ideas are too unseemly for a woman."

"Shalom!"

A voice hailed us from outside the house. As one we turned toward the source of the sound. I stood in the doorway and held the lamp aloft, illuminating the courtyard gate. I stared, tongue-tied, when I recognized the man standing in the shadowy street.

"Who is it?" Abba demanded from his chair. "Who comes so late?"

"Someone —" somehow I found my voice — "someone from Nazareth."

I stepped forward and opened the gate, then led Jude into the house. He hesitated at the threshold before bowing respectfully toward Abba and Aunt Dinah.

"Forgive my visit at this hour," he said, gesturing toward the gathering darkness outside. "But I am traveling to Capernaum and did not want to travel farther in the dark. I wondered if the donkey and I could pass the night in the safety of your court-yard."

"Of course," I said, speaking before Abba. "But you don't have to sleep outside, you can —"

"Tasmin."

Abba's voice held a rebuke, so I backed away from the door. "If Abba agrees, you may stay with us."

With an effort, my father pushed himself out of his chair and lumbered toward our guest. "I remember you," he said, looking Jude up and down. "You are one of Mary's sons."

Aunt Dinah's smile bathed our visitor in warmth. "Of course he should stay here. We can't have him traveling after dark."

"I wanted to leave sooner," Jude explained, spreading his hands, "but since I couldn't leave Nazareth until after sunset —"

"Come in, come in." Abba caught the door and opened it wider. "Tasmin will see to your donkey. Jude can have Thomas's bed. Can we get you water? Bread?"

I left them exchanging pleasantries while I brought the donkey through the gate, removed his halter, and led him to the watering trough. As I pulled the pack saddle from his back, I couldn't help but smile. Jude and I had formulated the same plan, but he had ended up here instead of Jotopata — and, all praise to HaShem, now I would have an escort.

When I returned, Jude was sitting on the couch with Dinah, a cup of water in his hand.

"Tell us about your plans," Abba was saying. "Why did you have to leave in such a hurry?"

Jude smiled at my father. "I had been home only a short time when one of the wealthiest men in Nazareth offered us a commission to build his wife a bed, a special gift for their anniversary. I'm going to find my brothers and give them the news."

"So you're going straight to Capernaum," I said, glancing at my father.

"I am."

I squeezed my father's arm. "You said Adonai would have made me a man if he wanted me to go to Capernaum. Suppose He *sent* me a man instead?"

Abba looked from me to Jude, then back. "How do you know this man wants company?"

I released my father and turned to our

guest. "I need to speak to my brother — I want him to come home. He has no business wandering around Galilee while Abba and I need him here. I cannot travel alone, but if Abba approves, I could go with you."

Jude's eyes widened slightly and then he glanced at Abba, whose face had gone red. "An unmarried man and woman traveling together . . ."

"Not proper," Aunt Dinah said. "Not seemly."

"It is but a day's journey," I said, speaking so quickly my words ran together. "We should reach Capernaum by nightfall. Then I can go my way and Jude can go his. I'll find Thomas, and he will escort me home. I will be safe, Abba, and Thomas and I should be home in two days. Please . . . give me your blessing to go."

What could the man say? He wanted Thomas home as much as I did.

He looked at Jude. "Promise me you will join other travelers as soon as you can."

Jude nodded. "We will."

Abba glanced at Aunt Dinah, who shrugged and lifted her hands. He then placed his hand on my forehead. "Be careful, daughter. Do not leave before sunrise, and return quickly."

"I will, Abba. I promise."

"You are no longer a child, so I will trust you both in this venture." He released a heavy sigh. "May Adonai keep watch between you and me when we are out of each other's sight."

Chapter Nine:
Jude

I tugged on the donkey's halter and wondered, not for the first time, if some part of me wanted to travel to Capernaum with this woman from Cana. I found her ready and eager to leave at sunrise, even before I could thank her father for the overnight accommodation.

I *had* planned to stop by her home. I turned down an offer of hospitality from Etan and Galya, quietly hoping Tasmin's father would agree to shelter me for the night. I *did* want to see the woman again.

But I was fairly certain I had not intended to escort her to Capernaum.

She did not say much as we set out, and I was grateful for a chance to sort through my thoughts without a lot of useless chatter. I glanced over at her — she was younger than me, probably by three or four years, yet far past the age when most young women were betrothed. Twenty-two?

Twenty-three? She was nearly as tall as her brother, easily able to look me in the eye, and the set of her chin suggested a stubborn streak. She wore her dark hair pulled back in a simple braid, and her tunic was light and unadorned. Excitement flushed her face, so I guessed she had not done much traveling outside the usual pilgrimages to Jerusalem, which meant she had likely never traveled without her family.

Tasmin's aunt had generously filled the donkey's pack saddle with water jars, bread, cheese, and dried fruit. I had brought several blankets in case my brothers and I had to sleep outdoors on the return journey. If Tasmin and I were not delayed, we ought to reach Capernaum by sunset, so she should not have to worry about spending the night in the open.

I slowed when we approached a fork in the road. The left branch proceeded due north through the wilderness with only a few villages along the way. The more traveled branch led northeastward and would take us by Tiberias, home of Herod Antipas and his palace. The second route offered more pleasant views, cooler weather, and the prospect of additional company on the journey, though I did not care about company.

Perhaps Tasmin did. And she had promised her father that we would travel with others . . . When I hesitated in a moment of indecision, she glanced up at me.

"Why are we stopping?" she asked.

"I'm thinking about the best route to take."

"What is the difference?"

I pointed to the left fork. "If we go that way, we will make better time."

She lifted a brow. "Thomas says the northern route runs through a dull desert. The heat will sap our strength and slow our steps. The eastern road might be longer, but we will walk faster and enjoy the journey more."

"Are you not enjoying it thus far?" I meant the comment as a joke, but when she did not smile, I abandoned my pitiful at tempt at humor. "I have no interest in mingling with Gentiles. My father avoided anything related to the first Herod, so I see no reason why we should travel past the city built by Antipas."

Her eyes widened. "I thought you were related to John the Immerser."

I frowned. "What has that to do with — ?"

"Have you not heard? The Immerser has been arrested by Antipas's soldiers. And where do you think they took him?"

My throat went dry. My mother had always been close to Elizabeth, John's mother, and she would want to know if something had happened to her kinsman.

"My mother would want me to see about John," I admitted. "So we will take the eastern route. But we should not enter Tiberias unless necessary. We ought to be able to learn the latest news by standing outside the gate."

Tasmin nodded. "Agreed."

We turned toward the east, and I found myself feeling grateful for her insight. I had forgotten how the land softened and greened as we proceeded eastward. Verdant trees rustled on the gentle hills, and the atmosphere cooled and sweetened. Even the donkey seemed in better spirits; his sprightly step lightened my mood to the point where I thought I might make an attempt at conversation.

"You are not as talkative as most women," I finally ventured. "You make a man wonder what is in your head."

She laughed. "I am used to talking to my brother, and with Thomas I don't have to say much. He can read my face like a scroll."

"You are close, then?"

"We are twins." She said it as if that fact should explain everything.

115

I waited, expecting her to continue, but she remained silent.

"We have no twins in our family," I said, shrugging. "And though I have siblings, I cannot imagine having someone in the same space as me. We are so accustomed to knowing our place as firstborn, second-born —"

"You?"

"Fourth-born. Not young enough to be the baby of the family, or old enough to be the most respected."

She nodded. "And the firstborn?"

"Yeshua."

"Second?"

"James."

"Third?"

"Damaris."

"Your sister," Tasmin went on, "when did she marry?"

I closed my eyes to recollect. "I was fourteen, so she would have been fifteen."

"I can't imagine having a family that large. Seems like it has always been me, Thomas, and Abba. And Aunt Dinah, when she is able to join us."

"Your mother?"

"Died."

She spoke without grief or inflection, and I marveled at her detachment. "I'm sorry," I said. "When?"

She blew out a deep breath. "Thomas and I were five. After that, we grew even closer. We've never needed anyone else."

I lifted a brow, not knowing how to respond to her answer. I thought she would give me details — where, when, and how her mother had died, but Tasmin practiced economy of speech when it suited her.

"What should we do now?"

I looked up and saw her pointing to another intersection. I recognized it as the place where our road met the well-traveled highway that led south to Samaria. We would continue north, yet the incoming highway was not so crowded that others would slow our pace.

We had to reach Capernaum by nightfall. This woman's father expected her home in two days, and I did not want to be responsible if she did not make it back in time.

"You say you and Thomas have never needed anyone else," I said, guiding the donkey around a large rock in the road. "Would he agree with you?"

She cast me a sharp glance, then returned her gaze to the road. "I used to think so. Now? I don't know, and that is why I am going to Capernaum."

CHAPTER TEN: TASMIN

When we spotted the thick walls of Tiberias, we stopped, tied the donkey to a tamarisk tree, and climbed a hill for a better view. The city was everything I expected from a ruler infatuated with Rome — surrounded by tall, thick walls and heavily guarded. Gleaming marble buildings. Red-and-gold flags mounted above each gate.

"We're not going inside, right?" I said.

"Why would we?"

"I don't know. I only wanted to be sure."

While the donkey browsed the grass beneath the tree, Jude took a bag from the pack saddle and offered me bread and cheese.

I had just taken a bite of bread when I saw him dip a cup into one of the water jars. He offered the cup to me, but I only grinned. "What, no wine?"

He flushed when he realized I was jesting. "No wine," he said, stressing the words.

"And, by the way, Etan drained his water jars after the wedding feast. I suppose he didn't want his next guests washing their feet in good wine."

"That would have been extravagant." I broke off a bite of cheese and popped it into my mouth, glad to know this man could joke about a sensitive subject. So maybe he wouldn't mind if I asked a personal question.

"So," I said, "you and your brothers have carpentry work to complete. Is that the only reason you're going to Capernaum?"

Jude glanced at me and brushed bread crumbs from his beard. "Isn't that enough?"

"Perhaps. But I can admit to another reason."

"Such as?"

I leaned back against the tree. "I want Thomas to come home and stop dodging his responsibilities, yes. But I also worry that he is following someone who might get him in serious trouble. I can admit that possibility — can you?"

A flicker of surprise widened Jude's eyes, followed by a flash of fear that tightened the corners of his mouth. "You are not shy, are you?"

"I've never had a reason to be."

"Most women . . . are more subtle."

119

"No one ever taught me that womanly art. And Thomas would agree with you — he is always saying I should not be so forthright."

Jude chuckled. "I don't mind. In some ways, you are a relief." He took a deep breath, his shoulders rising and falling with the effort. "I have not wanted to admit it, but I daresay you are right. If I can persuade Yeshua to come home, a tremendous burden will be lifted from my shoulders. From all of us."

"Even your mother?"

"Especially my mother." He blew out a breath. "I fear, however, that Ima is lost to us. She has supported Yeshua in everything he has ever done, so I find myself trying to save her as well as my brother. But Ima comes first. She is innocent of his madness."

I blinked, surprised by the unexpected tremor in his voice.

"You think he might be truly mad?"

"No. Yes. I don't know." He looked at me, and in that moment I saw lines of heartsickness and weariness around his mouth and eyes. "We have been watching Yeshua for months, noting changes, trying not to make too much of them. But now that he has begun to collect followers, we don't know what he is doing. Or planning. And the possibilities are enough to keep me awake at night."

Desperate to offer some kind of comfort, I snatched at the first words that came to mind. "I was beginning to think he wanted to be a wine merchant."

Jude stared at me, bewilderment on his face, then tipped back his head and laughed. The release must have been good for him, because he smiled when he looked at me again. "I am probably worried about matters that will never amount to anything," he said, looking to the road ahead. "And we should not forget why we are walking by Tiberias — we need to learn what happened to John."

"All right." I pointed to a man and woman who had just come through the city gates. "Should we ask them if they know anything?"

"And if they don't?"

"We ask someone else."

"That will take time." Jude glanced at the sun. "The day is half spent and we still have a considerable distance to cover."

"He is your kinsman, so you choose. We don't *have* to find out what happened to John. You could share the rumors with your mother."

"And your father wants you home in two

days. I would hate to disappoint him."

I lifted my chin. "My father knows I am stubborn and will not quit until I have accomplished the thing I set out to do."

Jude turned to study the gates of Tiberias. "My family will want to know the full story. Yeshua thinks a great deal of John. He will want the truth."

"Then we'll stay," I said, "for as long as it takes to learn everything. And if it takes longer than two days to find out what we need to know, we will be late."

Jude looked at me and nodded. "So be it."

CHAPTER ELEVEN:
JUDE

John's story had been part of my life for as long as I could remember. My mother loved to talk about his parents, Elizabeth and Zechariah, and how she had visited Elizabeth when they were both with child. Mother had been present for John's birth, then had returned to my father in Nazareth.

Five years later I was born. By then Yeshua was four, James two, and Damaris one. I learned to walk among cedar shavings and sawdust. I fell asleep to the sound of pounding nails and whining wood. When he was not working, Abba taught us Torah, while Ima made our home as pleasant as she could. She had a fondness for bright colors, and once when I asked why she wore bright oranges and blues when no one else did, she replied that Egypt had influenced her tastes and she never wanted to forget the time she lived there. James and Damaris had been born in Egypt, she reminded me, but then she and Abba had come home to Nazareth, where they would remain unless Adonai willed otherwise.

As I grew with my brothers and sisters, I heard stories about John, who grew up in the hill country of Judah. Ima said he was being raised as a Nazarite, never drinking any intoxicating beverage and maintaining ritual purity because he had been filled with the Ruach ha-Kodesh since his birth. "Many of Bnei-Yisrael will turn to Adonai because of John," Ima always said. "And he will go before Him in the spirit and power of Elijah, turning the hearts of fathers to the children and the disobedient ones to the wisdom of the righteous, preparing the people for Adonai."

"He will go before *who*?" I once asked, but Ima only smiled in response. "You will see," she said, smoothing my hair. "You will see."

John remained more of a locust-eating legend than cousin until a few months before the wedding in Cana. Yeshua wanted to visit John in the desert because we'd heard he was calling people to be baptized for the repentance of sins. I knew John's message was timely — everyone knew that many of the priests and leaders of Israel had black hearts and unclean hands. Since returning from the exile in Babylon, our people had lived through generations of infighting among prideful men who wrestled for power, first in the Temple and then on the throne. Those struggles had not ceased with the arrival of the Romans. Israel no longer had a king — Ima said we would not have another until the promised king arrived — but our religious leaders seemed to care more about currying favor with Roman leaders than with HaShem.

Our religion had become a series of laws that grew ever more complicated. Like everyone else, I read the Scriptures — the teachings, the prophets, and the writings — and determined never to do what our forefathers had done and forget the Law. They forgot and fell into sin; so we read and learned and memorized and put laws *around* the Law so we would never offend in one jot or tittle. But somehow, like many others, I sensed that in all our efforts to learn and work and obey, we had forgotten something elemental. Something important.

Yet John was drawing crowds in the wilderness. Had he found what we were missing?

Yeshua invited all of my brothers to visit our kinsman, yet James and Joses were busy with an order, and Simeon had no interest in traveling. To satisfy my curiosity, I decided to join Yeshua.

As we traveled southward, following the Jordan, at one point he looked at me and said, "A voice cries out in the wilderness, 'Prepare the way of Adonai, Make straight in the desert a highway for our God.' Do you remember the prophecy?"

I struggled to place the words. "Isaiah?"

He nodded. "This highway" — he indicated the paved road we walked on — "is nothing compared to the work of John."

We hadn't gone far when he quizzed me again. " 'Behold, I am sending My messenger, and he will clear the way before Me. Behold, I am going to send you Elijah the prophet, before the coming of the great and terrible day of Adonai. He will turn the hearts of fathers to the children, and the hearts of children to their fathers . . .' " He glanced over at me. "Remember?"

I blew out a breath. "Zechariah?"

"Malachi. And I tell you, Jude — these are things you will see with your own eyes, this very day."

I did not know what to make of my brother's comments, but Yeshua had always been given to odd pronouncements. He was also prone to wander off when there was work to be done. Often James or Joses or I would find him staring at the horizon as if his thoughts were focused on some realm we could not see.

But on the day we found John, Yeshua remained firmly in the moment. Step by step we moved down the road that led us to a place outside the village of Salim. A crowd had gathered on the rocks that lined the bank of the River Jordan. Among the crowd I saw representatives from every level of society: soldiers clad in leather armor with daggers hanging from their belts; mothers with young children; wealthy merchants and tax collectors attired in richly adorned robes that screamed of wealth and privilege.

One couple caught my eye because I could not readily identify their station in life. They wore simple linen clothing without ornamentation, but the man and his wife wore their hair curled in the Roman fashion. They did not appear wealthy — they wore no gold bracelets, earrings, or chains — but carried themselves with dignity and were exceptionally well groomed.

Yeshua must have noticed my interest in the couple. "Chuza," he said, nodding in the man's direction. "And his wife, Joanna."

"Are they from Nazareth?"

Yeshua shook his head. "Tiberias. They are servants at Herod's palace."

I lifted a brow, about to ask how he had gathered this information, but at that moment a man with waist-long hair stood and walked to the river's edge. He wore a rough garment of animal skins, inexpertly stitched and ragged at the lower edge. His laced sandals revealed muddy legs, his beard was long and untrimmed, and his eyes blazed with inner fire.

"Why have you come here?" he asked, lifting his voice until it floated above the crowd. "Did you come to hear the voice of one crying in the wilderness? For that is who I am, the one who shouts, *Make straight the way of Adonai,* as the prophet Isaiah foretold."

I glanced at Yeshua, impressed that he had quoted the same Scripture.

"Repent of your sins," John shouted, his bony finger picking out various people in the crowd. "For the kingdom of God is at hand. Come and be immersed in these waters, leaving your sinful ways and rising to walk in repentance. Confess your sins so that the Ruach ha-Kodesh, the Spirit of Adonai, can purge you with hyssop and make you clean. He will wash you, and you will be whiter than snow."

A flurry of movement caught my eye. I turned in time to see a group of dark-robed

Pharisees join the crowd at the riverbank. Their faces were tight with disapproval, their mouths frozen in unyielding frowns.

John must have seen them, too. But instead of ignoring or pandering to them, he pointed at the eldest and most disapproving of the lot and said, "You brood of vipers! Who warned you to flee from the coming wrath? Produce fruit worthy of repentance, and do not think you can say to yourselves, *We have Abraham as our father!* For I tell you that from these stones God can raise up children for Abraham. Already the axe is laid at the root of the trees; therefore every tree that does not produce good fruit is cut down and thrown into the fire!"

Was he threatening our religious leaders with eternal destruction? I listened with rising amazement as the Pharisees bristled.

"But, John," a common man called, "how can we produce this fruit?"

John met the man's question with a smile. "Whoever has two coats, let him give to the one who has none; and whoever has food, let him do the same."

Another man stood, his ostentatious clothing declaring him to be a tax collector or merchant. No one else would advertise his wealth in such an obvious display. "What shall *we* do?" he asked.

John made his way through the crowd and rested his hand on the man's shoulder. "When you take the taxes, do not take more than you are supposed to. Do not think to enrich yourself with the money of others."

"What about us?"

I searched for the speaker and saw that the voice belonged to a soldier — one of the Jews who served in the Roman militia. John walked toward him, a man most Jews would purposefully avoid. "Do not take things from anyone by force," answered John, "do not falsely accuse anyone, and be content with your wages."

As John paused to drink from a water jug, murmurs rose from the crowd. "Is he the messiah?"

"Are you the Christ we have been waiting for?"

John lowered the jug, then turned and waded into the river until the water reached his waist. He turned again and fluttered his fingers over the surface. "Who will come to be baptized for the remission of sins? As for me, I immerse you in water for repentance. But the One coming after me is mightier than I am; I am not worthy to carry His sandals. He will immerse you in the Ruach ha-Kodesh and fire. His winnowing fork is in His hand, and He shall clear His threshing floor and gather His wheat into the barn; but the chaff He shall burn up with inextinguishable fire." John lifted his hands again. "Now, who will come to be baptized?"

I looked over the crowd. The tax collector stood, followed by another man, and another. Women stood with their husbands, and children followed the example of their parents. The soldier stepped forward, as did a wealthy merchant.

But the leading Pharisee did not stir, nor did any of his companions.

"So this is our cousin," I murmured. But when I looked at Yeshua, his gaze was fixed on John.

I stood and brushed the dirt from my tunic. "I'm going to take a walk," I told Yeshua. "Going back out to the road. Perhaps I can find someone from Nazareth, even pick up some business for the family."

Yeshua nodded, and I left him to think his thoughts as I went on my way.

I'm not sure what people thought as Tasmin and I waited for information outside the gates of Tiberias. Perhaps they considered us beggars, since we were both covered in grit from the road. We tried to approach Jewish families, but most of the travelers who passed through the gates wore tunics and togas in the Roman style, while we looked undeniably like Jews, and poor Jews at that.

Most of the men I tried to stop stared at me as if I were a stray dog that had suddenly bared its teeth. I sank onto a rock, discouraged, and Tasmin clicked her tongue in sympathy. "Let me try," she said, lifting her chin. She used her head covering to wipe the mingled sweat and dust from her face, then arranged her features in a pleasant smile and walked to the road. Another group was approaching, a handsome litter carried by four servants and guarded by two horsemen.

"Shalom!" she called to the man riding in front. "Will you wait a moment, please?"

The horseman reined in his mount and scowled. "What business have you here, woman?"

"I am in search of news," she said, her smile disappearing, "of one called John the Immerser. I hear he has been arrested."

Behind the horseman, a bejeweled hand parted the curtain on the litter. Instinctively I gripped my wooden staff, not knowing what sort of person lay behind the disguising fabric.

A man peered out — Roman, from the

look of his aquiline nose — and beckoned Tasmin to come closer. "Who asks about John?"

"I do." Tasmin stepped forward but remained out of the man's reach. "And my companion, who is John's kinsman."

I stood as a pair of dark eyes met mine, then shifted to Tasmin. "You have heard correctly," the man said. "The prophet has been arrested and imprisoned in Herod's palace. He is safe but will probably not remain so much longer."

"Why is that?"

The man lifted his shoulder in a half-hearted shrug. "If Herodias has her way, she will convince Antipas to take John to Machaerus, a prison by the Dead Sea. She cannot abide the sight of the man."

Tasmin nodded and backed away, murmuring her thanks.

After the litter moved on and entered the city, Tasmin turned to me. "I don't understand why Antipas's wife hates the Immerser."

"I can guess," I said, taking a cup from the pack saddle. "I would imagine it has something to do with John's insistence on pointing out her sin. Not only did her marriage make Antipas an adulterer, it also made her guilty of incest. John was not at all reluctant to name her sin in public."

Tasmin lowered her head, then looked up at me, her face serious. "I have not paid much attention to politics or affairs of government."

"You should pay attention," I told her. "Because you live in a world that changes from year to year and day to day. But Ha-Shem's laws do not change, and John has never been shy about exposing sin. Yeshua would say Adonai sent him to be a voice in the wilderness, not a diplomat in the palace."

"But why would he insult Herodias? I have heard she is a beautiful woman —"

I cut her off with a snort. "Does beauty make a woman good? Antipas's wife may be beautiful, but apparently she is also ambitious. Though married to Philip, after meeting Antipas, she saw an opportunity and seduced him. Philip divorced her, Herod married her, and thus she climbed to a position of greater power."

"I had no idea," Tasmin said. "I have never known any woman like that." She glanced at the glowing horizon. "Oh! Darkness will soon be upon us and we are nowhere near Capernaum."

"We will have to stay here." When I caught the look of unease that rippled over her face,

I hastened to assure her, "I am no more pleased than you, but I will find an inn where you can safely spend the night. I will sleep in the town square."

"Will you be safe there?"

I touched the knob at the top of my staff. "I will."

"But the expense! I did not plan on staying at an inn —"

"Do not be concerned. HaShem has made provision for us."

She stammered in protest, but when I pulled the donkey toward the city gates, she followed.

Chapter Twelve:
Tasmin

After the longest night of my life — a night in which I slept on the floor and shared a tiny room with three women, four children, a baby, and two goats — I rose, braided my hair, and prepared for the final segment of our journey to Capernaum. I had not expected this detour, so I had not been able to come up with a reason why we should not spend a night in Antipas's capital. But surely Jude was now as anxious as I to reach our destination.

I found him waiting for me outside the inn. I wished him shalom, then lifted my small bag to my shoulder. "Did you sleep well?"

"As well as I could, considering I slept on paving stones." His gaze ran over me in swift appraisal. "You appear to be rested."

"I am — and thank you for paying for the inn." I gave him one of my brightest smiles and gestured toward the city gates. "Shall we be on our way?"

I realized his plans had changed when he did not respond. Instead he glanced over his shoulder, then looked at the ground and shifted his weight. "I think we should wait here a day or so," he said, not meeting my gaze. "My mother will want to know about what's happened to John. I cannot leave here without taking the time to see if I can help in some way. I should at least try to see him."

I stared, unable to believe I'd heard him correctly. "You think we would be allowed to see one of Antipas's prisoners? Do you expect to walk up to the palace gate and ask for permission to enter?"

Jude made a face, acknowledging the inherent difficulty, then kicked at the ground. "I have to try. If I tell my mother what we've heard about John, the first thing she'll ask is what I did to help. How can I tell her I did nothing?"

I blew out a slow breath, understanding his quandary. The tight-knit families in Galilee depended upon each other, and a man who did not care for his kin was worse than an infidel.

"I understand why you *want* to see him," I said, speaking slowly. "What I don't understand is why you think you *can* see

him. You are a not a Roman, you are a Jew
—"

"So is Antipas, or so he says," Jude interrupted.

I ignored the comment. "You'd have more
success if you were Roman, or wealthy, or
even a Pharisee from Jerusalem. But you
are from Nazareth, one of the poorest towns
in Galilee."

"You don't have to remind me." Jude
exhaled heavily, then met my gaze without
flinching. "At least allow me to do this —
let us go to the palace and wait to see if
HaShem will grant me an opportunity. If
He does, we will walk through whatever
door He opens. If He does not, at least I
can tell my mother that we went to the
palace on John's behalf."

I bit my lip and considered his proposal.
Jude was not a careless man — clearly he
wanted to do the right thing. He was not
purposely trying to frustrate my desire to
reach Thomas, because he also had urgent
reasons for reaching Capernaum . . .

"All right." I threw my scarf over my hair
and looked around. "Where did you leave
the donkey?"

"He's in the stable. We can pick him up
on our way out of the city."

"Good."

We turned onto the main street and walked deeper into the city Antipas had built, rumor had it, on the graves of Jews from an ancient town called Hammoth. Many Jews refused to enter Tiberias because they considered the place unclean, but I suspected the real reason had more to do with wanting to avoid the tetrarch. My father was always quick to point out that although we often referred to him as our king, he was not a king like his father, for his power was limited and his decisions closely monitored by the Roman emperor. As much as Antipas might want to be the ultimate power in Judea, we knew he never would be. The first Herod made certain his authority would be divided after his death, so that none of his heirs would ever be as powerful as he was.

The streets became wider and smoother as we ventured into the heart of the city. The white paving stones, gleaming in the morning sun, had sunk in spots, causing the occasional wagon to jounce heavily over the street. The buildings, all faced with white stone, looked more Roman than Judean, and I wondered how long they would maintain their polished façades beneath our blistering sun.

We turned a corner and stepped onto a

broad avenue. On an elevated plateau — the highest point in the city — stood a grand building that had to be the tetrarch's palace. Resplendent in white marble, with over a dozen Greek columns standing guard along the front, the sight of the place staggered me. Wide steps led from the street to a porch, while banners emblazoned with Antipas's emblem fluttered from poles attached to a second-story balcony. Like the buildings and homes around it, our ruler's palace looked sturdy, Roman, and indisputably new.

"If Antipas built this place to intimidate his people," I whispered, "he must be pleased with the result."

Jude snorted in agreement, then surprised me by taking my hand as we began to climb the steps. I marveled that he had dared to touch me — most men would not touch a woman unless they were betrothed, siblings, or ill-mannered. None of those situations applied to us, and when I looked up I saw nothing but grim determination on his face.

He was not thinking about me; he was thinking about John.

He had taken my hand reflexively, as if I were a sister he meant to help up the stairs. He probably didn't even realize he had done it.

Because I was accustomed to Thomas doing the same thing, I did not pull away.

We were not the only people on the stairs. Others climbed the steps with us, though I could not tell if they were petitioners, nobles, merchants, or servants.

Once we reached the open area leading to three pairs of golden doors, we waited with the others — for an audience with Antipas, I presumed. A hushed stillness hung over the gathering, and I couldn't help but wonder if everyone expected to see the tetrarch. I would have asked the man next to us why he had come, but when I turned to the fellow, Jude jerked me back to his side.

"Remain silent," he hissed through clenched teeth. "We do not want to draw attention."

"Why not?" I whispered, but he did not answer. A moment later he inclined his head toward a man and woman who stood several feet away. "I know them," he said, his eyes widening. "They were at the river when Yeshua and I went to visit John."

I peered at the couple, but they were strangers to me.

Jude led me across the open area until we stood beside the couple. He bowed and placed his hand on his chest in a formal gesture. "Shalom. Excuse the interruption, but we might know each other. I saw you near the Jordan when John was baptizing. My brother saw you, too, and told me you were one of Antipas's servants."

The man flushed and glanced quickly around. "I . . . I do not know you, friend."

"Perhaps you know my brother. He is called Yeshua."

At the mention of Yeshua's name, the man's mouth opened and the woman gasped. The man grabbed Jude's tunic and led him down the steps until they stood apart from the others. Bewildered, the woman and I followed. When Antipas's servant seemed sure no one else could hear, he clapped Jude's shoulders. "You are the brother of Yeshua?" he said, managing a wavering smile. "And this is your wife?"

My cheeks went hot as Jude stammered a reply. "Yes, I am Yeshua's brother, but this woman is a friend, not my wife. We are traveling to meet our families in Capernaum. But we heard about John's arrest, so we came here to see if we could do something to comfort him."

The servant's face fell. "I only wish you could. Last night Antipas's men put John on a wagon destined for Machaerus. Antipas always leaves Tiberias in late spring because the summers here are stifling. But where are my manners?" He patted his chest. "I am Chuza, steward to Antipas, and this is Joanna, my wife." He gestured to the woman, who bowed her head and smiled. "We will travel with the royal family when they leave for the summer palace later this week. If you would like, I might be able to give John a message from you."

Jude looked from the man to the woman. "You are quite certain John is no longer here?"

"I am in charge of Antipas's household." Chuza's voice overflowed with humility and sorrow. "Trust me, your kinsman is gone. They will keep him in the summer palace until . . . until Adonai's will is accomplished."

"But why was he arrested?" Jude crossed his arms. "I have heard the man speak, and he did not speak of insurrection or rebellion. Surely Antipas has no reason to fear a man who preaches repentance."

"Ah." Chuza lowered his voice and leaned closer. "Antipas *himself* sent us to hear John. Not only us but also his best friend from childhood, a man called Manaen. Antipas wanted a firsthand report of John's activities, so we told him the truth when we returned."

Jude's brows flickered. "What truth did

you tell him? I did not hear John say anything deserving arrest and imprisonment."

"Antipas's action was spurred by Herodias." Joanna's brown eyes had sharpened. "She could not abide a truth John frequently mentioned — that Antipas was guilty of incest and adultery. Antipas disapproves as well, because John's words disprove the man's claim to worship Adonai. How can you worship HaShem and not obey His Law?"

Chuza nodded. "Antipas was fascinated by our reports of John and earnestly desired to see some miracle performed. He would have commanded a miracle if he thought John would perform it — sometimes I wonder if that is why he wants to keep John close by."

Relief flitted across Jude's face. "So Antipas will let him live, he's in no danger."

"Danger is never far from any of the Herods," Chuza said, "but Antipas fears the people more than he fears John. He knows John is popular, so by keeping him alive and in prison, he does not rouse the people's anger and he prevents the Immerser's fame from spreading." He rested his hand on the edge of his robe, then gave Jude a conspiratorial smile. "So you were there that day? You saw the skies open when Yeshua came out of the water?"

I turned to Jude, eager to hear his response, but a line had appeared between his brows. "I did not see anything."

"You didn't see John baptizing Yeshua?"

Jude slowly shook his head. "I had gone for a walk."

"Ah, my friend." A shadow of regret entered Chuza's eyes. "I am sorry you missed it, but I was a witness. So were Joanna and Manaen. We will never forget what John said about the Lamb of God."

I was about to press the man for details when the gilded doors of the palace swung open, the screech of metal hinges rending the air. As the crowd on the landing surged forward, Chuza looked up. "We must go."

"Wait." Joanna grabbed her husband's arm, then looked at me. "You are on your way to meet your families?"

I nodded. "My brother is with Yeshua. Jude's mother, too."

"And they are in Capernaum?"

Jude nodded.

"Oh, Chuza." Joanna turned wide eyes on her husband. "Let me go with them. You will soon leave with the king, and I have never enjoyed the summer palace. Let me go with these two so I can serve Yeshua. With so many following him, he will need people to arrange for food and shelter, to handle the details of daily living. I could be helpful."

Chuza patted his wife's hand. "Perhaps these two have made plans of their own."

Joanna smiled. "Perhaps they would like a chaperone. I'm surprised the girl's father let her travel in this man's company, considering they are not even betrothed."

"We meant to take only a single day for the journey," I said, my cheeks burning, "but we were delayed by the news about John —"

"I do not doubt your virtue," Joanna said with a smile. "Still, with an older woman along, no one else will have reason to doubt it. Please, let me go with you. When we arrive in Capernaum" — she transferred her gaze to Jude — "perhaps I can be of some comfort to your mother. I may also be of help to your brother."

Before I knew it, our traveling group of two had become a group of three.

Abba would be pleased.

While we waited for Joanna to gather a few belongings, Jude purchased flatbread and cheese to break our fast. We sat in the shade of a terebinth tree and ate, neither of us saying much. I kept wishing Chuza had said more about when he and Joanna went to visit John because I desperately wanted to know what really happened when the Immerser baptized his kinsman. Did they see a dove light upon Yeshua's shoulder? Did they hear a voice or thunder? Did the river become wine?

At least this unexpected delay had not been altogether unprofitable. We would not be able to see John, yet we had picked up a fellow traveler. Having a third person along might be good. Jude, being a man, had to be prodded to make conversation.

He elbowed me, interrupting my musings. "Tasmin" — a dark note shadowed his voice — "do not be obvious, but slowly look toward the cart where I purchased the bread. Do you know the man standing there?"

Alarmed, I lifted my head and pretended to look for Joanna. I spotted the man Jude mentioned — he stood near the flatbread cart but wasn't buying food. Instead he seemed to be studying us, his arms folded, an intense expression on his face. He was clean-shaven, like most Gentiles, but something about him seemed alien. I shuddered when I realized what it was — he had only one eye. In the spot where his right eye should have been, I saw only a dark, gaping hole.

I turned back to Jude. "Do you know him?"

"Do you?"

"I have never seen him before."

Jude cleared his throat. "I saw him earlier, when we were speaking to Chuza. He was watching us then." Jude swept the street with a slow look. "He had been climbing the stairs, and when he saw us talking to the steward, he stopped. He watched us until Chuza went into the palace."

We sat in silence for a few moments, finishing our morning meal, and all the while I felt the pressure of the man's eyes — his *eye* — on us.

When I had finished, I brushed crumbs from my lap. "Is he still there?"

Jude nodded. "He has moved away from the bread cart, but he is still watching."

"If Thomas were here, he would know what to do."

I looked up and saw Joanna approaching us with a basket in her arms. She had covered her head with a scarf and managed to wave when she saw us.

"I am eager to be on our way," she said when she drew closer. "Do we need anything else before we go?"

"Just one thing." Jude turned his back to the one-eyed stranger, then discreetly jerked his thumb over his shoulder. "The tall beardless man over there, the one in the blue tunic. He has been watching us all morning. Do you know him?"

Joanna glanced over Jude's shoulder, then looked at me with worry in her eyes. "He is a stranger to me."

"Are you certain? Could it be Manaen, the man who went with you to hear John?"

She gave Jude a slightly exasperated look. "I know Manaen well — he grew up with Antipas and is always at the palace. He is a good man, trustworthy. That *other* man I do not know, but I have seen him with Herodias."

Jude lifted a brow. "Surely she is not unfaithful to her —"

Joanna snorted. "Not with him. This man is a eunuch who has served her since her marriage to Philip."

"Why would a eunuch be interested in us?" I asked, edging into the conversation.

Joanna shook her head. "I have no idea, unless Herodias asked him to spy on Chuza. He probably saw you, didn't recognize you, and now he wants to pick up a juicy morsel of gossip for his mistress. Fortunately, he will hear no gossip about us." She shivered slightly. "I wonder if this is a good time to leave. If Chuza is under suspicion —"

"Why would he be?" Jude asked. "He went to see John the Immerser because Antipas asked him to go."

Joanna nodded. "Still, anyone who favors the prophet is destined to be abhorred by Herodias. She cannot tolerate anyone who speaks for HaShem."

"If you would rather stay here —" I began, but Joanna shook her head.

"I will not let Herodias ruin my opportunity to serve Yeshua," she said. "Come, let us go. Capernaum is not far, but we should not tarry when daylight is wasting away."

I gave Jude a questioning glance, and he shrugged. Joanna was a mature woman who knew her own mind. If she wanted to go with us to Capernaum, who were we to dissuade her?

"Chuza will send word if trouble is afoot," she said, adjusting her basket on her back as we walked toward the gate. "And I will pray for Chuza's safety while I am away."

Chapter Thirteen:
Tasmin

Magdala, another primarily Gentile city, was but a short walk north of Tiberias. Although we planned to avoid it, we had to pass by its gates on our way to Capernaum. The shining sea to the east — which Antipas had recently renamed the Sea of Tiberias to curry favor with the emperor — lay at our right, while Magdala loomed at our left. The settlement was not new and stately like Tiberias, and yet Roman visitors loved its marketplace, famous for its salted fish and beautifully dyed silks and woolens.

"I hear you can even buy pork at that market," Jude said, glancing toward the watchtower that gave the city its name. "The sellers of Magdala have no regard for the Law."

When I mentioned that I loved salted fish and colorful silks, Jude firmly shook his head. "I am sorry," he said, "but we spent far too much time in Tiberias. We must keep walking if we are to reach Capernaum by day's end."

I sighed, knowing he was right. Joanna wisely remained neutral, voicing no opinion on either fish or fabrics, so we passed the city gates and kept walking. We soon came upon the city's burial ground, and I shuddered at the desolate look of the place. A dead tree stood in the center of the walled graveyard, lifting skeletal arms to the sky. The near-constant wind had scrubbed the carving from ornamental bricks on the wall and several family sepulchers. I could not spot a single speck of green in the place, nor a living shrub or weed.

We had only gone about ten paces past the graveyard when the heavy silence surrounding the place shivered into fragments. I whirled around, terrified by the sound of a blood-chilling scream, and Jude reached for a stick he had strapped to the donkey's back. Joanna jumped and fell against the startled beast, upsetting the pack saddle and scattering our belongings on the road.

Amid the confusion, a woman rose from behind the wall and ran through the gate, her arms upraised, her hands curled like the talons of an eagle. Her tangled dark hair rose in a wiry thundercloud from her head and shoulders, and her tunic, or what remained of it, fluttered in the fierceness of her attack. She launched herself at me, her piercing eyes boring into mine, and I could see nothing but those dark orbs. I threw up my hands to protect myself as my ears filled with the stream of undecipherable words spewing from her cracked and scabbed lips. Was I to die without ever seeing my brother again?

I did not die, because Jude sprang into the space between me and the madwoman. He held up his stick as a warning, which the woman did not seem to notice. She ran into him, spitting and snarling, and knocked him to the ground. With no room to wield the stick, Jude released it and caught the grasping hands that tore at his garments. In the dust they rolled and grappled, struggling in a frenzy of sound and fury. The quiet melancholy of the graveyard vanished, replaced by a flood of foul language, some of it in a guttural voice that seemed more suited to an animal than a creature created in HaShem's image.

Stunned, I stared at the living tableau before me, idly wondering how an emaciated woman could have the strength to wrestle a strong young man. She seemed a part of the graveyard and must have been living off scraps tossed by passing strangers . . . unless she had been eating the vermin that frequented the tombs at night. A long, angry scar ran the length of the inside of her arm, and I wondered whether someone had cut her or if she had wounded herself.

Time seemed to slow as Jude and the woman continued to scuffle. Then from the corner of my eye, I sensed other movement. Joanna had picked up Jude's stick and now held it with both hands, raised and ready. She approached the pair on the ground, hesitated, and finally brought the stick down on the woman's head.

Joanna's blow had little effect. The enraged woman did not stop fighting but turned from Jude to Joanna, her lips twisted in a snarl. Joanna whimpered as the woman sprang to her feet. But Jude stretched out his arm, caught the woman's ankle, and brought her down again. Amid more curses, the woman twisted and reached for Jude, yet he managed to roll out of the way. She leapt onto all fours and lunged toward him, raking her ragged fingernails across his face just before I picked up the stick and hit her across the back, finally bringing her down.

As she lay at our feet, silent and still, the three of us looked at each other. Jude, slick with dust and blood and perspiration, slowly rose to his feet and wiped his face with his cloak. Joanna covered her mouth and backed away while I dropped the stick and stared, unable to believe I had struck another human being. Even though Thomas and I had played rough games over the years, I had never hit him.

We stood in silence, gasping and trembling, for none of us knew what to do. I then spotted blood trickling down the side of Jude's face, and my stomach roiled in response.

Finally, Joanna spoke in a quavering voice. "Did we kill her? HaShem knows we didn't intend to —"

"She lives." Jude pointed to the woman's chest, which rose and fell in a natural rhythm. "She breathes."

"What — what was wrong with her?" I asked, feeling weak-kneed. I clung to the crumbling cemetery wall for support. "What made her act like that?"

"Madness," Joanna said.

Jude lifted his chin. "Or an unclean spirit. She was probably forced out of her village and reduced to living here."

"This is living?" I glanced around at the forlorn place. "No one lives in a graveyard."

"No one *in her right mind* lives in such a place," Joanna corrected. "This woman is not in her right mind."

I ran my hand through my hair, trying desperately to think of a reasonable course of action, and came up with nothing. We couldn't take her with us when she seemed intent on killing us. We couldn't take her into a city, because they would immediately put her out, if we could even get her past the gate. If she had a home and family, we had no way of finding them . . .

Thomas would know what to do, but where was he when I needed him most?

"Let us move her back into the graveyard," Joanna said. "At least she will not be in the road."

Jude knelt and placed one of the woman's arms around his shoulders. "Perhaps she will attack a pair of Roman soldiers. They will not hesitate to do whatever should be done."

I shuddered, knowing what soldiers would do. They'd probably take their pleasure with her and then end her life.

Jude carried the unconscious woman back to the burial ground, then closed the sagging gate and secured it with a leather strap. "There," he said, tightening the strap. "Perhaps the next traveler will now have a moment to prepare for her attack."

My hands were still trembling when we

gathered our scattered belongings and continued on our way.

Still rattled by the madwoman's attack, I fell into step beside Joanna, hoping that conversation would take our minds off our frightening ordeal. "So you want to help Yeshua," I said, offering her a polite smile. "Do you believe he is our promised king?"

Her eyes lit with eagerness. "I hope he is. I only know what I saw the day we were at the river. I heard John proclaim Yeshua to be the Lamb of God, and I heard a voice from heaven when the Spirit lighted on Yeshua's shoulder. Whoever he is, he was sent to us from Adonai. And if I can help him, I am willing to do it."

"Your husband feels the same way?"

She nodded. "Chuza and I talked about following Yeshua together, but Chuza did not want to leave his work. Manaen agreed with him. Who knows? One day Yeshua might need a friend in Antipas's palace. With Manaen and Chuza, he will have at least two."

I studied the lady as she talked. She and her husband were older, probably in their early forties, and anyone could tell that neither of them had ever walked behind a plow. She spoke like an educated woman

157

and could probably converse in Greek as well as Hebrew and Aramaic. She frequently gestured with her hands as she talked, and with one glance at those long manicured fingernails, I knew she had never chased a chicken or scrubbed clay pots. She lived an easy life . . . so why had she decided to follow Yeshua and serve his ragtag band of followers?

Perhaps by studying Joanna I could learn the secret to his charisma.

We were only a short distance from Capernaum when I heard an odd sound from the high grass at the roadside.

"Wait." I stopped and peered into the grass. "I think I heard an animal. It sounded hurt."

An anxious frown crinkled Joanna's brows. "I'm not sure we should search for a wild animal."

"But it sounded like a *small* animal." I pushed at the tall grass and studied the slope that ran down to the seashore. I saw nothing unusual.

Jude sighed as Joanna retreated behind the donkey. "The sun will set soon," he reminded me.

"I am eager to reach Capernaum, too," I reminded him. "I only need a moment."

I stepped into the grass, aware that I might

encounter a rabbit, a snake, or a rat. My sandals offered no protection from a snake-bite, and if I discovered a rat's nest, Jude would never stop for me again. But the cry I heard sounded bigger than a rat or rabbit, and more urgent . . .

I took another step into the tall grass. Maybe I had imagined the cry. Thomas was always accusing me of hearing things, so I closed my eyes and listened in a silence so thick the only sound was the quiet pounding of my pulse. We were alone. No fishermen were on the lake, no boats or nets waited on shore. This desolate area lay between two cities, so any sound must have come from an animal, and animals knew how to fend for themselves.

"You should make noise," Joanna called. "Chuza says a snake will flee if he hears you coming."

"That is good to know." I lifted my voice, hoping Chuza had given his wife sound advice. "If you are a snake, please leave . . ."

Ahead of me, something shivered the grass, and my heart nearly stopped beating.

Jude must have seen the movement, too. "Tasmin!" His voice thundered in rebuke. "Get out of there."

I was about to turn and retreat, but then I heard a distinctively human cry. Tiny fingers

159

parted the grass in front of me, and I saw a little boy crouching among the stalks. He wore no clothing, and bloody scabs marked his pale skin — wounds from sharp reeds, I presumed, or insect bites. Liquid dripped from his noise, mottled scabs covered his lips, and his brown eyes were deep enough for me to fall into . . .

"Oh!" I fell to my knees and gestured to him. "Come here, little one. Why are you hiding in the grass?"

The boy hesitated, then stood and staggered toward me, crying in earnest. I gasped in surprise when his arms went around my neck. I awkwardly patted his back and felt sharp bones beneath the thin covering of skin. Whose child was this, and how long had he been out here?

I met Joanna's wide gaze. The sight of the child had startled her as well, but now she opened her arms. Gratefully I walked over and gave the child to her, then watched as she murmured soft words and lowered the boy to the ground. Together we knelt and looked him over.

"How old do you think he is?" I asked.

"Two or three years, I would say." She ran her hand over his thin arms and legs. "No broken bones. No cuts other than these bites and scratches."

"Who would leave a boy out here?" I asked. "Or could he be lost?"

Joanna shook her head. "His family might have been part of a caravan, so he could have been lost along the way. Sometimes children wander when their families stop to eat. The family moves forward again, unaware that their child has slipped away."

"So we need to find his family."

She nodded, then inhaled a sharp breath. "There is another possibility. Most children are weaned at three. If his family could not afford to feed him, they might have abandoned him in the hope that someone else would take him in."

I stared at her, stunned. "How could anyone do that?"

"The concept is an ancient one — the Greeks and Romans still leave unwanted babies for the wild dogs."

"But surely no Jew —"

"We are not blameless in this matter. When our fathers turned from HaShem, they sacrificed their children to Molech, placing their babies in the fire. The prophets were horrified — *HaShem* was horrified. Such things should not be done, but when men turn their thoughts from Adonai, they place their pleasures above the holiness of God-given life." She ran her hand over the

161

boy's tousled hair and pulled a burr from his curls. "Do you have a name?" She smiled at him. "Are you called . . . Jacob?" The child shook his head. "David?" Again a headshake. "Why don't you tell me what your name is?"

The boy stared at her, his eyes filling with tears. He stuck his thumb in his mouth and began to wail in earnest.

"Poor thing." Joanna drew him close, cradling his head against her breast. "I'm sure he's terrified."

I tilted my head. Joanna was old enough to have adult children, and she was free to travel. Perhaps she was free enough to raise another child . . .

"Do you have children?" I asked. "You seem to know what you are doing."

The flicker of a smile rose at the edge of her mouth, then faded away. "We had a daughter and a son, but both died from a fever. Adonai has not seen fit to bless us with others."

"I'm sorry. I wondered because you seem so comfortable with the boy."

"Comfortable? Yes. And heartbroken. But HaShem is faithful, and His mercies are new every morning."

She rubbed the crying boy's back and looked at me. "What about you? Have you younger siblings?"

"None. I have a twin brother, though, and he is my other half. That's why I have to find him in Capernaum and take him back home."

"If Adonai wills." She looked over at Jude, who had led the donkey down to the lake for water. "Jude? We are willing to go when you are ready."

Jude pulled the donkey from the water and led him up the hill. When he drew closer, he looked at the child in Joanna's arms and lifted a bushy brow. "And what are we doing with him?"

"Taking him with us," Joanna said, clearing a space for the boy on the pack saddle. "Perhaps someone in Capernaum will either recognize him or be willing to take him in. But we cannot leave him here."

Jude glanced at me, then nodded. "Let us go, then, and hope Adonai leads us in the right direction."

We finally spotted Capernaum, an old city shining in the melon-colored tints of the setting sun. This thoroughly Jewish town was located just off the highway that ran from the Great Sea to Damascus, so the settlement was well fortified. A Roman garrison — a smaller structure than the massive complex in Jerusalem — had been built into the city wall, and soldiers walked on its flat roof, keeping watch over the highway. On the ground, just outside the gate, a group of elders sat in a semicircle, enjoying the honor accorded them, while a group of women sold their wares in a booth not far away.

As the women eyed the setting sun and put away their goods, an energetic group of Torah scholars argued about a point of the Law, their hands moving in emphatic gestures and occasionally slamming an open palm. A few of the older men, quiet and dignified in their long gray beards, cast inquisitive eyes on us as we walked past, yet no one stopped us or inquired about our visit.

From snatches of conversation that reached my ear, I learned that news of Etan's wedding had traveled faster than we had. "I heard it from eyewitnesses," one merchant was saying. "The Nazarene took water from a common cistern and turned it into wine!"

"I have seen him at the well," another man said, "and he looks as ordinary as you and me. What makes him a king? His mother is a common woman, and his father was a carpenter."

"He lives with Simon Peter's family," a woman inserted. "Would a king live with a fisherman?"

"He comes from the house of David," another man argued. "His father was Joseph, son of Matthat, son of Levi, son of Melki, son of Jannai, son of Joseph, and so on until David. Did Adonai not promise us another king from the house of David?"

Ahead of me, Jude guffawed. I grimaced, hoping none of the men had heard him. The last thing we needed was an argument with one or more of these strangers. They had no idea that Jude was Yeshua's brother, but Jude, who had probably grown weary of the conversation of women, might be eager for a robust argument with men who held strong opinions about Yeshua.

When I saw him turn and stare at one fellow, I quickened my step and caught his arm. "Please don't." When he scowled at me, I pinched the flesh beneath his sleeve. "We have no time for this sort of thing. The sun will soon set, and we have yet to find our families and prepare for the night."

Jude cast a derisive glance at the men, then nodded. "You are right; it would be wiser for me to avoid a confrontation. Perhaps you should ask those women about our families."

Leaving his side, I walked over to a table where a woman was packing up a collection of clay bowls. "Shalom," I said, smiling. "We are looking for Yeshua of Nazareth, who is traveling with a large group. I believe they arrived here two or three days ago."

The woman's round face relaxed in a smile. "I saw them camped on the lake shore."

"Good." I pointed to a road that appeared to lead toward the lake. "Is this the best way to go? Around the town?"

"You could go to the lake that way," she said, "but you won't find Yeshua there. He and his people left this morning."

"They've gone?" I gaped at her. "But they invited us to join them."

Jude appeared at my side. "Where did they go?" he asked, his voice rough.

The woman arched a brow. "If you want to know that, you should have arrived earlier. People leaving Capernaum do not always tell me where they are bound."

Jude flushed. "They must have told someone —"

I placed my open hand into the space between Jude and the woman. "Thank you for your help," I told her while pulling Jude away. "We will go into the city and ask a few others. You have been most helpful."

I released Jude's arm when we reached the donkey. While he sputtered in frustration, I grasped the donkey's halter and led him, Joanna, and the boy into Capernaum.

"She had to know where they went," Jude said, trailing behind the donkey. "Women like that know everything."

"Why would she lie to us?" I countered. "Perhaps she was home when they left the city. Perhaps she didn't ask because she doesn't care. But your brother lives here now, so someone will know where they were going."

The streets of Capernaum were clearing as we ventured into the heart of the city. We walked past shuttered shops and homes where lamplight fringed the doorways. Joanna stayed beside the donkey, keeping a steadying hand on its passenger — the boy had fallen asleep on the pack saddle.

"We should find a place to rest," Joanna said, nodding toward the child. "And we need to find food — we have an extra mouth to feed, and this boy will be hungry."

"The woman said Yeshua camped on the shore," I reminded her. "Maybe we should set up a camp there. One of the fishermen might have overheard their plans."

Jude snorted. "Fine. But we need to make camp before dark."

We followed the curve of the road and soon came to the eastern edge of town, where a well-worn path led toward the lake. Breathing in the mingled scents of water and fish, I led the way to the shore. I peered down the path, hoping to spot some kind of shelter, but all I could see was sand, shrubby bushes, and a few overturned boats.

"We can camp there," Jude said, pointing at the boats. "I'll help you set up, then I'll go look for food. I'll have to hurry before they close the gates."

"Go now," I urged him, leading the donkey toward the boats. "Joanna and I will build a fire."

"Are you sure?"

"Of course."

Jude hesitated a moment, then turned and left us alone in the gathering darkness.

As Joanna and I unloaded the pack saddle near the overturned fishing boats, I struggled to hide my disappointment. I had hoped to be spending the night in Thomas's company, surrounded by a sizable group. Instead I was camping outside with a man, woman, and child I barely knew. I was not afraid — I trusted Jude and Joanna — but I had been confident that Thomas and I would be reunited before sunset.

Countless times during the day I found myself turning to look for my brother, but then remembered he was not around. I frequently bit back words I would have said, words he alone would have understood. A hundred times I had swallowed *Thomas always says* and *If Thomas were here . . .*

Would I ever find him again?

When everything had been unpacked, I sat on a blanket and rested my elbows on my knees. Thomas's absence was so overwhelming, so palpable, I felt like his shadow sat beside me, a mocking, taunting remnant of my twin. Wherever he was, did Thomas feel my absence? Did he miss me as much as I missed him? What had it been now — four days? Four days without Thomas. Endless, frustrating days.

My gaze drifted toward the east, where the setting sun had spangled the sea. Waves crested rhythmically against the shore, a soothing sound that would soon lull us to sleep . . .

For Thomas's sake, I would not mind sleeping on the narrow beach. I knew the lake could occasionally spawn fierce storms, but the wind was warm and the sky clear.

Joanna took the sleepy child from the donkey and set him on a rock. I helped her roll out blankets. Since she had a blanket of her own, we put ours together and created a space large enough for two women and the boy to stretch out. "I suppose we could crawl beneath one of those boats if it rains," she said, one hand on her hip as she looked over the area. "But with a fire, it might be more pleasant to sleep under the stars." She lifted a brow. "Do you think Jude is capable of defending us if necessary?"

I laughed. "Capable? Sure. But perhaps the question is not whether he *could,* but whether he *would.*"

"Why? Is there some trouble between you two?"

I blinked at her. "I don't know why I said that. I suppose I was thinking of my brother, who would defend me from anything. I . . . I suppose I didn't think anyone else would want to defend me."

She sank to the blanket. "You and Jude have something in common, then. You are both seeking a brother."

I nodded. "He wants Yeshua to stop traveling and return to the family business. I want my brother to come home and stop following this would-be messiah. Thomas has no business leaving me and our father alone."

Joanna nodded as she filled a small clay lamp with oil from a stoppered pitcher. "This will do in place of a fire," she said, placing the lamp in the sand. "As for me, I don't think Yeshua is a would-be messiah. I believe he is the One we have been waiting for."

I shot her a questioning glance. "Because you heard a voice from heaven?"

"In part." She bent her knees, then locked her arms around them as she looked at the watery horizon. The setting sun behind us had turned the eastern sky purple and pink, a glorious ending for a long day.

"Is this not the right time for the messiah to appear?" she asked. "Our people returned from exile after proving we could not keep the Law. We learned we could not, so why have we become so determined to keep it now?" She laughed softly. "Manaen and Chuza have spent hours discussing these things. When we went to the Jordan to see John the Immerser, we did not go to be convinced of anything. Chuza hoped to tell Antipas that the Immerser was simply another fraud. But then we saw Yeshua — quiet, simple, and lowly — and we heard John declare that 'Yeshua is the Lamb of God, the One who will take away the sins of the world.' "

I looked up, confused. "What does that mean?"

She waved her hand, clearly at a loss for

words. "I'm not sure. But if HaShem has sent him to take away sins, then that is what he will do, for how could HaShem fail in his purpose?"

A flush raced like a fever across her lovely face. "The prophet Jeremiah testified that Adonai would bring us back from exile because He loves us, and He always will. And the Lord said, 'Behold, days are coming when I will make a new covenant with the house of Israel and with the house of Judah — not like the covenant I made with their fathers in the day I took them by the hand to bring them out of the land of Egypt . . . After those days I will put my Torah within them. Yes, I will write it on their heart. I will be their God and they will be My people . . . for I will forgive their iniquity, their sin I will remember no more.' " She tilted her head and smiled. "Does that sound like a Lamb of God who will take away the sins of the world?"

I blew out a breath. "Lambs are meant for sacrifice. Do you think Adonai would send our messiah only to have him die?"

A momentary look of bewilderment crossed Joanna's face. Then she shook her head. "Chuza and I have asked ourselves the same question. We don't have all the answers, but I know one thing — what

Adonai has promised, He will do. And if John says Yeshua will take away the sins of the world, then he will. How will He do it? I am content to wait and see."

We sat in silence for a few moments, then the child began to cry. Joanna gave him a pitying glance, hugged him, and patted his back. "I can feel his ribs," she whispered. "And I have nothing to give him."

"Wait." I pulled a half-finished loaf of flatbread from my bag. "I have this."

Joanna took the bread and broke off a piece, then offered it to the boy. He brought it to his mouth, but instead of biting it, he licked it like a ravenous dog.

Startled, I looked to Joanna for an explanation. "Why does he eat like that?"

"I don't know."

She pulled the boy's hand away from his face and tipped him backward to better see inside his mouth. "He has teeth," she murmured, "though they are not arranged as they should be. Wait." A frown darkened her face. "I have never seen anything like that."

"What?"

Gesturing for me to come closer, she tipped the boy's head toward the lamplight. I saw a few teeth in his pink gums, then I gasped. The boy's tongue was . . . wrong.

Deformed. Instead of being long and rounded at the end, the tongue had *two* ends, neither of which seemed to reach his front teeth.

I recoiled in horror. "Is this the child of the devil?"

"Of course not." Her mouth dipped into an even deeper frown. "But he was born with some kind of deformity."

"How can he eat with a tongue like that?"

"Or talk?" Joanna shook her head. "No wonder he couldn't tell us his name — I wonder if he can speak at all."

Horror ran down my spine as I realized yet another reason he might have been on the side of the road. His parents might have left him because they could not repair his tongue. A mute child who could barely eat would face a short and dismal future . . .

I am ashamed to admit it, but in that instant I wished I had not stopped to investigate the sound in the grasses. Some other woman's problem had just become mine and Joanna's, and I was less equipped to deal with it than the boy's parents had been. How could I care for a child like this? How could Joanna, and what would her husband say if she brought him home?

I drew a deep breath, drowning in waves of guilt. "My father" — I lowered my voice

— "says I tend to fill my plate with more than my stomach can hold. This time I have outdone myself."

Joanna had already proven herself a kind woman, but even she had no answer for our dilemma. Distress filled her eyes, and I was fairly certain she was experiencing the same regret. What could be done for this boy? A surgeon might be able to remove the tongue, but having no tongue might be worse than what the boy currently had. A doctor might try to sew the two pieces of tongue together, but the result would undoubtedly be clumsy and might leave the child in an even worse condition.

I broke off another piece of bread, but before giving it to Joanna, I pressed it into the thinnest layer possible. Maybe he could manage it . . .

"Do not be afraid."

I started as a male voice came out of the darkness. Joanna and I had been so focused on the child, we had not paid attention to the area outside the tiny circle of lamplight. A man stepped forward, a tanned and grizzled fisherman, I surmised, for he carried a basket of fish in one hand and a net in the other.

He nodded to us. "I did not mean to frighten you, but I got a late start coming back. I will just pass by . . ." He hesitated, looking at the flattened bread in my hand, then glanced at our spare campsite. "Have you nothing else to eat?"

"Our companion has gone into town to get food," I said, not wanting this stranger to linger.

"But you are hungry now. Here." He opened the hinged lid of his basket and pulled out a handful of small fishes. "These are delicious roasted over a fire. And they are tender, for the young lad."

I thanked him and accepted the fish. "I am Tasmin of Cana, and this is Joanna of Tiberias. We came here to find Yeshua of Nazareth, but we have heard he is gone. Do you know where he went?"

A change came over the man's features — his polite smile melted into welcoming warmth. "Of course I know. My sons went with him to Jerusalem, where they will celebrate the Passover. I would have gone, but these weary legs can no longer make the journey." He sank onto the ground and crossed his legs. "I am Zebedee, father to James and John. We were mending our nets right there" — he pointed to a spot next to an overturned boat — "the first time Yeshua came through this area. He called to my sons and asked if they wanted to be fishers of men." The old man laughed. "I'd never heard such a question, and neither had my sons. They got up and went with him, leaving me and the hired hands to finish the nets. I thought I might not see them for weeks, but two days ago they were back, more convinced than ever that Yeshua is our promised deliverer."

"But they're gone," I said, my voice echoing with despair. "All the way to Jerusalem."

Zebedee shrugged. "What is to stop you from following them? With Pesach approaching, you won't be alone on the road. Everyone who is able will be making the pilgrimage."

I looked at Joanna, and from the weary aspect of her eyes I suspected we were thinking the same thoughts — Jerusalem was a long walk over ground we had already traveled. The roads would be crowded and the walk slow. The Passover pilgrims were usually a happy bunch, for the festival was a highlight of the year, yet I would not be happy, and neither would Jude. With every step, my distress over Thomas and my antipathy toward Jude's brother would strengthen.

And yet if I wanted Thomas to come home, I had to go. I had no other choice.

I didn't know how Jude would feel about

traveling on, but one thing was certain — we all had good reasons for moving forward, so we would go to the Holy City. But when Jude and I finally found our wandering family members, we would not be happy with them.

CHAPTER FOURTEEN:
TASMIN

The first thing I heard when I awoke was the trill of birdsong. The notes had never seemed so clear, so crisp, and so — I opened my eyes — loud. The bird serenading me was perched on the bow of the boat not three paces from my head.

I sat up into a peaceful spring morning. The rhythmic *swoosh* of the waves was broken only by the sounds of Jude rummaging through the pack saddle. Next to me, the boy slept on his tummy, his thumb in his mouth. Joanna lay next to him, her face slack in repose but still lovely.

I watched Jude for a moment, then hugged my knees. "Are you looking for something?"

He glanced over his shoulder and shook his head. "A fishhook. I thought I might catch something to break our fast."

"No need." I uncovered the basket of dried fish Zebedee had left with us. "We met a fisherman last night."

Something that looked like a smile twitched in and out of the tangles of Jude's beard. "Why did you not say so?"

After waking Joanna and the boy, we shared a light meal and packed our belongings on the donkey. Before we set out, however, Joanna picked up the child and crinkled her nose in distaste. "He needs a bath," she said, holding him toward me. "Bathe him in the lake, please. I want to discuss our provisions with Jude."

I lifted a brow, wondering why she didn't trust me to discuss our provisions. Certainly she knew more about bathing babies than I did. But because I knew Jude was watching, and because the child *did* smell, I wrapped the boy in my blanket and took him down to the shore, where a faint white edge of lapping wave proved to be the perfect place for bathing a child. The steady slush and suck of the water filled my ears as I removed the blanket, then lifted my tunic and knelt at the water's edge.

"Ah." I gasped at the unexpected coolness of water on my knees, then smiled at the boy. "It's cold, but we'll get used to it, won't we?"

He didn't answer but put his finger in his mouth and turned, his large brown eyes soberly regarding the sea.

180

"I'm sorry this will be cold." I dipped a corner of the blanket into the water. "But we have to make you clean."

The boy's skin was caked with dirt, his little bottom red and irritated from filth and bug bites. Not certain how to proceed, I used what I had — water to soften the dirt, mud to gently rub the skin, more water to rinse the mud away. The boy's teeth chattered when I moved him into water that reached up to his knees, though he did not resist me.

"You're a good boy," I told him, smiling. "And as soon as we can, we'll get you something nice to wear."

When I could no longer find dirt in every cranny of his little body, I wrapped the dry area of blanket around him and scooped him up in my arms. Jude and Joanna had finished loading the pack saddle, so I draped the blanket over the boy's shoulders and sat him on top of the mound.

"There." I crossed my arms and looked around the campsite for anything we might have missed. "I suppose we're ready to go."

"What about him?" Jude pointed to the boy. "We have to go through Capernaum, so should we find someone to take him? The journey to Jerusalem is taxing enough without adding the burden of a child."

"We could stop by the well," I said. "Most of the town's women will be there getting water. One of them might be willing to take him."

"Wait." Joanna gave the boy a cloth filled with tiny bits of salted fish, then looked at me and Jude. "If Yeshua can change water into wine, he might be able to heal this child."

I scowled and Jude guffawed. "I don't believe he turned water into wine," I said, shaking my head. "Jude and I attended that wedding, and we are convinced he conspired to trick the groom and the guests."

Joanna smiled. "Conspired with whom?"

"Well . . . we're not sure."

"Did you discover some proof of this trickery?"

"Well —" I glanced at Jude.

"I believe," Joanna went on, "it would be easier for a prophet to work a bona fide miracle than to implement the sort of trick you have implied. Since it is easier to believe in mystery than the trick, why not accept the miracle?"

"Look." Jude turned to face the older woman. "I have lived with Yeshua all my life. While I can admit he's a righteous man and a skilled Torah scholar, he was not sent from God. We are sons of Joseph and Mary, and we are as ordinary as sand. Not wealthy. Not connected to anyone powerful. We are simple men from Nazareth, one of the least remarkable towns in Judea."

"But Isaiah wrote of John the Immerser," Joanna argued. "A voice cries out in the wilderness, 'Prepare the way of Adonai, Make straight in the desert a highway for our God.' Isaiah wrote of John, and John testified of Yeshua."

"Then John was mistaken." Jude grabbed the donkey's halter and pointed at the boy, a shadow of annoyance crossing his face. "If you want to take this child to Yeshua, you will have to care for him along the way. Do not let him slow our pace. I have an important job waiting at home."

Joanna took a step toward Jude and looked up into his eyes. "Have you no heart, young man? This child has his entire life before him. If Yeshua can help him —"

"I have a heart," Jude replied, his voice going hoarse. "And it is focused on my family. Unlike others, we must work to eat. We have a job waiting in Nazareth, a commission that could feed us for months and take care of our mother. Even Yeshua would profit if he would only return to the work our father left us."

My stomach clenched when Jude and

Joanna turned to me. "*You* found the boy," Joanna said, lifting a brow. "What would you like to do with him?"

I looked from one flushed face to the other, then crossed my arms. "We could spend all morning trying to find him a home in Capernaum, but we could also find him a family on the road to Jerusalem. So let's take him with us. If we haven't found him a home by the time we reach the Holy City, we can take him to the Temple. The priests might be willing to train him for Temple service."

My suggestion might not have been the best answer, although it seemed to satisfy Jude — because it would not delay our progress — and Joanna, because the boy would probably be with us when we located Yeshua.

"One thing remains," Joanna said, smiling at the child. "What do we call him?"

"Nothing," Jude said. "We will let his new family name him."

Joanna shot Jude a twisted smile. "We can't just call him *boy.*"

"We can," I answered, not wanting to argue about the name for another hour. "We can call him *boy* until we find him a home. He'll know we're talking to him."

With the issue settled, we started out,

knowing we would walk for days before reaching Jerusalem. If heaven smiled upon us, however, we might encounter Yeshua — and Thomas — on the road.

Finding comfort in that thought, I fell into step beside the donkey.

Zebedee had told the truth — a single day made quite a difference, and the road was much more crowded than it had been when we walked to Capernaum. Because of the approaching feast days, families had packed their donkeys and set out, most of them in high spirits as they traveled toward Jerusalem. Passover was a time of rejoicing, yet neither Jude nor I felt happy about our reason for the trip.

Every time I saw a familiar sight on the road, memories of other journeys to Jerusalem passed through me like an unwelcome chill. If Yeshua had not come to the wedding in Cana, Thomas would be walking with me now, the two of us taking yet another trip to the Holy City. Abba would ride in the wagon, due to his age, while Thomas and I walked together, sharing memories and laughing at the joyous Passovers of our childhood. We would stay with a distant cousin in the Holy City, the home where we had eaten countless Passover meals in previous years, and Thomas would tease me about Amos, the young cousin who never failed to stare at me as if I were as beautiful as Esther. After the festival, all the way home, Thomas would tease me about marrying Amos, and I would reply that if he did not stop teasing, I would go back to Jerusalem and look for my cousin. "Then you will see," I would say. "You will miss me when I am gone!" Thomas would laugh, because we both knew I would never leave him, as we were too closely bound together . . .

Now Thomas was gone, and I was not laughing.

Even though we were among scores of families on the road, we might have been one of the more somber groups. Jude walked in front, leading the donkey, while Joanna and I walked on opposite sides of the beast, sharing responsibility for the boy on its back.

We were about ten furlongs out of Capernaum when Jude turned and caught my eye. "Don't say anything, but we have picked up an acquaintance. He has been following us since we left Capernaum."

Joanna glanced at us. "What acquaintance?"

"You know him, too," Jude said, keeping

his eyes on the road. "We met him first in Tiberias."

I turned, pretending to look at the scenery but glancing at the travelers behind us. My stomach tightened when I spotted the one-eyed man we had seen outside the palace — the eunuch who worked for Herodias. He was walking behind a family and their wagon, yet he kept veering to the side of the road to keep an eye on us.

"The eunuch," I reminded Joanna. "The man who was spying on us."

Annoyance struggled with fear on her fine-boned features. "Why would he follow us? I thought he would grow weary of watching us in Tiberias."

I shrugged. "He must have nothing better to do."

"Or he has heard we are acquainted with John the Immerser," Jude said. "I tried to warn Yeshua that John would attract trouble. If someone is following us, you can be sure others are following Yeshua. The authorities do not like men who could agitate a crowd."

"What should we do?" I scanned the road ahead. "Maybe we could join a larger company. We could disguise ourselves or buy different clothing —"

"We have another choice," Jude said. "Instead of heading east to Scythopolis and the Jordan, we will take the route that goes through Samaria and Lebonah. Near Mount Gilboa we will stop and appear to make plans to stay at an inn, and then we will leave under cover of darkness. The next morning he will assume we have taken the road that avoids Samaria, so he will travel east."

I nodded, agreeing with his logic. The Jews and Samaritans had a history of bad blood, and few Jews willingly traveled through Samaritan territory even though the route was a more direct path to Jerusalem.

"We may arrive at Jerusalem before Thomas and Yeshua." I smiled at the thought. "My brother will be surprised to find me waiting for him."

"My brother, too," Jude said, though he did not smile when he said it.

We did exactly as Jude said. The one-eyed eunuch, apparently traveling alone, remained a consistent distance behind us as we passed by Taricheae, Dabaritta, and Nain. So as the sun lowered in the west, we stopped at an inn near Mount Gilboa. We went inside and ordered food, fed the baby, and unsaddled the donkey. The eunuch disappeared — probably, Jude said, to find an out-of-the-way place to sleep — and once

Gilboa appeared silver under the moon, we retrieved the donkey and slipped away from the inn.

Fortunately, the road to Jerusalem was paved, thanks to the Romans, and clearly visible in the moonlight. Tension fueled our footsteps, helping us make good time despite our weariness. Jude had fashioned a bed from our blankets and strapped it on the pack saddle. The boy slept most of the way, helping us in our effort to be quick and quiet.

We passed the point where most Jews turned east for Scythopolis and continued on to the ancient city at the heart of Samaria. When dawn crept up in streaks and splashes over Mount Ebal, we stopped at a stream to refill our water pitchers, then spread blankets on the ground and stretched out for a rest.

A few hours later, the boy's crying woke us. I sat up and looked at the road, where I saw only two Roman wagons and a farmer leading a pair of yoked oxen. I nudged Jude. "We no longer have a one-eyed follower."

"Your plan worked," Joanna said, pulling the boy into her arms. "Thanks be to Adonai for giving you a quick mind."

Jude said nothing but rested his arms on

his bent knees and studied the western horizon.

After we had broken our fast and watered the donkey, we took to the road again.

An hour passed when I realized the brief rest had done little to replenish our strength. The boy slept slack-jawed on the donkey, and Joanna appeared to concentrate on putting one foot in front of the other. Even Jude seemed to be dragging his feet.

I was about to suggest that we find a place to rest again when Jude said, "Sychar is just ahead. It's a Samaritan city, but I think we can find an inn. I would rather get proper sleep than collapse on the road."

"Good." Exhaustion cracked Joanna's voice. "I am spent."

We found an inn just outside the city, and the Samaritan hostess greeted us with a smile — an unusual approach, I thought, to greeting a trio of Jews.

"We have space for you." She opened the door wide. "You are most welcome to spend the day and night."

Jude pulled his purse from his belt. "I can pay."

The woman held up her hand. "I couldn't charge you tonight. No one in Sychar would charge you tonight."

Surprise blossomed on Joanna's face. "Why?"

The woman's smile broadened. "Because Yeshua was here. He met Photini by Jacob's well and spoke to her. He told her such amazing things that she came into town and told us we had to hear him ourselves. We all went out to the well, and after hearing him we begged him to stay with us. He stayed two days, and none of us will ever be the same." She tipped her head back and sent a stream of infectious laughter rippling through the air. "After hearing what Yeshua had to say, I have faith in the future. I have faith" — she took my hand — "that Jews and Samaritans can be united under God."

Joanna smiled and sank onto a stool. "What did Yeshua say?"

"Yes," I echoed, frowning. "What did he say to make so many follow him?"

The innkeeper's wife chuckled. "Well, let me think. First, he told Photini everything she had ever done, though most of us could have given him that information. Photini was not exactly known for righteous works."

"Two days?" Jude interrupted. "He was here two days?"

She lifted a brow. "Yes. He left this morning."

Jude turned to me. "We may be able to

catch them before they reach Jerusalem — especially if Yeshua stops to teach in every town along the way."

"Wait." I rubbed my forehead, troubled by a thought that had just occurred to me. "Why did he come through Samaria? No one takes the western road without a good reason."

"Perhaps he wanted to take the most direct route," Jude replied.

"Or perhaps he went where he was most needed," Joanna said, lifting the boy onto her hip. "Clearly he was needed here."

Jude scrubbed his hand through his hair, then sighed. "We will have to catch them tomorrow. Let's get some sleep so we can leave early in the morning."

"You won't be able to miss him," the Samaritan woman said. "A great crowd follows him now."

Jude frowned. "How many? A dozen?"

She laughed. "A hundred at least. Everyone wants to hear him, and most people believe he is the Messiah. The way he explained God's truth, we couldn't help but believe in him."

"That's it," Jude said, heading toward the door. "I'll bring the blankets so we can get our rest."

Leaving Joanna and the Samaritan woman

inside, I hurried after Jude, grateful that I would be able to catch him alone. "Wait," I called, lengthening my stride. "I would speak with you before we sleep."

He stopped and turned, revealing a face marked by exhaustion. "Yes?"

I pressed my hands together and searched for the right words. "Does this not bother you? So many people follow him now — and many of them are Samaritans. How can your brother expect people to believe he is the promised king of Israel when he welcomes *them* to join him? I do not understand his message, and I cannot find a valid reason for his appeal —"

"And you think I can?" His voice, like his face, was wracked with weariness.

I sighed heavily, then shook my head. "I just keep asking myself: why would Thomas go with Yeshua? It is as if he heard a command I could not hear."

Jude stared at me for a moment, then nodded and turned toward the barn. "Exactly," he said.

CHAPTER FIFTEEN:
TASMIN

The next morning, the innkeeper and his wife kindly gave us fruit and cheese to break our fast. Joanna and I took turns chewing the figs and giving small bites to the boy.

"I wish we could put some meat on his bones before we reach Jerusalem," Joanna said. "But at least the tunic covers his ribs."

We had picked up a small tunic at a market in Capernaum, and though the garment wasn't extravagant, it did disguise the boy's gaunt frame. With a clean face, smoothed hair, and closed lips, he almost looked like a normal child. Until he smiled.

"Come on, little one." I picked up the boy and settled him on my hip. "One more day on the donkey for you."

"Wait." Joanna placed her hand on my arm and tilted her head toward the innkeeper's wife. "She is kind, and I haven't seen any children around this place. Do you think . . . ?"

Leave the boy here? Two days ago I would not have hesitated to ask the woman if she wanted a child, but now?

"I thought you wanted Yeshua to see the boy," I said.

She lifted a brow. "I thought you didn't believe."

"I don't. But if anyone can help him, I'd like to give him a chance. Even the priests at the Temple could pray for his healing."

Joanna sighed. "Come on, little one, it's off to Jerusalem we go."

We had just placed the boy on the pack saddle when we saw an old man running toward us, leading a little girl by the hand. "Wait! Do not leave!"

"What's this?" Jude muttered under his breath. He glanced at me. "Have you been picking up other children?"

"No." I squinted at the man, not recalling his face. "Let us see what he wants."

"Ah, friends, thank you for waiting." The old man stood before us, breathing heavily. When he had caught his breath, he pulled the little girl forward. "I am Ziv," he said, dropping his hands to the girl's shoulders, "and this is my granddaughter, Rahel. I have heard about Yeshua and the people he healed, but he was gone before I returned from a neighboring city. The innkeeper says you are going to find him. Please, I beg you — may we travel with you? I promise we will be no trouble."

Jude's brows rushed together as he looked at me, then we both turned to Joanna. She shrugged as if to say, *What does two more matter?* Jude sighed and gave a nod. "We want to travel quickly — can you keep up?"

"I will," the old man said, "and Rahel is a fast walker. Sometimes I think she has more energy than I do." He released a strained laugh, and the little girl looked up at us with wide eyes. Seeing her, so innocent and young . . . how could anyone refuse them?

"Jude —" Joanna began.

"It's fine. Come with us, then."

Wasting no time, Jude took the donkey's rope and led the animal to the gate. Joanna and I moved to our usual places, and the old man fell into step beside me.

"I am sorry to intrude," he said, his voice rasping. "And forgive me for being out of breath. I ran up the road because I was afraid you would get away before I could catch you. I would make the journey myself, but the roads are not safe for an old man and a child. The lestes, you know. And the Romans."

I nodded. "I know."

When the girl stumbled, Ziv swung her

196

into his arms. We hadn't taken more than fifty steps when he eyed the boy on the donkey. "I wonder if the beast could manage another child," he said, breathing more heavily than ever. "I wouldn't ask, but the girl is like dead weight when she sleeps, and she's sleeping now . . ."

"Jude, will you stop?"

Jude tossed a frown over his shoulder, but halted. The old man struggled to lift the girl — she must have been five or six, so she was not small — and Jude helped him. With water jugs dangling from both sides of the pack saddle, we had to position Rahel's legs in front of the water containers and place the boy in front of her.

"Poor donkey," I whispered to Joanna. "We will owe him an apology after this."

Joanna's mouth twitched with amusement. "I'm praying the Lord doesn't give him the gift of speech like He did for Balaam's beast. He'd be sure to complain."

We settled into the journey, knowing we still had quite a distance to walk. Yeshua and Thomas had to walk it as well, I reminded myself, so I ought to calm my anxious heart and rest in the knowledge that we would soon find them. After all, a handful of people could travel more quickly than a hundred.

The countryside around us basked in sunshine that hinted of a scorching day to come. Even though we were surrounded by brown sand and white rocks, occasionally I spotted patches of wild grass and splatters of colorful wildflowers. Behind us, shreds of gray clouds hung like rags on the shoulders of Mount Ebal, where Joshua once built an altar to HaShem.

Though Jude was anxious to reach Jerusalem, he exhibited a thoughtfulness that must have frustrated his desire to reach the Holy City. When we grew thirsty, he stopped so we could drink and rest in the shade. When the boy cried from hunger, he stopped so Joanna and I could feed him. And when Rahel fell off the donkey in the grip of a fit, Jude stopped and allowed the old man to comfort her until the fit passed. Then Jude found a stream so Joanna could clean the tunic the girl had soiled while in the grip of the demon.

For people who were planning to reach Jerusalem before sunset, we took a very long time. Finally, Jude and I realized we would not reach the Holy City in time to celebrate the Passover with our brothers. The next day, Nisan 14, would find us hours away from the Holy City.

We swallowed our disappointment as best

we could.

"Perhaps Yeshua will linger in Jerusalem," I told Jude. "We may still find them."

"Perhaps," he agreed. "And if not, we will ask people where they have gone." He released a weary laugh. "I'm sure they will have heard about Yeshua's arrival. He has a gift for attracting attention."

"I am in no rush," Joanna announced, running her fingers through the boy's curls as he slept on the donkey's back. "I will offer to serve whenever we find Yeshua. All will be as Adonai wills."

The old man said nothing but clung to Rahel's hand as we searched ahead for a place to spend the night.

The city of Ephraim was not near the highway, but it was a Jewish settlement and in Judea, so we headed toward it as the day of Passover drew to a close. We passed through the city gates in late afternoon, and Jude asked one of the elders if he knew of a family who would welcome strangers to their dinner. The elder introduced himself as Abel and invited us to his home. "I have come from the Holy City to spend Passover with my aged father," he said, leaving his seat to escort us to his house. "I will count it an honor to have guests join us in our meal."

Abel, his wife, his father, and his eldest daughter lived in a modest home near the center of the city. We were warmly welcomed by Abigail, Abel's wife, and the daughter hastily arranged for more seating. A series of trays stood in the center of the main room, and each held an element of the traditional Seder: the unleavened bread or matzah; the bitter herbs to represent the bitter lot of the Hebrews under Egyptian slavery; and the mixture of fruit and nuts, the *Charoset,* to represent the mortar the Hebrews used to build monuments for the Egyptian kings. We were missing the sacrificial lamb, which would only be obtainable by those in Jerusalem.

Abel poured a cup of wine for Elijah and set it on a tray, then propped open the door of his house in hope that the prophet would appear. "As Malachi wrote," our host began, "Adonai said, 'Behold, I am going to send you Elijah the prophet, before the coming of the great and terrible day of Adonai.' May the prophet come, and hasten the arrival of our messiah."

After the traditional ceremony, as the men relaxed and the women took the dishes away, the talk turned to what had happened in Jerusalem the day before. As his aged father reclined on a couch and slept, Abel leaned forward, his dark brows arching into triangles. "Never has anyone done anything like it! Right in front of the chief priests and Pharisees, with everyone watching, a Galilean walked up to the money tables and flipped them over! His face was as red as blood, and he shouted, frightening the animals and setting the shepherds to flight." He rubbed a finger over his lips as he laughed. "You've never seen so many doves flapping about — their cages broke up when the tables went over."

Jude gave our host a bleak, tight-lipped smile. "This act was committed by a man from Galilee?"

Abel narrowed his eyes. "I never learned his name, but he had a group of men with him — women, too. They shrank back when he began to overturn the tables, but some of them looked as though they might be willing to add to the mayhem. But before anyone could do anything to stop him, the man slipped through the crowd and disappeared."

"What —" Jude squeezed the bridge of his nose — "what reason did this man give for causing such destruction? Or did he simply create a disturbance and flee?"

Our host's eyes shone as he leaned forward. "Oh, he was not afraid to speak his mind. He stood in the center of the outer court and shouted, 'Is it not written, My house will be called a house of prayer for all nations? But you have made it a den of robbers.' " Abel barked a laugh. "I've always thought it a sin to charge double for the animals we have to sacrifice, but no one has ever protested such cheating. Yet this man did it in front of the chief priests and the teachers of the Law. And everyone, I tell you, was amazed. Everyone wanted to know who he was and where he came from. I'm sure the word is all over Jerusalem by now, yet all I have learned is that the man was a Nazarene."

"Are you certain" — Jude's voice sounded strangled — "he was from Nazareth?"

Our host grinned. "Right. Everyone started looking for him, but he and his people slipped out of the city before anyone could stop him. I left, too, because I had to get home. I kept hoping I would see him on the road." He reached over and patted his father's hand. "I had to be home to be with Abba and my family."

The old man sleepily patted his son's hand, then went back to snoring.

"We are glad you were here." Joanna

smiled. "And we are grateful for your hospitality. We will trouble you no more, but we ought to make our way to the city square."

"You will not leave us," the wife said, rising. "You will sleep here. Abel, get blankets and fresh straw. I cannot let you sleep outside, not with the girl and the little boy."

I smiled at Joanna, grateful she had mentioned sleep. My eyelids were so heavy I could scarcely keep them open, and sleeping in the city square was neither comfortable nor safe, especially for women and children.

We split the front room, with Ziv and Jude on one side, and Joanna, me, and the children on the other. Once we had bedded down and our hosts had gone to sleep, Jude reached out and tapped my shoulder. "This is what I tried to warn him about," he whispered, and I knew instantly who he was talking about. "He believes he is on a mission from God, but he's going to create more enemies than converts. If what Abel said is true —"

"It must be," I interrupted. "Why would he lie?"

"Then this is just the beginning of trouble. I'm sure your brother was with him in the Temple court — along with James and John,

Peter and Andrew, and others who will soon be sorry they decided to follow him."

"Don't worry." I was so tired I was beginning to slur my words. "We will find them soon, and we will bring them home. They have not yet been arrested. Perhaps they never will be."

"They can be arrested whenever the authorities decide to step in," Jude said. "I can only pray we find them first."

Because Nisan 15 was the Feast of Unleavened Bread and a special Sabbath, we remained with Abel and his family, worshiping at the synagogue in Ephraim, then returning to Abel's home to rest. I watched Abel's respectful interaction with his aged father — how they conversed during the meal, and how Abel tenderly guided his father from the dining couch to his bed for an afternoon nap.

I closed my eyes to the sight as a surge of rage caught me by surprise. Thomas should be home with our father, not walking all over Judea in pursuit of a long-prophesied king. My brother should be home, working in our business, helping Abba oversee the date grove, helping me with my baking. HaShem could not possibly mean for Thomas — or any other sons of Israel — to drop their responsibilities and travel around the land stirring up trouble. Especially at the Temple.

On the first day of the week, my ninth day without Thomas, we rose with the sun, partook of the meal Abel and Abigail graciously offered, and thanked them again for their hospitality. Then we set out for Jerusalem, even though we realized Yeshua might have already left the city.

"I hope," Jude said, scanning the road ahead, "to see someone we know. I am certain the Temple incident has upset most of his followers. Surely some have deserted his cause and will be on their way home. If so, we may speak to them and learn of his whereabouts. Never fear, Tasmin, we will find those we seek."

Though we traveled against the prevailing traffic, when we stopped to rest we mingled with travelers who were eager to share the latest news from Jerusalem. We heard several reports about the disturbance at the Temple, and witnesses described it in terms ranging from "riotous" to "a righteous act of indignation." One man said a mob had invaded the courtyard, overturned the tables, and stolen the money in the treasury boxes; another said dozens of animals had been set free to roam the streets of Jerusalem.

"The Galilean made a whip out of cords," another man told us. "He drove every creature from the Temple area, sheep and cattle and bulls, and scattered the coins of the money changers as if they were forbidden objects. To those who sold doves, he said, 'How dare you turn my Father's house into a market!' "

"The Temple authorities came out immediately," a woman told us. "And demanded to know by whose authority he had ransacked the money tables. Then they demanded a miraculous sign to prove he had been sent by HaShem."

Jude scoffed. "I presume he gave them no proof."

"He gave them words," the woman replied. "He said, 'Destroy this temple, and I will raise it again in three days.' "

I lifted a brow, astounded by the alleged answer. Herod spent forty-six years building the Temple, so how could anyone raise it in three days?

When the woman left us, I glanced at Jude. "Has your brother gone mad?"

"It would appear so," he answered, his voice flat. "And I have heard enough. Come, let us get the others and be on our way. The sooner we find Yeshua, the sooner we can put an end to this foolishness."

Our goal was simple, our purpose forthright, but HaShem had other plans for us. As we neared the outskirts of the Holy City, we heard the strident keening of mourners. A few paces farther brought us to a group of weeping men and women, who sat in ashes and torn garments. When Jude asked about the cause of their lamentation, one of the men looked up and answered in three words: "John is dead."

Joanna's hand went to her throat. "John the Immerser?"

A weeping woman rose from her knees and staggered toward us. "It happened a few days ago," she said, struggling to find her voice. "At Antipas's birthday banquet."

Disbelief struggled with horror on Jude's face. "Antipas executed a prophet at a banquet?"

When the woman dissolved into fresh tears, another man, presumably her husband, stepped forward. "Antipas had invited all his officials and military commanders to the dinner. That odious wife of his commanded her young daughter to dance for him, and the girl pleased Antipas. Wanting, no doubt, to appear generous before his guests, he promised the girl he'd grant her request, no matter what she wanted. She asked for the head of John the Immerser on a platter."

I gasped and Joanna fainted. Jude and I hastened to attend to her. When she finally opened her eyes, she sat up and ripped the neckline of her tunic in grief. "My poor Chuza," she said, tears streaming over her cheeks. "He is surely suffering over this."

"He must be accustomed to Antipas," Jude said. "Surely he has learned to mask his revulsion."

"He has," she whispered, her voice raw. "But what did John do to deserve such a fate? He spoke the truth, he called people to repent, and for that he lost his head?"

"The sin should be charged to Herodias," the man said, his voice rough with disgust. "The girl was merely a pawn in that woman's hands."

Jude and I helped Joanna to her feet. She walked directly to the weeping woman and put her arms around her. "I met him," Joanna whispered, her voice broken. "My husband and I were at the river when John baptized Yeshua of Nazareth. I am now on my way to find Yeshua and offer my service to his cause."

The other woman swiped tears from her cheeks. "Do you think he could use another pair of hands? I was a friend to Elizabeth, John's mother. Now I would willingly serve

Yeshua."

A thoughtful smile curved Joanna's mouth. "What is your name? Would your husband come, too?"

The woman managed a trembling smile. "That is my brother, not my husband. I am Susanna, and a widow. I would gladly go with you."

Joanna's hand slid into Susanna's. "Come with us and we will find him."

Two things struck me in that moment — first, that Susanna's brother was by her side, comforting her, while my twin was nowhere to be found. Second, that our traveling party seemed to be growing by the hour.

I looked to see if Jude shared my surprise, yet he seemed unaware that we had gained another traveler. He stood by himself in the road, eyes down and brow furrowed, clearly thinking hard about something.

I learned what had occupied his thoughts when we neared the city gates. As we walked amid a crowd of those who sang the traditional songs of ascent, Jude pulled me aside. "You do realize," he whispered, "that my brother no longer puts his followers in danger of prison or censure — now their very lives are at stake. Antipas executed John. How long before he or the procurator decides to execute Yeshua?"

I blanched. "Rome has seen so-called messiahs before. Usually these men and their movements fade away."

"Not without a confrontation of some sort," Jude responded. "Remember Judas the Galilean? The Egyptian? And there are the lestes — I'm surprised they have not already infiltrated Yeshua's group. They are eager to shake off the Roman harness, and if they think Yeshua could lead a rebel army" — his mouth spread in a thin-lipped smile — "they will persuade others to follow him. When the Romans intervene, they will happily die, seeing themselves as martyrs."

I frowned. "Thomas will not want to be a martyr. I do not know anyone more sensible. He cannot make a decision until he has investigated every option. He cannot purchase a cow until he has seen the sire and dam. He would not buy a house until he checked the foundation and the roof —"

"Thomas may soon be so committed he cannot withdraw," Jude said, a muscle twitching at his jaw. "I only hope my brother has the good sense to realize he may be attracting men who would rather fight than fade away."

We entered Jerusalem, but despite our inquiries, all we found of Yeshua and his followers were rumors, questions, and accusations. Thousands of people still thronged the city, so we moved carefully over the cobblestone streets, dragging our recalcitrant donkey through groups of pedestrians, narrow alleys, and open courtyards. Everywhere we went, people were talking about the incident at the Temple and asking questions about Yeshua. Some speculated that he was Elijah, come to fulfill the prophecy of Malachi; others said he was John the Immerser, somehow escaped from prison. Some claimed Yeshua was a prophet; others insisted he had come to free Israel from Roman rule.

The last rumor strummed a shiver from me as I remembered Jude's dire prediction. How well did Yeshua know the men following him? Did he speak to them individually, test their hearts to know if their motives were pure? Thomas was a righteous man, if momentarily misguided, but what of the others? My mind kept returning to the night we met Zebedee, who said Yeshua met his sons, said, "Follow me," and they dropped their nets in obedience. Didn't Yeshua want to know what sort of men they were before issuing his invitation? And from where did he get such powers of persuasion?

The people of Jerusalem were also talking

about John the Immerser. The Temple authorities remained silent on the subject of his execution, because, it was rumored, they didn't know whether to mourn him as a prophet or condemn him as a lunatic. And yet they could not deny his popularity among the people. John was one of the few leaders in Israel who had been willing to expose sin no matter where he found it — in Antipas's palace, among the leaders of the Sanhedrin, or in Rome.

I had never seen the city more divided. Public opinion varied widely even regarding the villains of John's story. Some said young Salome had played the part of a wanton seductress and danced like a harlot; others said the girl was little more than a child and completely innocent of John's death. Only one report went undisputed: Herodias had definitely initiated the girl's request for John's head, and the daughter had — whether easily or reluctantly — obeyed her mother's command.

We heard that Antipas was truly upset by John's execution, though he took pains to remain composed while in view of his wife and his guests. "But I know," Joanna told us as we broke bread that night, "Antipas admired John a great deal. When he summoned Manaen and Chuza to report on their visit to the Jordan, Antipas listened to them, then said he would like to meet the prophet himself. Once John was finally brought before him, Antipas asked him several insightful questions. He did not seem to grasp John's message, but he could find no fault in him. He did nothing to deserve execution."

Jude sipped from his cup and looked around at our group — a grandfather and granddaughter, Joanna and Susanna, a little boy and me. He lifted his head, like a dog scenting the breeze, then announced that we would begin our return to Galilee on the morrow. "I am sorry to disappoint you," he said, smiling without humor. "We have come a long way and have nothing to show for our efforts. If the rumors are true, Yeshua and his followers are traveling north. If HaShem wills, we may spot them on the road. But if we do not, I am sure we all have work waiting for us. You are free to do whatever suits you best."

A man sitting at a table near us turned at the sound of Jude's voice. "Shalom," he said, looking us over. "I could not help overhearing that you are looking for Yeshua."

Jude nodded. "We were."

"I know," the man said, "where he was going."

Joanna released an involuntary squeak. "Where?"

"Nazareth." The man smiled at her. "He plans to speak in the synagogue on the Sabbath."

Jude shook his head. "Full circle," he murmured, catching my gaze. "I should have waited for him at the house."

A thrill ran through my senses. Yeshua and his followers were going home. Perhaps I would walk into my house and see Thomas sitting with Abba. He would tell me he had come to his senses and would never leave again.

I looked at Jude. "So we are going back?"

He nodded. "We are going home."

CHAPTER SIXTEEN: TASMIN

Jude was true to his word. The first pale hint of sunrise had only brushed the eastern sky when I heard movement outside the women's chamber. I rose, packed my few belongings, scooped up the boy, and stepped outside to meet Jude. To my surprise, Ziv was already beside the donkey, adjusting the pack saddle while Rahel waited.

"I am sorry, Ziv," I said, shifting the boy to my hip, "that we were not able to find help for your granddaughter."

The old man's eyes filled with tears as he nodded. "It is as HaShem wills," he said, placing a folded blanket on the saddle. "Blessed be the name of the Lord."

I sighed, realizing that more appropriate words had never been spoken. If we had found Yeshua and he failed to cure the girl of her fits, what would Ziv feel then? His disappointment would be a thousand times worse.

"Will you go home now?" I asked. "Or —"

"I'm going to Galilee with you." Ziv placed his hand on Rahel's head. "I will find Yeshua or die on the journey."

I lifted a brow, then smiled and moved away. Susanna and Joanna would continue with their search for Yeshua, of course, but what should we do about the boy?

Jude appeared out of the shadows and nodded a greeting as Joanna and Susanna followed him.

"The innkeeper's wife has given us food," Joanna said, nodding at the basket in her arms. "Since you are anxious to be under way, we can eat as we walk."

I peeked in the basket and spied bread, cheese, salted fish, and eggs. The boy would like the eggs, for they were soft and easy to swallow.

"That's it, then." Jude took a last look around, then helped Rahel mount the donkey. "On to the Temple, and then we will leave the city."

I was about to place the boy in front of Rahel but then hesitated when prickles of uneasiness nipped at the back of my neck. "Why do we need to go to the Temple?"

Jude eyed me with a curious expression. "The boy, of course. You said we could leave him with the priests if we did not find a home for him."

My uneasiness swelled into alarm. I could not deny what I had said, but that idea no longer seemed reasonable or right. I could no more leave the boy with a stranger than I could cut off my own arm. Neither, though, could I raise him. I was an unmarried woman who knew nothing about children or motherhood.

"We still have the return journey," I said, settling the boy on my hip again. "And you yourself said we might find Yeshua on the way. If he can't help the boy, surely one of his followers could provide him a better home than the Temple priests."

"As you wish." A smile played briefly on Jude's lips before he turned and led the donkey toward the street and the city gates.

Once we were out of Jerusalem, we set as quick a pace as our weaker members would allow. Joanna and Susanna had formed a solid friendship, and I listened halfheartedly as they discussed husbands and homes, baking and sewing. Susanna confessed that when her husband died, he left her a valuable estate that allowed her to travel wherever she pleased.

Ziv and his granddaughter were not wealthy, the old man told me, though he had managed to set aside a few coins for their journey. "I have long waited for Israel's redemption," he said, "and I would walk from Tyre to the Dead Sea to find our promised messiah."

"But how do you know the messiah can help Rahel?" I asked. "I know some believe Yeshua is the promised king from David's house, but —"

" 'Bless Adonai, O my soul,' " Lev said, reciting a psalm I knew well. " 'He forgives all your iniquity. He heals all your diseases. He satisfies your years with good things, so that your youth is renewed like an eagle.' " He smiled at me as if I were a small child. "If our messiah is from HaShem, how could he *not* help Rahel?"

Since I could not argue with the Scripture, I remained silent.

A long stretch of wilderness lay between Jerusalem and Lebonah. We were not alone on the road — other pilgrims were walking home, as well. Life had returned to normal, and often fast-moving horses and heavily loaded wagons forced us to the side of the pavement as they blew by. Once I heard a man laugh as he galloped past us, and the dark sound of his laughter chilled my bones. When I looked up, I could see nothing of the rider but his striped head-covering and the back of his tunic.

After the energy of the morning wore off, we walked mostly in silence, each of us preoccupied with our thoughts. I did not know Susanna well enough to know what caused a frown line to appear between her brows, but with one look at Joanna I knew she was grieving John the Immerser. For her sake, I hoped we would soon find Yeshua, so she could set her grief aside and put her hands to useful work.

Ziv and his granddaughter walked ahead of me. Rahel must have been glad to be heading home, for she seemed more animated than usual, looking for birds and trying to name them as they flew overhead. Apparently Ziv had spent a great deal of his life in the wilderness, as he seemed to know the name of every bush, tree, and creature we saw. His granddaughter obviously adored him, and I wondered about her parents. Did they think Ziv was foolish for taking her to see a would-be messiah, or were they quietly hoping and praying for a miracle?

Jude, leading the donkey up front, was doubtless planning the magnificent bed he and his brothers would build for the wealthy merchant. Several times during the journey I caught him drawing sketches in the sand,

and though sand was not the best medium for communicating a creative idea, even I could see that the bed would be worthy of a king. The joy of fulfilling an artistic vision, coupled with the generous monetary reward, provided more than enough motivation to go after a much-needed brother.

I glanced at the boy on the donkey. The child rode like a sultan now, his legs expertly bent over the pack saddle, his back straight, his eyes on the road ahead. He had even woven his fingers in the donkey's short mane to maintain his seat. "You are a fast learner," I told him, my heart overflowing when he answered with a lopsided smile. "What a good boy you are!"

I had made no inquiries about a home for the child, not because I wanted to take him, but because I had begun to see him as a test for Yeshua. A trickster or charlatan would have a difficult time concealing the sort of disfigurement that afflicted the boy. But if Yeshua could heal this child of a deformity that had tormented him since birth, then perhaps Yeshua *was* more than an ordinary man.

As darkness rose up from the earth, filling first the ridges by the roadside, then the shadows beneath the shrubs, we decided to spend the night under the stars. Jude said he would rest easier if we made camp on a high point, so we set our sights on the crest of a hill that lay ahead on the road. As the swollen sun dropped toward the shimmering horizon, I focused on the line where the road met the sky, the place where we could finally turn aside and take a much-needed rest. I was ready to close my eyes and surrender to exhaustion, forgetting everything for a few hours.

We had nearly reached our destination. Forcing myself to hold my head erect, I placed my heavy hand on the donkey's back, ready to pull the boy off and lay him on my blanket. I knew I would be asleep before my head touched the earth. Weariness engulfed my body. My legs moved on their own volition, my mouth tasted like grit and sand . . .

A shrill scream sliced through my stupor. The sound was so unexpected, so out of place, it seemed to go straight to the center of my head. I blinked, and when I looked up at the road, I saw a line of mounted men with fabric wrapped around their heads and heavy clubs in their hands.

I knew immediately who they were: lestes.

And they were waiting for us.

CHAPTER SEVENTEEN: JUDE

My stomach lurched at the blood-curdling sound. Ahead, silhouetted by the setting sun, stood a line of armed bandits, and I knew I could not hope to win a fight against them. Like jackals, they had lain in wait along this desert road, hoping for a group like ours — only one young man to guard an old man, women, and children. They could beat us into submission without even dismounting.

I turned to face the frightened people under my protection. "Women, scatter into the brush, hide as best you can. Ziv, take your granddaughter and see if she can climb yonder tree. Tasmin, take the boy, hide him, and then run away. Do not return until you hear nothing from this spot."

Pulling my staff from the pack saddle — the only weapon I had — I crouched to face those who would attack us. Leering like demons, the lestes galloped down the hill, leaning to the sides of their saddles, displaying their athletic prowess as they brandished their clubs. Behind me, I heard the sound of breathless running, frantic scrambling, and a bewildered bray from the donkey. Someone must have pulled the beast off the road to prevent him from being stolen.

I alone remained in the road. One stick against half a dozen.

I grimaced as the thundering hooves stormed closer. My coins — all that remained of the two talents from the merchant — were hidden in the hem of my tunic. If they found the money, I would lose nearly everything we had to buy materials for the merchant's anniversary gift. My brothers and I would have to make a bed out of the few planks of cedar and sandalwood I had already ordered.

On they came, the center man rushing toward me, club in hand, and though I tried to dodge the blow, it crashed into my face, sending a shower of dancing lights through my head. My mouth opened in a scream, but there wasn't enough air in my lungs to push sound out of my throat. I fell backward, dimly aware of churning hooves, dust, and rough men spinning and laughing and dismounting.

Sandaled feet and rough pieces of timber

walked toward me. Someone called me an unspeakable name, then a club struck my stomach, forcing the remaining air from my lungs. I tried to inhale but couldn't as a blow to my rib cage made pain rise inside me like flames, flinging sparks in every direction.

My eyelids fluttered, and as color ran out of the world, I twisted my head and saw one thing clearly — the face of the one-eyed eunuch.

CHAPTER EIGHTEEN:
TASMIN

Run! Obeying Jude's instruction, I held the boy close to my breast, lowered my head, and ran into the wilderness, dodging bushes, leaping over holes, trying not to stumble over broken branches and wayward rocks.

"Run," he had said, *"and don't return until you hear nothing . . ."*

He had also told me to hide the child first, but I could not leave the boy behind. These men, whoever they were, were not likely to care about the boy. If they found him, they would take one look at that cloven tongue and kill him. And I would not, could not, allow that.

I ran until I thought my heart would pound out of its cage of ribs, then I turned and hid behind a boulder. I heard nothing — no pounding steps, no hoofbeats, no cries or shouted threats.

"There now, boy." I set him on the ground, where he looked up at me with wide eyes and a quivering chin. "Do not cry. HaShem is watching over us."

Crouching behind the boulder, I leaned to the side and peered beyond the rim of rock. The invaders had gathered in a circle and were milling around the place where Jude had fallen.

My panic suddenly turned into a deeper and more immediate fear: what were they doing to Jude? Would they kill him?

I slapped my hand to my forehead, desperately trying to remember everything I had heard about the lestes. They were more than bandits, because they took pleasure in terrorizing their victims. Many of them were motivated by politics, leading them to attack Romans or Jews who cooperated with Romans.

So why had they attacked us? We were not allied with Rome. We were simple people, poor and harmless . . .

I gasped as another thought crashed into my consciousness. Jude and I might be harmless, but Yeshua was not. With every miraculous act and audacious action, his popularity among the common people grew. The authorities had noticed. Perhaps some had heard that Jude was Yeshua's brother. People had been passing us all day on horseback, so perhaps someone had recognized him. Perhaps this attack was an indirect way of sending Yeshua a message . . .

I shook my head — the *why* did not matter now. What mattered was saving Jude and the others.

I leaned out again and searched the area, looking for Ziv and Rahel, Susanna and Joanna. I spotted Ziv and Rahel hiding behind a tree near the road — apparently they hadn't managed to run far. Joanna and Susanna had hidden behind a sparse bush farther away, but if I could see their colorful tunics, so could those vile bandits.

HaShem. I closed my eyes. *As you guided Gideon and David, as you used Deborah and Michael — guide my steps, too, Adonai, and direct my path.*

Girding myself with courage, I picked up the baby, set him on my hip, and crept toward the rock where Joanna and Susanna were hiding.

Joanna whirled around as rocks crunched beneath my sandals, her eyes wide with fear. "Tasmin! You should not be here."

"I need you to watch the boy." I crouched behind the scrawny shrub and placed him in Joanna's arms, then ran my fingers over his curls. "I'm going down there to make sure they don't kill Jude. Stay here and stay hidden. Keep the boy quiet."

"Jude said you should run." Susanna looked at me with reproof in her eyes. "How will he feel if you are attacked by these ruffians?"

"Not as bad as I will feel if they kill him." I gulped a deep breath, then stood and lifted my chin. If the lestes saw me — *when* they saw me — I wanted them to see a daughter of Israel who was not afraid.

I moved straight toward the circle of ruffians, pointedly ignoring Ziv and Rahel's hiding place as I passed. If any of the lestes turned in my direction, I would not betray the anxious grandfather with a glance.

As I strode forward, I could clearly see what they were doing. Jude was on the ground, curled up like a sleeping dog, while they kicked and cursed at him. They kept asking questions, but he did not answer.

I had nearly reached the pavement before one of them looked up. "Orien," he said, tapping another man's shoulder.

The second man pulled out of the circle and turned. I flinched when I recognized the face beneath the striped head-covering.

"So." The one-eyed eunuch eased into an oily smile. "I knew you wouldn't be far

228

away. You two have been inseparable for days."

"What do you want?" I asked, trying to be as composed as Herodias, the only woman I knew with ice in her veins. "We are not wealthy people."

"Aren't you?" He opened his palm, showed me a handful of coins, then chose the largest and flipped it into the air, neatly catching it with his other hand. "This is a nice profit for a day's work."

I had no idea where the coins came from, but I would not let him see my surprise. "Take what you have stolen and go." I crossed my arms. "We are no threat to you."

"Indeed, you are not." He stepped closer, then slipped his arm around my back and drew me to him. "What is your name, pretty one?"

His sour breath brushed my cheek as he held me tighter. I leaned away, pressing my hands against his chest, but I knew I was no match for his strength. *HaShem!*

"Orien!" one of his men called.

"Hush," the man replied. "I am sampling the sweets."

"I'm — I'm not afraid of you," I stammered. "You're a eunuch."

He released a bitter laugh as his grip tightened. "I am, but they are not." He jerked his head toward the men standing behind him — men who were staring at something beyond us, something on the road.

"Orien, look behind you!"

The eunuch did not budge, but bent his head to nuzzle my neck. As I struggled, I heard the sound of footsteps and the creak of saddles. Then Jude charged at the eunuch, launching himself at the man's middle. The eunuch released me, turned, and bent over, clutching his stomach. Jude kicked him in the rear, sending the man to the ground.

Jude looked at me, his eyes blazing above a bloodied face. "Are you all right?"

My stomach swayed at the sight of the blood, but I managed to speak: "Behind you!"

He turned just in time to block the dagger coming at him. He and Orien struggled, a deadly dance marked by blows, slashes, and indiscriminate splatters of spit and blood. Orien trapped Jude, sending him to his knees, and before Jude could regain his feet, the one-eyed eunuch wrapped his arm around Jude's throat. He brought his dagger to Jude's neck and grinned at me, then looked past me and his countenance changed. His mouth opened; the dagger fell from his hand as he released Jude and staggered backward, then turned and ran for his mule.

While Jude held his throat and gasped, I knelt beside him, grateful for whatever had startled the eunuch and his men. When I was sure Jude had not received a fatal wound, I looked at the road behind us and saw no one but Ziv and Rahel, Joanna, Susanna, and the boy emerging from their hiding places.

"Why did they run?" I looked to the others, then to Jude, yet none of them understood what I meant. "The lestes saw something on the road — something that frightened them away." I stood and searched the southern horizon. The air had gone shadowy and blue with the approach of dusk, and I saw nothing but wilderness and empty road.

"Whatever they saw," Ziv said, resting his age-spotted hands on Rahel's shoulders, "we must praise HaShem for it."

"We should praise him for more than that," Jude said, pointing to the road.

I glanced down, and in the fading light of the sun I saw a trail of coins. I looked up to see the look of relief on Jude's face. "HaShem's provision?" I said, remembering what he had said when we set out.

He grinned and knelt to gather the money. "HaShem's mercy, I would say."

Jude was not well. But the next morning he refused to admit he suffered from the prolonged beating he had endured. "We go on," he said when I suggested we take a day or two for him to recover. "If we want to catch Yeshua in Nazareth, we have to keep going."

"We can find Yeshua later," I told him, firmly pushing him back to his blanket. "He is your brother — do you think he will not speak to you when you finally find him?"

"You don't know him," Jude murmured, but his smile held no malice.

We camped for two days, resting and living off the wilderness. I knew Joanna was thinking about John the Immerser when she and Rahel walked through the shrubs looking for food — she brought back a basket of wild locusts and a honeycomb. Though I made a face and refused to eat the insects, Jude, Ziv, and Rahel ate and declared them quite good.

"Crunchy," Rahel assured me. "Noisy in your mouth."

We set out on the fifth day of the week, hoping to reach Nazareth by the Sabbath. Jude seemed better, and no longer winced with each deep breath. I walked behind him, observing his stride to see if I could detect any weakness in his limbs. Fortunately I could not.

We were a short distance from Nain, a small village south of Nazareth, when Ziv's granddaughter stiffened and fell from the donkey, taking the boy with her. I hurried to pick up the boy and checked him for bruises as Joanna, Susanna, and Ziv gathered around the flailing girl. For some reason the donkey began to bray and kick and struggle when the girl fell. Jude gripped the animal's halter with both hands.

When I was certain the boy had suffered nothing more than superficial scrapes, I lifted him onto my hip and watched helplessly as the girl convulsed on the ground. "Tasmin," Joanna called from where she knelt by the girl's side, "can you get me a stick or something? We must keep her from biting her tongue."

"Hold the animal," Jude said, placing my hand on the halter.

I set the boy on the ground as Jude stepped off the road and returned a moment later with a branch, which he broke into a piece as long as my hand. I gave him control of the donkey, which calmed once Jude led him a good distance away from Rahel. I knelt by Joanna, the stick in my hand.

Without warning, Rahel's wild eyes focused on me. "You seek your brother," a deep and guttural voice roared, "because you have an unholy love for him. Go ahead, tell them why you want your brother by your side. You want him in your bed!"

Repulsed and stunned, I recoiled from the girl. Joanna, likewise astonished, lost her grip on Rahel's arm. The girl, who must have been stronger than she looked, wrenched free of Susanna's grip and sat up, striking Ziv in the face. The old man staggered and might have collapsed had not Jude intervened, positioning himself between the grandfather and the girl, who had crouched in the middle of the road like a lion about to spring.

I blinked and scrambled away, terror lodging in my throat. In all my years, I had never seen anything like the scene before my eyes. I had never *imagined* anything like it.

"Rahel," Ziv cried, reaching out to her from behind Jude's back. "Come back to me!"

The child — or demon — gnashed its teeth and roared again, then sprang for Jude. His arms shot out to catch her, and she fell against him, limp and unconscious.

Jude laid the girl on the road, and the rest

of us gathered around. A stream of blood ran from Ziv's nose and dripped onto his beard, a sight that made me feel faint. He paid no attention, but instead bent over Rahel and listened for the sound of breathing.

I looked at Susanna, Joanna, and Jude and tried to maintain an erect posture. The event had happened so suddenly I had no words to react; then I remembered what the girl had said.

"It's not true." I looked at my friends, desperate to convince them. "What she said about my brother — none of it is true."

"Pay no attention to the ravings of the demon," Ziv said, tenderly pushing wet hair away from his granddaughter's soaked forehead. "The unclean spirit loves to accuse and destroy. It always lies. It torments. And that is why we must find Yeshua."

I waved the matter away, pretending not to care, but in truth, the girl's accusation had burrowed deep into my head. Did Jude and Joanna think I had an unnatural love for Thomas? I loved him, certainly, but I had never even imagined anything beyond familial affection.

Thomas and I did have a shared secret, but that truth had nothing to do with incest. It was far simpler and perhaps even more horrible . . . which was why we never spoke of it.

I sank back and looked at Jude, my mind reeling. Was he thinking about his brother now? What could a carpenter's son from Nazareth do in the face of this evil? We should have left Rahel and Ziv at the Temple; surely the priests would know what to do.

For what did we common people know of demons? I knew nothing, and I was certain that neither Jude nor Thomas nor Yeshua was any better equipped than me.

CHAPTER NINETEEN:
TASMIN

I squinted at Ziv, examining the growing lump beneath his right eye. "Are you all right?" I asked, my voice trembling. "I — I have never seen anything like that."

Now that the attack had passed, the old man had gone pale beneath his beard. "The fits are not always so bad," he said, brushing sand from his tunic. "Most of the time she does not speak, but bites her tongue and spits blood at us. But today — I don't know what happened. I am sorry."

"It . . . is not your fault."

"But if you had not been kind enough to accept us, you would not have been subjected to the sight of such evil." He sighed and gestured toward a scrubby terebinth tree. "Rahel will need to sleep for a while." He looked at her limp form, still stretched out on the road. "If you do not want to wait, you may travel on without us."

Jude bent and picked up the girl. "We will

wait with you," he said, carrying Rahel to a shady spot beneath the tree. "We will not leave you alone."

Joanna moved toward the donkey. "We have bread and cheese to share. We might as well eat while we rest."

While Joanna and Susanna set out the food, I picked up the boy and wavered between Jude or Ziv. Which would most welcome my company? Or would they both prefer that the woman accused of perverted love keep her distance?

Jude caught my eye and jerked his head toward the empty space next to him. I walked over and sat down.

"You seem upset," he began.

"I'm not."

"Disturbed, then. What you saw — have you never seen a person possessed by an unclean spirit?"

I shook my head, grateful he had broached a subject that seemed too horrible to discuss. "I —" I swallowed hard — "I am beginning to think I have lived a very small life."

He did not mock me, but simply looked at the ground. "The world is full of strange situations. Adonai blessed you with a father who sheltered you, just as Adonai shelters us under His wings."

"Adonai could have sheltered me better if He had not taken my mother." The words spilled from my mouth before I had the intention of forming them. I shook my head. "I'm sorry. I try not to feel sorry for myself. But as I was growing up, all the other girls had mothers —"

"While you had Thomas."

I nodded, for he was beginning to understand. "Thomas and I had Abba."

"And that is why you are close."

I gave him a careful nod. "We are twins, after all."

"Yet neither of you has married."

"You are not married, either, and you are older than Thomas."

"Women usually marry at a younger age. And yet" — his eyes narrowed — "you have not."

"What of it?"

"I'm only wondering —"

"Ziv said the demon lies. It lied today."

"You mistake my intention. I am not wondering if your feeling is unnatural; I am wondering why you and Thomas are so close. I have sisters, but I would not travel the length and breadth of Galilee in search of them."

"Yet you are traveling in search of your brother."

Jude chuckled. "Only because we have a job to do. I am not searching because I miss him."

His words, spoken so easily, struck me like a blow. *Miss him?* I missed Thomas dreadfully. I missed his strength. I missed having his outlook on everything from daily events to my nightmares. I missed his humor, his belches, his voice, and the way he rubbed his nose when he fought off a sneeze. I missed the way we could read each other's thoughts with a single glance, and the way we would laugh at some sight or sound only the other would find humorous.

And I missed sharing my guilt with him . . .

"You're not a twin." I heaved the words at Jude as if they were stones. "Twins are different. They are unusually close."

"Are they?" His gaze lowered, as did his voice. "Jacob and Esau were twins, but they were not close. One was smooth and one hairy. One was chosen of God and the other was not. One was his mother's favorite, and the other his father's —"

"Perhaps they were an exception."

"Or perhaps you and your brother are close only because you had no mother when you needed her to guide you into womanhood. Perhaps the bond between you and your brother is not such a good thing, because eventually most twins separate and live their own lives."

I flinched at the implication. "Are you saying I shouldn't miss my brother? That I am wrong to want him home with us?"

"I did not say those things. You did."

I clenched my hands. "We are close because after Mother died, we had no one else. Father was always busy in the grove, and we had no other siblings. We were each other's playmate, fellow student, and best friend."

Jude's eyes softened. "You had no friends among the village girls?"

I shook my head. "They were always with their mothers. Aunt Dinah visited sometimes, but she had her own children to look after. I had Thomas. Only Thomas."

"He did not attend Torah studies with the other boys?"

"Yes, after a while. When he was young, Abba taught him. Abba taught both of us."

"Then you were blessed indeed. I was nineteen, a grown man, when I lost my father, and sometimes I struggle to remember his face. At least I have my brothers and sisters to keep his memory alive. And our mother, of course."

I studied his countenance, searching for

any sign of cynicism or condemnation yet saw nothing but interest . . . and kindness.

At the sight of that kindness, tension began to melt from my shoulders. "You will soon be with your brothers again," I said. "And since Yeshua has undoubtedly heard the news about John, perhaps he has decided to go back to woodworking. Your mother will be relieved, and Thomas will come home to care for our grove and help me."

"You want him to manage wedding feasts?"

I snorted. "I want him to care for Abba's date palms. I will bake, Thomas will tend and harvest, and Abba will take the orders and collect the payment. We will provide dates for the market, festivals, and export. I will bake and oversee the occasional wedding feast. We will be very busy — and happy."

"Really?" Jude did not look at me but smiled into the distance. "And that will be enough for you?"

"It is enough for anyone."

"Suppose Thomas wants to marry?"

I shrugged. "Fine. We will both live in Cana, so we can work together by day and go home to our families at night. One day our children might play together." I smiled, hugging my elbows in pleasant anticipation. "This is the life our father wants for us. It is the life we want."

"Are you certain?"

The question hung in the air between us. When I did not answer, Jude stood, wiped the sand from his tunic, and walked toward the donkey.

Though we were making good time, we stopped when we spotted another group coming toward us. Not knowing who or what could be hiding in the ox-drawn cart, Jude pulled the donkey to the side of the road and gripped his walking stick.

We could see a woman and a boy in the cart, their sandaled legs dangling over the front, while a young man led the ox. A few people followed, but they traveled on foot and did not carry weapons.

We relaxed when we realized they did not pose a danger.

The woman in the cart hailed us, her smile unusually bright for someone traveling one of Judea's dusty roads.

"Blessed be he that comes in the name of the Lord," she called, her voice ringing like happy bells. "Where are you heading, friends?"

I glanced at Jude and saw bewilderment

on his face. "We are on our way to Nazareth."

The woman clapped and lifted her gaze to the sky. "Blessed be Nazareth, the city on a hill, and blessed be the One who grew up within its walls. Praise Adonai for His goodness."

"Excuse me." Jude stepped forward and addressed the young man leading the ox. "Is this woman well? I have never heard anyone bless Nazareth."

The youth cracked a smile. "My aunt has good reason for what she says. See the child with her?"

Jude nodded.

"Last week that boy was dead. My aunt was traveling this same road, accompanying her son's coffin to the cemetery. We were almost there when we saw a group coming toward us. They stopped when they heard the mourners, then one of the men called out a greeting and told her not to weep."

Jude eyed the youth with a stern expression. "Where was her husband? He should have prevented a stranger from interrupting a funeral procession."

The youth shook his head. "No husband; she's a widow. We were all so astonished by the fellow's authority that the men carrying the coffin stopped in the road. Then the man walked over, placed his hand on the box, and said, 'Young man, I say to you, get up!' "

Jude flinched. "I hope someone rebuked him for his cruelty."

"We praised him for his mercy. Because the boy — my cousin — pushed away the lid of his coffin and sat up, then looked down and asked his mother why he was riding in a box."

Jude stepped back, silenced by surprise, but Joanna had not lost the power of speech. "I would hear more," she called. She walked over to the mother and son and reached up to grip their hands. "Tell me — was it Yeshua you met? Yeshua of Nazareth?"

The widow nodded, her eyes filling with tears. "We began to praise HaShem for His goodness and mercy. We knew a prophet had appeared among us, and when we heard he was from Nazareth, we gave thanks." She looked over at Jude. "Do not doubt it — HaShem has come to earth to help His people."

Jude did not respond to her, but gripped his walking stick and set his eyes on the road ahead.

Before we reached Nain, I had almost convinced myself that Yeshua had changed his mind and decided to return to his brothers' business. After all, who would want to continue such dangerous work after Antipas executed the Immerser?

But after we encountered the widow and her son, I knew Yeshua would not walk away from the work he had begun. Even if the so-called miracle was the result of a man waking a child from a deathlike sleep, people would always believe Yeshua had brought the child back to life. That elevated him to the status of Elijah, who had resurrected the widow of Zarephath's son.

When we finally entered Nazareth on the first day of the week, I expected to find the townspeople dancing and praising Adonai outside the synagogue. The news about the boy's resurrection must have reached them, for Nazareth lay between Nain and Cana. Wouldn't they be thrilled to know one of their men had brought a child back to life?

Instead, silence greeted us as we walked down the main road, an oppressive stillness that hovered over the city like a cloud. Every person we saw wore a surly expression, and Jude's frown deepened with every step we took.

"Where are we going?" I asked, looking around. "Is your brother here?"

"I'm beginning to think not," he snapped,

then turned the corner. He led the way up the narrow, steep street where he lived and stopped in front of his house. "Home," he said simply, looking at Joanna, Susanna, and Ziv. "Let me go inside and see if anyone has been here."

A few moments later he returned, accompanied by his brothers. "Tasmin, Joanna, Susanna, Ziv." He nodded to each of us. "I'd like you to meet my brothers — James, Joses, and Simeon."

Each of us politely bowed in greeting, yet I knew we were all wondering about the family's missing members. "And your mother?" I asked.

"She is with Yeshua." Jude shifted his gaze to the horizon as if he could see them on a distant mountain. "They have gone north — no one knows exactly where."

James, the tall, lanky man I remembered from the wedding, stepped forward. "I know you must be exhausted," he said, stepping into the role of host. "Jude told us about your latest trials, and we hope you will spend the night with us. My sister Damaris will bring food, and tomorrow you can decide what you want to do. Please come inside."

Ziv hitched the donkey to a post, then sighed in appreciation when Joses untied the beast and led him toward the first-floor stable. Joanna brushed wayward hair from Rahel's forehead, slipped an arm around the girl's shoulders, and led her up the stone steps. Ziv's eyes welled with tears at Joanna's kindness.

I patted the boy, who had been sleeping on my shoulder ever since Jude pulled him from the pack saddle. A rest would be good for all of us. Tomorrow we would consider our options in the clear light of day.

As we went inside, a man passing on the street stopped and stared. "A curse upon your house," he shouted, wagging a finger at the siblings on the stairs. "If your brother enters Nazareth again, he will be stoned! Make sure he knows we will not tolerate blasphemy!"

I looked at James. "Blasphemy?"

He shook his head. "Yeshua was here on Shabbat and went to our synagogue. He opened the Scriptures and taught a lesson from Isaiah —"

"Later," Jude interrupted. "You can tell the story over dinner, but I would rather you kept silent now. Why burden our guests with bad news?"

I looked from one brother to another. "Yeshua's message was not well received?"

James shook his head and walked into the house.

Chapter Twenty:
Tasmin

Over a meal of roasted vegetables, bread, figs, and honey, James explained what had happened at the synagogue.

"Everyone was eager to hear Yeshua speak," he began, breaking off a piece of bread and passing it to Jude. "He had been away for months, and people had heard rumors — we've heard all kinds of stories. So Yeshua read from the prophet Isaiah:

" 'The *Ruach Adonai* is on me,
because He has anointed me
to proclaim Good News to the poor.
He has sent me to proclaim release to
    the captives
and recovery of sight to the blind,
to set free the oppressed,
and to proclaim the year of Adonai's
    favor.' "

Susanna, Joanna, and I waited for an explanation of James's frown. "It is a familiar passage," I finally said. "Did he read anything else?"

James lowered his bread. "Yeshua rolled up the scroll, gave it back to the attendant, and sat down. Everyone in the synagogue waited, ready to hear what he had to say. Then he looked up, scanned the room, and said, 'Today this Scripture is fulfilled in your hearing.' "

I had no idea. I looked at Joanna, wondering if she understood what Yeshua meant.

"Before that moment," James went on, "everyone had been impressed with his gracious speech and understanding of the Scripture. After all, John the Immerser often referred to the prophets' writings, as well. But then Yeshua looked at our friends and neighbors and said, 'Doubtless you will say to me this proverb, *Doctor, heal yourself!* and *What we have heard was done at Capernaum, do as much here also in your hometown.*' "

"That's not offensive," Jude said. "So why — ?"

"He went on," James added. "He said, 'Truly, I tell you, No prophet is accepted in his own hometown. But with all truthfulness I say to you, that there were many widows in Israel in the days of Elijah, when heaven was closed for three and a half years and there came a great famine over all the land. Elijah was not sent to any of them, but only to Zarephath in the land of Sidon, to a widowed woman. There were many with *tzara'at* in Israel in the time of Elisha the prophet, and none of them were purified apart from Naaman the Syrian.' "

Jude blanched. "I can imagine how the people reacted."

James's mouth flattened into a grim line. "Of course, they were enraged at the implication. He practically said they didn't deserve to be healed or receive miracles because they didn't believe. They leapt up and drove Yeshua out of the synagogue and out of the town. They drove him toward the top of the hill overlooking the valley, and despite my entreaties, I was certain they were about to push him off the cliff. But just as I thought he would surely perish, a hush fell over the gathering. Yeshua said nothing but walked right through the crowd without anyone saying a word to him. His disciples followed, and all of them left the city."

I swallowed hard. "Was — was Thomas with them?"

James nodded. "He was."

"He . . . he *left* with them? The display of violence didn't dissuade him?"

Smoothing his beard, James offered me a compassionate smile. "He was one of the first to follow Yeshua as he walked away."

We sat in silence, each of us considering James's story. I couldn't believe that Thomas — ordinarily so careful, rational, and persuasive — could have gone with Yeshua after the man's neighbors and friends nearly killed him. The people of Nazareth should have been Yeshua's greatest defenders. For years they had known his siblings, his mother, and his late father. They had known him since his boyhood, so why didn't they support him?

When Jude spoke again, his voice trembled. "I cannot believe," he said, speaking as one carefully choosing his words, "that one in our family has lost his mind. Our father would tear his robes if he heard what Yeshua said in the synagogue. To think that a son of David, of the tribe of Judah, a son of Jacob, Isaac, and Abraham —"

"He may yet regain his senses." James held up a steadying hand and looked around the table. "I tried to convince our mother to stay home with us, but she insisted on leaving with Yeshua. I don't know why she goes with him — she is no longer young, and the travel cannot be easy on her."

"Perhaps," I ventured, "she is trying to

protect him. Perhaps she gives him advice."

Jude shook his head. "She has never given advice to Yeshua, and he would never ask for it. Of late she has maintained an odd distance from him — whatever he wants to do, she agrees."

I shifted on my couch, remembering what had happened at the wedding. Mary went to Yeshua and told him we had no more wine, then she looked at me. *Whatever he says to do, do it.* Why would she encourage his folly?

"Do you honestly think he is mad?" I looked from James to Joses and Simeon. "And do you all agree?"

"What else could it be?" Joses shrugged. "He spends hours in the wilderness by himself, and then he travels through Galilee inviting fishermen to follow him?"

"Fishermen," Jude repeated, looking at me. "Not teachers, not scribes, not men who are highly educated. Simple, unlearned men who barely had time for Torah school."

"Then he goes from place to place, speaking to the poor," Simeon said. "He tells them they will be comforted and inherit the earth. No wonder the crowds throng after him."

"He rebukes the tax collectors and Pharisees," Joses added. "This endears him to the common people because they hate tax collectors and self-righteous Pharisees, too."

"What about the miracles?" I asked. "How *did* he turn the water into wine?"

Jude shook his head. "I haven't learned his secret, but I'm sure there's an explanation. Perhaps he poured something into the cistern before the water was drawn out."

"And the boy raised from the dead?"

James lifted his hand. "He could have heard a noise from inside the coffin. Perhaps he knew the boy was only sleeping. After all, isn't that what he said?"

My thoughts whirled in bewilderment. I had heard so many stories from so many people, all of whom were convinced Yeshua was no ordinary man. And not all of them were poor and uneducated.

"I don't know," I finally said. "All I want to do is find Thomas and convince him to come home. My father is old and needs help managing the grove. Once I explain we need him, I'm sure Thomas will leave Yeshua's group."

"Adonai has smiled upon you, then," James said, the corner of his mouth quirking. "Because Yeshua has gone to Capernaum, where he stays with Simon Peter. If you leave tomorrow, you should be able to catch up with your brother."

Finally. Energized by a burst of hope, I caught Jude's eye and smiled. Soon, if all went well, we would find Yeshua, speak to our wayward family members, and bring them home.

All would be well. But, I had to admit, my world would seem small once I returned to Cana. I would miss the adventure of the journey . . . and at least one of my travel companions.

The next day we set out for Capernaum. We had gone as far as Taricheae when we stopped at the city well. I gave water to Ziv, Rahel, and the boy, then turned and saw Jude speaking to a man I did not recognize.

I left the bucket with Joanna and moved closer, curious about the stranger. The fellow Jude had engaged in conversation was older, with snowy hair and a beard to match. His hands moved in wild gestures as he spoke, and his eyes glowed with something that looked like wonder.

I stood at Jude's elbow and waited until he glanced down and acknowledged me. "Tasmin, this man is from Capernaum. He was telling me about what happened when Yeshua spoke in their synagogue."

"Did your neighbors chase him out of town, too?" I lifted a brow and smiled. "Did he offend your people?"

The old man laughed. "We were amazed at his teaching, because his words rang with authority. But the oddest thing happened — while he was speaking, a man stood and cried out at the top of his voice. 'Ha! What do you want with us, Yeshua of Nazareth? Have you come to destroy us? I know who you are — the Holy One of God.'"

I shivered as a creeping uneasiness rose from the bottom of my soul.

Jude cleared his throat. "What happened next?"

"I'll tell you what happened." The old man bent toward us, his eyes twinkling. "Yeshua said, 'Be quiet and come out of him!' The demon threw the man down and then came out without hurting him. The man who had been possessed sat up, blinked, and stared at us, then looked at Yeshua and began to praise Adonai."

Jude tugged on his beard, wished the man a good journey, then gently took my elbow and guided me back to the others.

"What do you think really happened?" I whispered, thinking of Rahel. "Does your brother truly have power over devils and demons?"

"I don't know how to explain it," Jude said, his voice clipped. "But soon we will find him and put an end to this."

More determined than ever to stop our wandering, we left Taricheae and set out for Capernaum. We walked over paving stones we had walked before, but this time I noticed details I had been too distracted to see during our first attempt to find Yeshua.

Capernaum, I realized, was a border settlement, which explained why the Romans had built a garrison in its wall. With Syria and Phoenicia to the north, Rome wanted the people of Capernaum to maintain the peace with its neighboring territories. To keep the people of Capernaum happy, Rome was generous with its gifts. Jude said the local centurion had gone so far as to sponsor the construction of a new synagogue.

Many of Capernaum's people were fishermen, while others were merchants and farmers, so the city was filled with shops and surrounded by well-tended fields of barley and spelt. I understood why Yeshua decided to move to Capernaum — the city offered more opportunities than Nazareth.

An old woman answered our inquiry about Yeshua by pointing to a house near the village square. The home's courtyard bustled with activity as people came and went. Among the odd mix of men in the courtyard was a group of masons and carpenters armed with the tools of their trade. Oddly enough, they sang psalms of praise as they shouldered their way through the crowd.

I nudged Jude and gestured toward the tradesmen. This was not normal behavior for men at work.

The reason for the workmen became apparent as we drew closer to the house. A ladder leaned against the structure, and from where I stood I could see bits of broken plaster and wood on the ground. Had the roof collapsed?

Jude tied the donkey to a post near the well and called to a man sitting on the low courtyard wall. "Shalom! We are seeking Yeshua of Nazareth."

The man turned, a smile gathering up the wrinkles at his aged mouth. "You have missed him. He was here."

"Can you tell me where he went?"

The man's grin widened, then he stood, jumped, and clicked his heels together. The other men, all of whom had turned when he began to speak, broke out in riotous laughter.

I looked at Joanna and frowned. Were they drunk?

Jude must have had the same thought. "Have you been at the ale so early?" he asked, his voice dry. "For surely you are not in your right mind."

"That's the beauty of it — my mind has never been clearer." The grinning man came closer. "I used to work with this crew" — he pointed to the men on the roof — "but one day I fell off a house and my legs stopped working. For five years I couldn't walk, couldn't work, couldn't feed my family, and couldn't worship in the Temple. But yesterday Yeshua came to town, and the crowds followed him to this house."

"He speaks the truth." I turned as another voice joined the conversation. A man who'd been standing in the front doorway came toward us — chubby with a round face that disappeared into an unruly beard. "I invited Yeshua inside, and the entire town came out to hear him speak. They were sitting on the windowsills, packed into the courtyard, perched on the courtyard wall —"

"My friends," the grinning man interrupted, glancing up at the workers on the roof, "wanted to get me to Yeshua, but they couldn't get me through the courtyard, so thick was the crowd. So they went around to the back of the house, lifted me up to the roof, and cut through the plaster and timbers. They rigged up a pallet and lowered me until I dangled right in front of Yeshua."

My mouth went dry. "And?"

The man's smile faded as a shade of uncertainty crept into his expression. "Yeshua looked at me and said, 'Son, your sins are forgiven.'"

Jude frowned. "He forgave your sins?"

"That's what the Torah scholars asked," the man said, spreading his hands. "'Who but God can pardon sins?' They said Yeshua was a blasphemer."

"This," Jude murmured to me, "is what worries me."

But the man had not finished.

"Then Yeshua said, 'Which is easier to say, Your sins are forgiven, or Get up, take up your mat and walk? But so you may know that the Son of Man has authority to pardon sins on earth'" — the fellow's grin reappeared — "he told me to get up, take up my mat, and go home. So I did. Even danced a little as the crowd parted to let me through. My legs felt so strong I could have walked all the way to Jerusalem without tiring."

I exhaled a slow breath as Jude lowered his gaze. I knew what he was thinking: we had been telling ourselves that Yeshua's healings were tricks, that people were only pretending to be healed. Yet this man was telling his own story, and the men around us had been witnesses to his accident, his helplessness, and his healing. How could we argue with them?

Jude cleared his throat. "Thank you for sharing your story. When Yeshua left this place, where did he go?"

"That is the most interesting thing." Our storyteller tugged on his beard. "He went out to the sea, where there was more space for people to gather. But as he was passing the tax collector's table in the town square —"

"Levi," one of the masons interrupted. "The man is called Levi."

"Yes, that's the one. Anyway, Yeshua looked at him and said, 'Follow me.' And the tax collector got straight up out of his chair and followed Yeshua to the water. And after he spoke a while, Yeshua accepted Levi's invitation to dinner. Many other tax collectors joined them, with sinners of every stripe —"

"A drunk," one of the men on the ladder supplied.

"A man who married his brother's daughter," another man added.

"A blasphemer," another called. "And a cheat."

The healed man laughed. "I thought maybe Yeshua had a secret whistle that called sinners as a mother hen calls her chicks. They all went into Levi's house, where they ate and drank together. All the righteous people — especially the Torah teachers — were astounded. They wouldn't break bread with a tax collector if you paid them and served peacock."

"Where —" Jude's voice sounded strangled — "is Yeshua now?"

The man looked over his shoulder, murmured something to one of his co-workers, then nodded. "He's looking for an open place that will hold more people," he said, turning back to us. "Last time Eli saw him, he and his men were walking toward Gennesaret. If you go there, you're likely to find him." Jude nodded his thanks and went to retrieve the donkey.

After placing Rahel and the boy on the pack saddle, he looked at Joanna, Susanna, me, and Ziv. "Why," he asked aloud, his hands tightening on the donkey's halter, "would Yeshua eat and drink with sinners?"

One of the men on the roof must have overheard the question. "He said the righteous didn't need a doctor," he called, his voice ringing out, "but the sick did. He didn't come to call the righteous, but the sinful."

Jude sucked at the inside of his cheek for a moment, then looked down at me. "My father," he said, lowering his voice so only I could hear, "was a righteous man and passionate for the Law. He never ate with Gentiles or sinners. He *did* do business with them, but would always purify himself afterward. He was fastidious about avoiding uncleanness whenever possible."

I nodded. "My father feels the same."

"Then why —" Jude paused and stared past me — "why is Yeshua behaving as though the Law no longer matters? Eating and drinking with sinners? I'm surprised he hasn't invited a Gentile to travel with him."

"All the more reason for us to find him." I gave him an assuring smile. "You will speak to him and remind him of your father's example."

Jude looked at me then, thought working in his eyes, then he nodded. "Let's go find him."

Together we led the others toward Gennesaret.

Chapter Twenty-One:
Tasmin

After leaving Capernaum, finding Yeshua was easy. Word of the lame man's healing had spread like a storm of locusts, and a steady stream of Galileans moved along the road that outlined the sea. As we made our inquiries, we asked several travelers why they were going to hear Yeshua. "We heard he is healing the sick on a mountain between Gennesaret and Capernaum," a man from Chorazin told us. "And we have a little girl who was born blind."

The people traveling to Yeshua seemed in remarkably good spirits, and none seemed to share the doubt that haunted me and Jude. We were a dubious minority in our own group, for Joanna and Susanna believed, and Ziv clung desperately to faith for the sake of his granddaughter.

"For your sake," I whispered to the boy riding on my back, "I hope Yeshua can do miracles, but I don't see how he can help you."

Once we reached the northern edge of the plain of Gennesaret, we were able to see the assembled crowd. Curiosity seekers had spread out over the hillside, clustering in small groups. Families unfolded their blankets and chose comfortable grassy places while children chased each other or jumped from the rocks jutting from the gentle hill. Except for the occasional shouts and squeals of the children, an unnatural silence prevailed, broken only by the sound of Yeshua's voice.

The man was already at work. Jude's brother stood on a rock halfway up the hill, proclaiming his message in a voice modulated to reach the edge of the crowd. I could barely hear him from where we stood on the road, but the people who sat closer appeared spellbound. Some of the children near Yeshua had even stopped playing and stood as still as statues while he told his stories.

We approached the gathering with the self-conscious awareness of people who had arrived late to a wedding. Jude hobbled the donkey, then let the animal browse the grass as he led us to an open area farther up the hill. We spread our blankets and sat facing

Yeshua — Jude, Joanna, Susanna, Ziv, Rahel, and me. I kept the boy on my lap. He had awakened during our walk through the field, and I hoped he would keep quiet so I would be able to hear what everyone else found so fascinating.

As Yeshua talked about loving one's enemies, I studied the people on the hillside. Along with family groups from neighboring villages, I spotted clusters of white-robed Pharisees who must have come from Jerusalem. A few in the audience wore the colorful garments and jewels of wealthy merchants; others wore rags and tattered papyrus sandals. I even spotted a couple of Roman women in silky tunics and elaborately styled himations, one accompanied by a pair of Roman soldiers. A politician's wife, perhaps, or a not-so-subtle spy.

I looked behind Yeshua, where other men stood and looked over the crowd with a self-important air. Yeshua's disciples, of course. I looked for Thomas, finally spotting him sitting with the fisherman Simon Peter. While Thomas listened intently, Peter seemed to think it was his role to cheer on his master. Every time Yeshua paused, Peter clapped and shouted approval.

"Do to others as you would have them do to you," Yeshua said. "If you love those who love you, what credit is that to you? For even sinners love those who love them. And if you do good to those who are doing good to you, what credit is that to you? Even sinners do this. And if you lend to those from whom you expect to take, what credit is that to you? Even sinners lend to sinners in order to receive back the same."

I leaned toward Jude. "Is your brother a moneylender? He seems to talk a lot about loans."

Jude snorted. "He has no money and cares little for it."

"But love your enemies," Yeshua said, peering earnestly into the faces of the people nearest him. "And do good, and lend, expecting nothing in return. Then your reward will be great and you will be sons of *Elyon,* for He is kind to the ungrateful and evil ones. Be compassionate, just as your Father is compassionate to you."

I could find no fault in what Yeshua was saying, so I blew out a breath and looked at the men behind him. I counted more than a dozen — at least fifty. Some sat while others stood in groups, their eyes scanning the crowd like guards on alert. When I considered a possible reason for their activity, a chill ran up the ladder of my spine.

Had Yeshua been threatened? Did they

fear an imminent attack?

Before leaving home I would never have considered the possibility that someone might threaten a simple man from Nazareth, but the fellow we saw in front of Jude's house had threatened to stone him. We ourselves had been attacked by the lestes without provocation, so evil could rear its head anywhere and threaten anyone. Why should Yeshua be exempt?

I shifted my position to keep an eye on Thomas and was surprised to spot a group of women working behind the disciples. Joanna had mentioned women who traveled with Yeshua's group, and I was amazed to discover so many. I recognized Mary, Jude's mother, who sat apart from the others. She was not focused on the work, but on her eldest son.

Joanna must have noticed where I was looking, because she leaned toward me and pointed to the women. "There," she said. "I would offer anything I have to work with them. Mine might be a small effort, yet I would happily give it to serve Yeshua."

She tapped Susanna and nodded toward the women, and the widow's face lit up. "Oh, yes," she breathed. "To be able to serve in practical ways . . ."

Before I could ask if they were sure about

what they wanted to do, Joanna and Susanna stood and began climbing the hill. With a sinking heart, I watched them go. This would be the place where they left us.

"Well?" Jude crossed his legs and jerked his chin toward the rocky knoll where the disciples stood. "Do we go up there and wait for Yeshua to finish, or do we stay here among the people?"

I looked at the hundreds of people in front of us, each of whom had come here for an important reason.

"I think these people would be unhappy if we kept them from Yeshua. Let us wait until he takes a break with his men, then we can go up. I'll find Thomas while you speak to your brother."

Jude sighed and stretched out on the grass. "Good. Until then I will rest."

The boy grew restless in my lap, so I let him stand and move around. He walked over to Jude, placed his hands on Jude's cheeks, and laughed in his quiet way. He stopped for a moment and turned to look at Yeshua, then returned to me, dropped into my lap, and gave me a slobbery kiss. I felt my cheeks burn, then glanced at Jude, who was watching. "He is a good lad," he said, smiling. "I wish Yeshua could help him."

The wind caught the teacher's voice and brought it closer. "A farmer," Yeshua was saying, "went out to sow his seed. As he was scattering the seed, some fell along the path; it was trampled on, and the birds of the air ate it up. Some fell on rock, and when it came up, the plants withered because they had no moisture. Other seed fell among thorns, which grew up with it and choked the plants. Still other seed fell on good soil. It came up and yielded a crop, a hundred times more than was sown."

I crossed my legs at the ankles and leaned back on my elbows, trying to figure out what the story meant. Was it a riddle?

Yeshua lifted his hand. "He who has ears to hear, let him hear."

I glanced at Jude. "Did you hear the story?"

"Yes."

"Do you know what it means?"

Jude shrugged. "How can anyone understand the rambling stories of a madman? He speaks of common things — seeds, farmers, and weeds — and people behave as though he is explaining the mysteries of Adonai's universe. How is that possible when not even the best Torah teachers can understand Adonai's thoughts? His thoughts are not our thoughts."

At that moment one of Yeshua's followers walked over and said something to the teacher, so I returned my attention to the boy. He was walking through the grass, trailing his fingertips over the wildflowers, smiling in the rare moment of sunshine and security . . .

My heart swelled with a feeling I did not understand. Inexplicably, I found myself feeling . . . grateful? Yes, *grateful* for my eighteen days without Thomas. As odd as it seemed, I was thankful my brother left and gave me a reason to go after him. Soon this chapter of my life would end. Thomas and I would return home to do what we had always done and be the people we had always been. But I would never forget the deep feeling of gratitude that rocked my soul in that moment.

A woman seated across from me saw the boy and smiled. "He's a handsome lad," she said, leaning toward me. "He reminds me of my oldest. Is he your first?"

I opened my mouth, about to say, *Would you like to have him?* but the words stuck to the roof of my mouth. What was wrong with me? I had taken the boy with every intention of finding a home for him, and there had never been a better time than now. This woman was interested, she had other children, and she would know how to make the boy happy. But for some reason I could not bring myself to speak.

Before I could force myself to react, Joanna tapped me on the shoulder. "Come with me," she said, looking at Jude. "Your mother wants to see you. Tasmin, you and Ziv must come, too. Bring the children. The women who travel with Yeshua have prepared a meal, and they want to share it with us."

The thought of food made my empty stomach growl, so I gave the inquiring mother a farewell smile, then scooped up the boy and followed Joanna up the hill.

The women, I saw when we drew closer, were sorting through baskets of flatbread, dried fish, and assorted fruits. I expected Mary to rise and greet Jude with a warm embrace. Instead, she only flashed him a quick smile and returned her attention to Yeshua.

I frowned. I had no idea what other mothers would do in the same situation, but her lack of concern for Jude seemed disrespectful. Shouldn't a mother greet all her children with love and affection?

Joanna handed me a wooden bowl loaded with bread, nuts, and fruit, then gestured to an empty spot on a huge rock. "Sit there and fill your bellies," she said. "I am going to help the women. They still have to feed Yeshua's disciples."

I gave the bowl to Jude, who took it to the rock and shared it with the others. While Ziv, Jude, Rahel, and the boy ate, I stood in an empty space and hesitated. Thomas sat less than twenty paces away, and he had not noticed me. A week ago I would have run to him and blurted out my intention, but now I wasn't sure what to do. How could I greet him and ask him to come home while Yeshua was teaching? My interruption would not be welcome, and I needed Thomas to be happy when he saw me. I needed him to be homesick for Abba and Cana . . .

Surrendering to caution, I sat with my friends and nibbled on nuts from the bowl. None of the others spoke, so we could hear Yeshua clearly. He finished a story about a lamp on a hill, and then he sat on his rocky platform and opened his arms in invitation. At once, dozens of people stood and streamed toward him, many supporting friends or family members who could not climb the hill without help.

I watched, mesmerized, as Yeshua greeted each person with a word and a gentle touch. He would listen to them, then place his hand on a head or shoulder or arm and lift his eyes to heaven as he prayed. When he finished, the person with whom he prayed would look up and smile or shout or leap, depending, I supposed, on his nature. Those who had approached with a limp walked away with an even stride; those who had climbed the hill with bent backs left standing straight. People with indiscernible illnesses left with confident smiles, even shouts of joy and praise to Adonai.

I looked at Jude and wondered how he could calmly eat without wondering about his brother. Had Yeshua truly healed those people or were they mad, as well?

I threw a pistachio at Jude. Startled, he looked at me. "Is there some problem?"

"Will you speak to your brother now?" I asked. "This might be a good time — you could get in line with the others and catch him off guard."

Jude snorted softly. "I don't think anyone can surprise Yeshua. But no, this is not a good time. He will not take time for me as long as someone waits to speak to him. How else will he build his following?"

As we ate in silence, I realized Ziv and Rahel had slipped away. I stood and searched, spotting the old man in the long line snaking up the hill. Rahel stood by his side, her face as blank as parchment.

The sight of the girl's stony face sent a tremor scooting up the back of my neck. "Jude" — I kept my eyes on Rahel as they inched closer to Yeshua — "do you see Ziv? He's down there."

Jude rose and came to stand beside me. We watched in silence as Ziv stepped closer, now only ten paces away, then eight. Rahel's face remained blank, but one of her arms had begun to jerk spasmodically.

"Jude . . ."

When Ziv stepped toward Yeshua, Rahel arched her back and released a scream that pierced heart and soul alike. She wrenched her hand away from her grandfather, then straightened and glared at Yeshua, her face contorting into a grimace unlike anything I had ever seen.

I stared, horrified, as Yeshua bent and said something to her. Whatever he said made her close her eyes. Her chest lifted and fell in a mighty heave as a flock of birds rose from a nearby stand of trees and took flight over the sea.

Yeshua placed his hand on Rahel's shoulder. The girl opened her eyes and smiled, then threw her arms around his neck.

Ziv knelt at Rahel's side and drew his granddaughter into his arms, tears streaming down his cheeks as he looked up at Yeshua.

Speechless, I turned to Jude, who had turned toward the sea. "That — that was impossible."

Jude lowered his gaze. "What?"

"What I saw — that was impossible. Rahel was in the grip of the demon, and then she was herself again."

Jude tugged at his beard. "Did you notice the birds? The entire flock dove into the water."

I looked toward the sea, but I saw only its silver-blue surface reflecting the sun.

"Rahel appears to be well. Yeshua healed her."

A muscle flexed in Jude's jaw as he crossed his arms. "I suppose Ziv will be leaving us now. He will be convinced — until the girl has another fit."

CHAPTER TWENTY-TWO:
TASMIN

We did not have an opportunity to speak to Yeshua that day. As the sun balanced on the western horizon, Yeshua disappeared, leaving just as Jude and I were getting ready to approach him. One of the women said Yeshua typically went down to the water's edge, where he could launch out in a boat and rest on the waves. The twelve had gone with him while most of the local people had gone home. Those who had come from a distance camped on the hillside, erecting makeshift tents and building small campfires.

Fortunately, we were accustomed to sleeping under the stars, so we did the same.

The next morning, we rose with the sun and climbed the hill in search of food for the boy. While I waited to see if Joanna or Susanna could find something soft enough for him to eat, I studied the women working with Yeshua. The women worked well together, putting their hands to whatever needed to be done: doling out water to the thirsty, comforting the sick who had come to be healed, preparing food, or directing those with livestock to the watering trough by the lake. One woman looked familiar — she wore her long dark hair tied back with a leather strip, and her tunic looked new. She appeared to be middle-aged and would have been pretty in her younger days, for her face was symmetrical and her eyes large. She did not speak much, but when she smiled, her eyes lit with unmistakable joy and something that looked like relief . . .

When she handed a dish to Joanna, I saw a scar on her arm, and the truth hit me like a blow to the belly: we had seen this woman outside Magdala. It was she who had roared up from the graveyard and attacked Jude. Only a few days ago, this woman had been a lunatic.

I tugged on Jude's sleeve and pointed. "Do you recognize her?"

He turned and looked. "Should I?"

"We saw her outside Magdala." His eyes remained blank. "She attacked you."

He blinked, then startled. "Not possible."

"I'm sure it's the same woman. She has the same scar on her arm."

I didn't realize how loudly I had been

speaking until Mary came over and sat next to Jude. She slipped her arm around his shoulder and pressed a kiss to his temple. "My son," she said, patting his hand. "I am so glad you have come. Have you greeted your aunt Salome? She is with us."

"Not yet." He blushed under his mother's obvious affection. "It has not been easy to find you, but I am glad we did. I wanted to see if I could convince Yeshua to come back to Nazareth."

Mary patted his hand again, then looked toward the woman with the scarred arm. "I noticed you looking at Miriam. From your reaction, Tasmin, I thought you might have seen her before."

It was my turn to blush. "We — we did encounter her," I admitted, stammering. "She attacked Jude when we passed by Magdala. But she looked nothing like — she looked very different."

"Yeshua delivered her," Mary said, a smile lighting her face. "She had been possessed by seven devils. Hard to imagine, but she's had a rough life. Trouble at home, broken family, a lost baby — she had gone to Tiberias to beg for an audience with Antipas, and there she fell into company with a necromancer. But that is all over, and now she is whole. Restored."

The woman looked up, undoubtedly feeling the pressure of our inquisitive eyes, and her face softened when her gaze met Mary's. She came over, squeezed Mary's hand, and went back to work.

"All of us," Mary said, gesturing to the women, "have decided to remain with Yeshua until he no longer needs us. We will do whatever we can to make things easier for him."

Jude's face darkened with unreadable emotions. I knew he worried about his brother and feared for his mother. If Yeshua ran into trouble with the authorities, the trouble would be of his own making. Mary, on the other hand, was innocent, a sincere woman who only wanted to support her son . . .

"Ima" — Jude reached for her hand — "you are no longer a young woman, and the family needs you. James, Joses, and Simeon are home in Nazareth where they belong. Damaris and Pheodora are with their husbands and children. They need you. Your grandchildren need you. Everyone is sick with worry about you —"

Mary patted his hand. "They do not need to worry about me, son. I don't expect you to understand, but I have spent years preparing myself for what is to come. When the sword pierces my soul, I will be ready."

"The sword pierces . . . what sword?" Jude scrubbed his hands through his hair in wordless frustration. Face flushed, he stared at his mother. "Ima, it doesn't take a prophet to realize that your eldest son has run afoul of the Torah scholars and chief priests. The Romans are wary of any Judean who claims to be a prophet. Have you forgotten what happened to John? Yeshua is on a path marked for trouble and . . ."

He broke off when a group of men crested the hill and stood silhouetted by the rising sun. There was Yeshua, flanked by his chosen disciples.

I felt a warm glow within me when I spotted a familiar form. After so many long days and restless nights, finally I would speak to the man I had been seeking. "Thomas!" I ran toward my brother.

"Ooof!"

I nearly knocked the breath from Thomas's body when I embraced him. "Thomas, you can't know how good it is to see you!"

"Tasmin!" His face brightened as he lifted me off the ground. "What are you doing here?"

"I came to see you."

He released me and gave me a warm

smile, then glanced toward Yeshua and the others, who were walking toward the women. They were no doubt hungry and ready to break their fast, but Thomas's stomach would have to wait.

"Brother." I pulled on his beard, forcing him to look at me. "I have been searching for you since the wedding. I have walked for days, slept under the stars, been attacked by a madwoman and a group of lestes, and picked up all sorts of stragglers, all of whom wanted to see this Yeshua who so fascinates you. So give me your attention, please. I need to talk to you."

"All that? I am glad you are all right." He drew a deep breath and gripped my shoulders. "I'd like to introduce you to Yeshua — or did you meet him at the wedding?"

"I was too busy working, if you recall. You would have been working with me, if you had not found other people more fascinating."

Though I tried to adopt a serious tone, I couldn't help but smile because I was overjoyed to see him. I wanted to remain angry about how he left without warning, yet I couldn't stay mad at Thomas. Everything could easily be forgiven and forgotten if he would agree to come home. We would pick up where we left off, working together, talking together, making plans for the future —

"Listen, sister." Thomas tightened his grip on my shoulders. "When I left, I told you I wasn't sure if Yeshua was the one we've been waiting for. But now I know he *is* the promised Messiah. I have watched him closely, and oh, the things I have seen! I have seen the lame healed. I have seen the blind receive their sight, even a man born blind! I have seen the dead restored to life and tax collectors repent of their thievery! One of them walks with us now. Like John the Immerser, Yeshua is changing the hearts of many, and I —"

"Hush." I pressed my fingertips to his lips. "I have been following *you,* so I've heard all the stories. I know Yeshua's fame is growing every day, but this kind of fame is not good. The Torah teachers and Temple authorities are not pleased with the way he has stirred up the people. I have been traveling with his brother Jude, and he fears for Yeshua. It is time, Thomas, for you to come home. Our father is not well, so say your farewells here and come home with me."

When he did not agree immediately, I realized I had not used the gently persuasive words I wanted to use or spoken the way I wanted to speak. I had hoped to get Thomas in a quiet place, where I could make him laugh, make him miss me, and tell him something that would soften his heart. Then I could have made headway; I could have worked on his sympathies. But I had taken advantage of an opportunity and now I would have to accept the result.

I lifted my chin and saw Thomas staring at me as if I had suddenly grown a third head. "Go home? I cannot leave."

"Of course you can. Are you a slave? You took no vow to serve this man, so bid him farewell and come home. He will understand. Any righteous man would understand that you need to see to your father's needs."

"No one," Thomas said, his voice softening, "who has put his hand to the plow and looked back is fit for the kingdom of God."

I stared at my twin, who suddenly seemed a stranger. How could this be the man with whom I had shared a womb? "What are you saying?"

"I am saying" — he spoke slowly, as if to a child — "that the work of God must come first. I have put my hand to the plow and I cannot look back."

Unbidden tears sprang to my eyes. "What of our father? Would you forget about the one who gave you life? Who has supported you in every endeavor without reservation?"

The thin line of Thomas's mouth clamped tight for a moment, then he swallowed. "My father is a righteous man. And if he understood what I have discovered, he would encourage me to remain with Yeshua. If he were younger, he would count himself blessed to be here with me. Oh, how I wish he had come with you, so he could hear the words of the Lord for himself!"

I took a step back, horrified and offended by his use of the word *Lord* for Jude's brother.

"I cannot believe what I am hearing," I said as a trembling rose from somewhere in the center of my chest. "I cannot believe you would commit such blasphemy and ascribe it to Abba, as well."

"I have been watching Yeshua," Thomas went on, his voice calmer. "You know me — I am not one to endorse an endeavor without being certain of it. I have seen the Scriptures fulfilled before my eyes, Tasmin! If you would only look, you would see the truth, too."

"I would not." I shook my head. "Not even Yeshua's family supports him, and they know him better than anyone. Jude says he has always been aloof, even odd, and all of this is bound to bring trouble to the family and destroy his mother. Look at Mary!

Think of her!"

Thomas smiled. "Mary believes in him. She does not speak often, but I can tell she knows things she has not shared with us. Even when Yeshua speaks of the trials that lie ahead, she holds her tongue and does not argue with him. What sort of mother would do that unless she understood he was called to fulfill a higher purpose?"

"I know little of mothers," I replied, struggling to overcome a sudden urge to weep, "and you used to understand that. You used to understand everything I felt, but here I am, trying to make you see what you need to do, and I feel as though I am speaking a language you no longer understand."

"I cannot go home with you." Thomas winced in remorse. "But you could stay with us. You could join the women here. I know the others would welcome you."

I looked at the women working on the hillside. None of them seemed anxious or unhappy — in fact, they seemed delighted to be doing such humble work. Joanna smiled as she wiped the faces of children who had gotten dirty while playing on the hill, and Susanna sang as she mended a tear in a woman's tunic.

Could I stay? I would be with Thomas . . .

Mixed feelings surged through me, then

one conviction became clear: I didn't want to share my brother with these people, and I had been away from Abba long enough. Clearly, I would need time to convince Thomas to leave, but I could not work for a man whose cause I did not support.

No more than I could allow my brother to delude himself.

"Thomas —" I turned him toward the sea so he would see no one but me — "I know why you left the way you did. I understand why Yeshua's message appeals to you. He speaks of new beginnings, repentance, starting over, and I know you would love to do that. But you can't run from the past. You can't run from what happened. You and I are guilty and we always will be."

His expression changed — memory hardened his eyes, and a somber thought tightened the corners of his mouth. For a moment I thought he would pretend he did not know what I meant, but how could he forget? I remembered every detail of that day and always would.

He shook his head. "That happened so long ago . . . we were children."

"But it happened. And we are both to blame."

He drew a deep breath and looked away, his hand patting his side in a frantic rhythm.

"Will we never be free of it, Tasmin?"

"How can we be free? Our mother died because of us. Our father has lived alone because of us. We owe him."

Thomas lowered his head and blinked back tears. "I know what you are saying is true, but Yeshua gives me hope. If HaShem has truly sent him, perhaps there is a way —"

"To forget? Impossible." I blew out a breath, then squeezed my brother's shoulders. "I will stay a little longer, but only because I want to spend time with you. I want to understand why Yeshua gives you hope. If you can explain it to me, maybe I can help Abba understand why you've left us."

"I haven't left you. You will always be my sister."

"*Being* and *being there* are not the same, brother."

Thomas waved my words away. "I am glad you will stay. I know Yeshua will welcome you. We've had people coming and going ever since we left Cana. One day we are a small group, the next we are over a thousand." He forced a smile. "Having another mouth to feed is not a problem. The other day Yeshua fed a gathering of more than five thousand men — *and* their women and children — with five little barley loaves and two small fish."

I scoffed. "That's ridiculous."

"I saw it with my own eyes. Andrew found a small boy who had packed a lunch. They brought the food to Yeshua, who took it, gave thanks for it, and broke the loaves and fish into pieces, then gave them to us to distribute. We kept returning for more, and the Lord kept handing out bread and fish until every man, woman, and child on the hillside had a full belly."

I gave my brother a reproving look. "I know what happened — once you began to hand out bread and fish, the people pulled out the food they had hidden among their supplies. Once everyone began to share, the food appeared to multiply —"

Thomas shook his head. "We gave out barley loaf and dried fish. The people ate barley loaf and dried fish. And when we took up the remnants, our baskets — *twelve* basketfuls — held barley loaf and dried fish. Nothing else. The people were so impressed by the miracle that they rose up to take Yeshua by force and proclaim him king. Realizing what they were about to do, he had to hide on the mountain." Thomas stroked his beard and looked at me, his eyes bright. "Can you not see why HaShem has sent him? The time might not yet be right, but imagine a king who can feed his army without having to haul supplies! A king who can heal the wounded and keep his army fit for marching. A king who can resurrect those who are struck down by the enemy. Other nations are terrified by the Romans, but Yeshua, son of David, will defeat them by the power of Adonai. And then we will enter into a new Israel, the kingdom of God."

Disbelief and loyalty warred in my heart as I stared at my brother. Yeshua had clearly convinced Thomas and the other disciples, and yet I knew the erstwhile carpenter was no warrior king. I had been traveling with Jude, and Jude was no fool. He knew the Scriptures, he knew his brother, and he did not believe Yeshua was meant to be a king.

He would have to help me convince Thomas to leave this dangerous imposter.

"I will stay a little while," I repeated, gripping Thomas's arm, "but whenever Jude is ready to return home, I will go with him. And I will be praying that you will agree to come with me."

"Pray all you want," Thomas said. "As for me, I will follow Yeshua until the end." He gave me a smile as he walked away, but it was not the smile of a happy man.

For someone who had just proclaimed his loyalty to Israel's next king, I had to wonder about the reason for his lack of confidence.

Chapter Twenty-Three: Jude

I waited until the growl of nighttime conversations ceased and the grumble of snoring began. All around me, the disciples slept on the ground, covered only by their cloaks and the security of their conviction that they had enlisted in a holy cause. I did not share their conviction, yet I had more in common with Yeshua than any of them.

When everyone had stilled, save the man who had been appointed to keep watch, I rose from my place, pulled my cloak around my shoulders, and went in search of my brother. I expected to find him near James and John, the two who seemed his closest confidants, but I spotted them sleeping near a fire. Neither was Yeshua near Peter, the overeager fisherman. I did not find him near Thomas, who seemed to frown even in his sleep, nor near Andrew or Judas.

Yet when I turned toward the moonlit lake, I spotted a solitary figure sitting atop an overturned boat, a mantle wrapped tightly around his shoulders. Brown hair fringed the top of the fabric — Yeshua.

I strode through the grasses until I reached the shoreline. Yeshua seemed not to notice my approach, for his eyes were fixed on the moon's wavering reflection and his lips moved silently, as if in prayer. When I finally stood beside the boat, my arms crossed in patient forbearance, the corner of his mouth twisted in a wry smile.

"Why can you not sleep?" He looked over at me. "We have worked all day, and you are bound to be weary."

"You have worked, I have listened," I countered. "*You* should be weary."

"I am. But I have things to discuss with my Father."

I exhaled an exasperated sigh. "Look, brother, I came here to find you. I have tried to speak to you several times, but apparently you have had no time for family."

The moonlight gilded my brother's face as he turned and stretched his hand toward his sleeping disciples. "There are my mother and my brothers and my sisters. Whoever does the will of my Father in heaven, he is my brother and sister and mother."

I spat on the ground, irritated by his answer. "Look — you are the eldest, you should be the most responsible, but you have left James, Joses, Simeon, and I to do the work our father trained us to do."

"Don't you know that I must be about the things of my Father?"

"Our father is dead." I blew out an exasperated breath. "I have received a commission — a bed for a wealthy merchant — and none of us is capable of doing the carving. We need you to come home and work for the family. For our mother's sake. For all of us."

A cloud moved in front of the moon, darkening the light that had lit Yeshua's face. "Where is your faith, Jude? If you first seek the kingdom of God and His righteousness, all the things you need shall be added to you. So do not worry about tomorrow, for tomorrow will worry about itself." He sighed and turned back to the sea. "Each day has enough trouble of its own."

What could I say? I had walked for days, eaten locusts, endured a beating, wrestled with a madwoman, and tolerated endless hours of chattering women for nothing. Clearly, Yeshua had no intention of coming home. Not only did he seem implacable, but my mother would refuse to help me convince him, for she seemed fully committed to his foolhardy campaign.

I had failed. I had wasted precious time and a lot of the money Chanon Phineas had given me to buy materials for his anniversary bed. The merchant would want his deposit returned, and how could I earn anything while traveling?

Yeshua had left me with no options. My other brothers were waiting for me in Nazareth, and time was slipping away. I had promised to deliver a bed worthy of a king, and unless someone could teach me the skills of a master craftsman in a very short time, I would have to break my word.

Our reputation would be ruined, if Yeshua's activities hadn't ruined it already.

"So be it." I lifted my head to meet Yeshua's eye. "We will simply have to accept the hard truth: you have abandoned us."

A rising breeze blew the curtain of cloud away, allowing the moonlight to illuminate Yeshua's face again. I saw pain in his countenance and hurt in his eyes, and wondered why he could not see the same emotions in me.

Chapter Twenty-Four:
Tasmin

Jude wanted to leave the next morning, but somehow I persuaded him to tarry a few more days. I wanted time to quietly work on Thomas — perhaps, I reasoned, seeing me would make him remember his obligations. He would think of Abba and the date palms that needed a younger man to mount a ladder and harvest the fruit.

Jude might have been thinking similar thoughts, because he spent hours listening to his brother's teachings. I did not have as much time to sit and listen — I kept busy feeding, entertaining, and chasing the boy, who was no longer the emaciated child we had found on the side of the road. Good food and consistent attention had put meat on his bones, and he had become quite active. Though he remained silent, he compensated for his lack of verbal skills with a flurry of gestures.

One afternoon, as the boy napped with

his head in my lap, a man in the crowd stood and asked Yeshua about his plans for the future. "We know you are the son of David," the man said, "so tell us about the coming kingdom of God."

Yeshua smiled and leaned forward, gripping the edge of the rock where he sat. "How should we picture the kingdom of God? Or by what story shall we present it? It is like a mustard seed when it's planted in the ground. Though the smallest of all seeds in the earth, yet when planted it grows up and becomes the largest of all the herbs. It puts forth big branches, so the birds of the air can nest in its shade."

I glanced at Jude. "What does that mean?"

Jude shrugged. "He woos them with elusive word pictures. If they don't make sense, no one can hold him to a specific promise."

I spotted Thomas sitting with several other disciples. His face bore an inward look of deep abstraction — he was thinking hard but not about me, for he hadn't looked in my direction all day.

In that moment I knew we would be foolish to wait any longer. "Whenever you say," I whispered to Jude, "I am ready to go home."

While Jude and I both knew we were not

likely to bring our brothers home, we also realized that once we left the coastal area, we might not see them for months. So, in a desperate effort to understand what had pulled them away from us, we spent the rest of the week with Yeshua and his followers.

Thomas and the other disciples seemed to support Yeshua without question, yet I often heard bickering when I walked among them, so they were far from being totally submissive to their master. I once heard Simon Peter mutter that he had forgiven a friend three times for the same offense, and there ought to be a limit to how many times a sin must be forgiven. James and John, the two boisterous sons of Zebedee, argued over who would have to keep watch during the night, and Judas Iscariot frequently grumbled that they had already spent plenty to feed the poor, so couldn't they pay for at least one night at a comfortable inn?

One day a large contingent of Pharisees approached the listeners, then stood in a dark, disapproving huddle as Yeshua taught his followers. We had spent all morning sitting in bright sunlight and we were hungry and hot. At midday, when the afternoon sun bore down on our heads, Yeshua stopped teaching. The local people pulled out food they'd brought from home, and Yeshua walked over to the women, who had been busy preparing a meal for the disciples.

Jude had walked to the nearest town and bought bread and cheese for us. I broke off pieces of bread for Jude, the boy, and myself, and watched, idly curious, as Yeshua took one of the loaves the women had provided, held it up, and blessed it. He then passed it to Simon Peter, who ravenously tore off a bite before handing it to John. The mood among the disciples was casual, and everyone seemed pleased to relax for a while.

Then one of the Pharisees pulled away from his fellows and approached Yeshua, his stern face a stark contrast to the disciples' easygoing smiles. "Teacher," he called, his voice lined with iron, "why do your disciples break the tradition of the elders? They don't wash their hands before they eat."

Yeshua hadn't washed his hands either, but apparently the Pharisees preferred to stop short of criticizing the man many considered a prophet. I rose onto my knees, eager to listen, and Jude stopped eating, his eyes thoughtful as he watched his brother.

Yeshua turned to his disciples with an exaggerated expression — *We didn't wash?* Then he looked at the Torah teacher, his expression shifting to seriousness. "Why do you transgress the commandment of God for the sake of your tradition? For God said, 'Honor your father and mother' and 'He who speaks evil of father or mother must be put to death.' But *you* say, 'Whoever tells his father or mother, Whatever you might have gained from me is a gift to God, he need not honor his father.' On account of your tradition, you make void the word of God." A warning cloud settled over his features. "Hypocrites! Rightly did Isaiah prophesy about you, saying, 'This people honors Me with their lips, but their heart is far from Me. And in vain they worship Me, teaching as doctrines the commandments of men.' "

As Jude and I stared at each other with wide eyes, Yeshua lifted his voice so the entire gathering could hear. "Hear and understand: It's not what goes *into* the mouth that makes the man unholy; but what comes *out* of the mouth, *this* makes the man unholy."

Yeshua turned back to the Pharisees and shook his head. "Make every effort to enter through the narrow door; for many, I tell you, will try to enter and will not be able. Once the Master of the household gets up and shuts the door, and you're standing outside and begin knocking on the door, saying, 'Master, open up for us,' then He will say to you, 'I don't know where you come from.' Then you will start to say, 'We ate and drank in Your company, and You taught in our streets.' But He will say, 'I tell you, I don't know where you come from. Get away from Me, all of you evildoers!' "

Some of the Pharisees bristled openly at this, but Yeshua had not finished. "Listen" — he held up a warning hand — "there will be weeping and the gnashing of teeth when you see Abraham and Isaac and Jacob and all the prophets in the kingdom of God, but you yourselves thrown out. And they will come from the east and west and from the north and south, and they will recline at table in the kingdom of God. And indeed, some are last who shall be first, and some are first who shall be last."

As the Pharisees gathered up their long robes and stalked away, I turned to Jude. "What *is* the kingdom of God? Has he ever explained it to you?"

Jude watched the departing Pharisees with an odd mingling of wariness and amusement in his eyes. "Never," he said, shifting his gaze to meet mine, "but we all know what Daniel wrote about the kingdom of God and the Son of Man. 'He will come with the clouds of heaven and will be brought into the presence of the Ancient of Days. Dominion, glory, and sovereignty will be given to Him that all peoples, nations, and languages should serve Him. His dominion will be an everlasting dominion that will never pass away, and His kingdom will never be destroyed.' "

"And . . . Yeshua is not the Son of Man."

Jude blew out a breath. "Do you believe my brother capable of establishing an everlasting kingdom?"

I bit my lip. "He cast a demon out of Ziv's granddaughter. And he may have turned water into wine."

Jude pulled his shoulders back and lifted his chin. "My brother is not the messiah, nor did he arrive in the clouds of heaven. No, Tasmin. If Yeshua ever has a kingdom, its people will be these." He extended his hand to the poor villagers on the hillside. "Do you see warriors? Do you see an army? No. You see common folk who yearn for hope and comfort. That is what Yeshua gives them."

"But they are willing to serve him," I remarked, looking toward the disciples. Thomas seemed perfectly at home among the twelve and would probably remain so until Yeshua retired from wandering about the countryside.

I pressed my lips together, remembering the Pharisees who had been furious when they departed. If they had their way, Yeshua's retirement would come sooner rather than later.

CHAPTER TWENTY-FIVE: TASMIN

After sleeping amid a symphony of snoring from those encamped nearby, I rose at sunrise, stretched my stiff muscles, and looked around. Most of Yeshua's audience had departed the day before, returning to their homes and families. Shabbat would commence at sunset, and I wondered if Yeshua planned to move to a new location before then. To travel any sizable distance on the Sabbath would be breaking the Law, and no devout Torah teacher would willingly do that . . . except, perhaps, Yeshua.

I had my answer not long after the women set out a platter of cheese and figs to break our fast. Yeshua's twelve disciples pulled their cloaks off the ground and tied them around their shoulders. A small group of donkeys stood nearby while Peter and Andrew, another pair of brothers, secured pack saddles on the beasts.

"I had no idea Yeshua could afford so

many animals," I remarked to Susanna as I observed the preparations. "At least a dozen donkeys?"

"They are not his. They belong to her." She inclined her head toward Mary, wife of Clopas, who was filling a basket with blankets. "She gives freely to support Yeshua's work. I would love to do the same thing."

I did not know Mary, wife of Clopas, but was she wise to give so much to support an uncertain work? "When all this is over, will she have anything left?"

Susanna's eyes widened. "When this is over? My dear Tasmin, do you not see that Yeshua will change Israel — no, the world — forever? HaShem has sent our Messiah to usher in the kingdom of God, and nothing will ever be the same."

I held up my hands in a posture of surrender and backed away. I did not want to argue with my friends; I only wanted to gather my things and go home. If Mary and Clopas wanted to give Yeshua everything they had, what business was it of mine?

Now, where was the boy? I looked for him among the women, who usually delighted in helping him eat his morning meal. "Boy, where are you?" I asked Mary, Joanna, and Susanna, but though they had seen him earlier, none knew where he had gone.

The hard fist of fear rose in my throat.

"Thomas!" Compelled by natural habit, I ran to my brother, who was packing one of the donkeys. "Thomas —" I struggled to catch my breath — "I have been taking care of a little boy, perhaps you have seen him? He is two or three, and something is wrong with his tongue so he doesn't speak. I have no idea where he would go in a crowd this size . . ."

Thomas stared as if I'd lost my mind. "How did you get a child?"

"We found him on the side of the road." Impatient, I turned and scanned the crowd. "I know you've seen dozens of children here, but this boy would be by himself. He's wearing a blue tunic —"

"I have not seen the boy, but I'm sure you'll find him. Ask the women."

"I already have."

He pointed toward the open field, where a few people lingered, probably hoping to witness a miracle. "Then look around. Children usually run to other children, so perhaps —"

I stumbled away, nearly blinded by a sudden rise of tears. What had happened to my brother? A month ago, Thomas would have done anything to help me with a problem. He would have known all about the boy, and he would have been as eager to find him as I was. But *this* Thomas, this stranger, was more interested in packing water jars than in helping me find the child who had become unexpectedly dear to me . . .

I took long strides down the hill, compelled by gravity and panic. My heart lifted when I recognized a familiar physique. "Jude!"

He turned at the sound of my voice, and a smile flitted across his face. "Ready to go?"

"I can't find the boy. Have you seen him?"

His smile vanished as he, too, scanned the crowd. "When did you last see him?"

"This morning. Joanna was helping him eat figs and cheese. She had him on her lap while all the other women made a fuss over him."

"And after that?"

I shook my head. "I didn't see him after that. We were all packing supplies."

"He can't have gone far." Jude squeezed my shoulder, then tightened the straps on his sandals. "Let's split up. You walk east and I'll walk west —"

"You — you don't think some family took him, do you?" I looked at the road beyond the hill, already filled with men, women, and children, many of them wearing disguising head wraps and scarves.

Jude's eyes softened. "Isn't that what you wanted? To allow some other family to raise him?"

"Yes, but not yet. I wanted —"

"You can admit it. The child has become precious to you."

I drew a breath, wanting to deny it, then snapped my mouth shut. "All right. Yes. I like him. Someone else would make a better mother, but I can't give him to a woman I don't know. I want to be sure he's going to a good home. I don't want someone to simply pick him up and run off with him."

"Like you did?" Jude's brows slanted the question, and I had to admit he had a point. Yes, I found the child, and yes, I took him even though I was probably the least likely mother to pass his hiding place. But still . . .

"Please." I clutched Jude's arm. "I can't leave without knowing he is safe."

Jude pressed his hand over mine. "We'll go to the top of the hill and search as we walk in a widening circle. If he is still here, we will find him."

My heart pounded an uneven rhythm as I matched Jude's long stride and half walked, half ran up the grassy hill. A few of Yeshua's followers still stood at the top, and they moved out of the way when Jude and I climbed to the rocky summit and slowly turned, shading our eyes as we searched the hillside below. "He is wearing blue," I said, not sure Jude would remember that detail. "And he is probably alone —" my voice broke — "unless someone took him."

"Don't think that way," Jude said, his voice firm. "We will find him. We will . . . wait." He pointed to a knot of people below us. "There. My brother is sitting with a group of children. Do you think — ?"

I didn't wait to hear more. I took off, running toward the rock where Yeshua sat surrounded by youngsters. Their parents stood at a distance, watching the scene with tender smiles.

I pushed my way through the parents and walked up to Yeshua, then fell to my knees in sheer relief. Yeshua was telling the children a story, and my boy was sitting in his lap.

How had the boy come to be with him? Had Yeshua picked him out of the crowd, or had the boy simply spied an empty lap and climbed into it? I had no idea, but my heart warmed when I saw how the boy looked up at Yeshua with wide, trusting eyes. Yeshua continued his story, and at the end he looked down and smiled at my boy.

Jude and I weren't the only people who

noticed how Yeshua had taken time to be with the children. Two of his disciples, men I didn't know, stalked over with hard frowns on their faces.

"How can you trouble the master with your youngsters?" one of them said to the group of parents. "Can you not see that we are trying to pack? Yeshua wants to teach in another place today."

I thought Yeshua would thank the man and send the children back to their parents. Instead, he held up his hand, silencing the disciple. "Let the little children come to me," he said, his voice surprisingly gentle, "and do not hinder them, for the kingdom of heaven belongs to such as these."

The kingdom of heaven . . . was for children? I frowned, trying to reconcile the image of a revolutionary army with toddling babies on a hillside.

Yeshua placed his hand on my boy's head and murmured a blessing, and then, while I watched in astonishment, he pressed his thumb against the boy's chin, gently opening the child's mouth. I stepped forward, afraid he would recoil when he saw the boy's deformity, but I was too late. Yeshua had to see the forked tongue, but he did not remark on it. He simply pressed his fingertip to the boy's lips and held it there for a moment. When he removed his hand, he smiled at the boy again, then helped him down so he could come to me.

"Child, I thought you were lost!" I drew the boy into my arms. "Don't ever wander away again."

I did not expect a reply; I knew the boy couldn't speak. But he lifted his chin, his lip trembling, and in a voice as clear as birdsong, he said, "I won't."

I blinked hard, then brought my own finger to the boy's chin and opened his mouth. The cloven tongue . . . had vanished. The boy's tongue looked as whole as any other, and the misaligned teeth had arranged themselves in the proper formation. He appeared as normal as any other boy.

I reached for Jude's arm as the world swayed around me. When I looked up and saw him staring at the child, I knew he had seen, too, and was as dumbstruck as I. He shifted his gaze to Yeshua as a deep frown settled between his brows.

How could something like this happen? Had our eyes deceived us *before* this moment or were they false to us now? Such things did not happen in Galilee, and they did not happen to people like us. This healing, if that's what it was, must be temporary. Perhaps Yeshua had pressed a tongue-colored leaf to the fissure, and we would discover the truth when the boy tried to eat.

But I had seen no leaf, no fabric, no disguise. And I could not explain.

I lifted the boy and carried him down the hillside as quickly as I could. Jude gripped my elbow with uncharacteristic firmness, helping me keep my balance as I dodged the many rocks that peppered the ground.

Our steps cut through the grass as we hurried to our donkey. "I promised," I muttered between clenched teeth. "I promised Thomas I would stay a little while, but I can no longer abide this sort of thing. If this is a trick, Jude — and surely it must be — it is a cruel jest, for who would do such a thing to a child?"

"Maybe it is not a trick. Maybe the child has been healed, but by dark powers. My brother is surely mad."

I had no answer for him. Only one clear thought filled my head: we had to leave as quickly as we could.

As the midday sun radiated heat only a lizard could love, Yeshua and his disciples moved south on the road to Jerusalem. Susanna and Joanna left with Yeshua and the women who supported his ministry. Ziv and Rahel had departed earlier in the day. Jude and I guided our donkey southwest, toward Gabara and Cana.

Now that we were alone except for the boy, Jude and I did not speak much. I don't know what thoughts occupied his mind, but I couldn't help thinking about how his brother had healed the boy in my care.

At first I assured myself that the healing was an illusion, a trick to deceive the eyes, but by the time we passed through Gabara, I could not deny that the boy's tongue and teeth had permanently shifted. Before the healing, he had barely been able to eat, but at Gabara, when I offered the boy a piece of flatbread, he bit into it and chewed with no trouble. The action so startled me that I asked him to open his mouth and show me his teeth. I then motioned to Jude so he could see that the child's mouth was no illusion. Jude was likewise mystified, and yet neither of us had an explanation.

"Perhaps," Jude said when we began to walk again, "we didn't notice how normal his teeth were because we were so shocked by the sight of his misshapen tongue."

"But he *couldn't* eat," I insisted. "He couldn't bite into a piece of bread."

"Then perhaps Yeshua healed him by some other power. Pharaoh's magicians were able to imitate the miracles of Moses."

"Now you sound like the Pharisees. They have been saying that Yeshua drives out demons by the power of Beelzebub."

"Perhaps it is true."

"Yeshua heard their rumblings. He asked them how Satan could drive out Satan without dividing his kingdom. 'But if I drive out demons by the Ruach Elohim,' he said, 'then the kingdom of God has come upon you.' "

"Driving out demons by the Spirit of God," Jude murmured, lifting his eyes to the horizon. "He is nothing if not audacious."

We walked the rest of the way in a heavy silence I found depressing for several reasons. First, neither of us had accomplished what we set out to do. I had not convinced Thomas to come home, and Jude had been unable to persuade his brother — or his mother — to give up their dangerous quest. Second, I had hoped to discover proof that Yeshua's miracles were only tricks, but what I witnessed left me more perplexed and confused than ever. Third, and perhaps most surprising, I had grown accustomed to Jude and could not imagine the emptiness I would feel when he left me at my father's house.

Though I felt an emptiness when Thomas

left, Jude's absence would create a different kind of vacuum. Thomas was my brother, as familiar as the back of my hand. Jude was . . . unpredictable. Clever. And a bit of a challenge.

Life in Cana would seem dull without him.

CHAPTER TWENTY-SIX:
JUDE

The worst aspect of returning home alone was having to tell my brothers about the job I had accepted on their behalf, and how I did not believe we could complete it without Yeshua.

After hearing the news, James sank to a stool and tugged on his beard for what seemed like an eternity. I knew he was struggling to come up with a way we could salvage the situation. "Would this merchant be content with a headboard fashioned like a row of pillars?" he asked.

"I could ask him," I answered. "But he would probably want to lower the price. The amount he offered reflected the intricate carving involved in the project."

James looked at Joses. "You have been carving a bit — could you learn enough to complete a headboard in eleven months?"

Joses blanched. "I could try, but what if my work doesn't satisfy? I would hate to carve something he despises, especially if we could find another way to please him."

"He likes the Roman style?" Simeon lifted his head. "We could hire a sculptor to do something in stone, then affix the stone to the headboard. What do you think?"

I was willing to consider the idea, but James scoffed. "A sculptor, here in Nazareth? We'd have to go to Tiberias or Jerusalem to find a skilled sculptor, and his fee would probably consume all our profit. And we'd have to pay to transport the stone." He looked at me. "Do not go to him yet, Jude. Give us time to attempt a small replica and get the frame completed. Perhaps HaShem will inspire us with an idea the man will like better."

Joses sighed and rested his chin on his hand. "If only Yeshua were here. He would come up with something and carve it with time to spare."

"He is *not* here," I said, my voice sharper than I intended it to be. "And though I tried everything to persuade him to come home, he is set on following his own path — no matter what the risk." I sighed. "I am afraid we may never see our brother again, at least not in Nazareth. His teaching draws more people each day, while his words for the Pharisees and religious leaders grow ever sharper. Mark my words, soon they will decide to make an example of him."

My brothers did not argue. Apparently they had reached the same conclusion, only none of us had ever admitted the truth aloud. My statement was met with a silence that was the rueful acceptance of a terrible truth.

After a moment, James lifted his head. "So what do we do about the merchant?"

I frowned and rubbed the back of my neck. "I will speak to him. It would not be right to disappoint him when he needs a gift for his wife, so I must tell him we will be unable to make the bed he ordered. If he is willing to accept an alternative, all will be well. And if he is not" — I shrugged — "then we have lost a client and we will have to repay his deposit."

I looked around the room and breathed in the scents of the cedar and sandalwood I had already purchased. "If you know anyone else who wants a cedar bed, stool, or worktable, tell them we can make whatever they need at a great price."

"Can we not save it?" Simeon asked. "Surely in the future we will need —"

"We have to eat," I answered. "And we cannot eat wood."

Chapter Twenty-Seven: Tasmin

Even with a child and an aging father to care for, life in Cana felt boring. I blamed my boredom on Thomas's absence and began to think of him not with affectionate longing but with growing irritation.

Aunt Dinah was overjoyed to discover I had returned. Though she was shocked to see a child in my arms, she embraced me with enthusiasm and proceeded to tell me that she was henceforth leaving my father's care in my hands.

"Your father became ill not long after you left," she said, frequently casting curious glances at the boy. "I think he missed you and Thomas, of course. But I have been exhausted, caring for him and seeing to my own family, as well."

"You no longer have to worry." I patted her arm. "I am home."

"And this" — she pointed to the boy — "is a surprise. Who is he?"

"He is a child I found by the side of the road."

"You cannot intend to keep him."

"Why not? No one else wanted him."

"But lots of families would love to have a boy to help in the —"

"*I* would love to have a strong boy, especially since Thomas is not likely to come home in time for the harvest. As much as I despise them, the groves are now my responsibility, as is the boy."

I did not tell Aunt Dinah about the boy's cloven tongue, his healing, or the other miracles I had witnessed during my journey. Since she would ask questions for which I had no answers, I thought it best to keep silent on such troubling topics.

I also thought it best not to mention the attack by the lestes or Thomas's blunt refusal to leave Yeshua. No sense in troubling her with matters that could neither be helped nor erased.

"Did you find Thomas?" she asked. "Is he well?"

"I found him near the sea, and yes, he is well. He is committed to following Yeshua . . . until Yeshua fades away, I suppose."

She drew her lips into a tight smile. "I have heard many things about that man, not all of them good. What is your impression of him?"

I lowered my lips to the top of the boy's head and idly breathed a kiss on his curls. My impression of Yeshua? How could I explain my conflicted feelings? "I do not understand him, Aunt. He speaks of farmers and kings and the kingdom of God . . . but I do not find him as fascinating as Thomas does."

"Is it true what they say? That he heals people?"

I nodded. "Apparently."

"And he raises the dead?"

I shook my head. "I don't know. Some say he raised a widow's son, but the child may have been sleeping and Yeshua woke him."

"Well. You are a bright girl, so if you aren't convinced he is our king, then I'm not convinced either." She stood and smoothed her tunic, then lifted a brow. "I shall leave you with your father and your boy, then. What is the child's name?"

I smiled. "Yagil."

"Did you give him that name?"

I laughed. "No. We asked him, and he told us."

"While you were asking, did you ask about his real parents?"

"As gently as I could . . . but he could not

answer."

When I presented the boy to my father, he blinked and his mouth fell open before he recovered. "You bought a slave?"

"He's not a slave, Abba. I found him by the side of the road."

Abba frowned and stroked his beard. "Is he circumcised?"

"Yes."

"So he is Jewish?"

"Yes."

His left brow rose a fraction. "I hoped my daughter would return with a husband, but instead she comes home with a boy?"

"He's a good boy."

Abba studied the boy's face, which had filled out considerably now that he could eat. "People will talk."

"I don't see why they would. Pharaoh's daughter adopted Moses when she found him among the reeds, so why can't I adopt the child I found by the road?"

"Harrumph."

The boy gave my father a shy smile, then looked up as Abba rummaged in a basket and brought up a handful of wooden blocks. "Here, child." Abba gave the blocks to the boy. "I give you Thomas's blocks."

When Yagil began to stack them, Abba sat back and smiled. "Soon we shall teach him

Torah," he said, gripping his knees. "And when he is old enough, we will teach him how to harvest the dates."

Our grove had been left to itself since Thomas left, yet palm trees did not require much tending except in autumn when the dates were harvested. Abba would not be able to participate in the harvest, so I would oversee the operation.

Caring for my father quickly became my full-time concern. Every morning I had to prepare his meal and strain his food, since he had difficulty swallowing. After he ate, I helped him dress. Both my father and I suffered a thousand humiliations when I had to help him to the privy — that would have been Thomas's job had he been home, but now the responsibility fell to me.

"I am sorry to be a burden," Abba said when I helped him into bed each night. "You should be caring for a husband and a child, not your father."

"I love you, Abba," I said. "I am honored to help you."

Days melted into weeks and weeks into months. Yagil, Abba, and I developed a routine that was not unpleasant, though I still missed Thomas and often felt lonely. Every day I took care of my father and Yagil. Every week I cleaned the house, then Yagil and I walked out to the grove to make sure no mishap had befallen the date palms. I accepted orders for baked goods. I did not agree to manage any wedding feasts, because I could not risk being away from home if Abba needed me. He called for me several times a day and often during the night, as he needed help getting out of bed to relieve himself.

One night Abba tripped over a clay pot Yagil had moved from its usual place. The false step sent my father tumbling into the corner of a bench. Awakened by the noise, I found Abba on the floor. Unable to lift him, I drew his head into my lap, wrapped my arms around his shoulders, and wept, drowning in a gulf of despair.

What was I going to do? If Thomas were home, he could help me get Abba back to bed and then go for the physician. But Thomas was gone and I couldn't leave my father, which meant he would remain on the floor until someone passed by the house and heard my cry. I had no way of determining the seriousness of Abba's head injury, and for all I knew he might be dying in my arms. What could I do to help him? Nothing. I could do nothing but think of Thomas and curse the day he met Yeshua.

Since returning home, I had managed to

shelve my emotions while fulfilling my duties. I had not allowed myself to dwell on my losses or revisit memories of seeing Thomas by the Sea of Galilee. The memories would be too painful, the emotions associated with them too raw.

That night, however, my anguish snapped the last threads of my self-control. On the floor, in the flickering light of an oil lamp, I found myself in a fitting place for tears, so I gave way and let them fall. I had earned this empty, joyless life, and the one person who might have lessened my burden had abandoned me. For as long as I could remember, my world had revolved around Abba and Thomas, and I was on the verge of losing them both.

After weeping until I felt empty, I leaned back against a chest and managed to enter a shallow doze. Wandering in the hazy world between wakefulness and dreaming, I walked from village to village, searching for Thomas amid hundreds of people, all of whom were as lost as I was. Yagil, who rode my hip, kept crying and tugging at my tunic.

"Tasmin?" My heart flooded with relief when I recognized the voice: Jude.

I blinked the sleep from my eyes and saw him kneeling in front of me. The sun had risen, flooding the house with light. My father's head was still in my lap and he was still breathing. Yagil was standing by my side, his thumb in his mouth and his face streaked with tears.

I gaped at my unexpected visitor. "Why are you here?"

The grim line of his mouth relaxed. "I came by the house and heard the boy crying. What has happened?"

"Abba fell and hit his head," I said, stirring to wake my sleeping legs. "I knew I could never pick him up, so I tried to make him comfortable . . ."

"Let me help." Jude examined the bump on my father's forehead, then slipped an arm around Abba's shoulders and sat him up. Together we carried him to his bed.

"I'll go for the physician. Where does he live?"

"Um . . ." Thoughts scrambled in my head. "Three houses down the road, the house with the yellow courtyard gate. His name is Nahum."

"I will return soon." He stepped toward the door, then hesitated. "Do you need anything? Are you all right? Is Yagil?"

I rested my hand on the boy's head. "We are well. While you get the doctor, I'll prepare something to break our fast. And, Jude?"

"Hmm?"

"You didn't answer me — why are you here?"

A familiar softness settled around his mouth, a sign that he was about to smile. "I came to check on the boy."

"Good. I really don't care why you've come, but I thank Adonai that you have."

He flashed me a grin, then left the house and hurried down the street.

Propped on his pillows, Abba narrowed his eyes at the bowl of gruel in my hand. "So tell me more about the young man in my house this morning. This Jude ben Joseph."

I moved the bowl closer to his mouth. "Jude was at the wedding. You gave me permission to go with him to Capernaum to find Thomas."

Abba took a grudging sip of the gruel, then made a face. "That is horrible."

"It's supposed to be good for you."

"Of course it is. Otherwise no one would eat it." He took another sip, then pushed the bowl away. "I am not hungry. Give it to Yagil. Surely he needs gruel more than I do."

"He won't eat it."

Abba laughed. "Smart boy, that one." He turned back to me. "So, you know Jude because he went with you to find Thomas?"

"That's right. Remember, both you and Aunt Dinah approved of it."

"We approved of a two-day trip, but you were gone a *month.*"

"Yes, Abba, but we were not alone. A woman joined us in Tiberias, and after that we traveled with many people."

"Did he behave like a righteous man?"

"He is a good man. You would have approved of his behavior."

"Yet he does not follow his brother."

I shook my head. "None of Yeshua's brothers follow him."

"That is significant." Abba lifted a warning finger. "When a man's family will not support what he does —"

"I know, Abba. I said the same thing to Thomas."

"Yet your brother did not come home."

"No." I set aside the bowl of gruel. "Are you sure you're feeling better? The doctor said the bump on your head could be serious."

"I am feeling as well as a man my age ought to feel — which is not so good. What is it Solomon said? 'The glory of young men is their strength, and the splendor of old men is gray hair.' That's all I have, Tasmin — and gray hair is good for nothing but making a man look old."

"Abba, you shouldn't —"

"I should, daughter, and some things I should have done long ago. You and your brother became close after your mother died and I approved, since you had been through so much together. But now you are of an age when you ought to take a husband and bear children, yet you keep longing for Thomas."

"Not so much now. I have come to see that he is not willing to come home. Not yet, at least." I lifted my chin. "And why shouldn't I miss him? He's my brother. My best friend."

"It is time you found another friend. I am old, daughter, and growing older by the day. Soon I will go the way of my fathers, and you will be left with nothing but this house, the grove, and this child, who is not even yours."

"Thomas will return . . . eventually." I smiled with a confidence I did not feel. "This Yeshua will disappear, just like John the Immerser and the false prophets of our past. When that happens, Thomas will come home because he will realize he belongs in Cana."

Abba did not speak for a moment, then he shook his head. "I am afraid I will not live long enough to see my son again. So I must know what is in your heart. What do you think about this Jude ben Joseph? You say he is a righteous man. Could you marry him?"

Stunned by the question, I stammered as my heart did an odd flip. "I — I have not thought about it."

"Then think, daughter. Think."

I closed my eyes and leaned back in my chair as Abba's words danced in the air. Could I marry Jude? He was a good man, strong and protective, and as practical as Thomas, in his way. He was concerned about his business and wise about his work. He had been gentle with me and the boy, and courteous to Joanna and Susanna and Ziv. And even though he disagreed with Yeshua, he had not railed against his brother, had not cursed him or exploded in raging frustration. My heart warmed whenever I saw him. But while he was a good man, I still could not marry him. How to explain that to Abba?

"You are right, Abba — Jude is a righteous man."

My father crossed his hands atop his blanket. "So whom should I visit? His father is dead, no?"

"And his mother travels with Yeshua."

"Who then?"

"No one." I lifted my hands. "You asked if I could marry him, but I do not think Jude wants a wife. None of his brothers are married, probably because they are working hard at their business. So promise me you will say nothing to anyone."

Concern mingled with confusion in Abba's eyes as he struggled to sit up. The effort made him cough, a persistent barking sound that lasted for several minutes. He brought his hand up to cover his mouth, and when the coughing stopped, he wiped his hand on his tunic.

I felt a sudden chill when I saw that his hand left a blood-tinged spot on the fabric.

"I will not live forever, daughter," Abba said, speaking slowly. "As the dust returns to the ground it came from, so the spirit returns to God who gave it. But before I return to HaShem, I would like to know you will not be left alone."

"Abba . . . I don't want you to worry about me." I closed my eyes, wishing I could give my father the assurance he wanted. Still, if it would please him to believe I would marry Jude someday, why not tell him I would be willing? Better Jude than some man I did not know.

Better yet that Thomas would come home.

"I would be willing to marry Jude ben Joseph," I finally said. "If he is willing to take me as his bride. So put your mind at rest, Abba — I will not spend the rest of my life alone."

Abba smiled and patted my hand. "All will be well, daughter. You must have faith in the future."

"Faith?" I nearly choked on the word but was grateful for an opportunity to change the subject. "Yeshua often talks about faith. One day two blind men were behind him, crying out for mercy. He asked them if they believed he could heal them. When they said yes, he said, 'According to your faith, let it be done for you.'"

"And?" Abba whispered. "Did they see?"

"They did. But I had to wonder if they were truly blind or if Yeshua's men had asked them to pretend for the sake of the crowd."

Abba sighed, a frown puckering the skin between his eyes into fine wrinkles. "What has happened to you? I have never known you to be so . . . distrusting. Did he perform any healing you did not doubt?"

Yes. With only a touch of his hand, he healed my boy's cloven tongue and enabled him to speak. I also saw him cast a demon out of a young girl, a demon who knew things the girl could never have known.

But surely I had missed something, because such things simply could not happen.

"I would doubt any man who did what only HaShem could do." I kept my voice light, not wanting to enter in to a debate. "I would especially mistrust him if he stole a girl's twin brother away."

"Tasmin." Abba's voice held a note halfway between reproach and entreaty. "Faith is believing that HaShem is willing and able to do the impossible. When asked to sacrifice Isaac, Abraham had faith that Adonai would spare his son. Moses had faith that HaShem would lead His people out of Egypt. Noah had faith enough to build an ark to save his family from the flood. Faith has always been what Adonai asks of us."

"I believe in HaShem," I answered, smoothing the covers over my father's chest. "And, like Thomas, I believe HaShem will soon send a messiah king to deliver us from the Roman oppression. But I do not believe Yeshua is that king." I kissed the top of his head. "Sleep well, Abba. I will see you in the morning."

CHAPTER TWENTY-EIGHT: JUDE

The merchant did not want an ordinary cedar bed. Once I explained that the only brother capable of completing the detailed carving refused to come home, the merchant was sympathetic but adamant.

"Every family has at least one wayward sheep," he said, smiling, "but I have promised my wife an exceptional gift, and a *slightly* unusual bed will not suffice. And of course I would like my deposit returned, because I will have to go to Jerusalem or Tiberias to find the craftsman I need."

"I would be happy to return your deposit," I said, opening my empty hands, "but I have spent it on cedar and sandalwood. I would gladly make you something else, if you would consider that an acceptable exchange."

The merchant frowned and stroked his beard. "A pergola," he finally said. "Something to give us shade in the garden. My wife saw a pergola in Rome and has been asking for one ever since."

Though I had no idea what a pergola was, I bowed in relief. "If you can provide a sketch, we will construct the most beautiful pergola in Nazareth," I promised. "My brothers and I will be at your home on the first day of the week, ready to begin the work."

The merchant smiled. "All except for the wayward sheep?"

"Yes. All but him."

So my brothers and I began the work at the merchant's house, putting our minds and hands to the first job we had undertaken together in weeks. While I hammered beams into place and worked the bow-and-strap drill, I realized how deeply Yeshua's defection had affected us. As a team of five, we could have completed the pergola in six days. But with only four to do the work, the merchant's project would take at least seven. Not only were we lacking a skilled pair of hands, we missed our brother's company.

We had been quietly mourning the loss of our elder brother and mother without even realizing it. The house seemed empty without them. Ima's absence was palpable, a void not even my sisters could fill when they visited.

As for Yeshua, as irritated as we were by his stubborn refusal to take our advice, I had to admit that he had often served as the heart and soul of our family. When our father died, Yeshua stood in the synagogue and spoke of the impact a righteous father could have on a son. With tears in his eyes, he talked about the great faith and piety our father had always demonstrated, and how he loved our mother respectfully and deeply over the years. "When tested," Yeshua had said, sweeping his audience with a piercing glance, "Joseph listened to the voice of the Lord and obeyed. But he gave God more than obedience: he loved Adonai his God with all his heart, with all his soul, and with all his mind. He also loved his neighbor as himself."

I had other memories of Yeshua — how we used to giggle when his voice changed from the high tones of youth to the deeper voice of a man. How we stared at him in awe when the seedling hairs on his chin sprouted into the beginnings of a beard. How we heard Ima make gentle *tsk*ing sounds when a growth spurt rendered his tunic too short for modesty.

And after our father's death, we went to

Yeshua with our questions about HaShem, women, and righteous behavior. He would sit and listen as we struggled to string words together. He would nod, finger his growing beard, and provide an answer we had never considered.

He rejoiced with our sisters and their husbands when he held his newborn nieces in his rugged hands. Whenever Ima seemed lonely, he would walk with her in the cool of the day, listening as she shared whatever was heavy on her heart and mind.

Yes, we were irritated with Yeshua for leaving the family when there was important work to be done. I began to understand what Tasmin meant when she said her brother's absence had left a hole in her life.

Yeshua's departure created an abyss in our family.

When we returned home after a long day of work on the merchant's pergola, we would pull food from the baskets Damaris had been kind enough to leave at the house. We would rip off chunks of dry bread with our teeth, not caring about our manners because there were no women to remind us of the proper way to eat and drink. We would snack on figs and grapes, carve huge slabs of goat cheese, and eat nuts by the handful, gorging ourselves until we could barely roll into our beds.

And while we lay there, all four of us in the same stuffy bedchamber, I wondered what it would be like to have a woman to restore civility to the house, to implore us to bathe and eat properly, to trim our hair and check the looking brass to see whether or not we had food between our teeth.

A woman to sleep with . . . to hold when I felt lonely, to share my happiness and disappointment, to lie with in the hope of creating a family of our own.

What would it be like to have a wife?

We finished the merchant's pergola during the harvest season, just before Sukkot. We received his wife's gracious compliments, then went home, grateful to have satisfied a debt and done a good job. Now that the work was done, we looked forward to the Feast of Tabernacles, one of the most festive occasions of the year. Soon we would begin our pilgrimage to Jerusalem, where with thousands of other visitors we would build makeshift structures and remember the days when our desert-dwelling forefathers lived in temporary shelters.

That night, just after we crawled into our unadorned bachelor beds, I spoke into the darkness. "Which of you has given thought to taking a wife?"

James snorted. "Are you thinking about it?"

"Perhaps."

Joses cleared his throat. "I was waiting on Yeshua. He should take a wife first, then I might think about it. But since he seemed in no hurry to marry —"

"Yeshua will never marry. Not now," James said, a note of finality in his voice. "He is on a path to destruction."

"Then it's up to you," Joses said. "You are the second-born."

James made a gurgling sound deep in his throat. "A bridegroom must have money for a dowry. And it would be nice to have a father who could negotiate those arrangements."

I knew what we were all thinking, though no one said it. Yeshua could have made those arrangements for us, but he was gone.

"Since we have no father," Simeon said, his voice heavy with resignation, "you should speak for all of us, James. Because I think Jude has found himself a bride."

"Truly?" A note of envy filled Joses's voice. "You have someone in mind?"

I folded my hands across my chest as Tasmin's image drifted across the back of my eyelids. She had been much in my thoughts of late — many times, as we worked at the merchant's house, I had imagined I was building a pergola for her, a place where she could sit in the shade and relax with her father and Yagil. Perhaps even with me.

"I might," I said, smiling at the image in my mind.

With a little encouragement, I would have confessed Tasmin's name to my brothers, but at that moment a sound startled us. My nerves tensed as I sat up and Joses lit the lamp. James threw off his blanket and stood, ready to investigate.

"The door," I said. "Someone's in the house."

The tension in the air evaporated when Yeshua's figure filled the doorway, his face shadowed by the flickering lamplight.

"Yeshua?" Simeon gaped at him. "What are you doing here?"

"Can a man not visit his brothers?" Yeshua came into the room, sighed, and dropped the leather pack he carried. While removing his cloak, he sniffed the air and frowned. "Brothers, how long has it been since you washed?"

James's smile deepened into laughter. "You should talk. You smell of weeds and sand and donkey."

Yeshua chuckled, then sank to his bed, which had not been occupied in months.

"Where's Ima?" I asked. "Did she not arrive with you?"

"She and the other women are staying with Damaris," Yeshua said. "Our mother did not want them to be alone in an unfamiliar town."

I understood Ima's reasoning, but it did not seem right for all of us to be here without her.

"So why have you come home?" James lifted a brow. "Are you here to stay?"

Hope lifted my spirits. "You've come to do the carving for us?"

Yeshua shook his head. "We are only passing through. The other men have gone on to Jerusalem, but I wanted to see you — all of you."

Swallowing the hurt that had risen in my throat, I looked at Joses, whose face did not make me want to scream in frustration.

"Where are you going next?" Simeon rolled onto his side. "Back up to Galilee? Perhaps to Tiberias for an audience with Antipas?"

Yeshua must have missed Simeon's sarcasm, because he shook his head. "The Feast of Tabernacles approaches, so I wanted to come home. Some in Judea are planning to take my life."

James caught my eye and lifted a brow —

so Yeshua knew he was in trouble. Why, then, did he continue down this perilous path?

"If you want to win people to your cause," Simeon went on, "you should go to Judea, so your public can see the works you are doing. No one who wants to be well known does everything in secret. If you are doing these things, show yourself to the world! Why remain hidden in Galilee? And why do you heal people and tell them to keep quiet?"

Yeshua leaned forward, his elbows on his knees, and gave Simeon a weary smile. "My time has not yet come, but your time is always at hand. The world cannot hate you, but it hates me because I testify that its works are evil. All of you go to the Feast. I'm not going, for my time hasn't yet fully come."

I looked at James again, then blew out a breath. "Well, go or stay, Yeshua, do what you will. We are leaving for Jerusalem on the morrow."

Yeshua smiled. "Then we should all get some sleep."

Joses blew out the lamp, and darkness flooded the room. A moment later I heard the sound of deep breaths from Yeshua's bed and knew he had succumbed to weariness.

One by one, my brothers began to snore. Anticipation, however, would not let me sleep . . . because I planned to pass through Cana on my way to the Holy City.

My steps quickened as we neared Cana, and my burst of energy did not go unnoticed by my brothers. "Look at Jude," James remarked, grinning as he jabbed me with his walking stick. "What could make his face flush at the thought of passing through Cana?"

"Perhaps it's the sweet water at the village well," Simeon jibed. "Or the thought of our friends, the newly married ones — what were their names?"

"I do not think Etan and Galya could evoke that sparkle in Jude's eye," Joses said. "So it must be the young woman."

I glared at the lot of them. "Tasmin," I said. "Her name is Tasmin, and I adjure you to treat her with respect. Better yet, take the donkey to the well and refill the water jars. I'll join you after I've spoken with her."

"Is this a quick visit," James asked, "or should we try to buy food?"

"Do as you will," I answered, lengthening my stride. "I will join you later."

I found Tasmin's house easily and called out a greeting at the courtyard gate. Soon Yagil appeared, his face splitting into a wide grin when he saw me.

"Hello, little man," I called. "How are you?"

"Fine." To my utter astonishment, he spoke as clearly as he had the day he met Yeshua. "Do you want to see Ima?"

So now he considered Tasmin his mother. Good.

"Listen to you." I stepped into the courtyard and knelt to look the lad in the eye. "You are talking so well!"

He gave me a shy grin, then jerked his thumb toward the house. "Ima is inside with Saba. Would you like to see them?"

"Please."

Yagil scampered into the house, and a moment later Tasmin came through the doorway, dark curls fluttering around her flushed face. "Jude!" She wiped her hands on the cloth draped over her shoulder, then gave me a smile. "I did not expect to see you — anyone — today."

"My brothers and I are going to Jerusalem for Sukkot," I said, the words coming out in a rush. "I thought — I hoped you might want to go with us. Yeshua will remain in Galilee, but his disciples have gone on to

345

Jerusalem. If you want to see Thomas, you might be able to find him —"

"Of course I will go, as long as I can bring Yagil. Abba cannot manage him alone." The color in her cheeks rose. "Is it a large traveling party?"

I nodded. "A family from Nazareth travels with us, and we will undoubtedly join others along the way. You can assure your father of your safety."

She pushed a strand of hair off her forehead and bit her lip. "I will have to get Aunt Dinah to look after my father. He is not well."

"Has he injured himself again?"

She looked away. "No, it is the old weakness. If he wants me to stay home, I will. But I think he would want me to visit Thomas. We have not heard from him, and Abba wants to see him."

"I will wait for you." I pointed to the town square. "I will go to my brothers while you prepare. When you are ready, come join us."

She gave me a quick nod. "Thank you for thinking of me. If Abba permits, Yagil and I will join you soon."

CHAPTER TWENTY-NINE: TASMIN

I pulled the linen towel from my shoulder and draped it over a chair, then smoothed my tunic and went into my father's bedchamber.

Abba was abed, his eyes closed, his hands folded across his chest. The muscles in his face had gone slack — and for a moment I feared he was gone. I gasped, then his eyelids fluttered and opened.

"Tasmin?"

"Yes." I forced a smile and knelt beside his bed. "I have come to ask your permission to go to Jerusalem for the festival. Jude and James have invited me to travel with their family, and I would like to go. Aunt Dinah has agreed to look after you."

A wry smile showed in the snowy thicket of his beard. "You want to see Thomas."

I nodded. "Jude says he is in Jerusalem with Yeshua's disciples."

"Will you try to find him?"

"Of course."

"Then . . . tell him I would like to bless him as Jacob blessed Joseph before he breathed his last."

I caught my father's wavering hand and held it. "I will tell him, Abba. I will bring him home. I swear —"

Abba lifted his free hand, cutting me off. "Do not swear, Tasmin. It is unseemly for a woman, and foolish when a matter is beyond your control. But HaShem knows my heart, and He knows I would like to see my only son before I die."

I tried to smile at him, but the corners of my mouth only wobbled precariously. "Then I will do my best, Abba. Before Adonai, I promise to do my best."

The journey to Jerusalem was like a dozen others I had taken with my father and brother, yet I had never traveled with such anticipation in my heart. We set out with little save the donkey, water jars, and baskets of food, and time passed quickly.

I had never really talked to Jude's brothers, so I enjoyed getting to know them. James, the second oldest, was a skilled storyteller, a man with heart. He entertained us on the journey with tales about five anonymous brothers and two sisters growing up in Nazareth.

"Of course, those stories are completely untrue," Jude assured me as he blushed. "James has a lively imagination."

Simeon, the brother closest to Jude in age, seemed a quiet, dreamy fellow with an eye for pretty girls. He spent a lot of time smiling at me, until Jude told him to watch the road lest he stumble into a wagon rut. Then he walked at the head of our group, where he seemed to admire the women in any approaching party. "Our Simeon," Jude whispered to James, "needs to be married. The sooner, the better."

Joses, the youngest of Joseph and Mary's children, loved to joke. Good-natured and observant, he spent most of his time marveling at the natural beauty along the road and was the first to point out situations the rest of us hadn't yet noticed — the cloud of dust signifying an approaching Roman wagon, the downed camel with the injured leg, the frantic man whose wife was about to give birth in a makeshift shelter. At Sukkot, like all the pilgrimage festivals, ordinary life took to the road and would not be put off.

Compared to the last time I traveled to Jerusalem, this journey seemed relatively uneventful. We walked with families whenever possible, and when we stopped to eat or draw water, we often overheard snatches of talk about Yeshua and the miracles he had performed in Galilee.

Fortunately, none of the men mentioned their missing brother, though Jude did tell me they left him in Nazareth. "For a moment, I thought Yeshua had come home to stay," Jude confessed, lowering his voice so the others would not overhear. "But he assured us he was only visiting. He knows the Temple authorities want him dead, and yet he persists in continuing his teaching." He shook his head. "I am sorry, Tasmin, because I know Thomas is caught up in Yeshua's foolishness. I wish it were not so."

"We cannot force other people to do our will," I replied, glancing back to check on Yagil, who rode on James's shoulders. "I suppose not even a king has that power."

"HaShem has," Jude remarked, staring at a distant point on the horizon. "But He bends us rather than forcing us to His will. Remember Jonah — he did not want to go to Nineveh. Though HaShem had the power and authority to pick him up and put him in that city, instead He invited a great fish to swallow the prophet. From inside the fish's belly, Jonah decided he wanted to go."

I laughed at Jude's sour expression. "I hope I am never that stubborn. How much easier it would have been to obey Adonai."

"Indeed," Jude murmured.

We passed through Aenon and Salim, the cities where John the Immerser had taught his disciples, following the Jordan southward. After several days, we finally reached Jericho, the last major city before Jerusalem. Only a little farther to go, through beautiful territory . . . if you liked palm trees.

Along the banks of the Jordan, palm trees grew wild in thick clusters. They were everywhere, their tall, graceful trunks arching gently toward the sky, their long branches falling from the crown like a starburst. Jude must have realized I had a connection with date palms, for he turned to smile at me. "I am sure you enjoy this landscape — palms as far as the eye can see."

I stifled a yawn. "Not particularly."

"I thought you would love palm trees. Surely you worked in the grove with your father —"

"Perhaps that's why I am weary of them. Why don't you tell me about your latest carpentry project?"

Jude would not be distracted. Noticing a towering palm to our right, he gazed up at the crown. "My father used to say that the palms were what HaShem meant when He promised us a land flowing with milk and honey. God was referring to the date palm, because the fruit is as sweet as honey."

"Could you stop talking about dates? I do not feel well."

He tossed me a look of concern. "Did you eat so many as a child that the thought of them now sickens you?"

"Something like that."

I lowered my head as my stomach clenched. I visited the grove only because I had to look after the trees if Yagil and I wanted to avoid starvation. The grove provided our livelihood, but I didn't have to like it.

I swallowed hard and lifted my head, trying desperately to think of something — anything — else.

"Thomas, that is mine!"

Thomas grinned at me, then bent his pudgy legs and crouched beside the irrigation channel where I had placed a perfect tamarisk leaf. The cupped leaf, shaped like a little boat, was sitting on a bit of sand, awaiting the moment when Ima would pour water into the channel. Then it would sail away, down the channel toward the date palms, and I would follow it to see where it landed . . .

But Thomas had spied my leaf, and his greedy little fingers were reaching for it. "Thomas!" I warned. "Don't take my leaf. Find one of your own."

"Why should I? I want this one."

"Get your own leaf."

"I will tell Abba that you're not sharing."

I glanced up at the mention of our father. I saw him by the well, where he had moved the big flat rock that served as a cover when we weren't drawing water. Ima stood beside him, holding the bucket and rope, preparing to flood the channels and water our thirsty trees.

"I wish you'd let me stay and help you," Abba told Ima. "In your condition —"

"Go on." Ima playfully pushed him away. "By the time you have finished paying the taxes, I'll be done here."

"So why don't you wait? You shouldn't be hauling water —"

"I've been hauling it for months, so I'll be fine. Besides" — she lifted the bucket — "it's not a large bucket. Little by little, I will get the trees watered."

Abba reached for her and kissed her, the bump at her mid-section like a rounded boulder between them. Abba put his hand on her belly, and Ima laughed. "Please,

353

HaShem," he said, lifting his gaze to heaven, "no twins this time. One baby will be enough."

When Ima smiled, Abba kissed her again, then walked away toward the mule. Ima watched him go and then looked down the canal to the spot where Thomas and I were playing. "Are you two all right?" she asked.

I looked at Thomas and made a face, my way of warning him that I'd tell Ima if he didn't leave my boat alone.

"We're fine," he yelled, grinning at me. He flattened himself on the ground, propping his chin on his hands. So he was going to watch with me. Good.

Pleased with my small victory, I stretched out on the dirt across from him, and together we waited for the water.

The flood did not disappoint. The water came slowly at first, creeping like a living thing over the sandy ground, but the more bucketfuls Ima emptied, the stronger the current grew. Finally it crested the bit of sand where my leaf rested, and my pretend boat rode the wave for several minutes, moving toward the intersecting channel.

Thomas and I jumped up and followed the leaf until Ima finished and the water had disappeared. I picked up my leaf and stroked it as though it were alive. "Good little leaf," I said, holding it close to my chest. "I will keep you and bring you along the next time we come to the grove."

"Come, children." Ima took my hand and Thomas's, placing herself between us. I was content to walk calmly by her side, while Thomas was determined to misbehave. He kept reaching across Ima, trying to snatch my leaf. But I closed my fingers and strained to keep it from his grasping hand.

"Behave, children. Thomas, stand still and walk straight ahead. Tasmin, whatever you have there, let it go. We don't need to bring back — Thomas!"

I did not turn until I heard Ima scream. Thomas, in all his lunging and twisting, had slipped out of Ima's grasp and fallen into the well.

"HaShem, help!" Ima ran to the well and dropped to her hands and knees, peering over the edge. "Thomas! Thanks be to Adonai, stay right where you are! Do not move!"

Bewildered and stunned, I stood frozen in one spot until Ima screamed my name. "Tasmin! Here." She fumbled with the rope, now piled in a heap by the edge of the well. "Take this" — she thrust the cut end toward me — "and tie it around that palm tree. Hurry! You must tie it tightly!"

I gulped, forcing down the sudden lurch of my stomach, and ran for the rope, took it, and sprinted to the tree. At five, I had never learned how to tie a rope, but many times I had watched Abba tie ropes to wagons, trunks, and mules. I wrapped the rope around the tree, then brought the end over and under and over . . .

When my work looked a bit like Abba's knot, I stepped away from the tree and nodded at Ima.

"Did you tie it tightly?"

I nodded again.

Mama smiled through her tears. "Good girl. I can't leave your brother because he's clinging to a brick and I'm afraid he will fall. So I must trust you to save him."

Ima took the bucket end of the rope and lowered it into the well. "Thomas, grab hold," she ordered, her voice echoing against the stone walls. "Don't look down, just take the rope."

Terror blew down the back of my neck as the sound of Thomas's agonized wail rose from the depths. "Ima? Is Thomas all right?"

Ima was barely listening because she had shifted to dangle her legs in the stone shaft. "Stop crying, Thomas, you will be fine. Just hold on to the rope. That's right. Hush, no crying. I am coming down for you."

By sheer force of will I forced my feet to move closer. After shedding her headscarf and sandals, Ima pressed her toes to the uneven bricks of the well. She grabbed the rope, tugged on it, and looked at me. "I'm going down to get your brother," she said, her eyes flashing with determination. "He's too afraid to move, but he didn't fall far. I'll send him up and come up after him, understand?"

"Yes," I said.

"Good." Ima took a deep breath, then gripped the rope and shifted her weight, appearing to balance herself between the rope, the wall at her back, and the stones beneath her bare feet. I saw her swing into the well and slide down, disappearing from my sight, yet her voice continued to call out encouragement, urging Thomas not to cry, not to let go, to remain calm . . .

I clapped my hands over my ears, unable to listen. I closed my eyes and sang, so loudly I could no longer hear my brother's cries or my mother's words . . .

Then Thomas was on the ground, flat on his belly, the front of his tunic marked with wet slime. He lowered his head and cried in relief.

I uncovered my ears and told him to be quiet, but he only cried louder. "Thomas," I yelled, "we have to be quiet for Ima!"

He stopped, wiped his nose with the back of his hand, and turned toward the mouth of the well. Together we crept toward the opening, but we heard nothing.

I looked around for the rope I had tied to the palm tree. Ima had to be at the other end . . .

But at some point between my brother's escape and the sudden silence, the rope — and our mother — had disappeared.

CHAPTER THIRTY:
TASMIN

The Holy City overflowed with pilgrims, just as we had known it would. Jews from all over the world filled the inns — families from Alexandria, Babylon, Perea, even Rome and Greece. Adding to the happy sense of confusion were the temporary shelters propped along the city walls and leaning against existing buildings and family homes. Everyone who wanted to participate in the festival would sleep in a shelter, no matter how rudimentary.

I laughed when I overheard a woman from Jerusalem complain about sleeping in her shelter on the street. On our journey, we slept beneath the open sky, so having *any* roof over my head felt luxurious. Too many mornings I had awakened with a dew-dampened face.

After spending our first night in Jerusalem in a simple shelter — Yagil and I bedded down with a gaggle of giggly sisters from

Tabor — we joined Jude and his brothers and went in search of a place to erect our shelter for the week. James had a friend who lived in Jerusalem, and he generously allowed us a space for our shelter in the narrow alley behind his house. Our shelter had two compartments — one space for Jude and his brothers, and a smaller one for Yagil and me.

After setting up our shelter, Jude and I took Yagil and walked to the Temple. With Yagil riding his shoulders, Jude snaked his way through the crowds while I took care to remain close behind him. His wide shoulders were easy to follow, and I lost my initial nervousness over the fear of our being separated. My only remaining concern was how to find Thomas in the throng of visitors. Where would Yeshua have sent his followers? And without him, what would they do in Jerusalem?

We had just passed through the Golden Gate and stepped into the outer court when I heard a familiar voice in the crowd. I whirled around, straining to place the source of the sound, then tugged hard on Jude's arm. "Over there," I said, pointing to a group of men beyond a line of Levites. "I think I heard Thomas!"

Jude gave me an incredulous look. "How

could you hear anything in this mob?"

"I know my brother's voice," I insisted. "Please, let's walk that way."

With difficulty we slipped through the gathering, then I gasped. Thomas stood in front of me, flanked by several of Yeshua's disciples. I recognized the sets of brothers — James and John, Peter and Andrew — as well as the fretful man called Judas.

"Thomas!"

He turned and blinked hard, then stepped forward, his arms open, and enveloped me in a hug. "Tasmin! What are you doing here?"

"Looking for you, of course." Remembering my manners, I gestured to Jude. "I traveled with Jude and his brothers. I thought — I hoped — we would find you here."

His forehead creased. "Is everything all right?"

I dropped my hand to his arm. "Can we speak in private? I can hardly think in this place."

When he nodded, I told Jude I'd return in a moment before following Thomas out of the Temple courtyard. Once on the street, he pulled me into an alcove between two Sukkot shelters. "What troubles you?"

"It's Abba." I forced a smile. "For months he pretended nothing was wrong, but now

361

he admits he is dying. I do not know how much time he has left. I would be surprised, however, if he is able to celebrate another Passover."

"Has he seen a physician?"

"The physician can do nothing but comfort him." I struggled to control the tears threatening to overflow my lashes. "What I am saying, Thomas, is this: Abba would like to give you his blessing before he dies. Will you come home with me?"

Thomas drew a deep breath and slowly released it. "I would love to see him, but I cannot desert Yeshua."

"Yeshua is not here. Jude said he chose to remain in Galilee."

"All the same — this is not a good time."

"What *would* be a good time?"

He shook his head. "We've been through this, Tasmin. You know what Yeshua says. In a disciple's life, someone will always be dying, someone will always need something —"

"And you will ignore them all." I knew I sounded harsh, but I no longer cared. "Very well, then. Ignore our father. If Abba dies without seeing you again, I will tell him not to worry — you will visit his grave when Yeshua has grown weary of playing messiah."

"Tasmin." Thomas caught my arm, then lowered his head. "Yeshua would say, 'Let the dead bury their own dead. But you go and proclaim the kingdom of God.' "

"The kingdom of — the kingdom —" I crossed my arms as anger beat a bitter rhythm in my heart. "You are playing a dangerous game, brother. It is not enough that you have forsaken me and Abba, you have forsaken common sense, as well. You know the Scriptures, so think! Have you ever read a Scripture about a prophet coming from Galilee? No prophet has ever come from our region, nor ever will!"

Thomas shook his head. "You are only parroting what the elders have said. But they have forgotten a prophet who *did* come from Galilee — Jonah. They only remember what they want to remember, and they do not want to remember anything that points to Yeshua as the promised Christ."

For that, I had no answer.

After Thomas refused to come home, I went back to Jude and Yagil. Jude did not ask about my discussion with Thomas — my face must have told him everything he needed to know.

Though we were in Jerusalem for "the season of our joy," a cocoon of anguish had wrapped itself around me. I had hoped this trip would be another opportunity to reunite our family, and once again my attempt had failed.

But the week of Sukkot was not over, and I was not ready to give up.

By the time we returned to our shelter, I had resolved to keep trying. We might encounter Yeshua's disciples at the Temple again. I might see Thomas again, and I would continue to urge him to come home. If I prayed, if I made him see how heartless he seemed, perhaps he would listen.

So we continued to attend the Sukkot services, singing with the others and waving our *lulavs* to the traditional prayers.

On the fourth day, halfway through the festival, Jude, Yagil, and I stood together as the Levites prepared to begin the morning service. The lively colors of green boughs and yellow citrons enlivened the assembly of men, women, and children. Mothers and fathers helped their little ones arrange the palm, willow, and myrtle branches. I breathed in the tangy scents of citrus and greenery and told myself that this might be the day I managed to break through Thomas's stubbornness.

Finally, a Levite stood to lead us in prayers.

"Barukh atah, Adonai Eloheinu, melekh ha'olam asher kid'shanu b'mitzvotav v'tzivanu al netilat lulav."

Blessed are You, Lord our God, King of the Universe, who has sanctified us with His commandments and has commanded us concerning the waving of the lulav.

"Barukh atah, Adonai Eloheinu, melekh ha'olam shehehiyanu v'kiyemanu v'higiyanu lazman hazeh."

Blessed are You, Lord our God, King of the Universe, who has granted us life, sustenance, and permitted us to reach this season.

After the prayers, we turned to the east, north, west, and south while shaking the lulav and saying, "Give thanks to the Lord, for He is good, for His lovingkindness endures forever."

I laughed softly as Yagil dropped his myrtle branch and Jude bent to pick it up. An abrupt thought skittered through my mind: Jude would be a good father for my boy.

We had lowered our lulavs and were preparing to move out to the courtyard when something caused a stir near the altar. Whispers rose and floated above the crowd:

"Is that the fellow?"

"The Galilean?"

"He is good."

"No, he leads the people astray."

When a man stood on a low step to address the crowd, the whispers faded and a Sabbath stillness reigned. Because so many people stood in front of me, I could see no more than the top of his head, but I recognized the voice immediately.

"My teaching is not from me," he began, and I gave Jude a glance of utter disbelief.

"I thought you said Yeshua stayed in Nazareth," I whispered. "Is that not your brother?"

Jude stretched to his full height and frowned. "He must have set out after we left, but I have no idea why."

"Perhaps he took Simeon's advice. He is certainly speaking to a larger crowd than he did in Galilee."

Jude's brows knitted together. "An audience of Torah teachers, Levites, and Pharisees? He could not have found a more hostile crowd."

We fell silent and waited to hear what he would say.

"My teaching is not from me," Yeshua repeated, "but from Him who sent me. If anyone wants to do His will, he will know whether my teaching comes from God or it is myself speaking. Whoever speaks from himself seeks his own glory; but he who seeks the glory of the One who sent him, he is true and there is no unrighteousness in him. Hasn't Moses given you the Torah? Yet none of you keeps it. And why are you trying to kill me?"

A collective gasp echoed through the crowd, and then someone called out, "You have a demon! Who is trying to kill you?"

Yeshua did not stop. "I did one good work, and all of you are amazed. Because Moses has given you circumcision — though it is not from Moses, but from the patriarchs — you circumcise a man on Shabbat. If a man receives circumcision on Shabbat so the Torah of Moses may not be broken, why are you angry that I healed a man's whole body on Shabbat? Do not judge by appearance, but judge righteously."

I looked at Jude. "He healed a man? Here?"

"I have heard nothing of it," Jude answered. "But I would not be surprised if he is up to his old tricks."

Whispers vibrated the air around us:

"Isn't this the person the religious leaders are trying to kill?"

"But look, he speaks openly and they're saying nothing to him. Can it be that the leaders know he is the Messiah?"

"How can he be the Messiah? We know

where this person is from. But the Messiah, whenever he may come, no one knows where he is from."

"I know one thing," Jude muttered. "The Messiah will not come from my family."

Without warning, Yeshua cried out, "You know both who I am and where I am from! I have not come on my own, but the One who sent me is true. You do not know Him, but I know Him because I am from Him and He sent me."

More murmurs rippled through the crowd, until Yeshua lifted his hand. "If anyone chooses to do God's will," he said, once the people had quieted, "he will find out whether my teaching comes from God or whether I speak on my own."

Jude nudged my arm, then inclined his head toward the entrances of the Temple. The Temple guards, intimidating in their white tunics with gold sword belts, had formed lines at the east and west and were moving through the crowd, gradually narrowing the distance between themselves and Yeshua.

My stomach tightened. Though I did not believe Jude's brother was the Messiah, I did not want to see him slaughtered in this holy place.

No one around us seemed to notice the

approaching guards. "When the Messiah comes, he won't perform more signs than this person has, will he?" a man near us asked. "Who else has made the lame walk and restored sight to a man blind since birth? Is this not what Isaiah prophesied?"

Yeshua lifted his hand again. "I am with you only a little while longer, and then I am going to the One who sent me. You will look for me but will not find me. Where I am, you cannot come."

With those words ringing in the air, Yeshua stepped off the stairs and threaded his way through the crowd, evading the guards and exiting the Temple. I stood on tiptoe, searching for Thomas or any of Yeshua's disciples, but apparently he had visited the service alone.

"Where is this person about to go that we cannot find him?" A man near us turned and looked at Jude. "He's not joining the Diaspora to teach the Greeks, is he?"

Jude shook his head. "I have no idea."

"And what did he mean by saying, 'You will look for me but will not find me'? He has the oddest way of talking . . ."

"So I have often thought." Jude offered the man a wan smile, then gestured toward the exit. "Shalom, my friend. We must be on our way."

■ ■ ■ ■

Despite my earnest prayers and frequent visits to the Temple, I did not see Thomas again. I did not know where he and the other disciples were staying, and no one seemed willing to divulge the information. Yet the city roiled with talk of Yeshua.

On the last day of the festival, Jude, James, Joses, Simeon, Yagil, and I went to the Temple for the final ceremony. To commemorate the drawing of water from the rock at Horeb during the exodus from Egypt, every morning of the Sukkot feast a priest carried a large golden ewer from the Temple to the spring of Siloam. He drew water from the spring and carried it back to the Temple as jubilant onlookers cheered. The priest stepped through the Water Gate and into the inner court, where Levites blew the ceremonial silver trumpets and other priests chanted the words of the prophet Isaiah: "With joy you will draw water from the wells of salvation."

For the first six days of the feast, the ewer-carrying priest circled the altar once, but on the final day he circled it seven times, then poured the water onto the altar, washing away the blood of the morning sacrifices.

The priests, all bearing willow branches, sang psalms of praise while sages juggled lighted torches and performed somersaults as an expression of their joy.

My father always said that anyone who had not experienced the final ceremony of Sukkot had never known true joy.

From Jude's broad shoulders Yagil watched, fascinated, as the trumpets blew, the priests sang, and sages somersaulted through an atmosphere bathed in golden lamplight. Laughter bubbled up from nearly every celebrant's throat, and I managed to set aside my disappointment in Thomas while I watched my little boy's eyes sparkle with happiness.

After the benediction, we turned to leave, but once again a lone voice halted us in mid-step. We turned in time to see Yeshua standing high on the stairs, in plain view of anyone who cared to look.

"If anyone is thirsty," Yeshua cried, addressing the crowd with a voice like restrained thunder, "let him come to me and drink. Whoever believes in me, as the Scripture says, 'out of his innermost being will flow rivers of living water.'"

I glanced at the altar, where the cleansing water still dripped onto the bloodstained steps below. What did Yeshua mean?

He did not explain, but disappeared into the crowd.

As we left the building, we overheard snatches of conversation.

"This man really is the prophet."

"This is the Messiah."

"The Messiah doesn't come from the Galilee, does he? Don't the Scriptures say the Messiah will come from the seed of David and from Bethlehem, David's town?"

I lowered my head and walked faster, yearning for the peace and quiet of the road home.

CHAPTER THIRTY-ONE:
TASMIN

With a heavy heart I bade farewell to Jude and his brothers, then went inside my father's house. Yagil slid out of my arms and ran to Aunt Dinah, happily allowing her to pull him onto her lap.

Aunt Dinah greeted me with a subdued smile. Sympathy filled her eyes as she gripped my hand. "Your father is failing," she murmured, her eyes probing my face. "Do not be alarmed when you see him. I fear he will not be with us much longer." She hesitated. "Did you see Thomas?"

I nodded.

"And?"

"He will not come."

When I walked into Abba's chamber, I saw at once why she had warned me. All signs of color had drained from Abba's face. His hands trembled as they rose to catch mine, and his dark eyes had gone cloudy. The figure on the bed was a mere remnant of the strong, robust man who had ruled my life and heart for so many years. Thomas and I should both be here to comfort him in death as he had comforted us in life, but now . . . he had only me.

"Abba." I sat by his bedside. "It is good to be home with you."

"Did . . . did you see your brother?"

"He is well. He is still with Yeshua."

Abba's eyes closed. "Is he content?"

"He says he is. You know Thomas — he is not thoughtless. He still believes Yeshua ben Joseph is the Messiah."

My father's chest rose and sank in a heavy sigh. "Then I understand. If I had found the Messiah . . . I would not forsake him, either."

"Wouldn't you?" My voice broke as I floundered in a maelstrom of emotion. "Abba, you must forgive me."

His eyes opened. "Forgive you? For what?"

A sob rose in my throat, blocking my voice. I brought my hand to my mouth, then let the words I had buried burst to the surface. "For Ima. Thomas and I — we didn't mean to, but we killed her."

Abba's eyelids fluttered as his hands trembled on the blanket. "No, child —"

"Yes. Thomas was roughhousing and fell into the well. Ima told me to tie the rope and I tried, but I didn't tie a good knot. So the rope slipped and she fell, and it was my fault. Thomas and I . . . everything is our fault. I'm so sorry."

Abba struggled to lift his head, then grasped my hand. "You were only children."

"But we caused it. And over the years I realized how much we took away from you and how we could never make up for your losses."

"Daughter, I will hear . . . no more of this. Adonai gave and Adonai has taken away, blessed be the Name of the Lord. So dry your tears and . . . be a good girl."

His eyes closed and his hands stilled. I stared at him, my heart breaking. Did he understand what I told him? Could he ever forgive me? "Abba, there is one more thing."

He drew a breath to speak but began to cough, a fit that left him exhausted and the blanket flecked with blood. I thought he would slip into sleep, but stubbornly he kept his eyes fixed on my face.

I forced a smile. "When you mentioned Jude ben Joseph to me, I had no intention of marrying anyone. But now — I think I love him. Nothing may come from these feelings, but he is the only man who has ever stirred my heart."

Abba sighed as his eyelids drew down like

curtains, and his lips curved in a weak smile.

The next morning, as Aunt Dinah and I washed Abba's body and prepared it for burial, tears streamed over my cheeks — tears of frustration, sorrow, and regret that Jude's brother had come between me and Thomas, between Thomas and our father.

We buried him at midday — Aunt Dinah and I, Abba's two brothers, and several neighbors, who agreed to carry the coffin to the cemetery outside the city. Standing on the dry sand beneath a cloud-heavy sky, I couldn't help wondering what Thomas was doing at that moment. Was he listening to Yeshua spin another ambiguous proverb, or was he wishing he had come home?

I would write a letter about Abba and send it with a traveler, yet I would have no way of knowing if Thomas received it unless he wrote me in return.

I looked southward. What was Jude doing? Was he eating with his sister's family or building something with his brothers? Was he thinking of me? I had considered hiring a boy to carry news of Abba's death to Jude, but decided such an act might be considered presumptuous. What if he felt nothing stronger than friendship for me? Abba would have told me that friendship would ripen to love, but what if Jude dreamed of a girl from his own town? Even now, Pheodora or Damaris might be arranging a betrothal between him and one of their friends, so who was I to intrude?

Then, a few weeks after burying my father, a thought occurred to me — one that had been pushed aside during the days of grief. I had spent my entire life believing I should never marry because I needed to atone for my mother's death and remain with my father. Now that Abba was gone, I was free — not from the guilt but from the obligation.

That realization unloosed a horde of pent-up longings that had been pushing at the boundaries of my consciousness. Ever since returning from my month-long journey, I had refused to indulge in thoughts of Jude, but he had persistently appeared in my dreams. In the irresponsible freedom of sleep, I had walked and talked with him, heard his laughter, and stared into the depths of his dark eyes. In sleep, memories of my day had mingled with explorations of Jude — by the sea, on the road, even in the date palm grove. I had held his hands, examined the calluses on his palms, run my fingertips over the hairs on his arm. I had lain on the grassy hillside where we caught up to Yeshua and looked up into Jude's face as he kissed me.

In the weeks following Abba's death, thoughts of Jude flooded my mind nearly every hour of the day. I saw his face when I looked at Yagil, I heard his voice through the shutters when people passed on the street, and I looked for him every morning when I went to the well. He had come to Cana before, so it was not unreasonable to think he might come again . . .

But he did not. I told myself he had forgotten me. When Yagil asked about him, I said Jude was busy working. If he and his brothers were not building the merchant's fancy bed, they were undoubtedly searching for other work, scrambling to provide for themselves while their eldest brother and mother traveled around Judea.

At night, I lay in my narrow bed and stared into the darkness, begging Adonai for some assurance of my future. I had always assumed that Thomas and I would live together as brother and sister, but that appeared more unlikely with every passing day. Perhaps that was why I refused to release Yagil, because somehow I knew I would soon be alone.

The boy gave me a reason to get out of bed every morning. But Yagil, as sweet as he was, did not quench the burning desire that had begun to glow in my heart. At night, when I removed my outer garment and stood before the looking brass, I ran my fingertips over my chest, my belly, and the curve of my hip. Why did HaShem give me a woman's body, if not to join with a man? If Adonai wanted me to spend my life with Thomas, He could have fashioned two boys in our mother's womb . . .

I thought of Etan and Galya, and of her happiness after their first night together. *"But didn't Adonai make Eve for Adam? And didn't He create a female for every beast on earth?"* Galya told me I didn't know what I was missing, and finally I believed her.

If Jude did not want me, who else would want a woman far past her prime? I suspected I had become an object of pity to many in Cana. I was the unmarried virgin, the orphan, the woman whose closest kin had deserted her. Strangers looked at Yagil and wondered how I had come to have a child. Had I given birth to him in secret and later summoned the courage to bring him home?

No matter what the rumors, one thing was clear — at twenty-three, I would be considered undesirable. No father would want me to marry his son when unanswered questions swarmed around me like flies around manure. No older man would want me for a wife when unblemished young virgins were as abundant as figs.

So unless HaShem worked a miracle and brought Jude back into my life, I would remain alone . . . with only a little boy and a house filled with regrets.

In Tevet, the ninth month without Thomas, the days grew short and the air chilled, signaling time for the date harvest. Though Abba would not have been happy to know that Thomas remained away from home, he would have been pleased to see that our palms were heavy with fruit.

I hired five young men to help in the harvest. Since the job usually fell to my brother, I had to show the hired men how to remove the fruit from a date palm.

The thought of climbing one of the date palms made a sludge of nausea churn in my stomach, but at least I would only have to do it once. If these hired men were any good, they could handle all the harvesting and I would oversee the drying fruit and the marketplace sales.

To demonstrate, I propped a ladder next to a tall palm, then climbed up with mesh netting and a short saw. I wrapped the first long stalk with the netting, secured it with string, and used the saw to cut the stalk from the tree. "You might be tempted to cut the stalk and let it fall," I called down to them. "But the fruit will be damaged if you do. You must protect the fruit at all costs." Then, with the heavy stalk tucked beneath my arm, I climbed down the ladder and set the stalk on a long wooden tray.

"And that is how it's done," I explained, hoping my hired workers were as agile as they were strong. "After we cut the stalks, we remove the dark purple fruit. If a fruit has not darkened, leave it to ripen on the stalk. We'll harvest it later."

We finished the harvest in a month, and I paid the workers from the money I earned selling dates at the marketplace. The fresh fruit would not last long, so most women bought the dates and dried them to last through the winter. I dried a generous amount myself and would sell them throughout the year or use them for baking.

As the winds began to bite and the stubble in the harvested fields went gray, we heard reports from Jerusalem: Yeshua and his disciples had been at the Temple during Hanukkah, the Feast of Dedication. As usual, Yeshua had stirred up trouble.

"I was there," the butcher told us when

he reported on his trip from the town square. "Yeshua was with his followers in Solomon's Colonnade when the authorities swarmed around him. They asked him, 'How long will you hold us in suspense? If you are the Messiah, tell us outright!' "

We waited to hear the answer while the butcher smiled, enjoying his role a little too much.

"Well?" Aunt Dinah asked. "Are you going to tell us or not?"

The butcher's brows slanted in annoyance. "The Nazarene said, 'I told you, but you don't believe! The works I do in my Father's name testify concerning me. But you don't believe, because you are not my sheep. My sheep hear my voice. I know them, and they follow me. I give them eternal life! They will never perish, and no one will snatch them out of my hand. My Father, who has given them to me, is greater than all. And no one is able to snatch them out of the Father's hand. I and the Father are one.' "

A collective shudder ran through the group, and Dinah gasped. "He was speaking of HaShem?"

The butcher lowered his chin in a grim nod. "And again, the leaders picked up stones to kill him. But Yeshua said, 'I've

382

shown you many good works from the Father. For which of these are you going to stone me?' "

"How did they answer?" a man asked. "How could they think of stoning the man who has healed so many?"

The butcher held up his hand. "They weren't stoning him for a good work, but for blasphemy. They said, 'Though you are a man, you make yourself God!' "

"That's true," another man said, crossing his arms. "That's what he meant."

"The Nazarene went on," the butcher continued, "and said, 'If I don't do the works of my Father, don't believe me! But if I do, even if you don't trust me, trust the deeds. Then you may come to know and continue to understand that the Father is in me, and I am in the Father.' "

Silence sifted down like falling leaves, until I found my tongue again. "What happened next?" I asked. "What happened to his disciples?"

The butcher, who knew Thomas, looked at me with a sad smile. "Yeshua ben Joseph walked away, and they did not stop him. As to his disciples" — he shrugged — "they have a talent for disappearing into the crowd. I looked around for them, and they had all vanished."

"Good," I whispered in Aunt Dinah's ear. Though Thomas might insist on traveling with a man who constantly attracted trouble, at least he had learned how to escape.

CHAPTER THIRTY-TWO:
TASMIN

The year passed, a stream of months that blended into a continuous blur with only the festivals to mark them. As the second Passover without Thomas approached, I struggled with nostalgic memories of the previous Passover, which I'd spent with Jude in Ephraim, but then a message from Nazareth brought considerable comfort.

We would like you and Yagil to join our family for Pesach, Jude wrote. *We will be spending the pilgrimage festivals at home this year, for Yeshua is certain to stir up trouble in the Holy City.*

That invitation opened the door for other visits, as I became better acquainted with Jude's brothers as well as his sisters and their families. Nothing was said about marriage — at least not in my presence — yet I sensed they were all waiting for Yeshua to return to his right mind. "Next year," Damaris had said during the Passover meal, "we will go to Jerusalem again. Surely by then Ima and Yeshua will be with us."

I hoped she was right. I felt . . . I think we all felt that our lives had been temporarily suspended while we waited for Yeshua to decide what he would do with his followers. Was he planning to mount an offensive against Rome, or would he quietly retreat to Galilee? I know his siblings felt pressure from those who were critical of Yeshua.

"Last week," Pheodora remarked one night at dinner, "I was minding my own business at the market when a man came over and asked me why my brother hated the Temple. I said my brother did not hate the Temple, and the man replied by saying the news was all over Jerusalem — Yeshua proclaimed that the Temple would be torn down, not leaving even one stone atop another."

James's mouth took on an unpleasant twist. "Surely the man heard a false rumor."

Pheodora shook her head. "He insisted it was true. I have been afraid to go to the market ever since. Everyone in Nazareth already hates us, but now they will hate us more."

"You should come to Cana," I ventured, offering a shy smile. "Most people in Cana are not sure what to make of Yeshua, but they do not hate him."

"This is our home," Jude said. "For better or worse, Nazareth is the best place for us. For now, at least."

I lowered my head as a blush burned my cheek. I know he meant nothing by it, but Jude had just rejected my offer in a way that felt like he was rejecting *me.* I told myself I was being overly sensitive. I was imagining things, allowing my head to fill with presumptions that ought not to be there.

But when I looked up again, I caught Damaris's gaze — and saw pity in her eyes. Realizing that she had witnessed and understood my disappointment, I stood and hastily excused myself.

"Where are you going?" Jude asked, surprise on his face. "You and Yagil have barely just arrived —"

"We must go home," I said, turning away so he would not see the tears brimming in my eyes. I would have said more, but I could not trust my voice.

"I will see you to the door." Damaris rose from her seat. She helped me find the bag with Yagil's toys, then walked us down the stairs to the street. "Do not be upset," she said, folding her arms as she surveyed the nearly empty road. "Sometimes men can be as thickheaded as planks."

I swallowed a sob and nodded. Her smile gentled as she squeezed my arm. "I will have a word with my brother."

"No, please. I don't want him to feel pressured —"

"Leave it to me, Tasmin. I know men, and I know my brothers especially well. Jude will never know we had this conversation."

That night, as I tucked Yagil into his bed, I could not stop thinking about Yeshua and his family. James and the others could not imagine their brother as a prophet because they were too familiar with him. But Jude and I had been in the crowd on the hillside. We had seen him work miracles, and we had heard firsthand testimony from people who had been healed by Yeshua's command.

I went to my room, crawled into my bed, and closed my eyes. Memories played in my head: Yeshua by the sea of Galilee, touching Yagil's mouth and healing him; Yeshua smiling at Rahel after the demons left her little body; the joyous mother and her resurrected son outside Nain.

At the wedding in Cana, I had been convinced Yeshua performed some kind of elaborate trick, but I could not deny what I saw when he touched Yagil. I waited for the boy's healing to prove false or temporary.

Instead, the boy remained strong, healthy, and showed no sign of relapse. His tongue, which I checked every night before putting him to bed, remained whole. His teeth continued to hold to their proper place.

I remembered what Yeshua said at the Temple at the Feast of Dedication: *"If I don't do the works of my Father, don't believe me! But if I do, even if you don't trust me, trust the deeds."*

One of his deeds lived in my house, and I could no longer doubt Yeshua's power.

Memories of our journey to find Yeshua crowded my head, pushing and jostling and competing for space. Who could heal Yagil but a prophet? Who else could cast a demon out of Ziv's granddaughter and restore a lame man's legs? Who else could raise a widow's dead son from his coffin?

And what did the Torah say? *I will raise up a prophet like you for them from among their brothers. I will put My words in his mouth, and he will speak to them all that I command him. Now whoever does not listen to My words that this prophet speaks in My Name, I Myself will call him to account . . . When a prophet speaks in Adonai's Name and the word does not happen or come true, that is a word that Adonai has not spoken . . .*

Yeshua spoke in Adonai's name, and

although he had said things that had not yet come true, he had spoken other things that did come to pass. He had told fishermen to let down their nets, and when they brought them up, fish spilled from the edges. He had told dead children to rise and lame men to walk. If that was not the mark of a true prophet, what was?

Those thoughts brought others in their wake. In the beginning, did I doubt Yeshua because I resented him for taking Thomas away? If Thomas had not gone with Yeshua, would I have been so skeptical for so long? Probably not.

So yes, I could admit that Yeshua was a prophet. But I could not believe his claim to be ben-Elohim, the son of God.

CHAPTER THIRTY-THREE: JUDE

James, Simeon, and Joses joined me in washing up. Afterward we put on clean tunics and walked to Damaris's house for Shabbat dinner.

"What is the occasion?" Joses asked as we strode up the hill to her husband's fine house. "I can't remember the last time she invited us."

I shrugged. "Who can know what is on a woman's mind? All I know is she said we should all come."

"She has something on her mind," James said, a dark note in his voice. "She isn't the nostalgic type."

"Then I guess we will soon know what it is," I answered. We climbed the steps to her front door and waited until she opened it, her face flushed with exertion. "You came!"

Joses grinned at her. "When have we ever turned down a good dinner?"

"Come in," Damaris said, pushing the

door open. "Girls, make room for your uncles."

I smiled as Damaris's five daughters — six, counting the baby on the floor — lined up to greet us. Amarisa, Bettina, Jemina, Jerusha, Lilah, and Zarah looked just like their mother and seemed to have inherited her calm disposition.

James, Simeon, Joses, and I went down the line, kissing each girl on the top of her head. Then the eldest, Amarisa, took James by the hand and drew him into the common room, where she showed him a flower chain she had made.

"Jude, I would speak with you a moment."

I turned to Damaris, hearing a note of authority in her voice. "Have I done something wrong?"

She rolled her eyes. "Nothing every other man hasn't done at one time or another."

Confused, I followed her to the cooking area at the back of the house. "I don't understand."

She turned and propped one hand on her hip. "You need to stop putting off what needs to be done. Can't you see she's suffering?"

I turned toward the girls gathered around my brothers. "Who? Is one of the girls — ?"

"Not them. You have been visiting Tasmin

for, what, a year now? She has been visiting us. You play with the child, you escort her to Cana and come back with a smile on your face — you love her."

I snatched a sharp breath, stunned by her declaration. "What?"

"You are not some young boy who needs to be betrothed before love happens. You are a man, and you love Tasmin. So get the rabbi and declare your intention to marry the woman. You are not being fair to her. You act as if you are betrothed, yet you are not. Everyone in Cana must wonder what you are up to, so do the right thing and make the betrothal public. If you care for her at all — and I know you do — you must do the honorable thing and marry her. The sooner, the better."

For a moment I could only blink in astonished silence, then I shook my head. "How can I ask Tasmin to marry me when Yeshua is wandering around the country like a revolutionary? His life — even our lives — are uncertain. What if the Romans sweep through Galilee and arrest him and his followers? What if they arrest us?"

Damaris sputtered. "Why would they arrest us? We do not support him."

"When have the Romans ever weighed the fine details of a situation? All they need is the word of two witnesses — even false witnesses — and we could be put to death. Especially if people hear what Yeshua said when James, Simeon, Joses, and I last went to visit him."

She narrowed her eyes. "What did he say?"

I blew out a breath. I had not mentioned our visit to either of my sisters because we were unable to speak to Yeshua. But still, word of his response reached us.

"We found Ima with the women," I said. "She is well, and she tried to take us to Yeshua, but we could not reach him due to the crowds. One of the disciples managed to get through and told him we were standing outside the house, waiting to see him. Apparently he had been talking about fertile soils and how those who hear the word of God bear fruit. And when he heard we were outside, he said, " 'My mother and my brothers are those who are hearing the word of God and doing it.' "

Damaris smiled. "That's not what I expected him to say."

"Nor I," I admitted. "At first, I was pleased he hadn't turned against us because we haven't been supportive, but then I realized his statement would be enough to make people think we are complicit in his plans."

"What plans?"

I shrugged. "Who knows? He talks about the kingdom of God, but he has not raised an army or trained soldiers. I don't know what he is planning, but I have not forgotten that would-be messiahs tend to die in the midst of their uprisings. So do those who follow them."

Damaris pressed her lips together and crossed her arms. "I understand that you may not want to marry while the situation with Yeshua is still uncertain. But you cannot leave Tasmin without assurance. She is alone and vulnerable, and you do her a disservice by not speaking to her."

"And what should I say?"

"You must speak to the rabbi first. Have him draw up a betrothal contract. Bathe and put on your finest tunic, then go to Cana and present the contract to her. Take a gift — a good one. And promise that as soon as you can, you will go get her and make her your wife."

I stared at her, considering her words, and then smiled. "You always were the bossy sister."

"I'm older than you," she replied, her eyes twinkling. "I am expected to be bossy."

"If I do this, will you help with the wedding feast?"

"For you, brother, I would do anything. Now go to Cana with the rabbi before some other man claims Tasmin first."

On the short walk home, I allowed Simeon and Joses to walk ahead so I could talk to James. "So," I said, lowering my voice, "I discovered why Damaris invited us. She presented me with a stern rebuke."

Even in the darkness, I saw James lift a brow. "Let me guess — she wants you to marry Tasmin."

"You knew?"

He smiled and shrugged. "She is right, you know. You are two grown people, you spend a lot of time together, and yet you are not betrothed? People are talking."

"But how can I marry anyone when Yeshua is attracting so much attention? I worry about him, and I do not want to put her in the middle of what might turn into a tragic situation."

"Did you make this objection to Damaris?"

"Of course. She said she understood, but I should at least arrange the betrothal."

"Damaris has always been wise in the way of women."

I hesitated. "There is another reason I have waited."

"Your poverty?"

I laughed. "Perhaps there are three reasons."

"Then what?"

"Thomas." I lifted my suddenly warm face to the coolness of the night air. "When I first met her, all she could talk about was Thomas. Thomas does this, Thomas says that. I have always admired Tasmin —"

"Of course. She is beautiful."

"Yes, but more than that. She is thoughtful. She is kind. Yet I kept asking myself how I would feel married to a woman who constantly talks about another man."

James glanced at me, then returned his gaze to the road. "You met her a long time ago, right after Thomas left with Yeshua. So ask yourself — does she still talk about her brother?"

I pressed my lips together. "Not as much."

"You see? Things change. No one remains the same."

I stared at the row of buildings ahead, our house jammed in between others. Where would I build a home for Tasmin? How would I build it? My brothers and I continued to work — we had built four pergolas since finishing the merchant's — but we were far from wealthy. I would need time to save enough to build and furnish a home for a wife.

"I cannot marry for months," I said. "Not only because of Yeshua but because I have no house. I cannot even build onto our home, for there is not enough space."

James nodded. "HaShem will provide, and when the time is right, you will know it. But our sister is wise — if you love this woman, you should declare yourself."

I smiled. "That, big brother, will be the easy part."

Two weeks later, with the *ketubah* in hand, the rabbi and I made the journey to Cana. "Couldn't you have found a woman close by?" the rabbi groused as we covered the furlongs. "Nazareth has virtuous women, too. Even a few who are beautiful."

"Tasmin lives in Cana," I answered, "and I cannot see myself with any other."

"Humph." The rabbi wiped sweat from his brow and glanced at the sun overhead. "I hope she has refreshments. Is she a good cook?"

I nodded. "She bakes for weddings."

"Ah, well then. Perhaps you will put on a few pounds. Nothing like a stout frame to show that HaShem has blessed you."

Finally we entered the city, attracting attention from everyone we met. While I was now a familiar face, the rabbi was a stranger. More than one villager guessed at our purpose. One young girl ran up to me, grinned, and asked if she should fetch Tasmin's aunt Dinah.

"Please do," I said, returning her smile. "Have her meet us at the house."

A few moments later, we stood at Tasmin's courtyard gate. Yagil heard our greeting and thrust his head through the doorway. "You want to see Ima?"

The rabbi frowned. "She has a child?"

"She found him by the side of the road," I said. "As Mordecai took in Hadassah, Tasmin has taken in Yagil."

"Then you have found a rare woman indeed."

Tasmin appeared a moment later, and her face went the color of a rose when she saw us. "Come in," she said, opening the gate. "I did not expect visitors today."

"I would have sent a message," I said, not moving from the street, "but it was easier to come myself." I bowed slightly and gestured to the rabbi. "This is Amon ben Eshkol, our rabbi."

Tasmin dipped her head. "I am honored."

I cleared my throat. "Tasmin," I began, aware that the neighbors were watching from their open doors and courtyards, "let me speak clearly and directly. We have come today bearing a ketubah, a contract of marriage between you and me. It has already been signed by the rabbi and another witness. In this document I have sworn to care for you, provide you with food and clothing, and not to require you to leave Israel unless you consent. The *mohar*, the bride price of two hundred silver dinars, will be paid to you if I divorce you or die . . . but I do not plan on divorcing you, and I hope you outlive me by many years. Ordinarily your father would agree to this contract, but since he is gone, I was hoping to speak to your aunt Dinah or perhaps one of your uncles."

At that moment, Dinah came rushing up the street, out of breath and trailed by half a dozen young girls. "Wait!" she called, waving. "Wait for me."

She stopped by my side and clasped her hands over her heaving bosom as I repeated myself. When I had finished, the rabbi lifted the rolled ketubah, presenting proof of my intentions.

Dinah looked at her niece, her eyes glowing. "Well, Tasmin? Are you going to let them in?"

Tasmin's eyes sought mine, and for a heartrending instant I thought she would say no. Then she smiled, somehow her hands found mine, and I knew my heart would find a home in hers.

"Come in, come in," Dinah said, pushing past me through the open gate. "We will make lemon water and serve date cakes. We have to celebrate. Tasmin, it is time you were a married woman! We have much to plan, much to think about."

Tasmin bent her head toward me, her words for my ears alone: "I prayed you would come," she whispered, her voice fragile and trembling. "And now you have. God is good."

CHAPTER THIRTY-FOUR: TASMIN

After the house emptied of friends, family, and neighbors, the rabbi discreetly took Yagil outside, so that Jude and I could have a few moments alone.

My husband-to-be took my hands, and his eyes caught and held mine. "I will build a home for you," he promised, "and then I will come for you. It may not be within the year, however. I would rather marry you when Yeshua is not teasing Galilee with the idea of revolt against Rome. I do not want controversy to spoil our wedding."

"I don't think anything can spoil what HaShem has brought about," I replied, my heart warming to the gentle look of love in his eyes. "And about your brother — I have been pondering his ideas. I look at Yagil, I know Yeshua healed him, but I also know that he is the son of Joseph, not the son of God. So I asked myself: if he is not our messiah and king, then what is he? And I think

I have found an answer."

Jude lifted a brow. "My brothers and I would certainly like to know it."

I led him to a dining couch and gestured for him to sit with me. "I believe," I said, gripping his hands more tightly, "that your brother may be a genuine prophet. Prophets have power. Didn't Elijah work miracles? Didn't Moses speak for HaShem? And didn't Moses tell us Adonai would send us a prophet?"

" 'A prophet from your midst, from your brothers, like me, will raise for you the Lord your God. To him you must listen,' " Jude recited.

"See? Doesn't Yeshua call himself a prophet?"

Jude nodded slowly. "No one is a prophet in his own village." He pulled free of my hands and leaned forward, his forehead crinkling. "Our people have been waiting for the prophet for hundreds of years. My father was always telling us that when the assembly resolved that Simon the Maccabee would be their leader and high priest, they said he would fill that role until a trustworthy prophet would arise."

"They may have been speaking of Yeshua." I shivered as gooseflesh covered my arms. "After a year of hearing about Yeshua, after seeing what he did for Rahel and Yagil, I cannot say he is an ordinary man. I have tried to figure out how he performs miracles, but, like Pharaoh's magicians when they could not replicate Moses's wonders, I have to admit that Yeshua's healings involve the finger of God. Yet knowing what the Scriptures say about the promised king, I cannot say Yeshua is the messiah. But a prophet — one who points the people to God and who works miracles by HaShem's power — *that* I can believe. What do you think?"

Jude seemed preoccupied, as if he were sorting through memories and prophecies, then he looked at me and smiled. "You may be right. Let me discuss it with James."

I squeezed his arm, then smiled at a sudden thought — this arm was now mine to squeeze. The cheek was mine to kiss, the mind mine to explore, for legally Jude was already my husband.

His thoughts must have been moving in the same direction, because as I quietly celebrated the idea that he belonged to me, Jude turned, wrapped me in his arms, and kissed me slowly, thoughtfully, and gratefully.

"Damaris was right," he said when he released me. "She said anyone could see how I loved you. I'm only sorry I was so slow to let you know it."

"I forgive you," I whispered. "You will always be worth waiting for."

CHAPTER THIRTY-FIVE:
TASMIN

As I waited for Yeshua to fulfill his ministry
and Jude to build our house, I kept busy in
Cana. Though my nights were often lonely,
my days were full because I had Yagil to care
for and Aunt Dinah to keep me company. I
still missed Thomas and I was desperate to
join Jude, but Yagil proved to be the medi-
cine that made my heart merry. The boy
made me smile when waiting grew tedious,
and his laughter filled my empty house with
life.

I found great joy in teaching my little boy.
Every morning we would kneel by his bed
and recite the *shacharit,* or morning prayer.
" 'Hear O Israel, the Lord our God, the
Lord is one. Love Adonai your God with all
your heart and with all your soul and with
all your strength. These words, which I am
commanding you today, are to be on your
heart. You are to teach them diligently to
your children, and speak of them when you

sit in your house, when you walk by the way, when you lie down and when you rise up. Bind them as a sign on your hand, they are to be as frontlets between your eyes, and write them on the doorposts of your house and on your gates.' "

"Why, Ima," Yagil asked one morning, "do we say the same prayer morning and night?"

"Because," I answered, "saying them in the morning is our acceptance of the yoke of heaven, the yoke of His commandments, and our reminder of the exodus from Egypt."

"What's a yoke?"

I sank to the floor and faced the boy. "A yoke is a wooden bar that joins two oxen together. They pull beneath it and serve their master. Accepting the yoke of heaven means that we are submitting ourselves to serve HaShem. We will obey His commands as they are written in the Law."

I'm not sure how much Yagil understood in those early days, but by the time he was five, he could recite all three paragraphs of the Shema without prompting.

Life settled into a routine, its ordinariness broken only by occasional reports about Yeshua. Every visitor who came to our village brought another story — about a miraculous healing, stories he had told, or people he had angered. Over the next few months, everyone in Galilee, from the wealthiest merchant to the poorest servant, seemed to develop an opinion about him: he was our promised messiah, or he was a fraud and a trickster.

I clung quietly to my conviction that he was a prophet sent from God.

One story resonated with me long after the telling. A visitor from Jerusalem told us that some experts in the Law wanted to trap Yeshua with his words. The Pharisees sent him some of their students and some members of Herod's party. They said, "Rabbi, we know that you tell the truth and teach what God's way is. You aren't concerned with what other people think about you, since you pay no attention to a person's status. So tell us your opinion: does Torah permit paying taxes to the Roman emperor or not?"

Yeshua, knowing their malicious intent, said, "You hypocrites! Why are you trying to trap me? Show me the coin used to pay the tax." They brought him a denarius, and he asked, "Whose name and picture are these?"

"The emperor's," they replied.

Yeshua said to them, "Then give the emperor what belongs to the emperor. And give to God what belongs to God."

Everyone listening at the well marveled at Yeshua's clever answer, and I held it close to my heart. The emperor wanted our taxes, and a portion of our money belonged to him. But what belonged to HaShem? Our offerings? Our tithes?

The question niggled at my brain for days. HaShem didn't want our offerings, for the psalmist wrote, "Sacrifice and offering You did not desire — my ears You have opened — burnt offering and sin offering you did not require." And tithes were paid by farmers within the Promised Land, ten percent of the crop to pay for tenancy on God's land. There was another tithe, paid annually, of ten percent of our crops, which we carried to Jerusalem and ate while we were in the Holy City. So what part did HaShem want of us?

I asked Jude the next time I ate Shabbat dinner with his family. I told them of Yeshua's response to the Pharisees, then asked my question. "If we are to give to HaShem what belongs to Him," I said, "then what do we give Him?"

The brothers looked at each other, then Jude smiled at me. "Easy, my love," he said. "He wants us."

"Us?"

"All of us."

"Everyone at this table, you mean?"

"Yes, and all" — he gestured from his head to his feet — "every part of each of us."

My mind blew open. HaShem didn't want my tithes of dates, though I was happy to give them. He didn't want the effort I took to offer my morning and evening prayers. He didn't want the token coins I tossed into the basket at the synagogue. He wanted *me.* All of me.

I did not talk much for the rest of the evening, but when Yagil and I went home at the end of Shabbat, I resolved to reimagine my way of thinking about HaShem. I had been parceling out bits and pieces of myself: my obedience to the Law, my required tithes of produce, my regular prayers. But when I was not performing my required duties, my life had always been my own . . .

Or was it? Jude knew better. My life had come from HaShem, so it belonged to Him. And He wanted all of me, all the time.

What did that mean? I moved through my days with a new awareness of God, of what it meant to wear the yoke of heaven. I was to serve Him in everything, not only when required to speak or act according to the Law.

As the months passed, I began to say

farewell to Cana. In a year or so, this city would no longer be my home. When Jude finally arrived to carry me to our wedding, Yagil and I would move to Nazareth, and this place, these people, would no longer be part of my daily life. The butcher who carved my meat behind a curtain so I wouldn't have to see the blood; the woman who bought more dates than she needed out of generosity, Aunt Dinah and my uncles, whom I rarely saw but were still part of my family.

What would the people of Nazareth think of me? Would they regard a newcomer with the same hostility they had displayed toward Yeshua, one of their own, or would they welcome Jude's wife?

I tried not to be anxious about the upcoming changes. Some things would remain the same. My house would stay in the family, for since Abba's death, it legally belonged to Thomas. The groves also belonged to Thomas and would provide a good income for him should he ever decide to settle down and marry. If and when he decided to return to his old life, he would find it easy to blend into village life. I would not be around, of course, yet Nazareth was not far away. Jude and I would always welcome him into our home, and he would make a great uncle for

Yagil and the other children HaShem sent us.

As winter warmed into spring and the third Passover without Thomas approached, Jude showed up at my house. For a moment I feared he brought bad news — had something happened to Yeshua? Had his twelve closest disciples been arrested?

But one look at his smile assured me that all was well. He greeted me with a chaste kiss on the cheek, then let me lead him into the house, where Yagil danced around him, clamoring for his attention. He talked to Yagil for a few moments before sinking onto the couch. He looked at the linens I had sorted into piles. "What are you doing there?" he asked.

I ran my hand over the top of the folded linens. "I am sorting through what I should take and what I should leave behind for Thomas. The finer linens will go with me, since I embroidered most of them and Thomas has no use for such things. One day, when he marries, his wife will undoubtedly bring linens of her own —" I halted when his face closed, as if he were guarding a secret. "What's wrong?"

He shrugged. "You do not need to be in such a hurry, that's all. Thomas is still with Yeshua. And my brothers and I have been so busy that I have had no time to look for a place to build our house."

I sank onto a stool and struggled to mask my disappointment. "We have been betrothed for nearly a year."

"And I warned you that we might have to wait a year or more. But all will come to pass in HaShem's perfect timing."

I pressed my lips together, restraining the impatient words that threatened to break free. He was right, I knew we'd have to wait a long time, but patience had never been one of my virtues. I had already spent months preparing to leave Cana; I had been sewing and planning and mentally decorating an empty house. I had even picked out names for our children . . . though I had not been bold enough to share those with Jude. One look at his face assured me that he would not be pleased to hear them.

"Jude." I leaned forward until he met my gaze. "Do you still want to marry me?"

"With everything in me, I do." He placed his hands on my knees. "I want to be your husband in every way. I want to worship HaShem with you, and have children with you. But the time is not right."

Somehow I managed a smile. "Then I will have to be patient. You should know this, however — I am living for the day when we are wed. I am older than most women when they marry, and I can't help feeling I have wasted too much time —"

"Time spent waiting on Adonai is never wasted," he said. Then, perhaps to take the sting out of his news, he leaned forward and kissed me.

CHAPTER THIRTY-SIX: TASMIN

As the fourth Passover without Thomas approached, a traveler brought me a letter. I broke the seal and read it at once.

Dearest sister,
Shalom! I hope this letter finds you well and at peace. I hope you can find it in your heart to forgive me for disappointing you so many years ago. But I am convinced I have committed my life to the true Messiah, the One spoken of by so many prophets. I hope you understand that, and I hope you can forgive me for disappointing you for not coming home when Abba was dying.

I am writing because our time with Yeshua is drawing to an end. Yeshua has said so himself. So, if we must die with him, I want to address the matters that stand between you and me.

We were camped by the Jordan, near

415

the place where John baptized, when we received word that Lazarus, a friend from Bethany, was sick. Yeshua is close to Lazarus and his sisters, so I thought we would leave at once to go to them. But Yeshua said no, Lazarus would not die. His sickness was meant to bring glory to HaShem.

I was not sure what he meant, but we remained in our camp two more days. Then Yeshua told us that Lazarus had fallen asleep, but he would go to Bethany to wake him. We argued, saying he should let the man sleep, for then he would feel better. Then Yeshua explained that Lazarus was dead.

Dead? Had he not said the man would live?

We are now preparing to go back to Bethany, which is only a short walk from Jerusalem. We are returning, though we barely escaped the Holy City with our lives only a few weeks ago.

I told the others we should reconcile ourselves to the fact that we will soon die with our master.

Lazarus is dead, and soon Yeshua will join him. By the time you receive this message, I may be dead, too, along with the others. The rulers of the Sanhedrin will not be satisfied until we have been silenced. They fear the Romans, who do not want anything to disturb the peace of Jerusalem, and they fear losing their power over the people.

And so, dear sister, I must ask you to forgive me for leaving you the way I did. I am not sorry I went with Yeshua, but I am sorry I could not make you understand. Please remember this: You have always been the dearest, closest person on earth to me, and I do not want to die without assuring you of this.

Your loving twin,
Thomas

Swallowing the sob that rose in my throat, I lowered the letter. Was Thomas dead already? No. If he had died, I would have felt something. When we were children and he skinned his knee, I felt the sting. When I got sick, he would vomit.

If Thomas were dead, I would have felt the loss . . . unless we had been truly cut asunder.

Could all the years apart do that to us?

I looked across the room and studied the doorway to our father's bedchamber. If Thomas were dead . . .

I clenched my hand in a sudden rush of

gratitude that Abba could not feel the wave of grief that threatened to overwhelm me.

The next morning I rose early, shared some fruit and bread with Yagil, then took the boy to Aunt Dinah's house. "I will be back before sunset," I promised, "but I have to leave Cana for the day." When she asked where I was going, I replied, "Nazareth," but said nothing more. No sense in worrying her unnecessarily.

I left Cana and walked south, tormented by *what if*s. What if Yeshua and his disciples had been arrested and imprisoned like John the Immerser? What if Thomas or the other disciples had been killed? But I had not heard such a report, and explosive news like that would spread like wildfire.

Winter had warmed to a promising spring, and the morning heat had begun to bake the hills by the time I left Cana. I walked quickly, my sandals kicking up small puffs of dust on the road. By the time the sun had moved over a quarter of the sky, I could see the rooftops of Nazareth. I glanced at the watchtower as I passed and saw an old man snoozing in the shade of its thatched roof. The city was not on alert, so perhaps its most infamous son still lived.

A donkey stood in Jude's courtyard,

contentedly chewing hay as he watched the street. I gave the donkey an affectionate pat and moved toward the stairs at the front of the house. Pheodora and her children had been living with her brothers for several months, so the house looked better than it had in days when the brothers lived there alone. Several chickens clucked and scratched in the courtyard, and from inside the house I could hear the sound of a bleating goat.

I went up the steps, knocked, and stood back to wait.

I had rehearsed my opening more than a dozen times. I would wish Jude a good morning, then ask if I might come inside to discuss something of great importance to both our families.

The door opened and I looked up into Jude's sweat-stained face. He had been working, for I glimpsed a small cut on his hand and sawdust on his cheek. Every word I had rehearsed fled my mind. "Are they dead?" I asked, the words tumbling from my lips. "I received a letter from Thomas, and he said they were going to Bethany. He fully expected to be arrested and stoned, since they barely escaped Jerusalem at the Feast of Dedication . . ."

Jude stared at me, then called for James.

"Come in," he said. He lowered his voice once we were inside. "When did you receive this letter?"

"Last night. A traveler brought it to Cana; a neighbor delivered it to my house."

"Are you sure it was from Thomas? That it is not some sort of trap?"

I choked back a sob. "The letter was written in Thomas's hand. He spoke of things only he and I would understand."

Jude reached out as if he would embrace me, then abruptly gestured to the bench at the table. "Sit. Rest." As I sank onto the bench, he poured water from a pitcher and offered me a cup. "Drink first," he said, intently studying my face. "And when you have caught your breath, tell me what Thomas said. Then we will decide what to do."

As I drank, James, Joses, and Simeon came from the back of the house and took seats at the table. I took the letter from my tunic and read it aloud, then lowered it and looked around, searching the brothers' faces for some sign of hope.

"He's done it, then," Simeon said, his voice flat. "If he wanted to make himself a martyr, this is the way."

"Yeshua is not a fool," Joses said. "And our mother is with him. He would not endanger her."

Jude propped an elbow on the table. "He could have her stay with one of his disciples' families. She could be in Bethany, perhaps with the sisters of this man Lazarus."

"Passover is approaching," James said, his forehead crinkling. "Consider the timing. Remember how John called him the Lamb of God? Yeshua could be planning to enter Jerusalem at the time of the feast. Passover requires a sacrifice. If the authorities kill him now, his name will forever be linked with the Passover lamb."

"I do not approve of what he's doing," Joses said, "but we urged him to go to Jerusalem to make a bigger impact. He acted on our suggestion once; now he is doing it again."

"But what can we do?" I asked, pressing my hands to the table. "Your brother may be intent on getting himself killed, but I don't want my brother to die. He's all the family I have left."

Jude raked his hand through his hair, then blew out a breath. "I don't know if we can get to Jerusalem in time to stop Yeshua, but we can try. Is there any reason we cannot leave at once?"

"The work," Simeon said. "The butcher has asked for another table, and he needs it before Shabbat."

"Fine." Jude nodded. "Simeon, Joses, and James can remain here. But Tasmin and I will go to Jerusalem. We'll do our best to find Yeshua and see if what we suspect is true. If he is planning on dying at Passover, we will stop him."

He turned to me. "Are you able to do this? I assumed —"

"I'll go," I answered, standing. "With a short stop in Cana, I can tell Aunt Dinah about our plans and gather what we'll need for the trip. Yagil will stay with her. If you are going to Jerusalem, nothing on earth will stop me from joining you."

We heard the first reports just outside Jericho from people who had come from Bethany. "Did you hear?" one man asked as soon as we were within shouting distance. "The latest news of the Nazarene?"

Jude and I glanced at each other and braced ourselves for the worst.

"He raised a man who'd been dead four days!" The old man chortled with delight. "The fellow's sisters were dumbfounded with joy, but the leaders of the Sanhedrin were livid."

Jude blinked as his mouth went slack. "What did you say?"

The old man grabbed Jude's arms, and for a moment I thought he was going to dance. "Lazarus was his name. Yeshua and his disciples came to Bethany, and the teacher insisted on going to the tomb. He asked the neighbors to roll the stone away from the tomb's entrance. The dead man's sister protested, saying the stench would be unbearable. Still, they did it, and the teacher said, 'Lazarus, come out!' A moment later, there he was, still wearing the shroud his sisters had wrapped around him."

I couldn't move, stunned by sheer disbelief at the joyous expression on the old man's face. When I finally found my tongue, I had to ask, "Were there witnesses? Could it have been a trick?"

The man laughed. "A trick? Tell me — how can a living man stink like a dead cow one minute and come running out of his tomb in the next? And yes, there were dozens of witnesses. Half the town followed the dead man's sisters out to the graveyard. Everyone knew Yeshua was close to that family."

I clutched Jude's arm. "I believe the story. A prophet who could heal Yagil could certainly bring the dead back to life."

Jude turned to the old man, his expression one of intense scrutiny. "Have you been drinking?"

The man laughed again. "Not a drop."

"Why would Yeshua go to Bethany when he knows the authorities want him dead? Bethany would only be a short ride for the high priest and his guards."

The old man shrugged. "I don't know why he went. A few weeks ago others were with Yeshua in Herod's territory and heard the Pharisees warn him that Antipas wanted him dead. But Yeshua said they could tell that fox that he was driving out demons and performing healings and on the third day he would reach his goal. But he had to keep going because . . ."

"Because why?" Jude pressed.

The old man's face went somber. "Because a prophet would never perish outside Jerusalem."

Wings of shadowy trepidation brushed the back of my neck as I looked at Jude. Again, Yeshua had spoken of death.

"Did Yeshua remain in Bethany," Jude asked, "or did he return to Galilee?"

The man shook his head. "From what I heard, he left Bethany. But before he departed, some heard him say, 'Jerusalem, you will never see me again until you say *Baruch haba b'Shem Adonai.*' Blessed is He who comes in the Name of Adonai."

Though Yeshua's words left me as confused as always, Jude and I thanked the man and continued on our way, walking with even more urgency.

"He hasn't gone back to Galilee," Jude said. "He's going to Jerusalem."

"Is that what he meant about the prophets?"

"Apparently he believes he is destined to die in the Holy City. So we must reach him before he does something foolish."

Traffic became heavier as we neared the city gates. Travelers on their way to Jerusalem were frequently excited, especially during festival time, but that day an almost palpable air of anticipation surrounded the surging pilgrims. Instead of the usual songs of ascent, they were singing another psalm:

"The stone the builders rejected
has become the capstone.
It is from Adonai:
it is marvelous in our eyes!
This is the day that Adonai has made!
Let us rejoice and be glad in it!
Hoshia-na! Please, Adonai, save now!
We beseech You, Adonai, prosper us!
Baruch haba b'Shem Adonai —
Blessed is He who comes in the Name of
    Adonai."

The reference struck me and Jude in the same instant. We glanced at each other as the words rang out: *Baruch haba b'Shem Adonai.* The exact words Yeshua had predicted.

"Do you think he's here?" I rose on tiptoe to look over the throng.

Jude climbed onto a roadside boulder and scanned the crowd ahead of us. "I don't see him. But if he appeared before this mob, he would be trampled."

He looked down at me, a muscle quivering at his jaw. "My brothers and I were only jesting when we told him he should perform his miracles in Jerusalem. Stubborn though he is, he is still my brother and I do not want him to die. I would give anything if I could persuade him to go into seclusion for a while."

I nodded. "I would do the same for Thomas. I still don't understand how he got involved in this. Until he met Yeshua, he was so . . . practical."

Jude climbed down and we walked on, struggling to rein in our frustration as it became difficult to move forward in the crowd. Then, from out of nowhere, we heard a roar from the direction of the city gate. Something was happening up ahead, something we could not see, but we could certainly hear the cheering. We could *feel* it, like a wave that started at a breakwater and washed over everything between it and the shore.

Jude found another boulder, then climbed up and balanced himself to survey the road ahead. "I can see the city wall," he called down to me, "and a heavy crowd fanning out around the gate. People are waving palm branches."

"Can you see what they're cheering about?"

He squinted into the distance for a moment, then his eyes widened. "I see a man — on a mule or donkey. The people are waving the branches as he passes. He's moving toward the gate now."

"Is it — ?"

"I believe so." Jude's voice went flat, and in his tone I heard resignation, anxiety, and regret.

He crouched on the boulder, bowed his head, and covered his eyes. I thought he might be weeping, but after a moment he slid off the rock and stood beside me. "When we enter the city," he said, lines of concentration deepening under his eyes, "we will look for a safe place to spend the night. But before that . . ."

"Yes?" I asked, wondering if he wanted to

go to Bethany and find Lazarus and his sisters.

"Nothing." He took my arm and guided me back into the crowd.

CHAPTER THIRTY-SEVEN: TASMIN

On Nisan 13, the fourth day of the week, I met Jude outside the crowded inn where we managed to find sleeping space. He looked like a man who had not rested, and I had to resist the urge to rearrange his tousled curls.

"What have you heard?" I asked, determined to keep the conversation centered on the reason for our journey.

He glanced away and blew out a frustrated breath. "That was Yeshua we saw yesterday. After entering the city with that cheering mob, he went to the Temple where he cleared the court of the money changers — again — and openly challenged the chief priests and elders. According to the witnesses I talked to, he said the Torah teachers and Pharisees were hypocrites, clean on the outside but inwardly full of greed and self-indulgence. Then he called them whitewashed tombs, snakes and vipers." Jude snorted with restrained mirth. "Not that they don't deserve such names, but foolish is the man who speaks the truth in public."

I bit back a smile and tried to imagine how Thomas would have reacted to Yeshua's truth-telling. "And then?"

Jude crossed his arms. "Apparently, Yeshua left the city and went to stay with Lazarus and his sisters. While there, the younger sister brought out a vial of perfume and poured it on his feet. One of the disciples complained that the perfume should have been sold and the money given to the poor, but Yeshua said she had done it to prepare him for burial."

"Burial?" My voice broke as I echoed the word. "Does he *want* to die?"

"It seems he is set on it." A muscle flexed at Jude's jaw. "I don't know what to do. If we find him, I doubt we will be able to dissuade him from whatever he has in mind. You could talk to Thomas, of course, but what if he is as obstinate as Yeshua?"

"He is." I underscored the words with iron. "Still, we have to try. We did not come all this way only to give up now."

Jude gave a nod and sighed. "I need to find my mother. I want to be sure she is well and see if I can persuade her to come with us. We could have dinner with her and, tomorrow, look for Yeshua and his men at the Temple."

"Your brother should be easy to find — the crowds will be drawn to him, for everyone is expecting him to perform a great miracle. It's as if they can sense that his time is at hand."

"I only wish he could give them what they want." Jude's voice turned rough, so he took a moment to clear his throat before speaking again. "Are we in agreement, then? We'll search for my mother today, and look for Yeshua and Thomas tomorrow."

"Agreed. But, Jude —"

"Yes?"

"Does your mother know about our betrothal?"

His brow furrowed, then he smiled. "I'm sure word has reached her by now."

"But you didn't tell her?"

"How could I? I haven't seen her in over two years."

I nodded and smoothed my wrinkled tunic, hoping Jude's mother would approve of our news when and if we found her.

Though we searched throughout the city, we did not find Jude's mother or Yeshua's disciples. Everywhere we went, however, we heard talk of Yeshua and the kingdom of God.

One man stood in the center of the marketplace and told his story: "I heard him say it was easier for a camel to go through the eye of a needle than for a rich man to enter the kingdom of God." The man grinned as the crowd laughed. "Good news for us poor folks, I say!"

"That's nothing," another man called. "I heard him say that tax collectors and prostitutes would enter the kingdom of God before the Pharisees."

Stunned silence greeted that report, then someone snickered. "That sounds bad, but when was the last time a Pharisee offered you comfort and a little kiss?"

Another man spread his arms and addressed the crowd. "I, too, heard Yeshua speak about the kingdom of God. Someone asked how much longer we would have to wait for it, and Yeshua said, 'The Kingdom of God is not coming with things observable, for the *Malchut HaShem* is within you.' "

A fat man in gaudy robes thrust out his swollen stomach and made a face. "Inside me? No wonder my belly is so big!"

The crowd broke into raucous laughter as Jude took my elbow and guided me away.

As the sun began to lower in the west, we returned to the inn in the Valley of the

Cheesemakers. The innkeeper and his wife invited us to share their evening meal, so we thanked them for their hospitality and joined them.

As a servant brought around a tray of stew, leeks, and dried dates, Jude made a wry comment: "If we were home in Galilee, we would be eating the *seudah maphseh-ket.*"

The innkeeper frowned. "The last supper?"

Jude nodded and dipped a handful of leeks in a cup of sauce. "The last supper before the fast that ends with the Passover meal. It's a traditional practice in Galilee, honoring the firstborn sons of our families. After all, not all Jews were in danger when the death angel passed over Egypt. Only the firstborns."

"A nice ritual. A shame we don't practice it in Judea." The innkeeper's wife smiled at Jude. "Are you a firstborn?"

"No." A momentary look of discomfort crossed Jude's face. "My brother is."

The innkeeper lifted his cup. "May he rejoice in his seudah maphsehket tonight."

With a sober expression, Jude raised his cup. "To his seudah maphsehket."

I couldn't help wondering where Yeshua was eating the last supper. Most of his disciples were Galilean, so wherever they were, I was sure they were observing the ritual.

After dinner, I went to the women's bedchamber while Jude stepped out to sleep in the courtyard.

At one point in the night I sat up, as awake as if someone had poured water in my face. I heard shouting outside, and the tramping sound of marching men. I crept to the door, opened the shutter, and peered out. In the yellow torchlight thrown by the lamp at the door, I saw Jude standing in the courtyard, one hand on the donkey and the other on his hip.

"Jude!" I hissed, not wanting to wake the household. "Did someone try to steal the donkey?"

He shook his head. "The trouble has nothing to do with us."

"But I heard something — soldiers?"

"Temple guards. They were marching out of the city."

The Temple guards were controlled by the Sanhedrin, not the Romans. Where had they been sent at this hour? If Jude wondered the same thing, he did not voice his thoughts.

I went back to my bed, but sleep remained elusive. Could the Sanhedrin have sent the guards to arrest Yeshua and his disciples? They would not dare arrest him during the day, not when so many admirers thronged around him. By night, however, Yeshua and his men could be arrested quietly and his so-called crime announced the next morning. They would hear his case in the Sanhedrin's chamber at the Temple, and two or three days later they would announce their verdict.

I sighed in relief. This was a better scenario than the one I kept imagining. I had imagined Yeshua instigating a riot in the Temple courtyard, which would have been answered by swordplay, bloodshed, and lawlessness. The disciples, including Thomas, would leap to their teacher's defense. The Temple guards would then cut down Yeshua and most of his followers in full view of their passionate public. When they all lay dead on the cobblestones, the people would learn not to set their hopes on anyone the religious authorities opposed . . .

Surely a quiet arrest was better, and nothing would come of it. The Sanhedrin did not have the power to put a man to death, and Yeshua had not broken any Roman laws. The emperor should have no quarrel with a prophet without political aspirations, and so the Romans would stay out of this religious disagreement. Yeshua and his men would likely be flogged, released, and warned not to preach in public again. Case closed.

After this brush with danger, Thomas would be free. Yeshua would return to Nazareth, and Thomas would go home to Cana. Jude and I would marry, and together we would raise Yagil and any other children HaShem sent to bless us.

Content to know all would be well, I closed my eyes and withdrew into a deep, dreamless sleep.

CHAPTER THIRTY-EIGHT:
TASMIN

On Nisan 14, the day of Passover, the sun rose with the warmth of spring on its breath. I rolled out of bed, eager to find our lost loved ones and save their lives by taking them home.

The innkeeper's wife had spread bread, fruit, and cheese on the table for her guests. When she saw me, she nodded toward the food, silently inviting me to break my fast, then turned back to the door where she was in earnest conversation with a woman in the street. "But what will they do with him?" I heard her ask.

I was too anxious to eat, and I knew Jude would be fasting in observance of seudah maphsehket.

I left our hostess to her conversation and smiled at the woman's little daughter, who sat in a corner playing with blocks. The child gave me a shy smile, and my heart tightened unexpectedly as I thought of Yagil.

What was he doing now? Was he sitting on Dinah's lap and asking about me? Did he miss me at all?

The innkeeper's wife sighed, bade farewell to the other woman, and came toward me, wiping her hands on a linen square. "Is there anything I can get you?" She gave me a polite smile. "The young man with you —"

"Is he awake?"

"He went down to the well to inquire about some business. He said you should wait here until he returns."

I thanked her and pulled up a stool to wait. This inn was more comfortable than others I'd stayed in, although one expected to find decent accommodations in a city as large as Jerusalem. People from all over the world came here to visit Herod's Temple and David's Tomb, so the local residents undoubtedly felt pressure to make things pleasant for visitors.

I was idly entertaining the possibility of opening an inn when Jude burst into the house, his face flushed. He gave the innkeeper and his wife an abrupt nod, then locked his gaze on me. "They arrested Yeshua last night," he said, his voice low and taut. "All the men with him fled, and the Temple guard took Yeshua to the high

438

priest's palace. I heard they might move him later today."

I rose from my stool, knocking over a honeypot in momentary panic. "We should go." I grabbed a square of linen and frantically swiped at the honey. "We need to stop this before it goes any further —"

"But what can we do?" Jude's face opened, and for the first time I saw honest fear in his eyes. He had always been certain his brother was a mere annoyance to the ruling powers, but now with the high priest himself involved . . .

"Go." The innkeeper's wife hurried over to clean up the mess. "Do what you need to do."

"Let me get my bag." I thanked our hostess with a smile and rushed to grab my things.

We had walked only a short distance when we heard an outcry in the street. A group of men stood at an intersection, hands fisted and arms waving as they questioned, accused, and retorted.

"What's this?" Jude murmured.

I stepped back, bracing myself against a wall as he insinuated himself into the throng. I heard his voice rise above the others in a heated exchange, then he emerged a moment later, his mouth set in a grim line.

"During the trial," Jude said, "the high priest asked him, 'Are you *Mashiach,* Son of the blessed One?' Yeshua answered, 'I am, and you shall see the Son of Man sitting at the right hand of the Powerful One and coming with the clouds of heaven.' "

I gasped as Jude gripped my upper arm and pulled me into an alley. "What will they — ?"

"At daybreak the council of the elders condemned Yeshua for blasphemy. They have taken him to Pilate."

"Why?" I asked, struggling to keep pace with Jude's long stride.

"Because the Jews do not have the authority to put a man to death."

My blood ran cold. "They want Pilate to kill him? For blasphemy? Why should the Romans care about our religious law? They do not believe in HaShem, and I've heard them blaspheme their own gods —"

"The council will come up with something," Jude said, moving faster. "They want my brother dead, so I fear they will *make* the Romans care."

A crowd had gathered outside the gate of the procurator's palace by the time we arrived. A trio of Roman guards stood in front of the gate, and from their sidelong glances and shifting feet, I knew the crowd made them nervous. "You are going to need reinforcements," Jude called, noticing the guard's anxiety. "Your governor is holding a peaceful man, one who has committed no crime."

The guard might have moved against Jude, but at that moment a trumpet blew and the guards stepped away to open the gates. We were forced back along with the crowd. While we watched, perplexed, a horse-drawn wagon rumbled over the cobblestone courtyard and moved into the street. Four guards sat at the corners of the open wagon, and in the center, on his knees, knelt Yeshua.

The sight of him, beaten and bruised about the head, felt like a punch to the center of my belly. I gasped, struggling to breathe, as the man I hoped to call brother-in-law lifted his head, saw me, and then shifted his gaze to his brother's face.

"W-where are they taking him?" Jude asked, his voice ragged.

He was not speaking to me, but to anyone who would listen. He looked around, frantically seeking an answer, yet no one in the crowd knew any more than we did.

Then a familiar figure came out of the courtyard and walked straight toward us.

Though I had not seen the man in years, the beardless face, the snarling smile, and the gaping eye socket had not changed. "They are taking him to Antipas," the eunuch said, reaching for Jude. "The same place I'm taking you."

Jude tried to resist, but two armed figures followed the eunuch, burly men in plain tunics with sword belts at their waists. They probably served Antipas or Herodias, and in that instant I realized they had been following us.

"Tasmin," Jude said, glancing over his shoulder at me, "run!"

I would have, but one of the burly men grabbed my arm in a viselike grip. I bit my lip to stifle a cry.

"You are coming with me," the one-eyed man said, "now that you have no friends coming to rescue you."

I had no idea what he meant, but he was right. In the sea of people around us, I could not spot one familiar face.

CHAPTER THIRTY-NINE:
TASMIN

For a frightening moment I feared we'd be herded into wagons and trundled off to Tiberias or Herod's prison near the Dead Sea. Then I remembered: Herod Antipas always came to Jerusalem for Pesach.

I walked beside Jude through the streets of Jerusalem, roughly escorted by the eunuch and his brawny henchmen. Though the day was warm, a coldness filled my stomach, an icy lump that did not seem likely to melt. Frightened as I was, I kept thinking about Thomas. Was he being marched somewhere against his will or had he managed to hide? What of the other disciples? Were they together in a safe place or scattered like sheep?

The guards dragged us over broken cobblestones, through ankle-deep puddles of filth and piles of manure, caring nothing for our safety or our dignity. Finally I spotted the grand palace of Herod Antipas, not far from the Temple Mount. Our captors led us through a gate and held us in a marble-clad vestibule while the eunuch went into another chamber. Then he reappeared, and we were forced through gilded doors into a reception hall, where Antipas was engaged with a prisoner.

Yeshua.

In that moment, I realized that Jude and I were not the main attraction, only a sideshow. The tetrarch did not even glance at us; his attention was riveted on Jude's brother.

Held in place by the two thickset guards, Jude and I stood at the back of the room and waited while Yeshua, clearly in pain from a severe beating, was forced to stand before Antipas, who sat on a golden throne and looked frustrated. A dozen or so retainers and officials stood behind the tetrarch, their eyes darting right and left, probably trying to remain on guard lest Antipas ask something of them. At the back of the room, a contingent of Pharisees and Temple authorities stood in a somber huddle, their garments proclaiming their righteousness with an overabundance of tassels and tefillin.

The ruler of Galilee and Perea leaned forward and peered at Yeshua through heavily painted eyes, then turned to the woman on the gilded seat next to him. "Here he is, love," he said, his mouth curling as if on the verge of laughter. "The one the Immerser told us about."

"Delighted," she said with a deadpan expression.

With a grin, Antipas looked at his prisoner. "I have longed to see you, Jesus of Nazareth," he said, using Yeshua's Greek name. "If you had not been captured last night, I might have had to arrest you myself. Of course, it would help if you would do something . . . arresting. Something miraculous. Something truly extraordinary." He arched a brow. "So? Will you work a miracle for me? I could have water brought, if you would turn it into wine. But no, you've already done that. What if I brought a goblet of donkey piss? Do you have the power to turn that into a pleasing vintage?"

Jude leaned toward me. "Even I might attempt that," he whispered, "if Antipas would sample the cup."

The tetrarch waited, as did everyone in the audience chamber, but Yeshua neither moved nor spoke.

"Forget the wine." Antipas waved the matter away. "Bad idea. But here are the crumbs from my lunch — a crust, two grapes, a half-eaten fig. This room is filled with, what" — he looked around — "thirty people? Will you take these remnants and feed all of us? Can you do that?"

He waited, but again Yeshua remained silent.

"How about this?" Herod's smile vanished as he pointed to a young boy who stood nearby, a platter of fruit in his hands. "If I have my guard cut out yonder slave's heart, could you put it back and revive him?"

The boy trembled, his face rippling with terror as the platter fell to the marble floor, scattering the fruit.

I inched closer to Jude, my head spinning in the horrified silence of an audience holding its breath.

Antipas propped an elbow on his knee and rested his chin on his hand. His face transformed, the polished veneer peeling back to reveal the violence inherited from his father. "Answer me, Jesus of Nazareth. What will you do to prove yourself?"

No one moved for a moment, then Herodias broke the silence with a giggle. "Apparently the Immerser overrated his successor. This one is not nearly as entertaining as his kinsman."

"But the reports! I've heard so many amazing stories." Antipas frowned and clasped his hands. "I heard you resurrected a man who had been dead four days. If my dear Herodias could remember where she placed John's head, could you restore it to life?"

I closed my eyes, silently grieving for Jude and Yeshua and John. Had Antipas no mercy at all?

Herodias yawned. "This one is not even interesting. Why is he here?"

"Pilate sent him," Antipas growled. "He must have been bored with him, as well." He gestured to his guards. "Send the prisoner back to the procurator."

"Wait!" One of the chief priests stepped forward. "This man has been disturbing the peace in Galilee. He has said he is God. He said we ought not to obey the Law. He said he could destroy the Temple and rebuild it in three days — your father's temple, Tetrarch!"

Another priest stepped forward and bowed to Antipas. "He claims to be a king."

The word *king* seemed to fill the throne room and echo in the vaulted chamber.

Antipas lifted his head, his eyes narrowing at the title he had never been able to claim. "You are a king?" His voice dripped with derision. "Then I must apologize for my lack of proper respect. You there" — he pointed at a servant — "bring one of my purple robes. The one laid out on my bed, if you will."

As the servant scurried off Herod glanced at his wife. "Have you anything to ask him, my love?"

Herodias regarded Yeshua with impassive eyes, then looked at the one-eyed man who stood in front of me and Jude. "I have no questions for the Nazarene," she said, "but my servant has brought a pair who follow this Yeshua. I would speak to them, if it pleases you."

Antipas smiled. "Everything you do pleases me."

Herodias rose with oiled grace, walked toward us, and stopped a few paces away. "Orien," she said, "you saw these two in Tiberias and again in Galilee. When you saw them in Tiberias, they were talking with Chuza, my husband's steward. Is that correct?"

The one-eyed man bowed. "Yes, my lady."

My stomach dropped when she shifted her attention to Jude. "Do you deny it?"

If Jude was anxious, he hid it well. "I do not deny it." He boldly met her gaze. "I met Chuza in Tiberias nearly three years ago. He wanted us to escort his wife to Capernaum. We agreed to let her travel with us."

The corner of Herodias's mouth quirked. "You are followers of this Nazarene, correct? As is Chuza?" She glanced around. "Where *is* the steward?"

A tall, dignified man stepped forward and bowed before Herodias. "Chuza is overseeing preparations for the royal dinner, my lady. Perhaps I can be of service?"

Herodias lifted her chin. "Perhaps, Manaen. Do you know this couple?"

I closed my eyes, desperately trying to place the man's name. I did not know his face, but I had heard the name before — from Joanna. He had gone with her and Chuza to see the Immerser and was impressed with what he had heard.

Manaen turned toward me and Jude, his eyes softening as he smiled. I felt a measure of anxiety leave my shoulders — a man who smiled like that could not mean us harm.

"I do not know these people," Manaen said. "I have not had the pleasure of meeting them."

"Still." Herodias frowned. "I do not like the idea of our steward consorting with followers of this Nazarene. If he did it once, he will do it again."

Jude barked a laugh. "A follower of the Nazarene? Excuse me, my lady, but I am no follower. I am his brother, and I have spent years trying to convince him to give up his teaching and return to Nazareth."

Jude's honest answer was clearly not what Herodias expected. She narrowed her eyes at me. "Is he telling the truth? Are *you* a follower of the Nazarene?"

Following Jude's example, I smiled in false confidence. "I went in search of him only to persuade my brother, one of the man's disciples, to come home and help with the harvest. I seek my brother still, which is why I have come to Jerusalem."

"But you believe this Yeshua is the son of God."

I shook my head. "HaShem is One. So how can this Yeshua be His son?"

Our answers seemed to satisfy Herodias, for she stepped away, dismissing us and our one-eyed escort with a flip of her hand. But before we were ushered out of the audience chamber, I saw the servant enter with a regal purple robe draped over his arm. He took it to Yeshua, who looked at us with understanding and compassion as he turned to watch us go.

I should have been happy to be released from Antipas's custody, but my blood ran thick with guilt. We had come to Jerusalem to help Yeshua and Thomas. Though our honest answers had saved us, we had done nothing to help our brothers.

As Jude and I left the palace, my heart twisted with a wretchedness I had known only when my mother died.

Jude and I were still outside Antipas's palace when the Roman wagon passed again, four guards at its corners and Yeshua sitting in the center, clothed in the tetrarch's purple robe.

"They're taking him back to Pilate," Jude said, his voice grim. "We could go there, but the governor might pass judgment before we arrive."

"What sort of judgment could he pass?" I asked, trying to sound hopeful. "Antipas did not find Yeshua guilty of any crime. Surely Pilate will do the same."

"We will see." Jude grabbed my hand and led me through the churning crowd.

By the time we reached the governor's mansion, the gates had been opened and a crowd filled the courtyard. We worked our way through the mob, then stood among the others as Pilate stepped forward to address the people. Pointing to Yeshua, who stood behind him in royal purple, Pilate said, "You brought this man to me as one who incites the people to revolt. But having examined him in your presence, I have found no case against this man regarding what you accuse him of doing. Nor did Herod Antipas, for he sent him back to us. Indeed, he has done nothing worthy of execution."

The mob around us surged forward, shouting, "Take this fellow away! Release to us Bar-abbas!"

I rose on tiptoe and shouted in Jude's ear, "Who are they asking for?"

"A rebel and a murderer."

Again Pilate lifted his hand. "But what shall I do with this Yeshua of Nazareth?"

"Execute, execute him!"

Pilate lifted both hands, attempting to speak, but the crowd drowned him out as they called for Yeshua's execution. I glanced up and saw a glazed look of despair spread across Jude's face. Unable to bear the sight of his pain, I closed my eyes and clung to his hand, knowing that each cry from the crowd had to be a stab at his heart. If they had been calling for Thomas's death, I would be groveling on the paving stones, sobbing, begging for my brother's life . . .

Finally, the mob stilled long enough for Pilate to speak. "Why?" He scowled at the discontented rumble that continued beneath his words. "What evil has this one done? I have found in him no fault deserving of death. Therefore I will scourge and release him."

Like water pouring through a broken dam, the crowd's disapproval roared over the dais where the procurator stood, accented by renewed calls for Yeshua's execution.

Pilate's features hardened in a mask of disapproval as he called for a basin of water. In full view of the chief priests and Temple authorities, he dipped his hands in the water and held them aloft, illustrating that he had washed his hands of the entire matter.

While Jude and I watched, the procurator released the criminal Bar-abbas, who had been jailed for insurrection and murder. Then he surrendered Yeshua to the will of the frenzied mob.

Roman guards dragged Yeshua from the elevated patio where he had been on display and took him away.

I will never forget what happened next. While Jude and I stood stupefied on the pavement, a howling cacophony of fiendish glee rent the air. Men's faces distorted into horrible expressions of devilish euphoria, derision, and unholy triumph. Those who had sought to destroy Yeshua waved their hands, clapped each other on the back, and pounded the paving stones in a mad dance of delight. Surely their hatred had been inspired by the father of lies . . .

I had not been one of Yeshua's followers, but I would never want to destroy him. How could I when he had healed Yagil, raised a man from the dead, and banished seven demons from Miriam of Magdala? Whatever his motivation, Yeshua met people in need and made them whole; he brought healing and hope to their lives.

These celebrating his downfall were not healers but coldhearted destroyers. Whatever their motivation, they were opposing everything Yeshua had worked for, and he had worked only for the kingdom of God, never for himself.

Somehow Jude and I managed to escape the uncontrolled mob. We spilled onto the street with a handful of others, then wandered aimlessly through crowds that roiled with news of what had happened in Pilate's courtyard. This Passover would be anything but a time of celebration for our people.

"What — what will they do now?" I asked Jude as we searched for an alley that would lead us back to the inn.

"They will kill him quickly, before the news becomes widely known," he said, his voice breaking. "By all that is holy, I must find my mother. She must not — must not see this."

"Where could she be?"

Jude tightened his jaw. "Knowing her, she is near him. If we find Yeshua, we will find her."

We did not know how to find Mary or Yeshua, so we decided to travel back toward Pilate's palace, hoping to learn some news on the way. As we walked, spurts of overheard conversations kept us apprised of all that had happened since we escaped the mob. We learned that after Pilate surrendered him, Yeshua had been stripped, beaten, crowned with thorns, and re-clothed in purple before being made to stand before a cohort of Roman soldiers, who mocked and spit on him.

Jude went pale when he heard each report, yet I could not tell if his distress sprang from sorrow or anger. But the hand wrapped around mine felt like iron, and his eyes burned with determination.

We halted in the middle of the street when we heard an old man say he had seen Yeshua with two criminals on their way to the execution site. "Where?" Jude interrupted, his throat bobbing as he swallowed. "Where did you see him and where will they die?"

The old man lifted his walking stick and pointed it toward the northwest. "Outside the city, at a hill called Golgotha. That's where the Romans crucify those they intend as a warning for the rest of us."

An anguished wail nearly escaped me, but for Jude's sake I sealed my lips as he lengthened his stride and hurried toward the city gate. I followed with rising dismay, dreading what we would see once we reached our destination.

As a child I once saw a crucifixion, and afterward Abba scolded me for stopping to stare. "The Torah says anyone hanged on a tree is a curse of God," he chided. "You should never look on anyone who is cursed."

But how could I not look on Yeshua, who had done so much for so many?

Jude and I worked our way through the crowds, moving toward the gate in the western wall. Because it was Passover, merchants, traveling families, Roman officials, and harried shoppers filled every street and alley. Everyone wanted to complete the day's business before sunset, because as soon as the first three stars could be seen in the night sky, the Passover meal could be shared and the Feast of Unleavened Bread would begin. Already the sun stood almost directly overhead.

By the time Jude and I passed through the city gate, we could see the Romans doing their evil work on a distant hill. "I know that place," Jude said, his eyes abstracted. "They call it Golgotha because it resembles a skull."

I stared at the desolate spot with tears in my eyes. Though my heart squeezed so tightly I could barely draw breath, I forced myself to speak: "The old man was right. They want us to see it and fear them."

His grip tightened on my hand. "Let us get closer."

My heart pounded as we wound our way through the tangle of travelers. Jude led me until we stood at the base of the treeless hill. A wide path, deeply rutted by the wheels of Roman wagons, led up to a clearing where a group of soldiers sweated and cursed as they fulfilled their heinous duty.

We could not see the condemned men from where we stood, so I assumed they lay on the ground. The majority of the executioners were occupied with hammers. Another, a soldier with gold embellishments on his breastplate, propped his hands on his hips and stared up at the sky, where a thin scarf of cloud did little to provide shade.

Jude and I moved off the road and stood on the wayside, uncertain of what we should do next. A small group of observers stood only a few paces from the soldiers. Four of them were women, their heads bowed and their arms around each other. Two men in traditional Jewish garb stood off to the side while a group of Pharisees and Temple officials stood near them.

I looked at Jude, willing to go wherever he wanted to lead me.

"There she is." He pointed to the women. "The woman in blue — that's Ima. She's with Aunt Salome, Mary, and Miriam."

I squinted to better differentiate between the figures. Yes — I recognized the set of Mary's shoulders, though now they were bowed with grief. Miriam of Magdala stood at her right hand with Mary, wife of Clopas. Salome stood at her left.

I stared up at Jude, recognized grief behind the indecision on his face, and decided to abide by his wishes, whatever they were. "Do you want to go up there?"

"I can't." He swallowed hard. "Yeshua would see me, and what do I say to him? I tried to warn him, HaShem knows I tried my best, but he would not listen . . ."

Tears welled in his eyes.

"We don't have to go." I slid my fingers over his. "Your mother is not alone. Miriam, Mary, and Salome will take care of her."

We stood in silence as the Romans lifted

the heavy beams supporting the two criminals and slid them into prepared holes. As each vertical beam fell into place, the movement wrenched the man nailed at the wrists and feet, and the criminal's scream reverberated across the bleak landscape. Passersby jeered at the sound, many lifting their fists in support of the Roman atrocity.

I felt a shudder run through Jude as the soldiers in the center huddled and bent to lift a third execution stake. The commander barked an order, and the soldiers lifted the heavy timber. A flash of wild grief ripped through me when Yeshua came into view — somehow I had hoped I would see a stranger — and when they lowered the stake into the prepared cavity, Jude groaned and Yeshua's face contorted in agony, but he did not cry out.

I lowered my head as nausea followed grief, rippling through my stomach, up my throat, and burning the back of my mouth. For Jude's sake, I choked it down. If I was sick with grief, what must he be feeling?

I looked up and saw that his eyes were wide and as empty as windows, as though the soul they mirrored had died.

Not knowing what else to do, I drew a trembling breath and forced myself to witness what I had dreaded for months.

Because the three men on the execution stakes bore their bodies' weight on pierced wrists and feet, they struggled to breathe. Even from a distance I could see them suffer renewed agonies every time they pressed on their broken feet to propel themselves upward and snatch a breath. After each inhalation they collapsed against the stake, their torn and wounded backs sliding over raw wood, starting the slow process all over again.

I kept looking at Jude, whose face had settled into stony lines. He might have been a statue, so still was his countenance.

Though the travelers behind us commented, jeered, or wept, we watched in silence. We saw the Romans hang a written placard above Yeshua's head, then gamble for his clothing. We saw the chief priests, the Torah teachers, and the elders walk forward to observe his near-nakedness and mock his humiliation. Their voices floated down to us: "He saved others, but he can't save himself?"

"He's the king of Israel! Let him come down now from the stake and we'll believe in him!"

"He trusts in God — let God rescue him now, if He wants him. For he said, 'I am Ben-Elohim, the Son of God.' "

A man on the road walked toward the execution site and shouted, "You who are going to destroy the Temple and rebuild it in three days, save yourself!"

We were not the only people watching from the roadside. Others stopped to question, curse, or criticize the Roman violence. As I listened to one man deride all things Roman, I remembered that one of our own kings, Alexander Jannaeus, had crucified eight hundred Jews, mostly devout Pharisees, while he feasted with his concubines. Violence was not a Roman trait; it was as human as the curiosity that compelled dozens of travelers to gawk at this exhibition of cruelty.

At midday, about the sixth hour, the nearly cloudless sky went dark. This was not the gray light of dawn or an impending storm — this was an eerie absence of light that left an oily darkness in its place.

Yeshua's words came back to me on a tide of remembrance: *"I am the light of the world. The one who follows me will no longer walk in darkness, but will have the light of life."*

A prophet was dying, but what prophet took the light of the world with him?

I reached for Jude's arm — as much to give comfort as to receive it — and watched as Yeshua said something to a man standing near the foot of the execution stake. When the man nodded and turned, I recognized him — John, one of Zebedee's sons. He slipped his arm around Mary's shoulders and led her and the other women away from the place of execution.

Even from a distance, I realized what had happened. Yeshua had asked the disciple he trusted most to care for his mother, a duty Jude and his brothers had forfeited. I brought my hand to my mouth, heartsick to realize how that knowledge would affect them.

"I cannot watch any more of this," Jude said, his voice dissolving in a ragged whisper. "I can't —"

"Let's go." I took him by the hand and pulled him toward the city gate, hoping we would reach the inn before the full measure of grief overtook him.

The man who had squirmed through the crowd like an eel now walked with a leaden step, his eyes glassy, his face a mask. We passed through the gate, where the guards carried torches and tried to make light of the foreboding darkness. "I think Tiberius forgot to sacrifice to Sol," one guard joked. "The god has hidden the sun in retribution."

As if in answer, a low growl rumbled from

beneath the earth, and the stones in the Jerusalem wall scraped against each other. Men and women ran out of nearby buildings while the earth trembled.

If that weren't enough, Jude and I were on a narrow street near the Temple when the air filled with tremulous bleats of pain and terror. My heart pounded until I realized it was the ninth hour on the day of Passover — the hour when the Temple priests began to slaughter the sacrificial lambs. For the next three hours, the priests would kill thousands of lambs and collect their blood for the altar . . .

I had never been able to watch the bloodletting. Yet earlier I had observed a far more tragic sight as the Romans executed an innocent man.

"It is nothing," I whispered to Jude, whose face had gone deathly pale when the dreadful sound wrapped around us. "It's only the Passover lambs."

"Does the earth move when the lambs die?" he asked.

I pressed my lips together and pulled him away from the haunting screams.

"It is over," Jude mumbled, shuffling forward with uncharacteristic clumsiness. "And what did my brothers and I tell him the last time we were together? 'You should take your show to Jerusalem, so more people can see you. You're wasting your time here in Galilee.' " He stopped and put his hand beneath my chin as if to bring me closer. "One thing I know, Tasmin — God had no part in this tragedy today."

Seeing him in such a fragile state, I pulled him out of the crowd, wrapped my arms around him, and drew his head to my shoulder as he went quietly and completely to pieces.

Jude and I eventually made our way to the inn, where the innkeeper had just returned from the Temple, his slaughtered lamb draped over his shoulders. Seeing him and his wife involved in such festive, ordinary preparations struck me as surreal. Could they not see that we had just endured an unthinkable horror?

"Ah, let me get the lamb cleaned and into the oven," the innkeeper's wife said, rubbing her hands in anticipation. She looked at me and smiled. "We would be happy if you would join us for the Seder."

Neither Jude nor I had an appetite, but it would violate the Law to refuse their hospitality, so we accepted and sat in the courtyard to wait for sunset. The earth itself seemed to share our shock, for the darkness that had descended at the sixth hour continued until the ninth, when the bleating of the lambs finally ceased.

From inside the house, I heard our hostess preparing the wood for her fire. Soon she would slide the Passover lamb into the stone oven . . . and somewhere, if he had been fortunate enough to die quickly, someone would slide Yeshua's body into a pauper's grave.

"The sun simply stopped shining." Jude studied the sky, which had returned to its usual color. "How can the sun not shine?"

"Sometimes we encounter mysteries," I said, searching the heavens for an answer. "Things only HaShem can explain."

"It was almost as if Adonai grieved for my brother," Jude went on, "as if he was more than a prophet. But if so, how could HaShem allow such a horrible thing to take place? If He protected Shadrach, Meschach, and Abednego from the flames of Nebuchadnezzar's furnace, shouldn't He have saved Yeshua from the Romans?"

The Passover feast was supposed to be a time of great joy, yet our hearts were heavy as we went through the motions of the ritual meal. Afterward I thanked our hostess for her kind hospitality and went back outside, where the walls did not seem as if they were closing in on me.

Before I left the house, the innkeeper's wife caught my sleeve. "We heard about what happened outside the city today." She stole a glimpse at my face. "From your expression, I assume you were there?"

I nodded.

She shook her head. "Such a nasty business. I do not go to the executions. Watching the Romans execute our people in such a way — it is too much." She gave me a fleeting smile. "Try to put it out of your mind. Tomorrow will be a better day."

If only that were true.

Jude and I did not sleep that night but sat in the courtyard, our ears attuned to the sounds of the city and the earth. I was certain that somewhere, someone in Jerusalem had heard nothing about what had happened at Golgotha, but by sunset most people knew the story. Strangers who passed by the inn's courtyard nodded to us and inevitably said, "Have you heard?" No matter how we responded, they proceeded to share yet another version of the day's events.

Nearly all of the stories were beyond belief. One man reported that the centurion overseeing the crucifixion became a believer in Yeshua after watching him die.

"What was so special about his death?"

Jude asked, pain shining in his eyes. "I was there. I saw him hanging on the iron nails. He suffered, he bled, he died."

"Few people can stand that kind of agony," the man countered. "Yet Yeshua refused the wine that would have dulled his pain, then begged HaShem to forgive the executioners for what they were doing. In all the public executions I have witnessed, I have never witnessed such a thing."

Jude lifted his head. "You were there until the end?"

The man nodded.

"The woman, Yeshua's mother, do you know where she went?"

The man placed his hand atop his walking stick. "The accused man placed her in the care of one of his disciples —"

"And where did he take her?"

To deflect Jude's rising emotion, I asked, "Do you know Yeshua's disciples? Do you know Thomas?"

"I do."

"Do you know where he is now?"

The man glanced over his shoulder, then shook his head. "Like frightened sheep they all fled when the Temple guards arrested Yeshua in the garden. Simon Peter followed at a distance, going as far as the high priest's house, but Thomas . . . I haven't seen him."

I thanked the man for his time and watched until he vanished into the darkness.

Once again we were surrounded by darkness, but this darkness exuded warmth and celebration. Lamplight pushed at the night from torches mounted near every door, and sounds of joyous laughter spilled into the street as families enjoyed their Passover dinners. We heard singing and laughter and happy voices . . . how was it possible?

Evil had won the day, and those who had opposed Yeshua — whether through jealousy or zeal for the Law above all else — were no doubt celebrating, lifting their glasses, telling themselves and their families that they had eradicated another threat to their positions and their religious rituals.

Yet Jude and I knew better. I closed my eyes and heard Yeshua's voice, repeating something he had said on the hillside in Galilee: *"But if I drive out demons by the Ruach Elohim, then the kingdom of God has come upon you. How can one enter a strong man's house and carry off his property, unless he first ties up the strong man? Then he will thoroughly plunder his house. He who is not with me is against me, and he who does not gather with me scatters."*

Jude and I could not believe Yeshua was

the son of God because we knew he was the son of Joseph and Mary. But neither did we agree with those who had persecuted him, those who mocked him and celebrated his death. And Yeshua himself said that if we were not with him, we were against him . . .

"Jude?"

"Hmm?"

"Is it possible Yeshua was the son of God? In some way we do not understand?"

Jude inhaled sharply, brought his hands together and bent forward, resting his head on his fists. Then he looked at me. "What does it matter now? He is gone. And this time we will never catch up to him."

I nodded and leaned my head against the wall. Jude was right; Yeshua's story was finished. We would mourn him, we would wonder why he said the things he said, and then we would look to the future.

We would probably remain in Jerusalem for a few more days. Tomorrow, Jude would want to find his mother and I would make inquiries about Thomas. Surely Thomas would come home with me this time — what choice did he have?

I might finally accomplish what I had set out to do, but I would find little joy in it. I had wanted Thomas to come home because he missed me, not because death had shattered his dreams.

Tomorrow would be a special Shabbat for the Feast of Unleavened Bread. While we would be limited by what we could do, it was better to remain active than to sit and mourn in silence.

I looked at Jude's torchlit profile. If Yeshua had not drawn Thomas away from Cana, Jude and I would not be betrothed. Over the last three years we had endured much together. I had learned what an honorable, righteous, and brave man he was, and apparently he had found something admirable in me.

Once we went home, he might not be able to look at me without being reminded of this shattering day. In the space of a few hours, he had lost a brother, failed his mother, and broken his promise to his siblings. Everything about this trip had ended in failure, and it might take months for him to recover from his losses.

I knew about loss, and I knew nothing was ever the same afterward. Jude would eventually marry me, for he was an honorable man . . . but he would be in no hurry.

I shifted in my chair and closed my eyes to the night, my hopes, and his promise that we would marry soon after Yeshua had ended his ministry.

CHAPTER FORTY:
TASMIN

"Shalom to you." The innkeeper's wife smiled and gestured to her table, already spread with food to break our fast. "I hope you rested well."

I glanced at the food but still did not have much of an appetite. "Thank you — you are very thoughtful."

"Will you be going to the Temple this morning?" she asked, pulling her cloak from a hook on the wall. "I would be happy to walk with you."

I closed my eyes and shuddered. Go to the place where the chief priests would be leading prayers and psalms of praise? Where they would smile secret, self-congratulatory smiles and gloat over their destruction of an innocent man?

"I do not think so," I said. "I will wait here for my traveling companion."

"Shabbat shalom to you, then." She tossed a smile over her shoulder and went outside, where her husband and children waited.

I sank onto a bench at the table and propped my chin on my hand. In a gesture born of habit, not hunger, I reached for the matzah and broke off a piece. I had just taken a bite when I heard footsteps behind me.

"Look who was asking about us."

I whirled around. Jude stood behind me, and with him was Thomas — looking tired, exhausted, and thoroughly defeated.

A cry of joy and relief broke from my lips as I rose and threw my arms around my twin. "I am so happy to see you."

"You have no idea" — he lowered his head to murmur in my ear — "how much I have missed you. Especially in these last few days."

"How did you find us?"

He shook his head. "People talk. And I had time on my hands . . . too much time." He uttered the words in a thick voice, then collapsed onto the bench. I released him and motioned to Jude, who sat across from us and folded his hands on the table.

"It . . . is over," Thomas said. "Yeshua is dead. I have spent three years following him, waiting patiently, but now . . . all is lost."

"What were you waiting for?" Jude asked.

"The kingdom of God!" Fresh misery darkened Thomas's face. "We were waiting for Yeshua to work the ultimate miracle, the one that would liberate us from Roman oppression. We had seen him do mighty miracles by the power of God, yet for the last few weeks, all Yeshua could talk about was leaving us. He said he was going away. I thought he was planning to go to Rome to challenge the emperor. He said he was going to prepare a place for us and then would come back for us. He said we would know the way, but when I asked how we were supposed to know the way when we didn't even know where he was going, he smiled and said, 'I am the way, the truth, and the life! No one comes to the Father except through me.' "

I shook my head. "Yeshua's words have always confused me."

"You are not the only one who feels that way." Thomas looked at Jude, his expression tight with strain. "He said he would send us a helper who would be with us forever. He said he would not leave us as orphans, but would come to us. But then the betrayer left our table —"

"Betrayer?" Jude's voice sharpened. "One of the twelve?"

Thomas nodded. "Judas Iscariot. He sold

Yeshua to the Temple elders for thirty pieces of silver."

A swift shadow of anger passed over Jude's face. " 'So they weighed out my wages,' " he quoted, his voice thin and brittle, " 'thirty pieces of silver. So I took the thirty pieces of silver and threw them into the House of Adonai, to the potter.' "

I recognized the passage from the writings of Zechariah, a section referring to the sum the prophet was paid for shepherding a flock meant for slaughter. The paltry amount — what the Law required if a man's ox gored another man's servant — was the value of a slave.

My temper flared. By offering thirty pieces of silver, the Temple authorities had shown flagrant contempt for Yeshua, yet Judas had accepted the token payment and betrayed a prophet of God.

"What happened to Judas Iscariot?" I asked, my voice ragged with fury. "Have you seen him since his betrayal?"

Thomas's eyes peered out from deep, shadowed sockets. "He is dead. Apparently he took the money back to those who had paid him, then went and hanged himself."

"A fitting end," Jude said bitterly. "If only he had experienced his remorse sooner."

"He led the Temple guards to Gethsemane," Thomas went on, "where he betrayed Yeshua with a kiss. That was the last time I saw our teacher. So I ask you — how is Yeshua supposed to establish the kingdom of God from the tomb?"

I glanced at Jude, whose eyes still smoldered.

"Thomas." I reached for his hands as compassion replaced my anger. "Do not despair. You know that grief eventually eases."

Thomas stared mindlessly across the room, and I could not tell if my words had penetrated the fog of grief in his head.

Jude clenched and unclenched his hands. "I am glad you found us. I want to know what was done about Yeshua's body. Most important, Thomas, I need to know about my mother."

Thomas blinked in what looked like dazed exasperation. "I — I only know what I have heard."

"So tell us, and start with my mother. Where is she?"

Thomas sniffed and ran his hand under his nose. "She is with John, at his house. Some of the other women are with her."

Jude nodded. "Will she come home with me, do you think? My brothers and sisters —"

Thomas shook his head. "I do not think she will leave Jerusalem anytime soon. Not before three days, at least."

"What? Why?"

Thomas winced. "The Pharisees were always asking for a sign. Yeshua told them, many times, that they would be given nothing but the sign of Jonah the prophet."

"What sign is that?" I asked.

Thomas sighed. " 'For just as Jonah was in the belly of the great fish for three days and three nights, so the Son of Man will be in the heart of the earth for three days and three nights.' "

Jude frowned. "Why Jonah?"

"He was a Galilean," I said, staring blankly at the tabletop. "And a prophet, like Yeshua."

Thomas cleared his throat. "As I said, Mary is not likely to leave Jerusalem until three days and three nights have passed."

"What happened to Yeshua's body?" Jude nailed Thomas with a sharp look. "Did the Romans throw him in a ditch?"

Thomas lifted his hand. "This I can answer with authority, because Peter made inquiries. A member of the Sanhedrin had come to see Yeshua before, a man named Nicodemus. He and Joseph of Arimathea, another member of the Sanhedrin, went to

Pilate and asked if they could have the body."

"Did no one think that his kin might want to care for him?" Jude asked.

Thomas frowned. "Did none of his kin approach Pilate? Did any of them argue for his life? Apparently not. Nicodemus and Joseph took the body to a garden tomb not far from Golgotha. They did not have time to prepare it properly, so they wrapped it in linen with spices and sealed the tomb with a stone. The women agreed to finish the burial properly, after the Sabbath."

Thomas turned to me. "The chief priests and elders have visited Pilate, as well. They warned that we disciples would try to steal the body and claim he had come back to life, so they asked for a cohort of legionaries to guard the tomb."

"Did Pilate agree?" Jude asked.

Thomas shook his head. "He told them they had their own guards, so to secure it as best they could . . . which they surely did."

I looked across the table at Jude. "Do you want to find the place where they buried him? We could search for it today —"

"For what purpose? The guards will not let us in. And even if we found a way to take the body back to Nazareth . . ." His voice faded away. "Let him rest here in

Jerusalem, the city that killed Isaiah and Zechariah ben Jehoiada. He belongs here." He gazed out the window with chilling intentness for a moment, then turned to Thomas. "So what will you do now? You've spent three years following my brother, but at least you escaped with your life. Will you go home or will you remain in Jerusalem?"

Thomas gave Jude a weary look, then turned to me. "I was glad when I heard you were here."

"How did you know?"

"Miriam saw you on the street. You met her in Galilee."

"I remember."

"Once it was . . . all over, I set out to find you. And here you are."

"Yes." I grabbed the matzah, broke off a piece, and offered it to him. "Eat, brother. You look as though you are about to fall over. Did you sleep last night?"

He shook his head.

"Neither did we, but now we face a new day. While what happened yesterday was unjust, we can do nothing to change things. We must move forward now. We must go home."

Thomas accepted the matzah and stared at it as if he'd never seen unleavened bread before. "I am the bread of life," he murmured.

"What?"

"Something Yeshua once said: 'I am the bread of life. Whoever comes to me will never be hungry, and whoever believes in me will never be thirsty.' "

"Thomas, you are always hungry. So eat. Drink something. Build up your strength. On the first day of the week you can return to Galilee with us. You can go home to Cana and pick up the strings of your life. The house is yours. The grove is yours. I will be with you until Jude and I marry, then you can take a wife and begin a family of your own."

He inclined his head in a morose nod, but at least he had agreed. Finally, Thomas was coming home. I had given so much to win my brother back, and soon he would be home again. If only he had come to his senses sooner . . .

"Yeshua gave me hope for Israel. And now my hope is gone." Thomas uttered the words in a hoarse whisper, as if they were too tragic to speak in his normal voice.

I watched in silence as the two men in my life thoughtlessly picked at the food on the table. Yes, I would have my brother again, but at what cost? Something inside him had gone silent, and the light in his eyes had been snuffed out. Time might heal his wounds, but until then he would be but a shell of the brother I loved.

Though we were only children when we lost our mother, the loss had not destroyed him. So why was he so bereft now? Had he believed that Yeshua could forgive our sin? The horror that had stained our souls for years?

If so, I could understand his quiet desperation.

I glanced at Jude, who looked even worse than Thomas. Jude's countenance had fallen, his eyes gone dark with despair. He was undoubtedly dreading the journey home, because he would have to tell his siblings that he had not found Yeshua and Mary in time. Worst of all, he would have to tell them about watching Yeshua die on a cursed execution stake . . .

I lowered my head onto my hand and rubbed my forehead. For three years I had prayed and done everything I could to bring Thomas home, and soon we would be again living under the same roof. I had finally succeeded . . . why, then, did I feel so defeated?

Chapter Forty-One:
Tasmin

Because the next day was Shabbat, Jude and I resolved to remain at the inn and rest in preparation for our journey home. Thomas stayed with us. When I asked him what happened to the other disciples, he said they had scattered throughout the city. "Several are staying with John Mark's mother," he said. "She has a house with room to spare. James is probably with John. And the women." He flushed. "Many are afraid the Temple elders will try to punish us, as well."

"Why?" Jude asked, a note of mockery in his tone. "You didn't claim to be the son of God."

"No." Thomas lowered his gaze. "So they might not kill us. But 'forty lashes minus one' can make you want to die."

I turned away as an unwelcome blush burned my cheeks. My brother had never embarrassed me before, but was he honestly hiding out of fear? I could understand being afraid when they arrested Yeshua. But now? After hearing how Yeshua bravely stood before Pilate and Antipas and his Roman executioners, never once recanting his words or his beliefs, how could Thomas fear a whipping?

"I'm going to the other room," I said, standing. "I may sleep for a while. May both of you enjoy a Sabbath rest."

I left Jude and Thomas with each other — I loved them, but both men were walking examples of the word *stubborn.* I kept thinking of Jude's refusal to approach Yeshua's execution stake to comfort his mother, and Thomas refusing to come home after Abba and I begged him. Did they hesitate because of male pride, or was there some other reason?

I pulled one of the mattresses from the stack in the corner and lay down, crossing my hands over my waist. The last three days had been difficult and sleep should have come easily. But it did not.

"I and the Father are One," Yeshua had said, but how was that possible?

"Hear, O Israel, the Lord our God, the Lord is one." I had been reciting the Shema since childhood; its words were burned into my brain. HaShem was one. One.

My mind searched through all the Torah

lessons I had learned. HaShem told Moses that he had filled the men who would create beautiful items for the Tabernacle with the Ruach Elohim, or Spirit of God. So God was Creator and Almighty, but He was also a Spirit who could indwell people.

I closed my eyes, recalling some of the first words of the Pentateuch:

"And the Ruach Elohim was hovering upon the surface of the water . . . Then God said, 'Let Us make man in Our image, after Our likeness!'"

Us. Plural. One but more than one. A mystery beyond my understanding.

"I and the Father are One."

Had any other prophet made that claim? Not to my knowledge.

"But seek first the kingdom of God and His righteousness, and all these things shall be added to you . . .

"If I drive out demons by the Ruach Elohim, then the kingdom of God has come upon you . . .

"Again, I tell you, it is easier for a camel to go through the eye of a needle, than for a rich man to enter the kingdom of God."

I closed my eyes in a vain effort to sleep.

Why was I tormenting myself with these thoughts? Thomas had been waiting for Yeshua to establish the kingdom of God in

Jerusalem on earth. But there would be no kingdom of God now. The promised warrior king had been unable to save himself, so Yeshua was not the messiah. He had not been crowned king, he would never establish a kingdom, and he clearly was not God, for God could not die.

Still, the memories filled my head.

"No one who has put his hand to the plow and looked back is fit for the kingdom of God . . .

"The kingdom of God does not come with signs to be seen. For the kingdom of God is within you . . .

"The kingdom of God is like when a man spreads seed on the soil and falls asleep at night and gets up by day, and the seed sprouts and grows. He himself doesn't know how."

Another mystery. A secret beyond my —

My father's voice: *" 'The Lord is our God, the Lord alone' puts you under God's yoke and brings you into the kingdom of God."*

I felt the answer all at once, like a tingling in my head. Where was the kingdom of God? Under God's yoke, Abba said. Within us, said Yeshua.

The kingdom of God was not on a map. It was our submission to HaShem. In our choice to obey Him.

The kingdom of God was *wherever God was king.*

It was within those who surrendered to His kingship.

It was where demons fled and little boys came back to life.

It was why Thomas left his home and father and sister. His commitment was real, but he had misunderstood Yeshua's meaning.

None of Yeshua's teachings ever made sense to me because, like Thomas, I kept expecting him to establish an earthly empire. Yet over and over, Yeshua said the kingdom of God existed within those who made God their king.

HaShem was not Pilate's king.

Despite their dedication to rules and regulations, He did not rule in the hearts of the chief priests and elders.

My only regret — and it ran deep — was that I had not supported Yeshua sooner. HaShem had not sent us a miracle-working prophet in four hundred years, so how could I have let the opportunity to follow him slip by?

Now he was dead, like so many prophets before him. But Thomas had listened. He would share his memories with me.

I stood and walked to the doorway, then

leaned into the common room. "Jude, Thomas — I think I have discovered what Yeshua meant by the kingdom of God."

486

CHAPTER FORTY-TWO: JUDE

I listened to Tasmin babble, aware that Thomas was listening with a confused expression on his face.

"Don't you see?" She smiled up at me. "We were expecting a messiah to establish an earthly kingdom, but Yeshua was a prophet who wanted to remind us that the kingdom of God has nothing to do with human kings. He had no interest in armies or power but in the condition of men's hearts. That's why the rich find it hard to enter the kingdom of God, and children find it easy. Whoever loves money or power more than HaShem cannot enter, but those who love HaShem, those who surrender to His will — they understand."

She pressed her fingertips to her temples, smiling as she turned to her brother. "Thomas, I am sorry. I thought you were being stubborn and unkind when you would not come home, but you were seeking the kingdom of God. You were with Yeshua, day after day, while I resented you." She shook her head. "I should not have pressured you. I should have put Abba in a wagon and taken him to Yeshua for healing. I was focused on what I wanted, but the kingdom of God isn't about what I want. If God is my king, I am his slave. I must focus on what *He* wants."

"And Yeshua?" Thomas asked.

"A great prophet. A man called and gifted by HaShem."

Thomas looked at her, a faint smile on his face, then turned to me. "I think," he said, "we should go see John."

"John?"

He nodded. "I believe we need to visit your mother."

John's house was on the far side of Jerusalem, and I balked when Thomas revealed its location. "Today is Shabbat," I reminded him. "The distance is too far to walk."

Thomas tugged on his beard and sighed. "Once we were walking through the fields on Shabbat, and Yeshua bade us pluck the grain to eat. The Pharisees saw us eating and asked why we were doing something not allowed on the Sabbath. Yeshua said Shabbat was made for man, not man for

Shabbat." He gave me a restrained smile. "I am sure Yeshua would approve of your walking to see your mother."

So, after my initial misgivings, the three of us set out. When we finally reached the house where John was staying, a cautious servant opened the door. "Is Yeshua's mother here?" Thomas asked. "Her son Jude would like to speak to her."

The servant opened the door and gestured to the main room, where Mary, John, Salome, and others were reclining around the remains of a Shabbat meal. Every face wore an expression of surprise, but Tasmin quickly explained our purpose in interrupting their dinner.

"Please forgive us for disturbing you," she said, pressing her hand to her chest as she looked at my mother. "But Jude wanted to be certain you were well."

Ima looked at me, and for a moment I could not speak. We had all suffered over the last three days, and I had imagined that she would suffer more than any of us. But Ima's face was smooth, her smile gentle. Her cheeks were paler than usual, yet she did not look like a woman in despair.

"Ima," I said, my voice breaking, "I know how much you loved him. I am so sorry."

"Jude." She rose and came forward to

embrace me, then rubbed my back and looked up into my eyes. "I love you, too, my son. And I have been concerned about you."

I made a vague sound in my throat as Ima turned to Tasmin. "I understand you are to be my daughter-in-law," she said, placing her hands on Tasmin's shoulders. "Welcome to the family. May HaShem richly bless you with every blessing."

Thomas stepped forward. "I believe," he said, clearing his throat, "that Jude and Tasmin need to know the story of Yeshua's birth."

Ima lifted a brow. "Truly?"

Thomas smiled. "I believe they are ready to hear it."

My mother gestured to cushions on the floor. "Sit, please. It is a long story, but one that needs to be told. I have not told you about it before now because . . ." She paused and looked at me, her mouth curving with tenderness. "I wanted you and your siblings to love each other as brothers and sisters."

I glanced at Tasmin, wondering if she was as confused as I was. She met my glance and lifted a brow, then sat on a cushion and made room for me to sit next to her. Those who had been reclining on dining couches made themselves comfortable as we all settled back to listen.

Ima sat on a bench, her back straight and her eyes alight. "My story begins when I was a young girl in Nazareth." She looked at me, her eyes softening with seriousness, a moment of absolute truth. "I was betrothed to Joseph, and he was working hard to finish our home. Then one afternoon the angel Gabriel appeared to me and said, 'Shalom, favored one! Adonai is with you. Do not be afraid, for you have found favor with God.'"

I caught my breath. I had always known my mother to be a righteous woman, but why hadn't she told me that she'd been visited by an angel? I leaned forward to hear more.

"The angel said, 'Behold —'" a small laugh bubbled up from her throat — "'you will become pregnant and give birth to a son, and you shall call His name Yeshua. He will be great and will be called Ben-Elyon. Adonai Elohim will give Him the throne of David, His father. He shall reign over the house of Jacob for all eternity, and His kingdom will be without end.'"

I blinked in the heavy silence. Outside the house, a man's sandals made soft popping sounds as he walked down the street, and I wondered where he could be going in such a hurry. To the Temple? To his mother's house?

"Ima," I began, shaking my head, "you have been under great stress."

"It is not your time to speak," John said, with a gentle note of reproof. "It is your mother's."

I stared at him, suddenly aware that my mother's story had not shocked him. He had heard it before! Perhaps they all had, because I seemed to be the only one who could not understand how Ima could believe Yeshua was the son of God. If he were divine, why was he resting in a tomb?

Ima smiled and continued her story. " 'But how can this be,' I asked the angel, 'since I am not intimate with a man?' And the angel said, 'The Ruach ha-Kodesh will come upon you, and the power of Elyon will overshadow you. Therefore, the Holy One being born will be called Ben-Elohim, the Son of God . . .' "

I sat perfectly still, ripples of shock spreading from my head to my toes as Ima went on, telling us about my father's astonishment when he heard she was expecting a child, and about how Elizabeth, John the Immerser's mother, had known about her condition even before Ima visited her. She told us how an angel appeared to Joseph in a dream, assuring him that the child she carried was holy and begotten of God.

Ima blushed when she spoke of my father, and her eyes welled with tears when she told us how he saved her and the child when Herod the Great sent soldiers to slaughter all the babies in Bethlehem. She spoke of the months they lived in Egypt, of reentering Judea, and finally returning to Nazareth because it was home. No one in Nazareth knew the unusual circumstances of Yeshua's birth, and everyone assumed her firstborn was Joseph's, as were the children that followed: James, Damaris, me, Simeon, Pheodora, and Joses.

When Ima's voice had gone hoarse after so much talking, she smiled and looked at me. "I know you think the story is over," she said, "but it is not." Her expression shifted to one of fond reminiscence. "When Joseph and I were still living in Bethlehem, before we had to flee, we went to the Temple for my purification sacrifice. While Joseph and I were offering our turtledoves, a stranger approached us, a Levite named Simeon. He took one look at the baby in my arms, lifted his hands and praised HaShem, saying he could die in peace, for his eyes had seen Adonai's salvation — a light for revelation to the nations and the glory of Israel."

Ima glanced down, and I knew she was once again seeing that baby in her arms. Then she spoke slowly, as though she were reciting something she had memorized: "Then Simeon came to me and said, 'Behold, this One is destined to cause the fall and rise of many in Israel, and to be a sign that is opposed, so the thoughts of many hearts may be uncovered. And even for you — a sword will pierce through your soul.' "

She looked up, her gaze roving over all of us who listened. "Watching my son die *did* pierce my soul, but Adonai is faithful, and He will keep His word. Before Yeshua was born, I told the angel, 'Behold, the servant of Adonai. Let it be done to me according to your word.' I told HaShem the same thing as I watched Yeshua hang on the execution stake."

She turned, and the look in her eyes pierced *me.* How many times had I resented her for treating Yeshua differently from the rest of us? How many times had I asked myself why Yeshua was her favorite? He was no more handsome or skilled or talented than James or Simeon or Joses . . . or me.

How many times had I harbored jealousy of my older brother? I resented the hours he spent alone in the wilderness, in the

fields, and on the mountains. I never understood anything about him *or* my parents,
and all the time he knew it . . . and repaid
my pettiness with grace. For though I was
mean-spirited and selfish, he never retali-
ated, never disdained me, never insinuated
that he was anything but a loving older
brother . . .

"Ima." With my heart too full for words, I
reached out and caught her hands, then slid
over and knelt at her feet. "I never knew
anything . . . until now."

Her hands fell on my head, and a moment
later I felt her lips on my hair. "All is
forgiven, Jude."

My thoughts, haphazard and painful,
centered on a remorse that went far beyond
tears. "But now he is dead, and I cannot
make things right with him. He will never
know how sorry I am —"

"Jude." Ima's small hand lifted my chin
until we were eye to eye. "He knows," she
said simply. "And soon you can tell him
anything."

"But —"

"Shh." Her fingertip touched my lips.
"Tonight is the third night."

CHAPTER FORTY-THREE: TASMIN

When the first three stars appeared in the violet sky, signaling the end of Shabbat, Jude, Thomas, and I went back to the inn, each of us lost in our thoughts. Dozens of people walked in the torchlit streets, performing tasks they had postponed until the end of the Sabbath. We dared not speak about what we had learned because we did not know who might be listening.

I kept hearing Mary's voice as she told us of Yeshua's birth. She told her story clearly and without hesitation, and I knew she had not shared it with many. How were ordinary people supposed to react to such a tale? Most would not believe her — Joseph himself had not believed until an angel settled his doubts.

I understood why she never told her other children about Yeshua's conception. Living with such knowledge would be nearly impossible, for how could human children live up to the holiness of the son of God? She had done her best to raise ordinary children in an extraordinary situation, and I admired her courage and wisdom. No wonder HaShem had chosen her to bear His son!

"The third night," Jude said, pitching his voice so it reached me and Thomas alone. "Does she truly believe he will rise from the dead?"

Thomas spread his hands. "The sign of Jonah — three days and three nights in the earth. That is what he said."

"Mary believes it," I added. "Watching Yeshua die distressed her, but she is not grieving. She is waiting." I looked at Thomas. "You heard him say he would rise again. Surely you are waiting, too?"

Thomas inhaled a long, slow breath, then shook his head. "He was a man," he finally said. "I saw him eat, drink, and grow weary. I heard him cough and feel pain. I saw him weep. I do not doubt Mary's story, but can a man — even one begotten by the Spirit of God — wake from death by crucifixion? I do not believe it is possible."

"He raised Lazarus," I pointed out. "And HaShem is the author of life, so HaShem has the power and authority to work such a miracle."

"But will HaShem raise the one chosen to

be our Passover Lamb?" Thomas asked. "Sacrificial lambs do not live again."

Troubled by Thomas's answer, I turned to Jude. He had not said much since Mary finished her tale, and I knew conflicting doubts filled his head. But one way or another, time would tell the full story . . . and tomorrow, the first day of a new week, would bring an answer to the question we cared about most.

Chapter Forty-Four: Tasmin

The new morning dawned bright and cool. With a rush of memory I realized the day was Nisan 17, the day set aside for the Feast of Firstfruits. Today every Jewish family in Jerusalem would go to the Temple with some of the first sheaves of harvested barley. They would wave the sheaves before the altar, thanking HaShem for His provision. After their Temple visit, men and women would go about their work as usual, and if nothing extraordinary happened, Jude, Thomas, and I would begin our journey back to Galilee.

I left the innkeeper's house and stepped into honeyed sunshine. The day would be perfect for traveling, and if HaShem willed it, we would cover a great distance before sunset.

But first we had to see if Yeshua's words would prove true.

Thomas had left the inn before sunrise

and remained away for several hours. I was itching to search for him, yet Jude bade me to be patient. "If we leave the inn, we are likely to miss him. It would be better for us to wait here and see if he has heard any news."

By the time Thomas returned at midday, my patience had been stretched thin. I spotted him from a distance and ran into the street to meet him.

"Well?" I asked, my pulse pounding with anticipation. "Did you see any of the other disciples? Did you see Mary or Miriam or Joanna?"

Thomas closed his eyes and opened his mouth, a signal that he was too overcome to speak. He dropped onto a wooden bench in the courtyard. "There have been," he finally said, "developments."

"What sort of developments?"

He blew out a breath. "I saw Peter and John near the house where we ate the last supper. I saw the women, too. All of them said Yeshua is alive. The women saw angels in the cemetery, and Miriam met the Lord herself, or so she said. Of course, she thought he was the gardener, and he may well have been —"

I grabbed his hand and squeezed it. "You're making no sense. Please, come inside. Gather your thoughts and start at the beginning."

Thomas did as I asked, and as he began to explain, Jude came out of the men's chamber and sat beside me, leaning forward to listen.

"Joseph of Arimathea buried Yeshua's body in a garden tomb," Thomas said, glancing from me to Jude. "Because the Passover feast and Shabbat were approaching, the women were not able to properly wrap the body until today."

"You have already told us this," Jude interrupted. "So what happened today?"

Thomas held up a hand. "I am trying to tell you, so be patient. Early this morning the women went to the tomb. When they arrived, someone had rolled the stone from the opening."

I frowned. "Are you saying someone stole the body?"

Thomas shook his head. "The Sanhedrin had stationed guards at the tomb, for fear of just such a thing. But the guards were gone when the women arrived, and two men in gleaming robes stood at the entrance. They asked the women why they were looking for the living among the dead."

Jude buried his expression in his hands as a primitive tremor shook him.

"So . . ." I swallowed hard, barely able to speak the hope that had begun to pound in my chest. "Does Yeshua live?"

"How could he? He died. He is gone. Unless I see the nail prints in his hands, put my finger into the mark of the nails, and put my hand in his side, I will never believe otherwise." Thomas breathed an exasperated sigh, murmured something about getting some sleep, and went into the men's chamber.

Jude and I looked at each other, then he asked the question uppermost in my mind: "So what do we do now?"

"We do not go back to Galilee." I folded my hands. "Not until we know for certain."

"And how are we to know?"

My thoughts scampered, then honed in on a strong possibility. "Who would he visit first? His mother?"

Jude's brow furrowed and he shook his head. "If what the women told Thomas is true, he has already appeared to them." He made a fist. "So he would go to his disciples. James and John, Peter — all of them."

"And Thomas," I added. "He must not go to sleep; he must join the others."

Jude smiled, and together we called for my brother.

Thomas did not go see the other disciples when we roused him. Instead he rolled over and went back to sleep, and I decided my brother was stubborn after all.

Jude and I went out to see what we could learn from others in the city. People were still talking about Yeshua, but today they were talking about his empty tomb. "His disciples came by night and stole the body away," a woman told me at the marketplace. "He said he would rise again, so his disciples would do anything to make him seem like a god."

Jude looked at me. "I do not think," he said, a smile playing at the corner of his mouth as he led me away, "that we should return to Galilee so soon. Let us stay in Jerusalem for a few more days, until we know the truth of this matter."

So we did.

The next morning the city was ablaze with news of two men from Emmaus. Quiet supporters of Yeshua, they had been in Jerusalem for Passover. "We were hoping he was the one about to redeem Israel," they were saying when we encountered them in the marketplace. "So as we walked to Emmaus, a man began to travel with us. We did not recognize him, so we told him everything that had happened in the city — how Yeshua had been a prophet, powerful in deed and word before God and all the people, and how the ruling priests and our leaders handed him over to be sentenced to death, and the Romans executed him. We told him also about the women who had seen him and claimed he was alive."

"The disciples stole the body," a man in the audience jeered. "The resurrection story is a lie!"

The men only smiled.

"We could not believe that the fellow walking with us had not heard about these things," the taller man went on, ignoring the scoffer. "Then the man said, 'Oh, foolish ones, so slow of heart to put your trust in all that the prophets spoke! Was it not necessary for Messiah to suffer these things and to enter into His glory?' Then beginning with Moses and all the prophets, he explained to us all the things written about the Messiah in the Scriptures."

"And then," the shorter man said, "the hour was drawing late, so we invited him to join us for dinner. And when we reclined at the table, he took the matzah, offered a blessing, and, breaking the bread, he gave it to us. And our eyes were opened — it was Yeshua! Once we recognized him, he vanished."

"Gone!" the tall man said, his smile beaming through his beard. "And we looked at each other and said, 'Didn't our hearts burn within us while he was explaining the Scriptures to us?' So we got up and walked back to Jerusalem so we could tell everyone that Yeshua is risen!"

"There is more," the short man added. "We found the disciples and learned that Yeshua had also appeared to Simon Peter. While we were telling our story, Yeshua appeared in the room with us and said, 'Shalom Aleichem! Peace be with you."

"The disciples were afraid," the tall man said, laughing. "They thought they were seeing a ghost. But we knew they were not, because we had seen Yeshua break the matzah. And then Yeshua said, 'Why are you so shaken? And why do doubts arise in your heart? Look at my hands and my feet — it is I myself! Touch me and see! For a spirit doesn't have flesh and bones, as you see I have.' "

"They were still terrified," the short man said, "so Yeshua said, 'Do you have anything to eat? So they gave him a piece of broiled fish, and he ate it before their eyes so they would know he was real."

"And alive," the tall man added. "He is definitely alive."

I stood on the street, Jude at my right side and dozens of strangers before and behind me, as the testimony of the two men echoed in my head. Didn't my heart burn when I listened to Yeshua explain the Scriptures? I had resisted him at first, but after witnessing his miracles, I could not deny his God-given authority and power. And who but God had the power to forgive sins?

"Are you Mashiach, Son of the blessed One?"

"I am, and you shall see the Son of Man sitting at the right hand of the Powerful One and coming with the clouds of heaven."

The realization swept over me in a wave, one so powerful I nearly fell to the ground. I caught Jude's arm as the pieces slipped into place.

" 'Yet I know that my Redeemer lives,' " I whispered, " 'and in the end, He will stand on earth. Even after my skin has been destroyed, yet in my flesh I will see God; I myself will see Him with my own eyes . . .' "

A shiver rippled through my limbs. Yeshua, the One foretold by prophets as long dead as Job, had been conceived of the Ruach ha-Kodesh and born to an obedient woman named Mary. The old man and woman at the Temple had recognized him in his infancy. The priests at the Temple had been astounded by his knowledge as a twelve-year-old. John the Immerser had paved the way for him. Yeshua had turned water into wine, healed the sick, demonstrated his power over demons and death, fed the hungry, calmed the storm, and cleansed HaShem's Temple . . . because he had the authority and power to do so. He was our prophet *and* our messiah, and those who submitted to him, HaShem's son, entered the Kingdom of God . . .

Did Jude see it? Did Thomas? The evidence had been before us for years, so how could I make them see?

I turned to Jude, my knees weak. "Thomas should have been with the twelve today. He would have realized the truth."

"Thomas is grieving," Jude said, his voice unusually husky. "He is not thinking clearly."

"But why should he grieve when Yeshua lives? He should believe Mary and Miriam and Peter and the men from Emmaus — he should believe *us*! I do not have to see Yeshua to know he lives. He is the son of God."

Jude looked down at me, and beneath the

rough surface of his face I saw motion and flowing as though a hidden fount were breaking through. He grasped my shoulders and stared at me, his eyes brimming with wonder, regret, and joy. Then he wrapped his arms around me in a fervent outpouring of emotion.

"Yeshua is the Son of Man," he murmured, his voice clotted with feeling. "The One Daniel saw, the One who came with the clouds of heaven. 'Dominion, glory, and sovereignty were given to Him that all peoples, nations, and languages should serve Him. His dominion is an everlasting dominion that will never pass away, and His kingdom is one that will not be destroyed.'"

I did not know the writings of the prophets as well as Jude, but I knew his eyes had been opened to the truth.

"You must give your brother time," Jude said when he finally released me. "It is not easy to believe what men consider impossible."

Chapter Forty-Five:
Tasmin

Eight days after the Feast of Firstfruits, Thomas joined the other disciples in the house where they had eaten the last supper. Because they were still afraid of the chief priests and elders, one of the disciples locked the doors.

Jude and I were not there, of course, but Thomas gave us the details. He said they were sitting in the room, talking about where they would see Yeshua next, when suddenly he appeared before them and said "Shalom Aleichem."

"He was looking directly at me," Thomas told us, tears welling in his eyes. "He had come, I think, for my sake."

"How do you know?" I asked.

A lone tear trickled down my brother's cheek. "Because he looked at me and said, 'Put your finger here, and look at my hands. Reach out your hand and put it into my side. Stop doubting and believe!'"

I gasped. "What did you do?"

"What could I do? I fell on my knees before him and said, 'My Lord and my God!' Then he said, 'Because you have seen me, you have believed? Blessed are the ones who have not seen and yet believe.' " Thomas's gaze moved into mine. "Blessed are you, sister, because you believed when I could not."

I swallowed the lump that had risen in my throat, reached for my brother, and held him tight. "It is enough that we both believe," I told him. "And soon others will enter the kingdom of God, too."

"Did he say anything else?" Jude asked.

Thomas wiped the tear from his cheek, then cleared his throat. "He said he would meet us in Galilee."

We went back to Galilee, but not quite as we planned. Instead of traveling in a cloud of gloom and sorrow, we went rejoicing, knowing that Yeshua would soon meet us again.

Our traveling party was a large caravan, made up of the twelve — including Matthias, who had taken the place of Judas Iscariot — the women who had followed Yeshua, Joseph of Arimathea and Nicodemus and many others who had come to

510

believe Yeshua was the Christ. Jude and I were pleased to be among those who not only knew Yeshua but also believed in him and understood his message.

We remained on the main highway, and as we passed by Cana and Nazareth, my heart yearned for my loved ones. I would have given anything if Abba could have met Yeshua, and I wanted Aunt Dinah to meet him. When I mentioned this to Jude, he smiled, took my hand, and pulled me to the side of the road.

"What are we doing?" I asked.

"We are going to Cana," he answered. "We are going to get your aunt Dinah and Yagil and anyone else who wants to come. We will do the same in Nazareth, and in every other town we pass along the way. Is there any better time for them to know their Messiah?"

With joy and anticipation, we went to my hometown and Jude's, inviting anyone who would listen. Dinah responded to our invitation, as did several of our neighbors, but many scoffed at us, saying we were foolish for believing a crucified man could live again. We received the same reaction in Nazareth, where several of the townspeople were openly suspicious of Jude for declaring that Yeshua was the son of God. "It's fraud," one man proclaimed, "and now the entire family is part of it."

James, Simeon, and Joses were willing to join us, though they were not ready to accept Jude's story. They came with us because they saw a change in him and, as Joses said, "We'd better find out if Jude is mad or if there is something to the story."

Yeshua had told the twelve where he would meet them, so we returned to the Galilean hillside where he taught so many times. As before, we constructed simple tents and cooked fish over small fires, occasionally lifting our heads and looking toward the summit, waiting for Yeshua to appear.

"So why doesn't he come?" I asked, looking around for Yeshua. The hillside was crowded with several hundred people. "Why is he waiting?"

Jude smiled. "Perhaps he is waiting for all those who are meant to be here."

We slept that first night under a dark canopy of sky, sprinkled with countless sparks of light. Lying on my back next to Aunt Dinah and Yagil, I sighed in contentment.

"I don't know why you're so happy," Aunt Dinah groused. "We should have brought more blankets. My bones do not like this uneven ground."

"Try not to think about it," I urged her. "Think instead of the beauty around us and the glory of the heavens. HaShem created all of it for us to enjoy."

Dinah grumbled only once more, allowing me to fall asleep to the comforting churr of insects.

The next morning I opened my eyes to a pink sky tinted by the rising sun. Yagil was sitting up, grinning at me, and without a word he pointed to the hilltop.

Yeshua.

He stood there, wearing a robe so white I had to squint to look at it. But his eyes were warm and human, and the smile on his face said *welcome*. All around me, people were waking and realizing that Yeshua had appeared among us. A palpable astonishment swept over the hillside.

Not far away, Jude had camped with Thomas, James, Simeon, and Joses. I rose to my knees and saw that their faces were blank with astonishment. James's face in particular was a study in shock; the rising sun highlighted the new lines grief had carved into his cheeks. What must he be feeling? As the oldest son of Mary and Joseph, he had been the man of the house after Yeshua left to fulfill his calling. Though

James had mourned his brother's death, he had steadfastly refused to believe . . . until now.

Yeshua began to walk down the slope, his voice ringing over the hillside as he came toward us. "All authority in heaven and on earth has been given to Me," he said, a smile emphasizing the laugh lines around his mouth and eyes. "Go therefore and make disciples of all nations, immersing them in the name of the Father and the Son and the Ruach ha-Kodesh, teaching them to observe all I have commanded you. And remember! I am with you always, even to the end of the age."

Somehow — I'm not sure how or when — I looked over and saw Jude standing beside me, his hand in mine as together we knelt before our risen Lord and King.

EPILOGUE:
TASMIN

"This," Aunt Dinah called, grinning as my smiling groom led me through the courtyard gate, "is the day you have been waiting for. If only your father could see you now!"

I clutched the top of my veil as the wind threatened to blow it away and leaned closer to Jude, who was ducking beneath a shower of flower petals.

"You have managed to collect quite a crowd," I yelled, barely able to hear myself over the shouts of congratulations from our assembled guests. "Where did you find so many?"

He cast a wicked glance over his shoulder and squeezed my hand. "With all your friends in Cana, and all mine in Nazareth, plus the brothers and sisters in Jerusalem — did you think it would be a small feast?"

"But how will we ever feed so many?"

He stopped in the center of the courtyard, turned me to face him, and lifted my veil.

His steady gaze bored into me in silent expectation, and before his appealing smile my anxieties melted away.

"Wife," he said, "have you any idea how long I've loved you? I began to love you the hour I found you snooping around the cistern, looking for hidden barrels of wine."

"Husband" — my heart hammered in my ears — "when I saw you searching, I knew you were no ordinary man."

And then, before my brother, my aunt, my boy, and all our assembled guests, Jude gathered me into his arms and kissed me well.

Jude never got around to building me a house. After Yeshua ascended to heaven, we married and went to Jerusalem. We tarried there until Pentecost, when the Helper Yeshua promised arrived to baptize us in His Spirit. Filled with the Spirit and power, we began to travel as the Spirit led us, sharing the gospel of Jesus Christ with everyone we met. My humble husband routinely introduced himself as "the brother of James," purposely choosing not to identify himself as Yeshua's half-sibling.

After seeing Yeshua resurrected on the hilltop in Galilee, James had a private meeting with the Lord. We did not know what they talked about, but James moved to Jerusalem and became the head of the church there. He also took a wife and raised a family in the Holy City.

Joses and Simeon also took brides and began to travel, sharing the news about salvation for all people everywhere.

In his later years, Jude wrote a book, a short epistle written to believers throughout the Roman Empire. In it he encouraged those who believed in Yeshua and warned against false teachers who were trying to infiltrate the church and mislead those who followed Christ.

The twelve disciples and their wives also carried the good news about Yeshua's resurrection throughout the world. Paul mentioned them when he wrote the church at Corinth: "Don't we have the right to take along a believing wife, as do the other emissaries and the Lord's brothers and Peter?"

Thomas, my twin, took a wife and traveled east to a land far away. Although we lost touch with him, I was often comforted to think that we met regularly before the throne of God in prayer. Jude and I prayed daily for Thomas, and I was sure he prayed for us.

Sometimes, when I became weary or nostalgic for the simple streets of Cana, I would remember how I used to believe my life could never be complete or fulfilled without my twin brother nearby. HaShem made it possible for me to learn otherwise — and for a blessed life with a loving, godly husband and children, I would always be grateful. But even if Jude went to be with the Lord tomorrow, I would still be content. My life was made complete in Christ.

AUTHOR'S NOTE

I realize historical novels often raise questions in the reader's mind: Did that really happen? I've tried to anticipate some of those questions and provide the answers here.

Q. Did Tasmin really exist?
A. Yes . . . and no. We have no record of a woman named Tasmin who did the things described in this novel.

But Scripture tells us that Thomas Didymus means *twin,* so apparently he had one. And while Peter and Andrew were brothers, and James and John, Thomas's sibling appears to be absent from the roster of disciples. Was his twin not a disciple because she was female?

Scripture also tells us that Jude, Jesus's half brother and the author of the New Testament book, had a wife (1 Corinthians 9:5). I have no proof that Thomas's sister and Jude's wife were one and the same, but one is allowed to conjecture in fiction.

One thing is certain: I do try to be as accurate and responsible as possible, because one day I will meet Jude and Thomas and their wives, and I don't want to be embarrassed about how I portrayed them.

Q. Did the Virgin Mary really have a sister?

A. Yes. See John 19:25 and Mark 15:40. By comparing these two verses, you can deduce which women were present at the cross: Mary, mother of Jesus; Mary's sister, Salome; Mary Magdalene; and Miriam, wife of Clopas *and* mother to Jacob and Joses.

Q. Did Jesus really have siblings? And did you use their actual names?

A. Matthew 13:55–56 names all his brothers and mentions his sisters, but does not name them, so I invented names for his sisters.

Q. What does Ima mean, and how do you pronounce it?

A. It's what a Jewish child calls his mother, pronounced *eemah.* The word for father is *abba.*

Q. Are the events of this novel true to the timeline of the Gospels?

A. Yes and no. Jesus ministered for a period of three years, beginning with the wedding at Cana and continuing through his death and resurrection. I have tried to place the events and miracles in approximate order, but since not all the events are related in all the Gospels, it is difficult to pin certain events down to a timeline. I did exercise a bit of poetic license in this, using actual events at times and in places that suited my story.

Q. Did I understand correctly — you have Jesus being crucified on a Thursday night instead of Good Friday?

A. Yes. I read an excellent answer for what has been called "The Passover problem," which details the Jewish feasts that coincided with the death of Christ. If Jesus died on Nisan 14, Thursday afternoon, Passover *day,* he died at the very hour the Passover lambs were being killed at the Temple. The people ate the Passover meal after sundown, on Nisan 15, which was a special Sabbath because it was the Feast of Unleavened Bread. The next day, Nisan 16, was a Saturday, a "regular" Sabbath, and the next day, Nisan 17, was the day after the regular Sabbath during Pesach — the Feast of Firstfruits.

If we follow this pattern, Jesus fulfills his own words found in Matthew 12:40: "For just as Jonah was in the belly of the great fish for three days and three nights, so the Son of Man will be in the heart of the earth for three days and three nights." If Jesus died on a Friday night and rose on Sunday, he was only in the heart of the earth for *two* nights, not three.

This is by no means a new idea; it has been around for years. But people are so accustomed to the traditional Easter story that they are surprised to realize that crucifixion on a Friday doesn't fulfill Jesus's prophecy.

Q. I've never seen Mary Magdalene described as Miriam. And many of the names you use disagree with the names in my Bible.
A. The conflict arises only because different languages are involved. Depending on which version you use, your English Bible was likely translated from Greek into English. The New Testament was written by people who spoke Aramaic, the common language of the day. But educated people also spoke Greek and/or Latin, and

many people born at that time had both Hebrew and Greek names, like Salome Alexandra (Hebrew/Greek) and Alexander Jannaeus (Greek/Hebrew). Some names were very common: Mary/Miriam (same name, but Greek and Hebrew variations), Joseph/Joses, Jacob/James, and Judah/Jude.

Rather than aim for consistency and use only one language for names, I opted instead to use different variants to avoid confusion. By using *Mary* for Jesus's mother, *Miriam* for Mary Magdalene, and *Mary, wife of Clopas,* for the third Mary, I hoped to make things clearer for the reader. In reality, all three women were known by the same popular name.

Q. Why do you refer to the cross as an "execution stake"?
A. To give a complete answer, I have to go back to my church high school hand-bell choir. One Friday night, Jim Whitmire, our minister of music, arranged for us — kids from a Baptist church — to play for the service at a synagogue. Before we left for the service, Jim reminded us that God promised Abraham that whoever blessed his descendants would be blessed, and whoever cursed them would be cursed

(Genesis 12:3).

Ever since that time, I've had a strong love for Israel and sincerely want to respect and bless the Jewish people. I have spoken at a Jewish book club and freely shared my faith. I have Jewish friends whom I treasure. I am open and honest with them, realizing that it is the Spirit who must bring them to salvation.

Since entering adulthood, I've seen far too many Christians unintentionally offend Jewish people by saying that the church has "replaced" Israel in God's plan (it hasn't!) and by forgetting that we have been adopted into *their* family tree. God, in His mercy, has allowed us Gentiles to partake of the blessings brought about by the Jewish people and their messiah, Yeshua.

Throughout history, overzealous Christians have used the symbol of the cross to force Jews to convert or die. Christian anti-Semitism has been all too real, and for many Jews the symbol of a cross elicits the same negative emotions as a swastika.

For that reason, I and the messianic Jews who put together the Tree of Life Bible use both "cross" and "execution stake" when describing the instrument on which Jesus died. Changing the wording is a small effort for me, but it might make a big difference in a Jewish reader's perspective. And if my small effort blesses them, I am blessed in return.

Q. Did Jesus really live in Capernaum for a while?
A. Yes, and I had never realized that before working on this book. But the evidence is in Matthew 4:13.

Q. Did they really eat peacock in Jesus's day?
A. Yes. Originally I wrote, "They wouldn't break bread with a tax collector if you paid them and served steak," but after doing some research I realized that steak was not on ancient menus. Peacock, however, would have been a delicacy fit for emperors.

Q. Wasn't James one of the twelve disciples?
A. Yes. James, brother of John and son of Zebedee, was one of the twelve. But James, half brother to Jesus, did not believe Jesus was the Son of God until after the resurrection, at which time he had a private meeting with the risen Christ (1 Corinthians 15:7). At that point he believed

and became the leader of the church in Jerusalem. He also wrote the epistle of James in the New Testament. In the letter to the church at Galatia, Paul mentions meeting James (Galatians 1:18–19). The half brother who grew up with Yeshua became one of the pillars of the early church.

Q. Does history tell us anything about what happened to Jude or Thomas?

A. Thomas is reported to have traveled to the land we know as India when it was the Satavahanan Empire. There he worked as an evangelist and was eventually martyred.

As for Jude, history has given us an interesting footnote, preserved by Eusebius, about Jude's grandchildren. "There were yet living of the family of our Lord," Eusebius writes, "the grandchildren of Judas [Jude], called the brother of our Lord, according to the flesh. These were reported as being of the family of David, and were brought to Domitian [Roman emperor from 81–96 A.D.] . . . For this emperor was as much alarmed at the appearance of Christ as Herod. He put the question whether they were of David's race, and they confessed that they were.

He then asked them what property they had, or how much money they owned. And both of them answered that they had between them only nine thousand denarii, and this they had not in silver, but in the value of a piece of land containing only thirty-nine acres, from which they raised their taxes and supported themselves by their own labor. Then they also began to show their hands, exhibiting the hardness of their bodies, and the callosity formed by incessant labor on their hands, as evidence of their labor. When asked, also, respecting Christ and his kingdom, what was its nature, and when and where it was to appear, they replied 'that it was not a temporal nor an earthly kingdom, but celestial and angelic; that it would appear at the end of the world, when, coming in glory, [Christ] would judge the quick and the dead, and give to every one according to his works.' Upon which Domitian, despising them, made no reply, but treating them with contempt, as simpletons, commanded them to be dismissed, and by a decree ordered the persecution to cease. Thus delivered, they ruled the Churches, both as witnesses and relatives of the Lord. When peace was established, they continued living even to the times of Trajan [emperor from 98–117 A.D.]."

Q. Will there be a sequel to *Daughter of Cana*?

A. Not exactly a sequel, but a companion novel. The next book in the JERUSALEM ROAD series will feature Pheodora, Jesus's sister, as the main character.

REFERENCES

Beck, John A., ed. *The Baker Book of Bible Charts, Maps, and Timelines.* Grand Rapids, MI: Baker Books, 2016.

Bradford, Tom. "The Passover Problem Solved." *Torah Class: Rediscovering the Bible.* https://www.torahclass.com/other -studies/47-other-studies-text/985-the -passover-problem-solved-by-tom-brad ford, accessed 3/14/2019.

Brisco, *Thomas V. Holman Bible Atlas.* Nashville, TN: Broadman & Holman Publishers, 1998.

Cargal, Timothy B. *So That's Why! Bible: New King James Version.* Nashville: Thomas Nelson Publishers, 2001.

Corbo, Virgilio C. "Capernaum (Place)." Ed. David Noel Freedman. *The Anchor Yale Bible Dictionary,* 1992.

Elwell, Walter A., and Philip Wesley Comfort. *Tyndale Bible Dictionary,* 2001.

Friedman, Joan A., Ph.D. *The Same But Different: How Twins Can Live, Love, and Learn to Be Individuals.* Los Angeles, CA: Rocky Pines Press, 2014.

Fruchtenbaum, Arnold G. *The Messianic Bible Study Collection.* Vol. 131. Tustin, CA: Ariel Ministries, 1983.

———. *The Messianic Jewish Epistles: Hebrews, James, First Peter, Second Peter, Jude.* 1st ed. Tustin, CA: Ariel Ministries, 2005.

Heitler, Susan. "Marriage: 6 Guidelines from Ancient Wisdom Texts." https://www.psychologytoday.com/us/blog/resolution-not-conflict/201304/marriage-6-guidelines-ancient-wisdom-texts, accessed 1/4/2019.

Inch, Morris A. *12 Who Changed the World: The Lives and Legends of the Disciples.* Nashville, TN: Thomas Nelson Publishers, 2003.

Lindsey, Robert L. "The Kingdom of God: God's Power Among Believers." https://www.jerusalemperspective.com/2445/, accessed 6/04/2019.

MacArthur, John. *The MacArthur Bible Handbook.* Nashville, TN: Thomas Nelson Publishers, 2003.

Malin, Joshua. "The 8,000 Year Effort to

Transport Wine Around the World." https://vinepair.com/wine-blog/history -wine-transport-8000-years/, accessed 2/19/2019.

Mercer, Henry C. *Ancient Carpenters' Tools: Illustrated and Explained, Together with the Implements of the Lumberman, Joiner and Cabinet-Maker.* Kindle edition. Mineola, New York: Dover Publications, 1960.

Mitchell, Elizabeth. "The Sequence of Christ's Post-Resurrection Appearances." *Answers in Genesis.org.* https://answers ingenesis.org/jesus-christ/resurrection/the -sequence-of-christs-post-resurrection -appearances/, accessed 4/5/2019.

MJL. "Feasting Before Passover." *My Jewish Learning.* https://www.myjewishlearning .com/article/fasting-before-passover/, accessed 3/15/2019.

Negev, Avraham. *The Archaeological Encyclopedia of the Holy Land,* 1990.

Nixon, R. E. "Thomas." Ed. D. R. W. Wood et al. *New Bible Dictionary,* 1996.

Schein, Elyse. *Identical Strangers: A Memoir of Twins Separated and Reunited.* New York: Random House, 2008.

Segal, Nancy L., Ph.D. *Entwined Lives.* New York: The Penguin Group, 2000.

Siegel, Richard. "How to Wave the Lulav

and Etrog on Sukkot." https://www
.myjewishlearning.com/article/lulav-and
-etrog-the-four-species/, accessed 3/12/
2019.

Simmons, William A. *Peoples of the New
Testament World: An Illustrated Guide.*
Peabody, MA: Hendrickson Publishers,
2008.

Spence-Jones, H. D. M., ed. "Jude." *The
Pulpit Commentary.* London; New York:
Funk & Wagnalls Company, 1909.

Utley, Robert James. *The First Christian
Primer: Matthew.* Volume 9. Marshall, TX:
Bible Lessons International, 2000.

Watson, Joann Ford. "Manaen (Person)."
Ed. David Noel Freedman. *The Anchor
Yale Bible Dictionary,* 1992.

Wright, Lawrence. *Twins and What They Tell
Us About Who We Are.* New York: John
Wiley & Sons, 1997.

Youngblood, Ronald F., F. F. Bruce, and
R. K. Harrison, eds. *Nelson's New Il-
lustrated Bible Dictionary.* Nashville, TN:
Thomas Nelson Publishers, 1995.

ABOUT THE AUTHOR

Angela Hunt has published more than 180 books, with sales exceeding five million copies worldwide. She's the *New York Times* bestselling author of *The Tale of Three Trees, The Note,* and *The Nativity Story.* Angela's novels have won or been nominated for several prestigious industry awards, such as the RITA Award, the Christy Award, the ECPA Christian Book Award, and the HOLT Medallion Award. Romantic Times Book Club presented her with a Lifetime Achievement Award in 2006. She holds both a doctorate in Biblical Studies and a ThD degree. Angela and her husband live in Florida, along with their mastiffs. For a complete list of the author's books, visit angelahuntbooks.com.

The employees of Thorndike Press hope you have enjoyed this Large Print book. All our Thorndike, Wheeler, and Kennebec Large Print titles are designed for easy reading, and all our books are made to last. Other Thorndike Press Large Print books are available at your library, through selected bookstores, or directly from us.

For information about titles, please call:
  (800) 223-1244

or visit our website at:
  gale.com/thorndike

To share your comments, please write:
  Publisher
  Thorndike Press
  10 Water St., Suite 310
  Waterville, ME 04901